PRAISE FOR LEE KELLY AND JENNI

T0249232

THE STARLETS

"The glamorous 1950s setting, the plot twists, the romp across Europe, the chemistry between Vivienne and Lottie, ambitious, at-odds movie starlets who must join forces to save the picture and their lives—everything about *The Starlets* is a sheer delight! This fast-paced caper from the writing duo of Kelly and Thorne is fresh, fun, and exactly the escape readers need right now."

—Marie Bostwick, *New York Times* bestselling author of
Esme Cahill Fails Spectacularly

"Kelly and Thorne are a phenomenal duo . . . two brilliant authors with boundless talent and a singularly remarkable voice."

—Elle Cosimano, *New York Times* bestselling author of the
Finlay Donovan series

"The glam of old Hollywood meets the empowerment vibe of Barbie in this fast-paced European adventure that turns on-screen rivals into off-screen allies. Energetic, funny, and loads of fun."

—Lori Goldstein, author of *Love, Theodosia: A Novel of Theodosia Burr
and Philip Hamilton*

"*The Starlets* captivates from the first sentence. Brimming with Old Hollywood glamour, a twisty plot, and feuding film stars navigating increasingly sticky situations, this atmospheric, engrossing caper is your next must-read!"

—Rachel Linden, bestselling author of *The Enlightenment of Bees* and
The Magic of Lemon Drop Pie

"Lights! Camera! Action! Once again, Kelly and Thorne have created a heart-pounding story of non-stop adventure and irrepressible fun.

In *The Starlets*, cinema icon Vivienne Rhodes and up-and-coming Lottie Lawrence join forces to save the day and steal the show. I enjoyed every moment of this 1950s glamorous adventure that whisked me from Hollywood to Italy, with a delightful stop in Monaco to visit America's favorite Princess Grace, and back to Hollywood again with two leading ladies who know who they are and have the courage to chase what they want. A must-read!"

—Katherine Reay, bestselling author of *The Berlin Letters*

"*The Starlets* is the most fun I've had inside the pages of a book in a long time. The novel flips 'friends to foe' on its head, putting two competing actresses in the spotlight, transforming the starlets from adversaries to allies as they race across Europe to take down a kingpin. Shenanigans, quick thinking, and a cat-and-mouse game ensue. A propulsive, page-turning romp perfect for book clubs."

—Jenni L. Walsh, *USA TODAY* bestselling author

"Well-crafted and deliciously devourable, *The Starlets* tosses you onto a Hollywood movie set filled with everything you'd expect and want—glitz and glamor, love, jealousy, extravagance, jaunts across Europe . . . and murder! Plot twists abound when archrivals unite as real-life heroines who must save the day or all is lost, including their lives! A page-turning, exhilarating wild ride of a story that I devoured in a single weekend!"

—Jennifer Moorman, bestselling author of *The Magic All Around*

"Glamour. Danger. Adventure. Enemies to besties. Yes, please! This book has just the right touches of killer (pun intended) locations that our heroines get to zip around like an exploded champagne cork. Throw in some Hollywood touches, Esther Williams vibes, and this story is served like the perfect cocktail."

—J'nell Ciesielski, author of *The Winged Tiara*

THE
STARLETS

ALSO BY LEE KELLY AND JENNIFER THORNE

The Antiquity Affair

THE
STARLETS

a novel

LEE KELLY
JENNIFER THORNE

HARPER MUSE

Published by Harper Muse, an imprint of HarperCollins Focus LLC.

This book is a work of fiction. The characters, incidents, and dialogue are drawn from the authors' imagination and are not to be construed as real. Any resemblance to actual events or persons, living or dead, is entirely coincidental.

Any internet addresses (websites, blogs, etc.) in this book are offered as a resource. They are not intended in any way to be or imply an endorsement by HarperCollins Focus LLC, nor does HarperCollins Focus LLC vouch for the content of these sites for the life of this book.

Library of Congress Cataloging-in-Publication Data

Names: Kelly, Lee author. | Thorne, Jennifer, 1980- author.

Title: The starlets: a novel / Lee Kelly, Jennifer Thorne.

Description: Nashville: Harper Muse, 2024. | Summary: "Real life is turning out to be stranger than a script for the silver screen"-- Provided by publisher.

Identifiers: LCCN 2024019502 (print) | LCCN 2024019503 (ebook) | ISBN 9781400240661 (paperback) | ISBN 9781400240678 (epub) | ISBN 9781400240685

Subjects: LCGFT: Novels.

Classification: LCC PS3611.E4498 S73 2024 (print) | LCC PS3611. E4498 (ebook) | DDC 813/.6--dc23/eng/20240429

LC record available at https://lccn.loc.gov/2024019502

LC ebook record available at https://lccn.loc.gov/2024019503

Printed in the United States of America

24 25 26 27 28 LBC 5 4 3 2 1

For the stars of our lives: Henry, Oliver, Penn, and Summer

STAR POWER

Tuesday, October 15, 1957　　　　　　　　　　　　　　　　Issue 147

SPOTTED: Vivienne Rhodes Letting Loose with New Beau, Teddy Walters!

Screen queen Vivienne Rhodes is known for a lot of things—her stunning looks, athletic prowess, and undeniable acting talent being just a few of them.

But "life of the party"? Most certainly not.

Unlike her man-about-town father, Olympic-swimmer-turned-leading-man Damien Rhodes, and her tobacco heiress mother, wild beauty Lia Braithwaite Rhodes, who were both L.A. nightlife royalty in their day (and can occasionally still be caught closing down Chasen's), Vivienne has always struck *Star Power* as far more serious, taking pains to avoid the Hollywood social scene. Looks like we're getting another side to her . . . with all credit owed to her dreamy Apex Pictures costar, Teddy Walters.

"They danced the night away, kept ordering a rum cocktail they concocted," said a bartender at Ciro's who served the couple on Saturday night. "Told me I should name the drink after *Beach Holiday*, in their honor. You ever see Miss Rhodes smile in person? I tell ya, it can light up a room . . ."

Variety

Vol. 209 No. 7   NEW YORK, WEDNESDAY, APRIL 23, 1958   25 CENTS

SHAKE-UP AT SHAKY APEX

Fresh off a string of box office disasters and with ballooning budgets for their current slate of pictures, including disaster-fraught intended tentpole *A Thousand Ships* currently prepping at Pinewood in London, Apex Pictures board members voted to oust longtime chairman Murray Steiner. Also out on the tide: the studio's general counsel and vice president of finance, with more resignations mounting by the day.

Insiders claim board efforts now focus on courting potential buyers for the studio. Without new money fast, the days of the once mighty Apex Pictures may well be numbered . . .

SHIP SHAPE NEWS FOR APEX

By Everett Kain

Apex Pictures' long-awaited epic, *A Thousand Ships*, may recount one of history's dreamiest romances, but countless sources contend production's been a nightmare—a runaway budget, Lina Belmont's departure, and reported creative differences between the studio and producer William Wagner—and if *Ships* doesn't smash at the box office, the major studio may find itself in deeper trouble.

Fortunately for Apex's new president and owner, seasoned businessman and Hollywood newcomer Jack Gallo, the former studio talent Vivienne Rhodes is now officially attached to the blockbuster. Rumors have been swirling over which character Rhodes will be playing, but who else other than the picture's regal star?

Things have been looking up for swimmer-turned-actress Rhodes, who scored an Oscar nod in March for her entrancing turn in last year's swashbuckling biopic *Bonny*. Is her ex, Teddy Walters, eating his heart out yet, or is he too enamored with his latest leading lady to care? Let's just say his reps have declined to comment . . .

1

The synchrony of the waves feels reminiscent of a grand musical finale, a choreographed celebratory number, whitecaps rolling into the bow, parting, splitting in time. Vivienne leans back against the ferry's bench, affording herself a rare moment to relax. To revel in the rightness, the earned inevitability of this moment.

"Helen," she whispers to herself, trying on the role for size again. She can't help the stupid giddy smile that breaks across her face. The princess of Troy is one of the most influential, remembered, beautiful women *of all time*, and she, Vivienne Rhodes, has been entrusted with the part. A role that will finally break open the world for her. Jack Gallo himself promised Vivienne she'd become "America's golden girl" if she returned to Apex for *A Thousand Ships*. Buster Smith, the head of production, told her agent that this film would turn Vivienne "radioactive," whatever that meant. And the pay . . .

Well, if money really talks, her promised *Ships'* salary is a battle cry. A new standard. Her old Apex contract-player checks were peanuts by comparison.

She adjusts her headscarf, tucking in a few flyaways of her long brunette hair, and lets the soft wind propel her to her feet, toward the boat's railing. All those years spent waking up for crack-of-dawn swim calls, playing bit parts and villainesses, the unforeseen heartache and drama with Teddy, the Oscar snub—it was all worth its weight in gold, she decides, because it led her right here.

Breathing in the salt-scented air, she considers the rocky green island of Tavalli taking shape before her. No wonder the studio moved production here from London's Pinewood Studios a few weeks ago. The Italian island's jaw-dropping, jagged panorama will be the perfect backdrop for the film's battle scenes, for the lush emotional saga of the Trojan War. Two months of filming on this island, and when it wraps, Vivienne will have unequivocally made it. On her own terms, and on her own.

"Papa!" The voice cuts through her mellifluous moment like the screech of a needle on a record.

Vivienne turns to find a little girl with dark hair in a bowl cut and a big smile emerging from the cabin, now squirming near the ferry's sun-hardened skipper. Since they left the shores of Corsica, the captain has dutifully played the role of stoic witness to Vivienne's introspective voyage, so she's surprised to find him grinning now at the girl squealing beside him.

"*Papa, es le strega de mare!*" The child giggles wildly, pointing at Vivienne. "*Sta per tuffarsi in mare!*"

"Me daughter adore the movies," the captain says apologetically.

Vivienne lets out a knowing laugh. What an auspicious sign— the girl wants an autograph. "Don't we all."

"She says you are . . ." He winces. "She says you are the sea witch."

The corners of Vivienne's practiced smile pucker.

"She says you should, ah, go back to the sea."

The girl points toward the waves, delighted. "Medusa *da Poseidon's Depths!*"

"She calls you—"

"I got that bit, thank you."

Blinking away her annoyance, Vivienne cranks up her smile wattage and with a finger motions the girl forward. She stoops to meet her eye to eye.

"Those aquatic picture days are long gone for me, my darling," she tells the confused, wide-eyed little thing. "Today Medusa's face is going to launch *A Thousand Ships.*"

The ferry slows and curls around a craggy curve in the coastline. Vivienne stands, her breath catching.

Nestled between two emerald-capped cliffs is the most stunning production set she has ever seen. A matrix of blanched, planked docks extends from a smiling lip of sand, where a skinny man in a patterned bow tie already awaits. In the distance, she can just make out a small, charming town hued in white and coral. In the foreground, a few dirt roads peppered with donkey carts and bicycles wind past giant tents and dozens of custom stage sets. And at the top of the hills, casting a long shadow across the maquis brush, is a majestic hotel with balconies and arched windows.

It is all, fittingly, epic.

Her eyes are watering furiously from the glare—she underestimated the searing Italian sun, having packed her favorite pair of cat-eyes in her luggage—but she still manages to keep her chin high and her hands firm on the railing as the boat nudges the dock. An entrance is everything, after all.

The waiting gentleman hurries forward, extending his hand to assist her. He's shockingly young, no more than twenty or so, with a big grin above that somewhat absurd bow tie.

"Miss Rhodes," he says breathlessly as a few strapping Italian teenagers slip by to assist with her luggage. "Welcome, welcome to Tavalli!"

Vivienne nods, heels slipping as she steps onto the planks, the balmy wind whipping the hem of her floral swing dress.

"Johnny Preem, *A Thousand Ships* producer. Er, assistant, um, producer. Oh wow, are you crying?"

She lets out a dismissive laugh. "Just the sun."

Johnny blushes and waves her toward the donkey cart waiting on the beach.

"You'll get used to the glare out here. Though I think most of Cassandra's scenes are interior, at least to start."

Vivienne balks at the odd comment. Why bother telling her about the priestess's scenes? She makes a mental note—he's most definitely the assistant—and takes to setting the pace.

"Mr. Gallo is so thrilled you've joined the cast," Johnny gushes, scrambling to keep up with her. "And I've been a fan of yours ever since your aquatic picture days. Since I was a little boy. Er, not that I'm implying you're old."

She rolls her eyes as Johnny helps her onto the cart. He slides beside her on the bench, snaps the reins, and they are off, trotting toward the hotel.

"So many production changes since Mr. Gallo took over." Johnny fiddles with his bow tie as the donkeys plod up the path. "Set's been a whirlwind, I tell ya. Mr. Durand is doing his darnedest keeping up, but—"

"Syd. Yes, I'd like to speak with him straightaway," Vivienne says, scanning the valley as they bump along the dirt lane. So many grand, sprawling set designs—obviously the gossip columns weren't wrong about *Ships'* budget. Is that a rendition of King Priam's palace? A Grecian temple beside it? There's a boxy, massive warehouse atop the distant cliff too—perhaps a remnant of the war?—into which a team of burly men are heaving a gleaming statue of Aphrodite.

"I want to discuss his directorial vision for Helen," she says absently. "Her inner life specifically, over and above her beauty."

Johnny leans forward, obstructing her view. "What do you mean?"

"I'd like to make a few changes to her dialogue," she says. "Well, perhaps more than a few changes. A creative overhaul."

"A Helen overhaul?"

"This is what actors do, Johnny." She laughs at his confused expression. He must be very new to this. "I analyzed her scenes on the trip over from Los Angeles. The dialogue between her and Paris needs to be completely reworked. Perhaps George can join the meeting too? This will impact him as Paris, of course."

"George Carvel?" Johnny's face falls. "But he can't join, Miss Rhodes. He's—"

"Of course he can. Georgie and I go way back, you know, to *Cabana Girls*. What a fun picture. Lots of those lines were mine, if you can believe it. That director, Ed Mann, trusted his stars. I do hope Syd will do the same."

The assistant begins feverishly pulling at his collar.

"George will make a fine Paris," Vivienne adds. "Once our scenes are tweaked."

They turn into the impressive entrance of the Albergo Tavalli, the hotel's expansive stone terrace bordered by archways, looming facades and balconies, ellipse windows adorned with flower boxes teeming with tulips. Johnny jerks the reins with a *whoa*.

"Miss Rhodes, I think, well, there have been . . . lots of changes. Very last-minute changes. Maybe we should see Mr. Durand straightaway—"

But Vivienne has already hopped down from the cart and is pacing toward the hotel's spacious, column-checkered lobby and what looks to be a bustling bar inside. She can hear laughter, the hum of conversation, clinking glass.

"Just a few moments to freshen up," she tosses over her shoulder. "Can you be a love and arrange a hair and makeup touch-up? Whoever's on hand will do. Then we can be off to see Syd."

"Miss Rhodes." Johnny hurries after her. "Miss Rhodes, wait, I really have this sense you're uninfor—"

"Vivienne! Hello! Or should I say *buongiorno*?"

Vivienne freezes. That familiar, distinctive, perky voice . . . no, it's just her imagination. She's on a tiny island in the middle of the Ligurian Sea, for God's sake, halfway around the world from Hollywood.

Still, she turns . . . and finds her.

Lottie Lawrence, in the flesh.

Lottie. Lawrence.

Vivienne lets out a tiny whimper. What the hell is she doing here?

The last time Vivienne saw Lottie was in March at the Academy Awards, arm in arm with the man Vivienne had convinced herself was her soulmate. Turns out Teddy Walters is quite a convincing actor after all, despite all those rags that insist he's just a pretty face. In January Vivienne would have bet her career that Teddy was planning to propose when he returned from filming *Madame Bovary* overseas. He'd seemed every bit as smitten as she was, with their long strolls down Sunset Boulevard, talking about anything and everything, the little ways he'd surprise her with candlelit dinners and dancing at Ciro's. Instead, Teddy's daily calls from the *Bovary* set quickly dwindled to once a week and then to never, before he had the gall to show up at the Oscar pre-party with that woman, a notorious floozy, his only pathetic explanation being that he'd finally found "true love." And Lottie hadn't even taken the high road after that. Oh no, she'd followed Vivienne around all night, firing little digs about how "fine" Vivienne looked and what "serious competition" she was (for Best Actress, ostensibly, but Vivienne knew what she really meant) as all of Hollywood looked on.

That night Vivienne swore to herself that she'd do whatever it took never to cross paths with Lottie again. Catalyst of heartbreak, merciless homewrecker. And yet here the girl is—all flushed apple cheeks and perfect blonde bob and those freckles, for Pete's sake—running out of the hotel toward Vivienne like a long-lost school chum.

"Welcome to Tavalli, Cassandra, soothsayer extraordinaire!" Lottie squeals louder than the little girl on the boat.

She kisses Vivienne's cheek and, beaming, drapes a necklace of fresh, heady-smelling orchids around Vivienne's neck.

"I had these welcome flowers made in town this morning. Only a ten-minute donkey ride away. The most darling people, I tell you, and the language, ah, I could listen for hours. *Orchidee, più soldi.*" Lottie laughs out her annoyingly smooth improvisation of an Italian accent, her big blue eyes twinkling. "Can you foretell we're all going to be very successful here? I'm thrilled at playing Helen, though I'm not sure this face could launch a single ship," she chirps, pointing to her gorgeous mug. "These bags under my eyes! I've hardly slept between the Cannes premiere, promoting *Bovary*, then touring the Riviera. More of a Grand Prix than a vacation, right? I suppose Ginger will work her magic with makeup. She's already here too. Isn't that grand?"

The piazza cracks open, the ground splitting wide. Vivienne must be falling through the world. Lottie. Here, in Tavalli, on *her* picture. And . . . wait.

Did she just say *she* was Helen?

Vivienne latches onto Johnny with a glare. "What's the meaning of this?"

The assistant raises his hands. "Miss Rhodes, as I was, um, I'm getting the sense you may be a step behind—"

She tears off the necklace, thrusting it at Lottie. "Allergic."

"Oh." Lottie blinks rapidly. "I didn't—"

But Vivienne is in motion again, hurtling through the lobby past a blurred throng: The gray-haired theater actor Charles Brinkwater, lecturing with a heavy slur two young actors on the importance of voice lessons. A few bellmen in uniform. A collection of unrecognizable actors—bit players, maybe, or even extras, as they all appear a little starstruck. One of whom is such an effective wallflower, she nearly trips over his boot.

"*Excusez-moi*," the middle-aged fellow mumbles, straightening the lapel of his tattered tweed jacket.

"I need a phone," Vivienne barks as she can sense Johnny still nipping at her heels. "In my room! I was specifically and unmistakably told I was cast as—"

She barrels straight into a man's firm chest as she rounds into the hallway.

"Viv?"

Vivienne steps back.

Her heart plunges down, down, down.

"They told me you were coming in today." Teddy Walters scoops her into a hug before she can get her bearings. "Island's gorgeous, right? Beyond anything I could've dreamed."

She stiffens into stone.

"Haven't seen you since the Oscars." Teddy pulls away, suddenly sheepish. "You look well, Viv, really well."

She can't quite meet his eyes—it might be worse than staring into the sun—so she focuses on his smile and his hard, right-angle jaw. She swallows, beyond flustered. How many times had she longed to run her fingers along that jaw? Her lips?

"How are you here?" she whispers.

"I tried calling, you know. A couple times, after." Teddy clears his throat. "We never finished that conversation, Viv. I—I want to explain. It's part of the reason I said yes, when the studio called about Georgie not working out—"

"Wait, George Carvel isn't . . ." She huffs. "Are you saying you're—"

"The new Paris? Of course." Teddy laughs, eyes wide with excitement. "You should have seen the crowds in Cannes, Viv. It was unreal, the reception we got for *Bovary*. Can't blame Apex for wanting to keep a good thing going. They flew me and Lottie down straight from the Riviera."

"I . . . wasn't aware you were on the picture."

Teddy's face contorts at that—with guilt or disappointment, she can't be sure.

"Oh my God, yes, this is"—Johnny huffs, catching up—"all above my pay grade. Miss Rhodes, I was led to believe you were aware of the latest changes to the cast."

She blinks, sobered, freshly mortified. "Won't you excuse us, Teddy?"

Spinning on her heel, she beelines for the cage elevator. Stabs the button. "My room."

Johnny winces. "That's broken."

"Which one is mine?" Vivienne throws up her hands and stomps to the marble staircase opposite.

Around them, the lobby has gone curiously silent.

"Miss Rhodes, please—"

"Room!" she snaps again. Just like a damn sea witch after all.

"Number 305, but wait, just hold on a minute. You don't have the keys!"

Vivienne finds the room in question at the end of the long, narrow hall, seething as Johnny fumbles with a large ring of mismatched keys. He stammers all the while about how very pleased Mr. Gallo was when she signed on, how essential she is to the production. Garbage. Typical Hollywood bullshit.

"I'm calling my agent." She hurries into the spare, though admittedly beautiful, suite containing a cotton-sheeted bed and cherrywood furniture. White curtains rustle from the breeze as she plops down at the desk.

"Miss Rhodes, if I may?"

"Please leave."

He does.

Her fingers fumble as she tries once, twice, three times to remember the correct way to call international. She dials Lew's home, given the late hour in Los Angeles.

"*She was made to play the world's greatest beauty,*" Buster Smith had assured them. She was in the room when he said it!

Vivienne snaps a bitter laugh as the shrill Italian ring morphs into a hollow drone.

"*America's screen siren,*" Jack Gallo had said. So earnestly. So damn convincingly.

"What a joke." She puts the phone in a choke hold, now pathetically crying as she waits for Lew to answer. Has she really traveled thirty hours on planes, trains, and ferries only to play the handmaiden to her fiancé-stealing archnemesis? In the biggest picture of the decade, no less?

"Hello?" Lew's voice is soft and muffled. What is it—4:00 a.m.?

"Did you know?"

"Ah . . . who is this?"

"Did you know I've been cast as that weird fortune teller in the Troy film while two-bit Lottie Lawrence is Helen, and the *kicker*, Lew, the kicker: Teddy Walters is her Trojan in shining armor!"

Silence.

"Lew!"

"Oh dear."

"What are our options?" Vivienne's voice cracks like a shell and she takes a breath, collecting herself. "Tell me you can get me out."

Lew, more awake: "I don't know, Viv. We signed. But I can try."

"How bad would it look?"

"The papers have run your involvement. No mention yet of Teddy and Lottie. It must have just happened." Lew lets out a weighty sigh. "I could beat their agents to the punch, give a call to Hedda Hopper. Tell her your part wasn't up to snuff. Gallo will be livid, though, and—"

"I don't care." She pinches her eyes shut with a groan. "Though Hedda will find a way to cast me as the scorned woman, I'm sure of it. Again."

"Hey, you liked Sam Zimbalist when you met with him, didn't you?" Lew says, livelier now. "The producer of *Ben-Hur*, your lunch back in December? They've just started shooting in Rome. I could make a call, see if they've got a part for you—"

"I'm done with 'parts.' This was supposed to be it, Lew, the beginning of a new era. Ten years in the business, all the hard work, ups and downs, dedication! I want epic leading lady, damn it—"

"This *is* a leading role, Vivienne."

The new voice, from mere feet behind her, startles her cold.

Vivienne turns around, phone still in hand, to find Jack Gallo himself leaning against her hotel room doorframe.

She hurries to stand from the desk.

"Lew," she murmurs, "I'm going to have to call you back."

As she nestles the phone in its cradle, the president of Apex Pictures crosses the room.

"Vivienne Rhodes." Gallo gently takes her hand. "I'm so very glad you've arrived."

Vivienne's thoughts swarm, then flitter away. She knew Jack Gallo had been taking a very involved role on *Ships*, considering it would be his first picture as president. And Lew had mentioned before she left that he was technically standing in as producer, seeing as William Wagner had apparently stormed off set soon after the picture was moved here. But she hadn't pieced together that meant the new studio mogul was actually here.

She first met Jack last month, back on Apex's Burbank lot, days after he had taken over the studio. She'd noted his looks then in an abstract, disassociated way, like one might register the beauty of an Oscar statuette. *Yes, yes, he's handsome, attractive,* she'd thought at the time. *But what does this shiny man signify? How is he going to catapult my career?*

Now that Gallo's standing in her hotel room, it's a bit harder to dismiss his charisma. He takes off his fedora, his wide brown eyes never wavering from hers, his tan physique accentuated by the loose white linen shirt he's rolled to his elbows. He's got a certain physical ease, a comfort in his own skin. She'd peg him as late thirties, maybe early forties.

He smiles at her, a lopsided, charming smile that reveals pearly whites and a dimple. It nearly takes her breath away.

She backs up a step, breaking their contact, refocusing.

"No need to buzz Lew when I'm right here." There's a playful note to his tone. "The last thing Apex needs is a runaway phone bill."

"You've made a grave mistake."

"Funny, from where I stand, everything finally feels picture-perfect."

"Oh really?" Vivienne snaps. "Were there *two* Helens of Troy in the history books?"

"Vivienne." He purrs her name, closing the space between them. "Cassandra *is* a leading role. A far better role for you, I realized. A more complicated, memorable role than Helen. More than a face. A presence, a force. We needed a real actress to play her. Thus . . . you."

She shakes her head, still ablaze with frustration. "I can count the priestess scenes on one hand."

"Not after our pinch hitter is done rewriting the script," Gallo presses. "He's an underutilized ace. Snatched him up between projects. And when he's done with it, the picture might as well be called *Cassandra of Troy*."

"No, I—I can't, I won't." Vivienne paces away. "I can't be here, trapped on set for months, with the two of them as Paris and Helen, and—"

"Is that what this is about? Lottie and Teddy?" Gallo laughs, surprised, his dark eyes sparkling now. "The execs told me you and Ted were a set-up romance promo for *Beach Holiday*. Am I misinformed?"

She falters, then gives a little shake of her head. Because he's not wrong. Not technically.

"Oldest trick in the book, am I right?" Gallo continues. "Though not necessarily fair, forcing you to play the happy couple. Pairing and switching and swapping you all like bride dolls." His expression warms as he gazes at her. "You of all people deserve true romance, Vivienne. A partner. The real deal."

Silence stretches a beat too long between them, until an errant butterfly flutters in her chest.

"Things are going to change," Gallo says. "Now that I'm at the helm, I swear, I'm going to turn this money pit of a picture into an honest-to-God blockbuster. And I plan to be right here, every moment of every day, to make sure it's a smashing success. To turn Apex's luck around."

He edges closer now, leaning on the desk. She can smell his aftershave. Notes of vanilla. Pine. She can see flecks of amber in those wide, dark eyes.

"And . . . yes, we've secured more talent, more glamour, to make that happen," Gallo adds. "Lottie and Teddy, riding the tide of *Bovary*'s success. Household names like Clay Cooper. Charles Brinkwater. But most of all, we need you, Viv. You're our brightest star. As soon as I came on board, I told them, 'I can't make this without her.'" His tone is as soft as the Italian breeze nipping at her neck. "I'll be damned if this doesn't land you that Oscar I know you're gunning for. The Oscar you deserve."

Please. This is an obvious snow job, right? The typical Hollywood BS once again.

And yet the way he's staring at her . . . she can't be sure. There's a spark there. Belief. In her, or else in the magic they might make together: a true, unprecedented epic. A few hours of total enchantment that could reach millions of viewers, change lives. And still change hers. Perhaps Gallo's right, *if* she can put her pride aside. Recalibrate her plan. Allow herself to soar.

"Will you knock this out of the park with me, Vivienne?" Gallo murmurs. "Will you stay and do what I know you can do?"

She lifts her chin, mind racing. "I'll . . . need more creative control over the role."

He flashes that showstopping smile once more, broadcasting relief. "I'd expect nothing less."

She sighs, weightily, and then nods. Just once.

"Good," he says, shoulders loosening fully. He gives her a wink and a quick squeeze of her forearm that spreads tingles across her skin. "All right then. I'll let you settle in."

A Thousand Ships

An Apex Pictures Film

(Cast and Crew–Working List–June 1958)

Produced by:

Jack Gallo, president of Apex Pictures

Directed by:

Sydney Durand

Writing credits:

Max Montrose

Cast:

Lottie Lawrence—*Helen*
Vivienne Rhodes—*Cassandra*
Teddy Walters—*Paris*
Clay Cooper—*Hector*
Charles Brinkwater—*King Priam*

2

Lottie sprawls inelegantly on the hotel bed, staring at sea light dancing on the ceiling. "Heya, Teddy?"

"Hmm?" he answers from the armchair across the room, his face obscured by script pages.

She wrinkles her nose. "I don't suppose you remember Vivienne having a flower allergy?"

A pitying snort is his only reply.

She sits up with a groan, adjusting her sundress. "I know, I know. I'm a born dupe, but I have to try, right? We're gonna be on this island together for two months. She's got to warm up sometime, and the sooner the better as far as I'm concerned."

Teddy sets his marked-up screenplay to the side with a sigh. "I'm with you, Lottie girl, but I don't know. It's starting to look like she's never going to forgive us."

"For what? For doing what the studio tells us? She might be a free agent, for goodness' sake, but some of us are still locked into contracts." Lottie flounces off the bed and stalks to the window. "I know you said there were feelings involved on her part, and I can't say I blame her; you are *you* after all. But surely when Buster told her your arrangement was ending—"

"Buster didn't tell her." Teddy furrows his forehead like a guilty child. "We'd become pals, you know. I was fond of her. Still am. So I thought it should come from me, not the studio. And then, I don't know, it came time to shoot *Madame Bovary* five thousand miles away, and it felt like maybe it might naturally just winnow—"

"But you did break things off with her." Lottie perches on the window seat, gripping the sill hard.

"I mean . . . yes? I told her I'd met someone, as a matter of fact. Leveled with her as best I could under the circumstances."

Lottie stares, horror dawning. "*When* exactly did you level with Vivienne, Teddy?"

He sits up straighter. "You have to understand—I felt like a real heel. I don't think she'd ever been set up before, and I might have played my role too well. The more I kept things gallant, polite, the more eager she seemed. Started talking about marriage, little comments here and there, and—"

"And?" Lottie shoves herself off the windowsill. "Theodore Andrew Walters, please do not tell me it was—"

"It was Oscar night." He hangs his head, waiting for punishment.

Lottie obliges, whapping him with his rolled-up script. "No wonder she was so awful. That little comment she made, how I looked like I'd already been given an award."

"'Omaha housewife wins Queen for a Day,'" Teddy recites, barely suppressing his chuckle. "You have to admit, that was a snappy one-liner."

Lottie stomps her foot, but a giggle breaks through her scowl. "You are a beast."

A telltale knock on the door interrupts, resounding musically: *boom, badda, bop bop.*

"Open sesame," Teddy calls, loud enough for their visitor to hear.

Max Montrose cracks open the door like a mouse checking to make sure the humans are asleep and slides inside just as furtively. "Oh dear, am I interrupting a lovers' spat?"

Lottie rolls her eyes. "Hilarious."

"Speaking of one-liners . . ." Teddy shoots Lottie a wink. "How long did it take you to work that one up, Maxy? Is this why they pay you the big bucks?"

"The extremely middling bucks, I'll have you know." Max leans against the door with an apologetic grimace. "Dare I ask? Have you seen her?"

"You dare not," Lottie lobs over her shoulder as she paces.

"It's bad, Max." Teddy's smile drops away. "She was blind-sided, didn't even know we were on the picture. Nobody told her."

"'Course they didn't." Max pushes his round glasses into place and claims an ottoman to perch on. "She'd have walked if she'd known. Smarter for Buster Smith to pull out his time-tested schmooze act, for Jack Gallo, our man of endless charms, to woo her all the way across the Atlantic, to get her here and *then* break the news. We're on a remote Italian island. It's a heck of a lot harder to take off than to just stay put and play nice."

"Billy Wagner took off," Lottie notes of the film's erstwhile producer, just as Teddy cuts in with "Man of endless charms, huh," a note of pique in his voice.

"Listen," Max says. "Getting me to come out of my professional sepulcher writing dime novels in Montmartre and back onto an actual working set was no mean feat, but Gallo managed it."

"I suppose I had nothing to do with it? Who do you suppose

told Jack about this swell screenwriter he met in Paris, an actual genius, an award winner, who needs a little income these days to pay for his coffee and cigarette habit."

Max smirks. "I always figured it was Lottie who recommended me."

As the boys play-bicker, Lottie paces, trying not to bite her fingernails, the hardest of her bad habits to break. "You know, I think it's worse than not knowing we were here. Vivienne seemed to think she'd be playing Helen."

At that, Max lets out a full guffaw. Lottie and Teddy both glare at him.

He shrugs in self-defense. "Can you imagine it? From star swimmer to sea sorceress to pretty little princess? I'd have to change the plot to have her in battle armor, taking down Achilles in single combat. Don't get me wrong, she's dead gorgeous. She's just not Helen."

Lottie laughs, breathless. "And I am? Come on."

"You're plenty good-looking," Teddy says, more dotingly than convincingly, but Lottie does believe Max when he squints appraisingly.

"You know, you're lovable. Everybody likes you. That's what makes you Helen."

"Likable isn't lovable." Lottie peers out the window at the waves, the sun, cheerful little boats bobbing in the distance—and a familiar, lissome figure stomping out to the shoreline, her face turned into the wind, dark hair billowing out behind her. "And not everybody likes me."

She feels Max and Teddy exchanging a look behind her back but perks up with effort, whirling around, cheerfulness back in place.

"So Vivienne Rhodes isn't a fan of flowers," she says. "Fine and dandy. I've got a backup gift that simply can't fail. Nobody doesn't like See's."

"You have candy?" Max clutches his hands to his chest. "More candies? Don't waste them on glamour girl—she'll be watching her figure."

"Play nice," Teddy chides.

Max ignores him. "Give them to me. I'll love you even more than I do now."

Lottie flicks Max's glasses. "I already gave you your box."

"Which you ate in one sitting," Teddy deadpans.

"Anyway, it's worth another try." Lottie makes for the door. "And you two need some alone time to go over . . . dialogue notes, was it?"

She winks over her shoulder, but she can tell that as far as they're concerned, she's already gone. As she slides the door shut, she sees Max amble over to Teddy, leaving the script discarded on the floor.

Max is smart to be furtive, Lottie realizes, as she takes in the bustle of activity in the hotel halls. Studio crew, assistants, shipped-in extras chat in the stairwells and doorways, passing on their way to meetings and meals. The walls have ears and eyes in every production, and as far as sets go, you don't get more closed than a remote island location.

She spots Clay Cooper pacing the hall, squinting intently at his script.

"Hard at work already?" she calls.

"'I dare not pour a libation to the immortals with unwashed hands,'" he recites, trying valiantly to hide his Texas accent, which has served him so well in his prior cowboy pictures. "Any idea what *libation* means?"

"It means a drink, which is where I'm headed." Lottie laughs, swiveling just as Charles Brinkwater emerges from his room, adjusting his silk foulard robe and matching cravat.

Upon seeing her, he clutches his heart, and by now she knows what's coming.

"Oh Lottie, 'she doth teach the torches to burn bright!'" Charles exclaims in a voice far too booming for the close proximity of the corridor. "'Like a rich jewel in an Ethiop's ear.'"

"My goodness," Lottie coos, clutching her own heart. "You make a wonderful Romeo."

Just sixty years too old for the part, but Charles preens under the compliment. "I played the role five times, you know, once before the king. Say, shall I tell you about it over a dram of Scotch? Mr. Gallo, Jack, you know, gifted me a bottle of vintage Macallan, a very good year. Wait right there while I find the bottle . . ."

He doubles back into his room, but wait Lottie does not, instead seizing eagerly upon his momentary absence to escape down the stairs.

A pair of grips descending the steps stop mid-conversation to give Lottie a grin and a welcome when she trots past. The tall one is Hal, and the one who looks like a squirrel is Frank. By now she knows almost everybody from the American contingent staying at the hotel. Brought them all candy boxes this morning, establishing herself as the cast and crew's beloved kid sister. It's a familiar script, one she's played out many times before, from the studio school into the Little Birdie Told Me shorts, through the Millie movies, all the way up to the last shoot, *Madame Bovary*.

It's old hat, all of this. But this time, and she can't quite pinpoint why, Lottie feels off-kilter. In over her head.

Is it Max? she wonders. He's a complication, no question, principally because of him and Teddy, but even leaving that aside, Max is a liability. For the past three years, since popping up on a list of Communist Party members, the name *Max Montrose* has sat ominously at the tippy-top of the Hollywood blacklist. Maybe things are finally changing, with new-breed moguls like Gallo willing to bend the rules and take some blessed risks. But as things stand right now, Max still has to doctor this script under a pseudonym—and, above all, hide any hint of his real relationship with the movie's matinee idol.

Lottie has been burdened with some pretty hefty secrets, but she can keep her trap shut. She'd have to be a real dummy not to. Teddy's not only her meal ticket, their "whirlwind romance" hoisting her several rungs up the studio A-list; he's also a pal. Quite possibly the best friend she's ever had. And when they met Max in Paris back in January and the real romance of the century began, she found herself quite happily rolling along with them as a third wheel.

Lottie frowns now, digging a line into the oak banister with her fingernail. No, the source of her stress isn't Teddy's current love interest. It's his "ex."

Armed with her box of chocolates, Lottie rounds the next stairwell and fields a "What did you find, Millie?" joke from a freckle-faced gaffer, clearly a well-meaning fan, referencing Lottie's recurring line from those popular "farm girl and her clever spaniel" pictures.

"Nothing for you," she teases, sliding past, quelling the urge to scream, "Do you see a dog? *Millie's not here!*"

She takes a shortcut through the hotel bar, opting for the side door to the property's picturesque gardens, and barrels straight into an unobtrusive middle-aged gentleman in a tatty tweed jacket.

"Goodness!" She laughs, patting his padded shoulders in apology. "I need to hold my horses."

He's startled pallid by the attention. "Not at all, Miss Lawrence. Happens all the time."

Lottie's not surprised to hear that. Poor fellow must blend into the woodwork everywhere he goes. Maybe he's here as a background actor. Or a tourist. He's tucking a camera into his pocket now, a skinny metal one, not a brand Lottie's seen before. Maybe he's just sightseeing and got more than he bargained for.

He notices her staring and smiles tightly. *"Buonasera."*

Lottie nods with a cheerful grin. *"Buonasera."* She walks out into the gardens, dramatically cloaked now in the long shadows of early evening.

She finds Vivienne still lingering near the cliff edge, staring fixedly out at the sea as if contemplating throwing herself in, returning to her natural element. *The sea witch,* Lottie thinks with a smirk, Vivienne's jibe from the Oscars still smarting. Still, there's something so majestic about the taller woman, especially in this moment, that Lottie feels like she should be approaching with a paper and pen for an autograph rather than a box of candy.

Like an Omaha housewife who's won Queen for a Day.

Vivienne glances back, spotting her, and Lottie has to suppress a flinch at the ice in her new costar's expression. Vivienne looks the other way, clearly seeking an escape route, but Lottie starts to jog, hands tight around the box, keeping it from jostling.

"A little taste of home," she calls out. "I had some chocolates sent along. Didn't want you to miss out."

Vivienne looks down at the cardboard box as if Lottie has just announced it contains live cockroaches. But when she looks up, to Lottie's surprise, her lips are curved in a smile.

"You know, I get it," Vivienne says. "Why they cast you as Helen."

Lottie sees it. The trap behind the sudden pleasantness. But what can she do but smile back and say, "Oh?"

Vivienne starts away slowly, strolling the cliffside, an implicit demand for Lottie to follow. Lottie does, but makes sure she's on the land side. One little shove could end it all.

"Well, if you think about Helen, everything she does, the recklessness, lack of foresight, selfishness big enough to shake the entire Western world to its foundations," Vivienne muses, almost to herself. "It takes a certain quality to portray that, doesn't it? A particular . . ." Here she turns to Lottie, as if only now remembering she's here. "Dimness."

Lottie can't stop color from rushing to her cheeks. Her studio school wasn't exactly an academic setting so much as a crèche for kid actors, and as for Lottie's education prior to signing with Apex, it could best be described as sporadic. Meanwhile, Vivienne Rhodes was LA royalty. The daughter of one of Apex's biggest action heroes, the iconic star of *Robinson Crusoe* and so many other films. In Vivienne's own right, a national teen swim champion who everybody thought was headed for the Olympics. According to the breathless profile in *Life* magazine, Vivienne also would have been up for valedictorian at the Westlake School for Girls if it weren't for all the swim matches competing for her time.

An impressive personage. And doesn't she know it.

"I see your point," Lottie says, feigning affability. "I mean, I'm certainly no Joanne Woodward." She turns to see Vivienne's hard blink as the other woman remembers who beat them both for the Academy Award a few months back. "But then, neither are you."

Vivienne freezes for a full three seconds, weathering the insult like a rung bell, before she smiles, shrugging her chestnut hair out of the wind. "There's another quality to Helen too, though, isn't there, beyond her lack of intellect? The homewrecker element."

Lottie breathes slowly through her nose. *Don't react*, she warns herself. *Visible anger is never the right play.*

Vivienne keeps strolling, casual as the breeze, kicking a pebble along as she goes. "I'm curious. When you heard Lina turned down Helen, who did you appeal to? Was it Jack Gallo himself? Did you go to his office on . . . bended knee?"

She glances back, pointedly arching an eyebrow, apparently pleased with herself for that bit of clumsy wordplay.

Lottie forces herself to keep walking. "I didn't go to anybody. I'm still just a contract player, Vivienne. I do what they tell me to do."

"Oh, gee whiz," Vivienne snaps. "Is that what you said to Ken Winters's wife? 'Gosh, Betty, it's not my fault—the studio made me do it.'"

Lottie's eyes blur with instant tears. For Vivienne to bring up that damn *On the Q.T.* article now, *here*, a full ten years later. Of course Lottie knows that everyone knows, but the reminders never cease to pummel her.

An impulse strikes Lottie. A reckless one. The urge to step forward and slap, or better yet, shove. Vivienne's on the wrong side of that cliff edge, after all.

Vivienne seems to realize it too, sweeping swiftly away past Lottie with a look of barely quelled alarm on her face.

Lottie clenches the still-unopened See's box and wills her burgeoning tears to dry up before they so much as touch her mascara. She breathes, watching Vivienne beeline away, straight back to the safety of the Albergo Tavalli.

And once again, Lottie finds herself alone. Feels alone.

She can't go back to the hotel, not yet, and not just because that's where Vivienne will be. Lottie can't face all those studio folks and wonder if they've called her a harlot behind her back.

She'll do it soon—she damn well has to—but not yet.

She worries at her fingernail, then lets her hand drop with a sigh of frustration. She will not let Vivienne Rhodes destroy her manicure on top of everything else. Lottie wants to partake in a worse vice than fingernail biting anyway. What she'd give for a cigarette. Even just a couple drags. She can trade chocolates if she has to. Truth is, she doesn't even like sweets.

She'd brought Billy Wagner one of his favorite Cubans as a thank-you gift for casting her, only to find he'd quit the picture before she arrived. Fleetingly, she considers claiming the Cohiba for herself, but no. America's kid sister can't be caught smoking a cigar like a third-rate Marlene Dietrich. Her wholesome image is everything, so she'll have to be covert. And creative.

Looking for coconspirators, she scans the island's shallow central valley below, where they've built an entire studio town and a backlot in a matter of weeks. In the course of preproduction, the population of Tavalli has more than doubled. Biggest thing to hit this sleepy little island since the war, but judging by the prices at the village market this morning, Lottie supposes the locals don't need any lessons in how to make the best of a fluid situation.

Lottie expected to see an active set today, crew members milling about making last-minute alterations before filming begins tomorrow, but most of the staff seem to be congregated up near the entrance to the wartime hangar that might serve as one of their soundstages.

The hangar sits perched so close to the island's western cliff face that it looks like a strong wind might blow it into the sea. Only thirteen years since the end of the war, but the structure's already gone to rust. To the north of it, a little path has been trod through the grass straight off the edge of the island. As Lottie passes, she peers over, catching a glimpse of a cutback trail leading down to the water's edge. She spotted an idyllic little cove—might you call it a grotto?—on the ferry ride to Tavalli. She'd bet dollars to donuts that's how you get down there.

First things first. She approaches one of the loiterers by the hangar, smile ready, mind trying to land on one of the phrases she remembers from her hastily purchased phrase book: *Per piacere, fumare?* While most of this picture's crew is American, the entire property department was hired from mainland Italy, some kind of measure to foster goodwill with the Italian government, no doubt, in exchange for the opportunity to shoot here on Tavalli. Not only do most of these locals appear brand-new to the movie business; only one of them so far speaks a word of English, and this fellow, leaning on the hangar wall, isn't him.

He downright gulps at the sight of Lottie, tosses his smoke in the dirt, grinding it out with his heel before hurrying off inside, calling out something she's got no hope of translating and leaving her to curse herself for not miming "Can I have a drag?" quickly enough.

Voices echo inside the soundstage. Curiosity strikes, but more than that. Wariness. Her stomach has clenched.

She can practically hear her mother: "*You get that feeling, Loretta, you know, the one in your tummy? Turn and run and you'll find me in our meeting place.*"

There hasn't been a parent to meet her anywhere since she was seven, but that feeling in her tummy has been a steadfast guardian all her life. Right now it's telling her that there is something not quite right about that hangar.

Swiftly, she edges around the side of the building, eyes and ears primed, but for nought. The only things she can see from this angle are crates and all she can hear is in overlapping Italian.

A spindly figure emerges quickly from the soundstage, hand resting on his pocket as if ready for a quick-draw duel. Lottie instantly adjusts her stance, leaning against the building, legs crossed at the ankles, the picture of insouciance even as her heart races in her chest.

Then she lets out a breath. It's the prop master, Ludovico Despetti. The one Italian here who speaks English.

"*Principessa*," he calls. "What do you need? We are working hard here."

His voice is jovial, but there's an edge to his smile. Most people wouldn't notice it. Lottie does.

"Oh gosh, I didn't mean to intrude. I know you have so much to do to get ready for tomorrow. First day of filming. So jazzed."

That seems to appease him, but his eyes are narrowing on her in a way that's not entirely respectful, his hand rising up to stroke his impeccably trimmed mustache.

Lottie pushes off from the hangar wall. "I was actually on the hunt for a cigarette."

He cocks his head, surprised. Maybe impressed.

"I'm happy to barter for chocolates, if you promise not to tell anybody I smoke." She winks and leans in with a coquettish whisper. "Our little secret?"

Ludovico laughs hoarsely. "You are a naughty one, aren't you? Millie's girl smokes cigarettes, look at that."

As she laughs back in agreement, he shouts behind him in Italian. One of the set hands rushes to his side, Muratti cigarette in hand, lighter ready with a flame.

Lottie beams. "*Grazie mille.* And do take the chocolates. I was only teasing about trading. They're meant for you."

As Ludovico and his assistant open the See's box, peeking inside almost cautiously, Lottie steals a peek behind them, then puts in a casual, "So what are you fellas so busy with in there?"

There's a tense moment of silence, both men watching Lottie with fresh alertness. She keeps innocently dragging on her cigarette until Ludovico smiles, wolfish.

"We are building a horse," he says. "A very, very big one."

Lottie claps. "The Trojan horse! Of course. Can I see it?"

"No, no, no, you are too naughty, *principessa*." Ludo chuckles, his eyes twinkling lasciviously. "Not until finished. A craftsman must keep his secrets. This is how we work."

"In that case, I will respect your artistic sensibilities," Lottie flirts back, even as the fine hairs on her neck stand up. There's something about the glance the two men shared, as if they're playing a joke at her expense.

She looks away to draw another drag, hiding her discomfort.

Another form appears on the track, south of the hangar. He's unmistakable even from here, cutting a fine figure in his expensive suit, his handsome silhouette limned in gold by the setting sun. Jack Gallo looks more like a film star than a mogul to Lottie—either way, not an unpleasant face to see on set every day—but as she turns back to the set hands, she notes with surprise their very different reaction to his arrival.

Ludovico's teasing smile has dropped into a tense scowl. He barks something behind him and the young man scurries away, shouting to the others, who hurriedly shut the two tall hangar doors.

Time to extract herself.

"*Buonasera*," she calls to a distracted Ludovico. Then she turns on her heel and walks away north, maintaining a sway in her hips in case there's still an audience watching.

And as soon as she's out of sightline, she fights the urge to run. She puffs on the cigarette and calms her pace.

Nothing feels safe lately. Her instincts keep telling her to get out of here. But if there's one mounting threat Lottie's prepared to confront head-on, it's her incredibly irritating costar.

Lottie squares her shoulders and makes for the hotel, determined to face whatever comes with dignity.

So Vivienne Rhodes insists on tearing her down? That's absolutely fine. Because Lottie Lawrence is far, far away from here. And in her place is a timeless, iconic, beautiful, powerful woman. A figure of legend.

From here on out, she's gonna be nothing but Helen of Troy.

THE REPORT
Behind the Headlines

APEX PICTURES COURSE-CORRECTS WITH GALLO AT HELM

BY JAY GRIER

JUNE 11, 1958

After a small parcel sell-off of the behemoth Apex Pictures campus in Burbank, as well as an influx of new money and enthusiasm from businessman and entrepreneur Jack Gallo, the major studio might live to fight another day. Newly minted board chairman Lex Augustine and head of production Buster Smith fully support the new president's progressive vision for the studio, which includes cutting the number of pictures per season and instead focusing on a smaller slate of historical epics and big-budget sagas, like Apex's upcoming tentpole *A Thousand Ships*.

"Mr. Gallo is precisely what Apex needs at this critical juncture: fresh blood with an inventive approach," Mr. Smith told the *Hollywood Reporter*. "His lifelong passion for this industry is palpable, and we're thrilled to have him at the helm, a maverick ready to steer Apex into its next era . . ."

3

Friday, June 13, 1958

Vivienne stares into the mirror while the set's makeup woman, Ginger, brushes glistening bronze powder across her hairline. Despite her young age, Ginger Banowski is clearly at the top of her game, a whiz with the brush and quite eager to collaborate. She barely batted her false lashes when Vivienne sat down in her chair this morning, on her first official day of shooting at long last, with a comprehensive visual overhaul for Cassandra, a way to elevate her character from "somber priestess" into "glamorous oracle." Dark, theatrical makeup; sculpted cheekbones; cascading waves.

Maybe Ginger's such an ace because she has to be as a single working mother. Vivienne had heard she was a war widow—likely true, as evidenced by the slew of joyful photographs taped around the mirror's frame, Ginger and the same smiling little girl captured during various milestones, and not one husband photo among the lot.

Ginger follows Vivienne's line of sight and smiles. "My pride and joy. Jackie. She's ten."

Children really aren't Vivienne's thing, but she's eager for Ginger to warm to her. She doesn't have many allies on this island; plus, good hair and makeup people are essential. "Adorable. I don't think I've seen her around set."

"She's back home," Ginger explains. "With my mom. Easier for everyone, but golly, I miss her."

"Got to be hard."

Ginger pastes on a cheery smile. "The new doll and dresses that Mr. Gallo sent along helped to soften the blow," she says wistfully. "Such a thoughtful fellow, I tell ya. Though before you go askin', it's nothing like that. He's a gentleman through and through. If I need to be away from my Jackie for two months, at least I know it's for a classy guy. Easy on the eyes, too, isn't he?"

"Is he?" Vivienne tries to keep her voice neutral. "Hadn't noticed."

Ginger laughs. "I suppose he's got some competition on this set."

"Oh. That's not what I—"

"Really, I've been dying to know, is it awkward? Working with Teddy again?"

Vivienne hardens into marble in her seat, though if Ginger notices, she doesn't let on.

"Everyone thought the two of you were gonna tie the knot," she continues, wrinkling her brow as she sweeps the brush down Vivienne's cheekbone. "Exquisite couple you made. The wedding . . . Ah, it would've been swoonworthy."

"Yes, well, not everything works out."

"Oh, come on. I know real love when I see it. And you, Viv, you were smitten."

Vivienne closes her eyes.

"Well." Ginger sighs out the word when Vivienne stays silent.

"Other fish in the sea. I could see you with someone far more so-phisticated. Ooh, like Gregory Peck. He's married, though, isn't he? All the best ones are."

While Ginger applies her eyeliner, Vivienne attempts to slow her breath, to regain control of her jumping pulse. Jack Gallo was right when they'd spoken in her hotel room last Friday evening, the night she'd arrived: her relationship with Teddy had begun as an arrangement, a strategic romantic pairing to whet audiences' interest in *Beach Holiday* during the picture's opening weeks at the box office. And though it was her first setup, Vivienne was far from naive; she'd been in the film business long enough to know these sorts of relationships were arranged all the time. Besides, she'd grown up with performative parents—her celebrity father and Southern belle mother—whose brief infatuation morphed into fiery mutual hatred before Vivienne had been old enough to walk, and still the pair relentlessly played the part of "Hollywood's power couple" for decades. Vivienne had told Apex that of course she'd date Teddy Walters for the good of the picture. A few dutiful dinners out at LA hotspots, a handful of arranged public appear-ances together, and then they'd both say sayonara.

The trouble was, despite everything, Vivienne desperately wanted the "real deal," as Gallo had so succinctly put it—the kind of cinematic, boneshaking romance at the heart of films like *His Girl Friday*, *The Philadelphia Story*, *Casablanca*. Those heady love stories she used to sneak out to watch at the Santa Monica Cinema when her parents were shrieking at each other; the kind of rela-tionship she'd daydream about as she swam freestyle laps, hours upon hours perfecting technique, in the Athletic Club pool.

And Teddy Walters, it turned out, wasn't just a looker; he was honest and kind, a rare combination in this business. An Iowa-born track star with modesty and aw-shucks charm. And he had such a backstory, as interesting and tumultuous as Bogart's Rick Blaine in *Casablanca*. Teddy's days spent running track, he'd confessed to her, were more like running for his life, as he grew up dirt-poor, the fifth child of a drunken, destitute farmer. Moreover, Teddy seemed lonely, like she was. Like he was searching for the real deal too. Their connection felt open and candid and surprisingly right. Vivienne fell for him easily, the whole affair as effortless as stepping off a ledge and plunging in.

So she hadn't worried, at least at first, when Teddy's check-in calls from France started dwindling. *Bovary* had a tight shooting schedule, after all, and their time zones were literally night and day. It didn't take long, though, before her worries turned all-encompassing, Teddy's name a constant mantra in her mind, her torturous mental games of "Why Isn't He Calling?" consuming most Saturday nights this past winter, along with multiple bottles of white Bordeaux. The next time she saw him was at the Oscar pre-party, when Vivienne literally smacked right into him, a tight turn in her floor-length piqué gown sending her colliding into Teddy's tux-clad chest. *What a perfect reunion*, she'd thought, swelling with happiness before registering Lottie Lawrence draped across his arm.

Of all people. Lottie. An actress who flirted with anything that moved, who everyone had whispered about since the girl hit puberty, who climbed the career ladder early on by having an affair with her married costar, Ken Winters. It had to be a setup for *Madame Bovary*. That was the only rational explanation.

But then Teddy confirmed her greatest fears, pulling her aside right in the damned middle of the red-carpet madness, stumbling through some kind of half-baked explanation for why he'd disappeared on her. Telling her that he had, in fact, finally found the real deal—just with someone else. As if she would be thrilled for him.

Losing Best Supporting Actress that night had been a breeze by comparison.

"Lips, love," Ginger orders.

Startled from her recollective trance, Vivienne puckers. A few quick sweeps of color, then Ginger adds, "There," and steps aside like a showgirl.

Vivienne blinks at her reflection in the mirror. "Glamorous oracle" indeed. The woman staring back is downright arresting, with piled brunette waves; wide, beguiling hazel eyes; razor-sharp cheekbones. A ruby-red mouth that somehow looks equally alluring and classic.

"Is this what you were imagining?" Ginger says.

"Even better."

Ginger matches Vivienne's smile through the mirror.

"Knock 'em dead out there." The makeup artist winks before sauntering out the trailer's flap door with a toss of her auburn hair.

Vivienne once more studies the stunning woman in the mirror.

"Cassandra," she says aloud, trying on the new name again.

Playing the priestess still feels like a consolation prize—she can't deny that, despite all of Gallo's assurances—and yet she won something far more valuable in their exchange. She's still electrified by the creative control Gallo promised her, buzzing with excitement to get to set. Vivienne's never been handed carte blanche freedom over a role. That's what he gave her, isn't it? Total authority over her character? She's spent the last six days on the island holed up in her room, reworking her scenes and monologues, hand-delivering her pages to Max or Johnny to pass along to Syd Durand, while the rest of the cast has been busy filming the opening sequence. After Vivienne's reimagining, Cassandra will no doubt be her finest role: a woman with vision, passion, and drive; a mastermind tragically ahead of her times. The oracle is her surefire ticket to that elusive Oscar, and *not* in a supporting category.

Vivienne bursts out of the makeup trailer, humming from an undeniable feeling of destiny. She sets off down the short dirt path, passing the wardrobe tents and the "promo room," as the crew has taken to calling it, where an assistant is arranging neat stacks of large glossy photos of every major cast member. Gallo really is pulling out all the stops. And he was right, the final *Ships* cast list is quite impressive, if a bit, er, eclectic. Veteran West End star Charles Brinkwater. The young king of the Hollywood West- ern, Clay Cooper. Lottie and Teddy, both beaming in their annoy- ingly perfect headshots. And Vivienne herself, a pile of parted red lips, eyes bewitched by some distant horizon.

She heads toward the custom sets tucked like a row of diora- mas into the valley's fold. The gilded Grecian temple. The lavish bedroom interior set. Then a palace atrium checkered with marble columns and a gleaming, gilded floor. King Priam's palace, scene five, she recalls instantly, having read the script so many times.

The introduction of Cassandra.

Cast members and extras already cluster at the base of the set's elevated stage, the lot of them looking cut from a history book in their costumes: royal Trojan cloaks, chitons, servants in their togas. There's a crowd buzzing around Sydney Durand, who appears flustered even from here, his tufts of gray hair standing on end, his shirt untucked and sweat-stained. Syd's directing a group of cameramen with increasingly exasperated hand gestures while discussing something with Johnny and an- other assistant, Vivienne assumes, a tall, bald man with a long, crooked nose. Behind them, set hands run back and forth across the stage.

Despite her lingering reservations, despite the clawing nerves digging into her insides, there is something wholly irresistible about the frenetic energy of a shooting set.

"Finally," Syd huffs when he spots her. "Vivienne!" He storms toward her. "You've gotta be kidding me with this."

"Goodness, Syd, I'm only five minutes late." She laughs lightly. "Please don't have a coronary—"

"The look, I mean. Your look is all wrong!"

Vivienne flinches. Just an instant. She's in the right here, after all. "Syd. As I've been stressing, Cassandra needs a wholesale re-imagining if this picture's ever going to soar. The Oracle of Troy cannot fade into the background—"

"Vivienne, what part of 'budget constraints' do you not understand?"

She grits her teeth. "Eyeshadow costs the same whether it's purple or brown—"

"That Palladium prophecy scene you added? We don't *have* a Palladium. No, we need to revert, revert, *revert*." Syd spins on his heel, yanking on his hair, shouting, "Ginger? Can one of you putzes get me Ginger!"

Vivienne's about to follow, argue her vision until it's canon once and for all—didn't Gallo explain the new state of affairs?—but Charles Brinkwater saunters in front of her path, looking disheveled in his King Priam cloak and feathered headpiece.

"Oh, Vivienne." He teeters a bit, kissing her hand with a conspicuous wink. "Don't you just look like this picture's star?"

"Charles." She nods, though that wink . . . it makes her uneasy. On Wednesday night, as she was working on the next round of pages, Vivienne somehow polished off the bottle of Chianti she'd had sent up from the bar. As she was tipsily attempting to deliver her latest reworked scene to Johnny, since Max was nowhere to be found, Charles spotted and snared her on her way out the door.

Charles Brinkwater is most decidedly a bad influence. He cajoled her into another glass of wine, along with two gin martinis, while he rambled on about all his turns playing Romeo; about how *Ships* would turn him into an international star to rival "that hack Olivier." He even attempted to include the hotel's bartender in the discussion, oblivious to the fact that the poor guy spoke nary a word of English. At some point Clay Cooper joined them at the bar, at which point Vivienne launched into her own diatribe about Lottie Lawrence not being highbrow enough to play Helen of Troy.

"The cast and crew agree with you about Lottie, you know." Charles takes Vivienne's arm, leading her through the crowd, up the steps, and onto the stage. Goodness, it's not even 10:00 a.m. and she can already smell the booze on him. Around them, the lighting team shuffles about, putting the finishing touches on a mood piece: an otherworldly green spotlight shining onto a gilded mosaic on the floor. The dozen or so extras have started filtering in, mulling about the columns, chatting, waiting for Syd's call.

Charles adds, in a much too loud whisper, "I did you the courtesy of taking a poll."

Vivienne snaps her head around, eyes narrowing. "What do you mean, a poll?"

"A survey of sorts. About whether Lottie is suited for the role." His British lilt dips into a slur. "More than fifty percent agree she's miscast as Helen."

"Oh, Charles, you didn't."

"All those rumors of her and Ken Winters, it's just so uncouth," Charles goes on, talking over her. "Shagging her way into the upper echelons. Not the kind of actress one imagines playing the Queen of Troy. Even Lottie herself seemed surprised by her selection when I put it to her—"

"What?" Vivienne hisses. "You told Lottie what I said?"

Charles furrows his brow. "Only seemed fair to include her in the official vote."

"Talking about me again?" Lottie's voice rings out. "Gosh, you two can't seem to stop."

Vivienne turns to find Lottie wearing a wide, clearly fabricated smile. Her swept-up hair and regal makeup are so perfect, so stunning, that all the words fall out of Vivienne's head.

"My, what a glamorous priestess you are, Vivienne." Lottie appraises her back with raised eyebrows. "Really, nothing says 'virgin prophetess' like a full mug of makeup."

Vivienne stiffens. "We're reimagining Cassandra. To be more of a central presence. A heroine. I'm sure you were made aware."

Lottie smirks. "And here I thought Syd was the director. Silly me."

Vivienne's heart starts beating in race mode, a starting pistol cracked. "My changes are for the good of the picture, Lottie, nothing more."

"Feels a little like mutiny. How exciting." Lottie cocks her head. "And is everybody with you on this? Should we take a poll?"

"Too late to fix this. Ginger's prepping the goddesses." Syd huffs his way between them, oblivious. "Full body paint, gonna take a while. We'll have to make do."

He motions for Teddy, who's joined them on the stage, to stand atop the mosaic.

Lottie sweeps next to Teddy. Possessively.

"All right, ladies, gentlemen." Syd steps forward, manically clapping his hands. "Let's lock it up! Rolling in five!"

Vivienne pinches her eyes closed, a headache blooming.

As she hits her mark on set, she inches toward Lottie to whisper, "I did not ask Charles to talk to everyone. For the record."

Lottie doesn't meet her eyes. "I just hope you know there's absolutely no reason to feel jealous of me. We're going to have equal billing. Or at least close to it."

"Jealous?" Vivienne squawks. "Of you?"

"You're literally green." Lottie gestures to the eerie, lime-colored spotlight with a sweet smile.

"Annnd . . . action!" Syd calls from the director's chair.

Vivienne's mind goes as quiet as the set. That's her cue, yes?

She looks around, trying to focus, to dash Lottie Lawrence and her passive-aggressive jibes from her mind. Charles has stumbled to his seat on King Priam's throne. Teddy and Lottie are standing atop the mosaic. After Vivienne's revisions, it should only be Lottie in the prophecy, but no matter, they can run it right next take. Time for her new monologue.

Vivienne pushes her cloak from her shoulders and turns away from her ex and his harlot. "I, Cassandra, am a mere conduit of the future. I foretell Paris's rash actions will bring great pain upon our people, his ill-fated infatuation with a temptress across the sea—"

"And . . . ah, cut," Syd calls. "Good start, Vivienne, but let's stick with Max's dialogue."

Vivienne resists the urge to look in Max's direction. Max Montrose, who's still on the Hollywood blacklist, for goodness' sake, is apparently Gallo's pinch-hitter scribe. She'd thought a man who'd been handed such a golden opportunity to resurrect his career would be open to collaborating, had assumed he'd accepted her notes . . . Although Max did gape at her, didn't he—looked horrified, really, now that she dwells on it—when she passed along her reworked scenes earlier this week, as if some Greek sea-demon kraken was hand-delivering him pages.

In her peripheral vision now, Vivienne can see Max feverishly pacing behind Syd's chair, shaking his head of dark curly hair, adjusting his glasses.

"Let's run it again as written," Syd calls before Vivienne can interject. "Scene five, take two . . . action!"

Frustrated, Vivienne tilts her chin and swishes forward. "I have seen the great despair Paris will bring down upon our people, as he listens to the call of the siren across the sea—"

"Vivienne, cut!" Syd takes a long, audible breath and slides out of his chair. "That's not what the script says."

"It's what the script *should* say."

Syd's eyes bug wide. "As I mentioned, doll, we're holding to *Max's* script iteration—"

"And as *I* mentioned, that iteration needs rewrites."

"I'm not taking rewrites," Max growls. And then a low rumble, "I didn't upend my life to play secretary to a mermaid."

From the stage, Teddy shoots him an admonishing glare. It oddly fortifies her.

"Mr. Gallo gave me full creative control," Vivienne presses, "and I intend to use it to save this picture."

"Ooh, are we all in trouble?" Lottie effects a gasp. "Should we call the police?"

The extras titter with laughter.

The director's face grows redder. "Vivienne, I think you're misinfor—"

Vivienne spins. "And you know what, Syd, now I'm thinking of a different prophetic vision altogether. Perhaps Cassandra could be foretelling Helen's death."

"Hey, I like this game," Clay Cooper calls from his spot near the columns. "Are we all allowed to make rewrites? Let's give ol' Hector a monologue!"

Max covers his face. "This is an actual waking nightmare. A Dali painting. A—"

"Mr. Durand," Teddy cuts in, exuding friendliness with all his might. "Maybe we take five?"

Syd, flummoxed now beyond speech, simply gives a slow thumbs-up.

"Right." Vivienne blinks rapidly. "Fine."

She steps back with a clearing of her throat, then promptly takes the set steps two at a time. Past Syd, past Max—quickly before anyone can see her fully unravel.

Didn't Gallo assure her this was her Oscar vehicle, her role to mold as she sees fit? So why is everyone treating her like she's really Cassandra? A.k.a., a raving lunatic?

She careens up the dirt road before tears come on. Huffing, scalding, the indignity reaching the boiling point. She needs water. Air. Space to think. But what looks to be the trio of sparkling, no-name young goddesses are heading down the path via Johnny's donkey cart from the wardrobe tents.

She impulsively ducks onto the matted grass, weaving instead toward the warehouse on the island's cliff, where she saw the Aphrodite statue being loaded yesterday. She spots Jack Gallo, president of Apex Pictures, of all people, here, out for a countryside walk. For heaven's sake, couldn't he have been on set, backing her up?

He looks tense. He's staring at the hangar, his dreamy face stitched, as if concerned.

She approaches quietly, not wanting to startle him, but a twig snaps.

Gallo starts and turns. "Vivienne?"

He attempts that charming smile of his as she approaches. But she can tell he's still unnerved, rattled by something.

"What are you doing off set?" he asks. "Wandering around over here?"

She could ask him the same thing. Instead, it all tumbles out.

"This isn't working," she croaks, wrenching a flyaway hair behind her ear. "I thought I could move forward, focus on the film. But this is the definition of slow torture, foretelling the tale of Lottie and Teddy's earth-shattering love. And Max and Syd are aggressively ignoring my notes, like I'm just some clueless actress, and Cassandra as envisioned now is a two-bit character. I know what you said about me and this film and I want, quite desperately, to believe you, but I'm getting that feeling I used to get in the water, when I'd hold my breath just a beat too long and—"

She swallows a gulp of air.

"And I can't tell if I'm sinking or this whole *Ships* is sinking, but I have this deep, mounting sense that I should walk away. While I have the chance."

As she recovers from her monologue—not the one she'd intended to give today—Gallo softly cups her shoulders. At his touch, she feels her tension melting away. She peers up into his warm eyes.

"It's my fault," he finally says. "I framed your creative involvement as advice to Syd. I thought that might land better, but . . ." He sighs. "To be honest, the picture, this set, the crew, it's, well, there's more to do than I ever anticipated. Producing isn't for the faint of heart, is it?"

He lets out an unassuming laugh, then glances back at the hangar, all traces of his smile falling away.

"Tell you what," he says, brightening as he refocuses on her. "I chartered a private yacht from Corsica last week. Figured I'd need some space for myself away from the cast and crew from time to time. A wise move or a foolish one, I'm not sure yet. Some of the local production crew are proving a bit hard to manage." His eyes flick to the hangar again. "Either way, useful to have a hiding spot. But for you, Vivienne, I will gladly extend an invitation."

He carefully covers her shoulders with the folds of her cloak. She nearly blushes at the tenderness of the gesture.

"Why don't you come to the docks around seven tonight?" he asks. "We'll have dinner, go scene by scene through your changes to the script to make sure I fully understand your new vision. Then I'll talk to Max and Syd, get them both in line. Give me one more chance. That's all I'm asking."

Now she's really blushing, in spite of it all.

Dinner. With the studio chief. She knows his offered meeting isn't just about the script. There's a force between her and Gallo she can't deny, like a magnetic charge.

And she can see it in his eyes: he'd like more from her.

She's been so burned from the Hollywood game of strategy masquerading as love, from playing it with Teddy and losing big. And she is not, nor will she ever be, a Lottie Lawrence type, sleeping her way into a better role.

She stares into Gallo's eyes, their warmth now searing.

Then again, who's to say that whatever is building between them has to be an either-or situation? Who's to say things would go the same way as her fling with Teddy? Why *couldn't* this end like all those pictures she worshiped as a child?

Gallo drops his hands, almost reluctantly, from her shoulders. "What do you think, Viv?"

She swallows. "I believe my calendar's open."

His lips curve into a smile once more. "Then it's a date."

She allows herself a smile in return only when Gallo leaves, trailing toward the water. Then she leaves herself, heading back in the vague direction of the set. Along the way, she hears a tiny thump, then a muffled curse.

She spins to find that extra she almost tripped over at the hotel when she first arrived in Tavalli. The inconspicuous middle-aged man in the tweed jacket, although now he's in his extra costume, a full-length toga, hiding behind a few marble statues clustered near the warehouse entrance. A strange, thin, metal device is in his hand. It's a camera, isn't it? The type they used back in the war.

The man takes off, camera in hand, toga flowing, darting back toward the set.

Leaving her completely bewildered in the maquis brush.

On the Q.T.

The Magazine That Tells the WHOLE Story

Vol. 11, Issue 4

JUNE 1958

WHY DID WILLIAM WAGNER WALK (AND WHERE IS HE)?

There's been no shortage of gossip and speculation surrounding Apex Pictures' big-budget epic, *A Thousand Ships*. *On the Q.T.* has been trying to track down the man we hope has some real answers for us . . . but unfortunately, nobody can seem to find him.

Ex-producer and Hollywood veteran William Wagner made headlines a few weeks ago for storming off the set of *Ships*, which had been recently relocated to the remote Italian island of Tavalli, though no one appears to know exactly why he quit. Was Wagner upset about Jack Gallo purchasing the studio? Stagnated by budget woes? Frustrated with director Sydney Durand and the picture's ever-revolving cast of stars?

Wagner's representatives have all declined to comment, but sources close to Wagner's family say that the producer has yet to return home from his failed post overseas, or even to reach out with an update on his plans.

"His wife is worried sick," confesses an anonymous source. "Apex executives assure her that he must be taking some time abroad, vacationing, but she can tell it's a flimsy excuse. No one has heard from the guy. It's like he's just gone up in smoke."

4

And that's a wrap on day five of *A Thousand Ships*," Syd calls out to smatterings of applause from the gathered cast and crew. Only Lottie is close enough to see sweat pouring down his neck and hear him add, under his breath, "Felt like day seven hundred and four."

He's not wrong, Lottie thinks as she grins and waves her way out of the set. And yet they're already behind schedule. What should have been a morning shoot of the big Cassandra scene with a break for lunch and then Paris and Helen's first meeting became an all-day battle among Vivienne and Syd and Max with everybody else as a captive audience. The moment Vivienne came back to set, she seemed reenergized. Ready to fight, and fight she did.

Every time Lottie thought she was done holding her excruciating pose, that surely, surely, this was a wrap, Vivienne would pipe up. "One more take, Syd, and I think we'll have it, but let's just adjust the staging here and perhaps more blue in the filters . . ." And once again, Syd would get his back up, Max would object to the script changes, and the worst part?

Vivienne was right.

Her ideas, her changes were better. Whenever Sydney gave an inch, out of sheer fatigue, no doubt, Vivienne improved the scene. And when he balked, Lottie felt frustration quite separate from the irritation of having to wait out yet another argument.

Listen to her! she was half-tempted to scream. From a stock theatrical prophecy scene, Vivienne was clearly trying to craft something dreamlike and uncanny, something implausibly close to actual . . . art.

Well, no, actually, the worst part wasn't Vivienne's talent; it was when she tossed Lottie a casual glare over her shoulder and sniped, "At least you didn't have any lines to memorize. I can't imagine script analysis is your favorite part of the gig."

"Sure isn't." Lottie snorted. "We're playing make-believe, Vivienne, not getting our PhDs. Although, if this scene doesn't wrap soon, we might all qualify for one."

The laughs of commiseration from the crew that greeted her quip, along with Vivienne's deep glower, helped boost Lottie's spirits for the next several hours of shooting. But now that they're out of their costumes and off the clock, she can't help but replay it.

Vivienne Rhodes calling her a dumb blonde. Again.

I'm not dumb, Lottie tells herself, even her inner voice coming out petulant. *I'm not even really blonde.*

Teddy hops down the steps of his trailer, rubbing a knot loose in his neck. "If only we were home. I could really use the studio physio today."

"Physio," Max repeats from where he waits, wearily cleaning his glasses. "That's a funny way of saying 'triple whiskey.'"

Charles Brinkwater leaps from his trailer like a genie summoned by a magic word. "Whiskey, you say? Jack gifted me a bottle of Macallan, you know, very good vintage. Might be a bit left in the bottle, or shall we just go to the hotel bar?"

He links arms with Max and drags him along.

Max looks over his shoulder to mouth, *"Help!"* at Lottie. She bites her lip around a pitying laugh and slows her step to avoid also getting pulled into Brinkwater's undertow.

Her smile only starts to droop at the corners once she's well off set, wind tousling her curls and no one in close sightline. Behind her she hears a rumble: the little rustic cart, driven by Johnny, bless him, the junior production assistant with his polka-dot bow tie who seems to have formed a bond with the donkey, if no one else. She perks up once more, waving for him to go on without her.

"I need the exercise!" she shouts, and if he's a little quick to nod in agreement, she doesn't let her irritation show. Maybe she does need the exercise. An exercise in strategy. If Vivienne keeps on restaging and rewriting, her Cassandra will get that coveted Oscar nomination, no doubt, maybe even a win, while Lottie Lawrence will be the actress who, after thousands of years, made all of Western civilization say, "Who is Helen of Troy?"

And she needs this, just like she needs Teddy. A starring role, a glamorous one, a character who tugs on the heartstrings. One that leaves no question about her value as an adult actress. Never mind her turns as Daisy Buchanan or Emma Bovary, the public still sees her as "Millie's girl," pigtailed and gee-whiz innocent. And she needs that too, she knows. She has to capitalize on that legacy while adding another element and then another and another, or Hollywood's going to roll right over her and past her, and what will she do then?

This is it for her. Hollywood, the last safe haven. One role and then the next, running from one identity to the other. If that ends—no more characters, no more shoots—then all she's got is herself.

And that's nobody at all.

Teddy's waiting on a sofa in the hotel lobby holding two martinis when she arrives. She thinks for a second he's being rather bold in sharing a public evening cocktail with Max, even with Brinkwater as a buffer, but when he rises with a sympathetic wince and extends the glass, she realizes he's gotten it for her.

"Thought you might need this," he says. "Immediately. Bartender doesn't understand a word we say, so I had to mime it. Hope it's good."

What a fella, Lottie thinks. No wonder Vivienne fell in love with him for real.

She herself was spared that fate fairly quickly. When Buster Smith called her into his office before she left for France, she knew it was another "dating" assignment, courting the press to keep promoting her image as a glamorous young woman about town. She was hugely relieved to hear it was Teddy Walters and not someone with a spottier reputation. She'd thought he'd been paired with Vivienne Rhodes, but apparently that had run its course and they wanted to boost publicity for *Madame Bovary* ahead of release.

None of the actual work of it—the public dates, photo ops, "caught canoodling" moments—were slated to start until they were back home in Hollywood, but when they boarded the flight to Paris, Teddy had the seat next to her.

"So," he said by way of introduction, "I take it we're an item."

She waited for the knowing leer, the eyes grazing her body, the ownership taken. In other words, the usual routine. But he was a complete gentleman. Lovely, friendly, engaging, and entirely platonic for the entire flight.

And she knew. Right there. She'd always been good at reading people. The only thing that shocked her, really, was just how much she liked him. They palled around Paris together whenever they weren't needed on set, and Lottie found herself spilling her life story to Teddy, more intimate than she'd ever been with anybody else in her life. Not everything, of course, but a whole lot. And Teddy shared his life too, his frustrations at being stuck in second-billing pretty-boy roles, his alienation from his family, his worries about having led Vivienne on, his fundamental loneliness.

Lottie hoped she could help allay that last bit a little.

And then, with one after-dinner stroll to a dingy neighborhood bar in Montmartre, that last bit got fixed entirely.

Coming back from the toilette, Lottie found Teddy perched on a barstool, in a tête-à-tête with a fellow American.

"Lottie, you'll never guess who I've found," Teddy called. She'd been tempted to make a Millie joke at her own expense but restrained herself. "Max Montrose! You know him; he wrote *The Big House, Life of the Party*. He's a genius." He swiveled to gaze at Max. "Where have you been?"

"Waiting for you, I suppose," Max said, two drinks in, it turned out, and emboldened by Teddy's obvious instant infatuation.

In Paris, Lottie realized, you could be that bold. You could be yourself. Even so, Teddy's eyes darted to hers, his expression tight with worry, tinged with hope.

Lottie plopped herself down on the next stool, winked at Max, and nudged Teddy, saying, "This one's worth the wait."

And that was that. She left them to finish a bottle of red and make their own rambling way home together, a routine they would repeat many times in the coming weeks. That first night, Lottie strolled back to the hotel, a little wistful, assuming herself discarded. But, to her delighted surprise, that never happened. Sometimes it was Teddy inviting her out; sometimes Max himself would show up at her hotel room unannounced, lie on her settee, and hold forth hilariously about the injustices of the universe until she teased him out of his rant. And then Teddy would appear and off they'd go to see the city, or out to the countryside, or to their favorite corner bar. They made for a strange trio, no doubt, but a happy one.

When filming wrapped and they returned to L.A., it was wrenching for all of them. But after the Oscars, Teddy and Lottie's first "official" date, it was easy enough to use the excuse of the Cannes screening to pop straight back to Europe and stay there, reunited with Max for as long as possible. And then came the offer to shoot *A Thousand Ships*, and here they all were. Still on cloud nine. Or would be, if it weren't for the ever-rumbling cumulonimbus that was Vivienne Rhodes.

"You were brilliant today," Teddy says now, passing Lottie her glass for a clink.

She allows herself a swift eye roll. "Please."

"You were," he insists. "Not an easy feat, stealing the scene from the rest of us while standing completely still, but you managed it."

Lottie slumps down next to him on the lobby banquette. "It's frightening what a good liar you are. Vivienne literally stole the scene. First of many, I'm sure. She'll somehow find a way to restage our romantic scene around a brilliant soliloquy she's written for herself and force me to do nothing for the rest of the picture but stand in the background like a statue at the Met. And the picture will probably be better for it."

It's childish to sulk; she knows that. But she wants to pout. So she does.

Teddy stretches his arm out behind her, grinning. "Don't knock standing still and looking pretty. It's damn hard work, and I've made an entire career out of it."

Lottie lets out a genuine laugh at that, nudging him with her elbow so that he gets tickled and nearly spills his drink, both of them giggling like children.

The percussion of sharp heels on the tile floor stops them cold.

Vivienne's coming through the lobby. She pauses at the sight of them nestled together on the sofa like lovebirds, and the hurt on her face is so unguarded that Lottie nearly jumps up to reassure her. But in the next blink, Vivienne regains her usual hauteur, and if her eyes are broadcasting any announcement now, it reads, "Danger. Do not approach."

Her getup only adds to the effect. She's about as chic as Lottie's ever seen her, shy of Oscar night. Her hair is pinned in a sleek updo, sapphires dangling from her ears, the exact shade of her flared charmeuse evening gown, twilight blue. She's even wearing elbow-high gloves. Lottie didn't pack anything that formal, and she came here by way of the Cannes Film Festival. Where in the hell is Vivienne going, dressed up like this?

Vivienne pauses, chin lifted like a *Vogue* cover model, waiting for eyes to turn, and they do, all over the hotel lobby.

Clay Cooper, peeking from the hotel bar, lets out a slow whistle. "Beg your pardon, Miss Rhodes, but you look like a million bucks. Where you headed?"

Lottie's ears perk up. She can't help it.

Vivienne tosses Lottie a laconic glance over her bare shoulder before answering low, "Dinner with Jack. To discuss the picture. Some changes we intend to make."

"What was that you were saying about a bended knee, Vivienne?" The words fly out of Lottie's mouth before her better angels can reel them back in.

Vivienne stiffens, no doubt preparing an eviscerating riposte, but before she can deliver one, Lottie slings her arm around Teddy and says, "Oh, Ted, we've both got the day off tomorrow, haven't we? We should pop back over to Monte Carlo and visit Grace. I still feel awful I had to miss the wedding. It was smack-dab in the middle of filming *Gatsby*, but surely she's forgiven me by now."

Vivienne blinks hard, whether with surprise or hurt, Lottie can't tell, but it's enough to make her own smile curl into a satisfied smirk as Vivienne sweeps through the hotel door into the soft summer evening light and away.

Teddy crosses his arms, one eyebrow raised. "That was beneath you, Loretta."

He only uses her real name when he's very miffed.

Lottie bats her lashes, all innocence. "What was?"

She's spared a full lecture by the arrival of Max, trotting down the stairs, freshly bathed and dressed for dinner. He pauses on the bottom step and locks eyes with Teddy before continuing into the bar. Teddy finishes his martini quickly, his foot tapping on the carpet.

Lottie downs her own and hands him back the glass. She stands and stretches, smoothing down the comfortable cotton dress she changed into after shooting wrapped.

"Any plans for dinner?" Teddy asks, almost apologetically.

"Invitations all over town, I'll have you know. Impossible to sort through them." At Teddy's hangdog wince, she lets out a genuine laugh. "I'm fine on my own, sweetheart. You know me. Go talk Maxy off the ledge."

She bends to kiss Teddy's cheek, gathering glances from passing junior cast members that might be described as "knowing," if they weren't the exact opposite. When he goes to join Max at the bar, as if meeting a friendly colleague by chance, Lottie's certain no one has a clue. She hesitates at the doorway to the bar and dining area, taking in the scene. Ginger's back from set, looking exhausted. No doubt she pulled some unofficial overtime creating Vivienne's freshly polished look. Or maybe she's just tired of fending off advances from dreary old Charles Brinkwater, who leans over her even now, probably regaling her with tales of his "definitive Hamlet performance" back in the last century. Poor lady. She's got a kid at home, a little girl she's the sole provider for, and Lottie's not so sure she buys the war widow angle Ginger's always selling. Not that she judges her in the slightest. Ginger's on the up-and-up, supporting her kid through entirely legal means, which is better than Lottie's own mother ever managed.

She could invite Ginger for dinner. A "girls only" table. But golly, if her encounter with Vivienne Rhodes hasn't drained Lottie of enthusiasm for girl talk.

She takes swift action to flee the scene. A bottle of Montepulciano from the bar, a glass swiped with a friendly wink to the bartender, then out in the Albergo's front drive, foraged goodies still left on the donkey cart from craft services tied in a cloth napkin like a peddler's pack. Lottie heads on down the road before anyone's the wiser.

This is all she needs. The open world, some nourishment, her own wits. Her own two feet. Her mom taught her that.

Lottie remembers it now, those days at the bus stations and suburbs and bustling city corners. Omaha, Kansas City, Columbus. Moving on when the heat got too hot. Sometimes Lottie would wander around, looking lost, bumping into the richest- and kindest-looking couple she could find. Sometimes in bad weather she'd drift into a church gathering as if fever-stricken, her hair plastered wet around her waifish face. Sometimes she'd plant herself on a busy intersection and sing plaintive songs with her hat out—her first public performances—until some kind soul stopped to inquire why she was all alone. Only once or twice was she threatened, and she learned real quick how to get out of those scrapes too. She used to think her mother was watching from a safe distance. Maybe she was, at first, when she was three, but later Rosa would leave her to it. Find a bar and drink the money they'd last swindled, hoping to meet a mark of her own.

Lottie's scam was simple. She and her parents had been traveling to their new home far away. They'd been on the bus or the train and Lottie had gotten confused. She'd gotten off early without them. She didn't have the money for a ticket to get back to them, but if these nice people wrote down their address, she was sure her daddy would repay them and then some, grateful for the return of his little girl.

On the best nights, she got to go home with the mark. They'd give her a warm bath and a home-cooked meal and tuck her up tight in a guest bed, and she wouldn't want to leave, but she did. She knew her mother would be waiting, fingers outstretched, expecting results.

Oh, Rosa. She wasn't a good mom. An even worse all-around person. Lottie was under no illusions about that. But she was who she was. Pregnant at fifteen, kicked out by Catholic parents, shunned by her own even-worse sister, Rosa was just using what she had on hand to get by, and Lottie was an ace in the hole. The best little actress there ever was.

A born scrapper. Even now. And look where it's landed her.

Lottie stops walking at the top of a hill, her dyed blonde curls blowing in the soft breeze. She turns in a sweeping circle, taking in the great turquoise sea, the picturesque village nestled into the harbor below, the film set behind her in all its grandeur. She breathes the salt air.

Look at this. The life she's wheedled for herself. If Rosa were alive to see her little girl now . . .

Well, Lottie would tell her to get stuffed. But still.

Her eye catches on the one eyesore here, that rusted old military hangar. With nobody loitering outside it at the moment, it looks more desolate than ever. Not the optimal dining spot.

But then she remembers the footpath. She picks her way gingerly to the edge of the island and peeks down. There's definitely an inlet at the end of the trail, tucked into the bottom of the cliff face, a perfect spot to privately take in the sunset.

Perfetto!

Lottie has a skip in her step as she makes her way down, even as she teeters a little in her kitten heels, catching her hand on the rocks to prop herself back up. The ground is loose here. Worn out recently. Lottie hopes nobody's got big plans to come down here tonight. This tucked-away spot is all hers, a little spit of rocky beach and gently lapping waves. Finders keepers.

She stops. Stares.

The cove—yes, you could definitely call it a grotto—is full, but not with people. With props.

Large amphorae. Painted Grecian chests. Wine jars and terracotta statues and huge fluted columns all over the little pebble beach. *Maybe this is a storage space for them*, Lottie thinks before quickly berating herself for her idiocy. It's too dank down here. Too wet. And all these items are strewn higgledy-piggledy over each other, like a trash heap.

That's what this is, she realizes, approaching one of the columns, taking in the gaping crack running down its side. *A dump.* All these props are broken. Even the pottery is reduced to chunky shards. They almost look real, broken like this. Odd that they'd just be piled here, like the already oversized prop department doesn't have time to perform simple repairs.

More alarmingly, there is a smell to this trash heap. Not the fresh paint and sawn wood scent of props, not even the salty bracken stench of low tide, but something far more sour. Something unnatural.

It doesn't take long for her to discover the source.

Behind a stack of planks, hidden away, but not well. Hastily. A long shape, wrapped in fabric. Seeping liquid onto the rocky beach.

Lottie drops the food. The wine bottle, the glass.

She's seen a lot in her life, but never a rotting corpse. First time for everything.

With no preamble, she leans over and heaves.

As she rises, wiping her mouth, her breath coming short, she hears a noise like the growl of some great beast out at sea, growing closer by the second.

Before her brain catches up to recognize it as a boat engine, heading straight for her, Lottie's body prepares to run—back up the rocky path, back to the hotel, door locked, picnic plans officially canceled.

But then, up above her, she hears footfalls. Grumbling male voices speaking Italian.

Her gut tells her to get out. The heat's gotten hot. The set hands, prop guys, they've killed someone, hidden him here. She's found the body, and they're about to find her.

But there's no running from this one.

She's going to have to hide.

5

Vivienne follows the dirt path down to the docks, trying to dash the image of Teddy and Lottie from her mind. She's been compulsively replaying the two of them, cheek to cheek in the lobby. Broadcasting their infatuation to the entire hotel, casually bragging about jetting off to see Grace Kelly, as if the two of them jaunting across the Côte d'Azur, calling upon nouveau royalty, is just a regular weekend occurrence.

Focus on the water, she reminds herself. Water has always calmed her, from the cut-glass, sparkling expanse of the Pacific— one of the only perks of moving to Santa Monica for her father's career, halfway through her fourth-grade year—to the turquoise glow of the indoor Athletic Club, her greatest solace during childhood. The trials of having no friends and of being the gangly new girl were always promptly forgotten as soon as she dipped her first toe into its shallow end. Every afternoon back then was about rhythm, chasing perfection, routine; each practice had its own steady, regular pulse. Even after her transition to acting, after signing on with Apex Pictures at the tender age of seventeen, water was her lifeline. The sets of *Atlantica*, *The Siren's Nemesis*, her breakout role of Medusa in *Poseidon's Depths*. She'd stand on the diving board above the studio pool, poised twenty, thirty feet in the air, dozens of bathing beauties swirling into choreographed shapes below her, and the ripples and sparkles of the water would still, magically, equilibrate her heart.

Now, though, the vast stretch of the Ligurian Sea does nothing for her. Her heart . . .

It still feels shattered.

"*Signorina* Rhodes, *bellissima!*" a distant voice shouts.

Vivienne looks down the long pier, past the sloops and powerboats, the stacks of production crates littered along the dock. At the far end of the marina is a regal, towering yacht, its sharp, gleaming white contours a puncture on the pastel palette of sea and sky. A young, dark-haired man dressed in a fitted tuxedo is waving at her, beckoning from the yacht's boarding ramp.

She tries to chase away her lingering remorse and pastes on a smile as she waves a satin-gloved hand.

"Good evening," she calls out, then tries out a "*Buonasera!*"

"*Molto bene!*" The young man laughs, beckoning her forward, a vibrant flush to his cheeks. "Vivienne Rhodes. What a movie . . . star." He tries out the words, sheepish, grinning. "A big welcome aboard our ship. *Signore* Gallo is waiting."

She walks to the ramp in her kitten heels, gratefully accepting the man's hand, who grins anew as he proudly escorts her across the yacht's expansive stern—the afterdeck, it's called, as she learned from her days on *A Fine Day to Set Sail*—and then around to an interior switchback staircase. She peeks below to find a tight stone-floored corridor, an open cabin door, a flash of black—Gallo himself, maybe, getting ready—as well as the corner of a tightly made bed. She darts her eyes away, cheeks warming, thoughts turning far too intimate for a business meeting.

They ascend a half-set of stairs and then another, until the steward leads her into a spacious salon with plush couches and coffee tables lining the perimeter. Across the salon there's an elaborately set dining table with lit candelabras, gold-threaded napkins, and fine china.

She stops, momentarily startled, feeling as if she's unwittingly walked into someone else's surprise party and potentially ruined it.

Is this all for her?

"*Signorina* Vivienne Rhodes," Mr. Gallo says smoothly behind them.

She turns to find Jack in a tuxedo, complete with bow tie and patterned vest. Thank goodness she decided to dress formally for the occasion. Gallo's dark hair is slicked back, his strong jaw softened by that disarming smile.

"I'm delighted you're here," he says, eyes warming.

"I'm delighted . . . that you're delighted."

He laughs and gestures toward their table for two, pulling out a chair for her to sit. "I hope I didn't keep you waiting too long."

"Not at all."

"I want to make sure we get to see the sunset from the decks. These unobstructed views . . . there's nothing like them. No place in the world, honestly, like this island." He lifts the Dom Pérignon Brut from the cooler and pours them each a glittering glass. "You look stunning, by the way."

You do too, she nearly says, managing to stop herself in time. She takes a gulp of champagne, attempting to calm herself. Her earlier anxiety over Teddy and Lottie clearly hasn't dissipated, only given way to schoolgirl nerves.

"Then I take it you've visited this island before?" She attempts an airy laugh. "I'll admit, I was surprised when my agent told me the *Ships* production was moving to Tavalli. This island's not exactly easy to get to."

"But it's perfect," Gallo says after a swig. "The locals are supportive. The shooting locations varied, accessible. The coastline, too, brilliant for battle scenes." He flashes that charming smile again. "I haven't been back in years, but I remembered the place from my childhood. My mother had some family here, so we'd holiday on Tavalli from time to time when I was young."

"You're Italian?"

He laughs. "Indeed."

Heat creeps across her cheeks. "Right. Of course. Your lack of an accent fooled me."

Which she realizes is untrue as soon as she says it. She has detected a singsong quality to Gallo's voice, a lilt to his tone. Tempered, though, quiet, like the breeze off the Ligurian Sea.

He nods. "I've spent several decades abroad for various business ventures. But coming back to Italy, this island, as a film producer . . . Well, let's call it a true full circle."

"How so?"

Gallo pauses while a waiter slides between them, another sheepish, youthful Italian man dressed to the nines and holding a silver serving tray. He proudly presents them with a large platter of fresh oysters, arranged in the shape of an anemone on a bed of pebbled ice.

"Movies have always been a lifeline for me," Gallo says quietly. "When I was young, when I needed an escape, I would walk an hour to the local cinema to see the latest moving picture. *Immagine in movimento*, as we called them." His eyes have turned glassy, now focused somewhere far away. "All those glorious stories with their happy endings. Their beautiful people. Their unbridled joy."

He smiles wistfully, refilling his glass, and turns to refill Vivienne's. She gladly accepts, leaning in.

"I felt the same way as a child. Movies saved me too, in a way. I mean"—she snaps a laugh—"there was no question I'd follow my father to Apex. It had all been sorted out for me, the same way my father had thrown me into the pool before I could walk."

"A man with vision, I suppose. You won all sorts of medals, didn't you? Quite an illustrious career for someone so young."

Her face warms again, though it is true. She's just surprised, happily surprised, that he's taken the time to learn about her.

"Nationals was as far as I got," she admits. "I think Dad had assumed I'd follow him to the Olympics . . . until the day I tagged along to the Apex lot. My swimming coach was sick, if I recall, had canceled for one reason or another. Buster Smith took an immediate shine to me, and my father was gleeful. 'The boss sees something in the chip off the ol' block.' He course-corrected my career as fast as a flip turn, and—"

Vivienne stops herself, embarrassed. She never talks about her family.

She peers back up through her lashes. "I only mean to say that, regardless of being steered to follow in my father's footsteps, I've lived for the movies ever since I can remember. And from the moment I stepped onto my first set—as an extra in *This Time for Keeps*, mind you—I just knew."

She blinks back the threat of impassioned tears, recalling how seamless, how right the career pivot had felt once she'd fully committed to acting, the deliciously dogged preparation she'd take for her scenes, so reminiscent of her time in the pool. Her early roles in particular, where she'd iterate her lines, adjusting her inflection, her pacing, just so, until the words felt honest, lived-in, real.

Much like a slight adjustment to her shoulders or a tiny lift of her head could change her freestyle stroke entirely.

"There's nothing else I'd rather do," she adds quietly. "Movies are the closest thing we have to magic. Every problem, complication, disaster solved in an hour and a half. Every hero deserving of love and redemption."

Gallo nods, his gaze smoldering now. "I could not agree more."

She clears her throat, struggling to remember why she's here, other than baring her soul to this enthralling man. This movie. This set. Convincing Gallo that *Ships* is *her* picture.

She fumbles through her clutch, dislodging a roll of script pages of tomorrow's scenes, marked with her notes. "Which is, ah, why I think we need to bolster Cassandra's story." She thrusts the pages between them. "Give her a desire line, an emotional arc of her own."

He takes the pages with a soft smile, repeating, "Desire line . . ."

Her breath hitches. "I appreciate Syd's and Max's efforts, really, but right now, Cassandra is just narrating the events, too helpless to do anything to change history," she goes on anxiously as Gallo ponders her notes.

He's biting his lip, his dark eyes squinting, studying her changes like a schoolboy taking a test. It is, frankly, adorable.

"I'd love to give her more power," she adds. "Make her a force to be reckoned with. A heroine who can see the future, yes, but who also has the ability to impact and direct its course . . . even if those efforts ultimately do end tragically."

"These are good," he finally says with a self-deprecating laugh. "Really good. I'll confess, so far producing my first picture has felt more like putting out fires than storytelling." He looks up at her. "But I want to get back to the magic, Viv. It's why I bought this studio in the first place. And I think . . . I think you, this"—he shakes the pages, handing them back to her—"is the way forward. I trust your vision here. Completely. Let me talk to Syd and Max again, ensure you have their full support."

Tingles break across her shoulders, cascade down her spine, those words of his more intimate than a kiss. And yet she suddenly finds herself wanting, more than anything, to actually kiss him. To leap across the table and pull him in, have him whisper those words—*I trust your vision . . . completely*—into her ear once more, to maybe push the oysters aside, dish clattering to the floor, candelabras shining around them, like the penultimate scene in *One Long Adventure*.

Instead, she raises her champagne glass to toast him.

As their glasses touch, in place of a clink, there comes a deafening, rattling *pop* louder and angrier than any starting pistol she's ever heard.

Panic consumes her. She startles. Drops the flute.

"Vivienne!" Gallo leaps to his feet as if to shield her.

Hurried footsteps and shouts sound off below. *"Fermare! Fermare!"*

The steward from earlier rushes across the salon. *"C'è un uomo a bordo!"*

Gallo rounds the table, grabbing Vivienne's hand. They follow the steward toward the stairs.

"Chi?" Gallo calls out. *"Come è salito a bordo?"*

Another shot rings out, and then another, a booming cacophony echoing across the violet sky.

"What's happening?" Vivienne cries as Gallo escorts her swiftly down the stairs.

"Someone's here, on board," he says. "You're not safe."

"What?"

"Dammit, I knew something was wrong." Gallo's grip remains firm as they take the next set of switchback stairs. He fixes her with a look that mirrors her terror. "I want you to hide in the guest room at the end of the hall until we sort this out. Understand?"

Several sets of footsteps pound across the ceiling.

"But what about you?" she blurts as they reach the bottom floor.

"Lock the door and stay there." Gallo's eyes are wide, emphatic. "I need to see what's happening. I'll be there soon."

"Wait, Jack—"

"Go!" Gallo says, bounding back up the stairs.

Vivienne can't help but trail him for a few steps. Then another shot rings out. She shrinks back, turning to follow orders, and barrels straight into someone hiding at the bottom of the stairs.

The man grabs her shoulders, startled. He wrests them both into a shadowed interior.

It's the extra from set, the one she spotted outside the hangar earlier today.

"Who— Let me go!" she cries. "Get off me . . . Stop!"

It's only once he's released her that she realizes her charmeuse gown is streaked with blood. She recoils, forcing him away. Is she hurt? No, no, it's—

"Oh goodness," she cries. "You've been shot!"

Sure enough, thick red is spreading like ink across the man's button-down. He staggers into a railing, rights himself, then lurches to fish through the pocket of his pants.

"Waited too long . . . I . . ." He gasps. "Need to warn—"

He stops, his color fading.

"Stay with me!" She grabs his shoulders. "Warn who? Gallo?"

"Yes." He wilts against her firm hold. "Gallo, I— The cargo. You must . . . help me . . ."

"No, no, no, you need a medic." Vivienne studies him wildly. She's never seen so much blood—*real* blood—before. The stairwell turns claustrophobic with the pungent, metallic smell of death. How can this be happening?

He groggily shakes his head, thrusting a small, cold object into Vivienne's hand. "*Je suis* Emeric . . . C-Corbin. Interpol—"

She reels back. "Wait, I don't understand—"

"Interpol. P-Paris. Please. Go." He rasps a hard-fought breath. "They're here."

The extra must use every last ounce of his dwindling energy to push her toward the stairs. Together they trip up the half-set of steps and onto the deck.

Coming toward them from the hull is a vaguely familiar man, bald head illuminated by the moonlight. One of the assistants from set? Surely he can help!

Spotting them, the bald man stops, raises his gun . . . and fires, the bullet whizzing past her right ear.

She ducks, shrieking, "Oh my God!"

Vivienne frantically scans the deck, then what she can see of the salon from her vantage point. *Where is Jack? Is he all right? Has he been shot too?*

"Waterproof," Emeric rasps beside her with fading exasperation. "Now!"

"Waterproof? How is that relevant?"

As soon as she says it, she realizes he's inching her toward the hull's railing, the edge.

And that his hand is now dropping. His whole body falling with it. Eyes glassy and staring. Blank.

Is he dead?

Out of the corner of her eye, she spots another man advancing in their direction from the yacht's stern. *Who is he? What's happening? Where can I go?* She's surrounded. The extra's right.

Where can she go but the water?

In a flash, she spins in her bloodstained gown and clambers to the boat's edge in her slingback heels, her hand still firmly wrapped around the small object that the extra handed her. She can finally see what it is now, shining in the lights.

A film canister.

The approaching assailant raises his gun.

Two more steps and Vivienne is airborne, leaping from the railing, angling into a swan dive, just like the final scene in *Poseidon's Depths*. Straight from the yacht's second-floor balcony . . . and into the Ligurian Sea.

A frigid, breath-stealing slap, then muffled gunshots as she descends.

Down, down, down.

STAR POWER

Friday, June 13, 1958   Issue 181

"SHIPS" ABLAZE!

New Apex Pictures president Jack L. Gallo already has a reputation for bold hiring choices—we've just heard through the grapevine that starring alongside Vivienne Rhodes in Gallo's epic, *A Thousand Ships*, are none other than her ex-beau, Teddy Walters, and Walters's latest *Madame Bovary* costar and arm candy, the ever-charming Lottie Lawrence. Given this trio's history, we're betting on serious drama (maybe more off-camera than on).

While Gallo is trying to keep his production closed to the press, *Star Power* was able to connect with Ms. Rhodes's agent, Hollywood veteran Lew Binkle. Binkle hasn't heard from Ms. Rhodes since she arrived on set last weekend but assured us that "Vivienne is a professional, and *Ships* is sure to be her finest work yet."

We're not so sure. What could be more brutal than being trapped on a remote island with your ex-beau and your professional and personal nemesis? We certainly can't imagine. Here's hoping they're all surviving the ordeal.

6

The cramps in Lottie's legs are pure agony. This sort of crouch was a heck of a lot easier to maintain when she was hiding from the cops at age six. Not that she ever had to share her hiding place with a rotting corpse before. The energy it takes to stopper her nose and quell the urge to empty her stomach yet again is considerable.

But Lottie knows damn well she'll share the same fate as this unfortunate cadaver if she doesn't hold out just a little bit longer.

Absolute ages ago, from behind this half-shattered but adequately spacious Grecian chest, Lottie watched as a sleek mahogany speedboat pulled into the cove a few yards from the lapping shore and its lone occupant hopped out onto the rocks to loosely tie a line around a jutting stone. This skipper was so enormous both in shoulder width and height that he had to crick his neck to avoid bashing his head against the jagged ceiling of the grotto. To add to the effect, he was wearing a comically small blue-and-white-striped nautical shirt that looked fit to burst at the seams. Lottie was surprised a boat like that, twenty-five feet tops, could even manage to float with someone that size aboard. As it was, it bounced cheerfully in the shallows, its idling engine's purr echoing throughout the grotto.

Abruptly, the giant boomed out a brusque greeting in Italian, aimed up the path.

Someone considerably smaller was leading the charge down the cliffside. When he turned in profile, the red sunset glow revealing his slim mustache, Lottie's heart sank in confirmation. Yes, indeed, Ludovico, with five of his supposed "property department" trailing him into the grotto, then fanning out like a squadron. How strange, seeing film crew hoisting guns that weren't dummies.

As Ludo and the hulking stranger launched into lively conversation, maybe even debate, Lottie seized the opportunity to adjust her weight without worrying about small sounds being caught. That was the last time she moved.

And however long later—ten minutes? A lifetime?—Ludo's still arguing with the striped giant, although the two occasionally break into raucous laughter before the conversation lapses back into the cadence of a debate, their Italian too rapidly overlapping for her to pick out even a single word. One of the prop hands is squatting like a bullfrog at the top of the trail, picking dirt out of his nails with a penknife and blocking off the only mode of escape Lottie can see. She manages to peek out at Ludovico once more between the golden handle of the chest and one of the thick plaster column props.

No wonder Ludovico got so tense watching Mr. Gallo approach the hangar the other day. Ludo was obviously hiding something illegal, something the studio boss couldn't see. They've all duped him thoroughly, it looks like, infiltrating this set while conducting an entirely different type of business right under his nose. But what business is it, exactly? And was this dead fellow one of them, victim of a deal gone south, or an innocent bystander who happened upon them?

Just like Lottie.

"*Avanti*," Ludovico snaps. *"Presto, prendetela."*

As Ludovico waves two of his men over to the boat, unloading something or other, Lottie grips the side of the chest with sweaty fingers, barely breathing, following their path with her eyes, ready for them to conclude whatever dubious business this is and leave already. Or, barring that, for them to create the tiniest sliver of an opportunity for her to get out unnoticed, back to the hotel, door locked. Safe.

If the fellow on the path ever decides to move—maybe Ludovico will call him to action—Lottie will need to be stealthy and swift. She slides out now, just a few inches, already grateful for that much more distance from her rapidly decaying roommate.

"*Qualcuno viene?*" Ludovico calls out to the man on the path, and Lottie holds her breath, praying he's said something along the lines of, "Get up and help, you lazy ass."

But the man only pauses in his nail cleaning to pull a gun from his pocket, glance up the hill, and answer, "*Nessuno.*"

Lottie exhales in frustration.

One of the film crew—*Gino? The key grip? Him too?*—turns in her direction.

Her heart seizes.

Still chattering over his shoulder, Gino grabs the column beside her and pulls it onto its side as if it weighs nothing.

Exposed but as yet unnoticed, Lottie creeps back around the other side of the chest, pinioned safely by other props. When her hip nudges what looks to be a solid stone plinth, it gives an ominous wobble, hollow inside, but isn't loud enough to attract alarm from the others.

Ludovico's argument with the delivery giant who came in on the boat is heated enough that Lottie wonders if bullets will start to fly. Regardless, this might be her only chance to sneak off before all possible hiding places are removed. But where? The only point of egress is . . .

The water. Oh jeez.

Lottie watches the group, waits for all backs to turn again, then silently slides one prop—half of a large amphora with a hydra pattern painted on the back—closer to the shoreline. Can she make it to the water? Swim to safety? Ha! She can barely muster a doggy paddle.

Wade, then. Something, anything. Hide behind the delivery fellow's boat. It's plenty big enough to conceal her. Maybe the giant will head up the path with the others once their argument is over. Join them for dinner. It's not much to pin hope on, but it's all she's got right now. A matter of timing. And luck.

She just hopes that her lifelong lucky streak hasn't finally run out.

One other factor in her favor is the mounting darkness. Sunset has now passed into full dusk, and these fellows haven't brought flashlights down here, so the shadows are piling atop each other, blanketing the whole scene in deep blue.

The giant is counting lire, the fourth pile that's been put into his fist thus far. He starts to argue again and Ludovico's own voice rises in answer. Lottie waits as the last chest is hauled out of the empty boat, this one requiring the two remaining goons, their backs turned as they pivot.

She beelines for the water. Smoothly. Silently. Into the gently lapping waves. Heels and everything, no time to worry about ruining her Chanel pumps, and then she's knee-deep, the hem of her sundress clinging to her legs. The sound of her moving around the side of the boat is disguised by the shouting between the men until she's nearly there and . . .

A popping noise echoes over the water.

Gunshots, Lottie has time to think, *but not here*, before she realizes all the chatter in the grotto has stopped.

Lottie peeks over her shoulder. The five Italians on the shore stare back. Their hackles are already up from whatever that sound was. And their guns are drawn.

"Thought I'd go for a moonlight dip," she coos, shooting them her absolute winningest smile. "Care to join me?"

"*Sparale!*" Ludovico shouts, and Lottie doesn't need a phrase book to work that one out.

By the time their guns are cocked, she's already wrenched herself up over the glossy hull of the giant's idling speedboat and down between the leather seats, lying on her belly, listening to bullets boom and zing past overhead.

"*Aspetti!*" she screams. "Wait!"

They don't *aspetti* one bit, and neither does Lottie.

She gropes upward for the dashboard, or whatever you call it—she's never operated a boat in her life!—and when her fingers find a metal handle, she shoves upward, rewarded by a roar from the engine and a sharp lurch backward.

She's moving! Away from them! In a boat!

And then she's stopping, hard. "No!"

The boat swings to the side, caught by the rope still slung around one of the grotto rocks. The boat's owner's snarling face appears over the hull as he tries to climb aboard, but he's floundering, treading water. The depth must have increased dramatically—Lottie can't see the bottom anymore, just deep blue—and when she frantically shoves the boat handle even higher, hallelujah, the rope slides free from the rock and she is off, knocking the massive man loose, possibly driving straight over him.

"Sorry!" she shouts.

Once the boat clears the little bay, she clambers up off her stomach, then ducks again as another bullet resounds from the firing squad in the grotto. The boat's throttle is in reverse, but the boat is racing backward in an arc rather than a straight line. Which is *bad*. She's heading back toward the island now at dangerous speed. They're close enough to hit her, or the boat, but maybe it's too dark to make her out?

"Mother f—"

Lottie stands up, desperate, cursing as loud as she likes, scanning all the bits and bobs on the dashboard, and opts for the simplest option. The silver handle is up. Reverse. She shoves it down. Forward!

The boat complies, moving in the right direction.

"Yes! Let's go, let's go!"

She grabs the wheel—that part's easy enough—evades one goon who actually swam out into the sea to try to intercept her, and, dimly registering Gallo's boat in the near distance, heads top speed toward the spot where the sun just sank into the sea. Where to, besides due west?

"Who the hell knows," she shouts into the wind. "Away, that's where!"

She's in a panic, and the boat's engine is roaring, but the sea is calm beneath her, like undulating black glass.

Lottie glances behind her at the looming silhouette of Tavalli, looking not as lovely as it once did. In the darkness, it could be mistaken for Alcatraz.

She turns forward, peering across the bow, and screams in shock.

There's a mermaid.

In the water.

Swimming toward her in picture-perfect strokes. Hair slick and streaming. Fish tail waving behind her.

"Twilight blue . . ." Lottie gasps.

She flips every switch, jams every button she can find, until she finally thinks to pull up the handle and idle the engine.

The boat bobs. Lottie leans over the side to offer a hand, but Vivienne Rhodes ignores her. She heaves herself inside under her own power, then flops on the deck like a gasping fish.

Then, as if her eyes have finally cleared, Vivienne takes in Lottie and lets out a sharp laugh. "What the hell are *you* doing here?"

7

Escaping?" Lottie answers, as if confused.

"Well," Vivienne says on a gasp, wringing out her hair. "That . . . makes two of us."

Lottie continues to stare, eyes widening. "Oh my goodness." She hurries toward Vivienne. "Is that blood? Are you hurt?"

"It's not mine." Vivienne gathers herself against the boat's hull, swallowing another gulp of fresh air. "The yacht . . . there was a man on board."

"A man?" Lottie says. "Where? Gallo's yacht?"

Vivienne rests her head against the side, too fatigued to elaborate. She's wholly spent, no reserves, after swimming relentlessly through a panorama of deep blue above, around, and below. Nothing but the hazy, bobbing lights onshore to guide her forward. Her muscles are aching, quivering from what must have been half a mile in open water.

It's been a long time since she swam outside of a pool, fighting, stroke by stroke, against a strong current.

"I barely survived," she huffs out.

"And once again," Lottie says, "that makes two of us."

With a groaning lurch, the boat careens backward, sending Vivienne sprawling across the deck.

She rights herself, snapping indignantly, "Why are you in a boat if you don't know how to drive? A Riva Tritone, no less!"

"Because," Lottie shouts, futzing with the boat's panel, "we're getting shot at!"

Vivienne's about to protest when a chorus of gunshots rings out behind them. "Oh no, no, no, not again!"

A crescendo of bullets smacks the water a few feet away in an unnervingly accurate line.

Vivienne whips around, fully expecting to see Gallo's hijacked yacht trailing them. Instead, it's an agile motorboat, veering in their direction with discomforting speed.

"Who are they?" Vivienne yells as she hits the deck, ducking for cover as the shots keep booming. "And why are they shooting at us? What the hell is going on tonight?"

"The prop master," Lottie tosses behind her. "Ludovico. I saw him in the grotto, on the beach. Caught him exchanging something, I don't know what, but it's gotta be something illegal, right? I skedaddled out of there and into the water; the depth drops right off. They couldn't catch me. There were all these men with guns and a dead body and—"

"A what?" Vivienne croaks.

"Yes! Dead for days, by the look of it."

"Who was it?"

"No idea, didn't look that closely." Lottie huffs, as if defensive. "You wouldn't have investigated either, let me tell you. The smell . . ."

Vivienne's empty stomach curdles. A corpse. A secret exchange. Is what Lottie saw on the beach somehow related to the attack on Gallo's yacht? This can't all be a coincidence.

She scrambles toward Lottie, their roaring motor drowning out the gunshots.

"One of the crew was also on the yacht!" she shouts. "And also firing a gun—"

"What? Who?"

"The angry-looking fellow. Bald? With a crooked nose? I think he's one of Syd's assistants, works with Johnny."

"I noticed him while we shot the palace scene. He looked like he'd rather be anywhere else, which—"

Another riddle of bullets pierces the sky, cutting Lottie off. Her eyes go wide.

Vivienne risks another glance behind her. The other motorboat is gaining on them, so close now that the passengers' voices are audible. She can hear shouted curses in Italian. "We need to go faster; they're right behind us!"

"Okay, okay." Lottie monkeys again with the control panel. "Um . . ."

Their speedboat careens forward shakily, a breakneck, jagged line into the open sea.

Seasickness from Lottie's rocky steering comes on like a swell. Vivienne puts her hand over her mouth, resisting a gag.

"Seriously, pick a heading and stick with it!"

"Oh gee," Lottie says, "what a nifty idea. What the heck does that mean?"

Vivienne lets out a frustrated groan, tucking the film canister she's been holding in a death grip into her brassiere. She stands and gently nudges her costar out of the way, assuming control. She increases the throttle.

The boat takes off at top clip, zipping gloriously now through the water, chasing the dark horizon.

"Say," Lottie marvels. "You really know what you're doing."

"I've always known my way around boats, but I became quite the skipper on *Fine Day to Set Sail*. Are we losing them?"

Lottie swallows. "Yeah. We actually are."

They look over their shoulders simultaneously, the island of Tavalli shrinking in their wake, the shadowed cliffs and sandy lagoons now appearing ominous in the eerie twilight. The Albergo Tavalli glows like a sinister lighthouse on the hill.

Vivienne shakes her head, recalling her first impression of the island. A land of potential. The site of her grand, inevitable ascent to stardom.

How woefully ironic.

"So, wait," Lottie calls out from her perch on a leather seat. "This assistant—Syd's assistant—was shooting at you? Where?"

"Gallo's yacht," Vivienne says.

"Right." Lottie purses her lips. "Your dinner date with the chief. Sounds romantic."

"Seriously, that's what you're focusing on right now?"

Lottie shrugs. "The whole thing feels very 'pot calling the kettle black' is all."

"It was a business meeting," Vivienne hisses, cheeks warming.

"Of course. Hence the floor-length gown."

Vivienne shoots her a glare. "*Anyway*, as Jack and I were discussing the picture, we heard gunshots from the lower decks. We ran out of the salon, he told me to hide until he could figure out what was happening, and then I—"

She stops suddenly, making a connection.

Her eyes narrow on Lottie, who sits anxiously biting her nails. "You said you witnessed an exchange on the beach?"

Lottie drops her hand. "Definitely."

Vivienne turns to the bow again, considering. "I wonder if

that's what he was talking about. Ludo's exchange. He said the word *cargo*; I'm sure he did."

"Who said *cargo*? Jack?"

Vivienne ignores her.

"Maybe he knew about Ludovico too," she narrates to the watery expanse. "Maybe that's why he was on board. Trying to warn Jack about the illegal activity—"

"Vivienne!" Lottie pastes on that beatific smile that Vivienne is starting to suspect is a form of weaponry. "Hi, it's me, your fellow escapee! Care to clue me in?"

"Fine, if you must know, there was another man on board," she grudgingly lays out. "One of the film's extras, or so I thought. A periphery player, had a fondness for tweed, not someone you'd ever notice in a crowd, but—"

"I think I did notice him," Lottie says, leaning forward. "Middle-aged? Incredibly ordinary-looking, but lurking around in funny places? Kind of gave me the creeps, to be honest. Why does a guy like that even want to be in the pictures—"

"He was shot dead on Gallo's yacht tonight."

"Holy moly." Lottie grips the railing. "Now I feel bad calling him creepy."

"I'm thinking he boarded the yacht to get to Gallo," Vivienne says. "To warn him about Ludovico."

Lottie considers this. "Okay, but—"

"And the gunman, Syd's assistant, must have followed the extra onto the boat, tried to stop him. Oh my God. Does this mean that Syd is involved?"

"Sydney Durand, criminal mastermind?" Lottie scrunches her nose. "Doubtful. The man has a nervous breakdown if his shadow looks at him wrong. And anyway, maybe the extra was the bad guy and working with Ludovico. Maybe the assistant gunman was only protecting Jack."

"Maybe." Vivienne remembers the small film canister she's tucked into her décolletage. She retrieves it, showing it to Lottie. "But I don't think so."

Lottie gets up from her seat to look at it more closely. "Where'd you get that?"

"The extra. He gave it to me. I think he'd planned on giving it to Jack." The man's dying words come to her mind. "The extra said he waited too long. Ostensibly because Jack was engaged. With me. In our purely professional business meeting."

As Lottie takes this all in, Vivienne glides the boat farther out to sea, the hull slicing through the steel-blue water like a butter knife. She glances behind her once more. The motorboat following them has now shrunk into a blip, thankfully, a tiny pilot light like a star in the black distance.

"If the extra *was* a villain, why would he give me this?" Vivienne tucks the canister back into her bra for safekeeping. "Bad guys don't just pass along key materials. Take *X Marks the Spot*, for instance. One of the islanders in the story, a cold, curmudgeonly fellow who the audience assumes is villainous, is actually the catalyst in stealing the treasure map from—"

"Vivienne? Maybe recent flicks aren't our best reference point?" Lottie says, though not unkindly.

Vivienne takes her point. "The extra . . . he also gave me a name. I'm assuming it was his. Emeric Corbin. And another word—*Interpol*."

"As in the international crime-fighting agency?"

Vivienne nods. "In Paris. That's what he said before he told me to get off the boat. To run."

"Hmm." Lottie bites her lip, her eyes widening. "Maybe he wants you to bring whatever's in that canister to Interpol."

"Me?" Vivienne clears her throat, suddenly feeling vulnerable, overwhelmed even, by that ludicrous suggestion. "I think that's a stretch. He was probably *from* Interpol. All I know is that this is all above our pay grades. I mean, you're a contract player, for God's sake."

"Good thing he gave it to you, then," Lottie says dryly. "He must have known you could call your agent for help."

Vivienne ignores the quip. The full unreality of the evening has just washed over her like another cold wave, those final minutes on the yacht crystallizing like ice in her mind. The gunshots. The extra, covered in blood. Jack's voice calling for her to—

"Jack." Vivienne's throat tightens at her last memory of him. His wide dark eyes. His palpable panic, even as he shouted for her to protect herself. "Oh, Lottie, do you think he's all right?"

"I couldn't begin to guess." Lottie runs a hand over her wind-whipped bob. "And jeez, what about the rest of the cast and crew?"

"Teddy," Vivienne supplies immediately.

Lottie nods. "Not to mention Syd, Johnny, Max? These men have killed, and given what we experienced tonight, they're clearly willing to kill again."

"Ginger. Oh goodness, poor Clay Cooper, and Brinkwater—"

"I'm not worried about Brinkwater."

At that, Vivienne barks an unexpected laugh.

Their eyes meet, twinkling. They both promptly look away.

"They all might be okay, Viv," Lottie says softly. "Whatever schemes Ludovico is orchestrating, he's clearly been managing them during production. Somehow using the set as cover. The two of us were happily oblivious, right, perfectly fine, until we literally floundered into their dealings. If no one else is the wiser, then maybe they'll stay safe. I don't think the cast will think anything of those gunshots. They'll just write off the noise as a prop test, Cooper especially."

"But what are they going to do about you and me?" Vivienne retorts. "And where does that leave Jack?"

Lottie shakes her head. "I don't know."

"You weren't wrong about my agent," Vivienne finally says. "It wouldn't hurt to call Lew. He'll know what to do. He can sort this out, reach out to the embassy. But first we should contact the local authorities. They'll want to talk to us directly, after all."

"I suppose that does make sense." Lottie gazes around at the open water, the darkness draped across the sea like a velvet shawl. "But where exactly are we finding these authorities, and a phone to call Lew? Corsica's closest, but—"

"They'll be expecting us to go there. And right now I'd be happy if I never set foot on another island for the rest of my life."

"Sing it, sister," Lottie groans in commiseration.

Vivienne scans the console until her eyes lock on the powerboat's gas gauge. "Hmm. If my estimations are right, based on my incoming journey to Tavalli, where I'm assuming we are coordinates-wise, Monaco should be due north. We have the gas. I think."

She points at the navigation system, trying to convince the both of them.

"Yes, we should be able to make it. Perhaps we can dock at Monte Carlo, use our connections there. You and Teddy spent a lot of time in the Riviera, yes, after *Bovary*'s premiere in Cannes?" she says, trying hard to bite back any bitterness in her voice. "That's good. You'll know your way around. We can figure out a way to get help and put an end to this nightmare."

"Can you imagine how bananas the Apex board is going to go over all this?" Lottie shivers. "Cast issues, budget woes, and now a murderous prop master? Jeez Louise. Tabloids are going to have a field day. At least we'll come out as the conquering heroines."

"I admire your confidence in this inevitable future," Vivienne says wryly.

"Fair point. One step at a time." Lottie considers Vivienne with those childlike blue eyes. "You really think you can captain us all the way to the mainland?"

Vivienne shakes her head. Really, this woman is a mistress of passive-aggressive digs. "I have two boat licenses, for goodness' sake."

"No, the emphasis wasn't on *you*, just anyone. I mean, is this possible?"

Vivienne glances behind her once more. The pursuing boat's light has now disappeared fully from the cobalt horizon. The island itself seems a distant dream.

Vivienne looks at Lottie again, fresh adrenaline, purpose, coursing through her veins.

Truth be told, Vivienne never feels comfortable unless she's captaining. Unless she's been given indisputable control of the wheel. And it's a long shot, yes, making the journey across the open unknown sea to Monaco, but what choice does she have? Out of the two of them, Vivienne's the only one who stands a chance of delivering.

She grips the wheel with one hand, rests her other on the throttle, giving as resolute a nod as she can muster in these circumstances. "Well, I'm sure as hell going to try."

STAR POWER

Friday, June 13, 1958

Issue 181

PRINCESS GRACE HOSTS SINATRA; BENEFIT CONCERT FOR THE AGES

Grace Kelly has been quite busy with her royal duties as sovereign of Monaco, but two years is a very long time to stay away from the glamorous world of Hollywood, even for a princess. Perhaps that's why this weekend, Princess Grace is bringing Hollywood home to Monaco!

Insiders tell *Star Power* that the princess personally summoned her old friend and *High Society* costar Frank Sinatra to come visit and to perform a charity concert like no other. The event, which kicks off at midnight tomorrow, will be conducted by Quincy Jones and is intended to raise money for the United Nations Refugee Fund. Sinatra is expected to sing several chart-smashing hits from his latest album, *Come Fly with Me*. Perhaps he'll be sticking around to promote *Kings Go Forth* too?

Just how many Hollywood glitterati will be in attendance? Well, as Sinatra would say, "Blue Skies" the limit. We at *Star Power* are crossing our fingers we get an invite to that after-party . . .

8

Saturday, June 14, 1958

Lottie didn't mean to fall asleep. She kept vigil for hours, honest she did, while Vivienne held the rudder, both of them praying there was enough gas in the engine to get them all the way across the Ligurian Sea and safely onto European mainland shores.

But now, as she gasps awake, she sees the first dim light of predawn, and with it . . .

She scrambles up beside a wilted Vivienne, still at the wheel. "Land ho!"

"No thanks to you," Vivienne murmurs.

Uh, mainly thanks to me, Lottie thinks. *Honey, you would have been swimming to Monaco without this boat.*

But she keeps her pleasant smile in place. "Fantastic navigating. I'd have had us spinning in circles."

Vivienne looks a little appeased by that.

"Where do you suppose we should dock?" Lottie adds, peering out at the distant landscape, tiny lights sparkling on hillsides, a canvas of faded pastels and sandstones in the waking light.

"I'm not sure." There's an unfamiliar wavering note in Vivienne's voice, and Lottie senses it takes a lot for her to admit to not knowing something.

Vivienne steers the boat due west, and Lottie crawls carefully to the bow to get a better look at the growing landscape. "Oh, now I remember. There's a little harbor there, do you see? A marina?"

Vivienne doesn't answer, but she does turn the boat toward it.

"Oh gosh, do you suppose we have to pay to dock there?" Lottie asks. "'Fraid I forgot my handbag while I was running for my life. Not to mention that this boat is technically stolen. Maybe better to just tie up on the rocks for now, like those fishing boats?"

Vivienne still doesn't respond.

Lottie looks askance at her. Vivienne's lips are white lines, her hands iron tight around the wheel. She looks positively shell-shocked.

"You okay, hon?" Lottie asks gently.

"Yep. Just peachy," Vivienne finally snaps. "I've been shot at, watched a man die, swam for my life in an evening gown, dried out in a criminal's speedboat . . . Oh, right, and spent the last few hours listening to you snoring. Couldn't be better."

Why do I even try? Lottie wonders with a sigh. Then, frowning, *Do I really snore?*

Her eyes catch on a building a bit farther up the coast. The morning's first light slides across the green patina of its domed roof, its glittering Beaux-Arts facade.

"Hey, look, Vivienne," she calls lightly, trying another tactic. "Isn't the casino lovely?"

"Please stop distracting me. I'm trying not to run aground on top of everything else."

Vivienne does look to be concentrating quite hard as she

navigates their way into a boat channel marked by subtle buoys on either side. Inside the harbor Lottie marks the marina to one side, lined with luxury yachts, and on the other, a shoreline where smaller vessels are beached and tied up. As Lottie had suggested, Vivienne lowers the engine and heads for the beach, picking her way between anchored boats until they hit sand with a gentle bump that still nearly sends Lottie slipping off her seat.

Lottie practically sprints off the bow and onto dryish land. She held it together all night, but now that her feet are back on an actual continent, she feels acutely the fear she's been holding at bay since she fled Tavalli. Not just the mounting suspicion that her whole life, career, plan has just been shoved off the tracks, not even the terror of finding a corpse and coming a hair's breadth from sharing a shallow grave with the poor guy, but the basic fundamental anxiety of a not-strong swimmer spending several hours aboard a tiny vessel on a choppy sea with *Vivienne Rhodes*.

But she's made it. She didn't drown. Or get murdered. They can set things straight now, right here, in continental Europe. Lottie feels so full of existential glee that she nearly grabs a smoothly dismounting Vivienne and plants a giant smooch on that pristine cheek of hers.

Nearly.

"First things first," Vivienne says, marching up the beach without even wobbling in her salt-stained heels. "We need to find a phone, get Lew on the line. He'll call the embassy, sort out our tickets home. And it's good you have a friend here who can contact the authorities. I don't speak the language, and I have to assume you don't either."

Pinballing between confusion and pique—*Why assume I don't speak French? Was that yet another dumb joke? I've spent most of the past six months in France, for goodness' sake, and Vivienne damn well knows it*—it takes Lottie a moment to blurt, "Wait, what? What friend?"

"Yes." Vivienne huffs, impatient. "Grace."

"As in Grace . . . Kelly?"

"Did you hit your head on the boat? Of course Grace Kelly! More pertinently, *Princess* Grace. She can order the local constabulary to alert Interpol, and I assume they could meet us here without too much fuss. I'll pass them this." She removes the metal canister from her décolletage and turns it over for inspection, like a jeweler with a gem. She tucks it away again. "And once they arrest Ludovico, if that's even his real name, we can all go back to normal."

"Sure sounds like you've got it all worked out," Lottie mutters, trying to keep from keeling over. Gosh but the ground still feels like water.

"You've been wanting to visit, you said." There's a downright manic edge to Vivienne's voice, possibly from lack of sleep, as she hurries along the fine city promenade. "You can take the lead, seeing as you're friends. I'm sure she'll forgive you for missing the wedding, if that's what you're worried about. Especially under the circumstances."

"There are an awful lot of circumstances," Lottie grudgingly agrees. Maybe it isn't the world's worst idea, taking refuge in an actual fortress with armed guards posted outside.

She draws her arms around herself as she trails Vivienne, rubbing out goose bumps from the early morning coastal chill.

"What's the quickest way to the palace?" Vivienne asks briskly, over her shoulder.

"I'm not sure." Lottie looks around. "We stayed near the casino when we were here."

Vivienne flinches a little at that "we" but recovers quickly. "We'll ask a local then."

But despite the dazzling lights of hotels and casinos, the streets of Monte Carlo are practically deserted. Lottie squints at the murky sky, trying to guess at the hour. Five? Earlier? The only thing moving at the moment are seabirds swirling in search of breakfast and a poster pinned to a lamppost, flapping in the breeze.

Lottie pauses to read it. The biggest words by far are "Frank Sinatra," followed by "14 Juin 1958, Minuit, The Sporting Club, Bénéficier United Nations Refugee Fund."

"Should have timed our escape a little earlier. Looks like we just missed a heck of a concert," Lottie calls to Vivienne, but she's well out of earshot, up the boulevard, approaching an elderly man standing outside a restaurant awning with a broom.

As Lottie draws nearer, she sees Vivienne wincing, apparently pained by her own ghastly attempts to ask for directions, but luckily, the old fellow seems to understand. He points up the hillside.

"*Pas loin*," he says.

"Not far." Lottie arrives in time to smugly translate.

Vivienne rolls her eyes.

As they continue up the hill, Lottie can hear the old man chuckling to himself, and it occurs to her for the very first time what the two of them must look like.

Lottie's cotton dress isn't too damaged but is certainly rumpled, and her hairpins slipped while she was sleeping, all of which probably adds up to an overall effect of a Kansas farmer's daughter transported via tornado into the Riviera.

As for Vivienne, while her exquisite gown is certainly more fitting for Monte Carlo by night, the look is somewhat spoiled by bloodstains and salt water. Her dark hair has been wrenched loose and dried into wild tangles by the salty wind, and her eye makeup has dripped into streaks along her cheeks like a sad clown. She still has those velvet kitten heels on, at least, despite her long swim to freedom, which is a miracle Lottie hasn't thought to marvel at until just now.

Another miracle is just how quickly Vivienne is able to walk up the steep hillside avenue in those heels. Honestly, it could be a new Olympic event. Lottie tries her best to keep pace, with little sprints that leave her instantly winded.

When they reach a sleepy pink piazza, shopkeepers just starting to open up for the morning, they turn onto a switchback road and head up the even more vertiginous hill path, and at that point, Lottie gives up the chase. Vivienne is the one who didn't sleep a wink last night, and yet she's an automaton, utterly unstoppable. All that swimming she did earlier in her career must have turned her into a fitness nut. Lottie admits she could take a page or two out of that book. Light calisthenics to maintain her waistline aren't helping her get up this darned hill without panting and sweating herself into a wrung-out mess.

Up on the ramparts there emerges a long line of vividly painted town houses lined with a low wall with a vista that spans all of Monaco's borders. *A peachy place to stop and catch one's breath*, Lottie thinks, and apparently Vivienne agrees. Lottie finds her up there, sitting precariously on the wall, looking so pale she's practically green.

"Quite a view," Vivienne says, aiming for breezy, Lottie guesses, but coming out breathless.

So she is human, Lottie thinks, though too winded to even muster a smirk. She leans against the wall with her elbows. "Hard to believe we crossed all that water in such a rinky-dink boat."

"Riva Tritones are hardly rinky-dink," Vivienne volleys back. "They're built to be ocean cruisers. There's even a little berth below the bow where someone can sleep."

"Now you tell me."

"I'll admit, your beauty sleep wasn't foremost on my mind," Vivienne drawls. "It is an incredible vessel, though. I've always wanted to take the wheel of one, just . . ."

"Not like this," Lottie supplies.

The sun is peeking up over the horizon now, casting the sea in tangerine. It's surprisingly peaceful standing here with Vivienne, gazing out over the wide world. Lottie's eyes trail the coastline, the little beach where they washed up rendered more lively by the morning's activity, four fishing boats now setting out, one coming in. And there's their Riva, hull gleaming in the dawn light. She rises with a smile, about to point it out to Vivienne, when—

"Oh no." Lottie feels the blood drain from her face. "No, no, nooooo . . ."

Vivienne stiffens beside her, instantly alert. "What is it?"

Lottie bites at her thumbnail, staring down at the large figure jumping into the shallows from the bow of the sole approaching fishing boat. More than large, absolutely hulking. And wearing a blue-and-white-striped shirt. Even from way up here, it looks ridiculously tight.

"Care to fill me in?"

"D-down on the beach . . . it's him," Lottie stammers. "The . . . the . . . deliveryman."

"Delivery?"

"The criminal whose boat we stole! He must have gotten a fisherman from Tavalli to bring him here."

"It's a coincidence," Vivienne says quickly, her lips going white. "It's got to be. I'm sure no one managed to follow us. He has no way of knowing we're . . . here . . ."

No way except the boat we just stole. From him.

Lottie and Vivienne watch in sickly silence as the striped giant spots his own boat. He stares for a moment, hand atop his head, then leaps into action, gesturing wildly before running up the boulevard.

"I think he knows," Lottie deadpans.

"It doesn't matter," Vivienne snaps back. "We just need to get to the palace. Not far now, I hope."

Rounding the intimidating battlement and medieval walls, Lottie runs as fast as her little heels will allow, feeling invisible eyes boring holes into her back all the way, but even with that burst of effort, Vivienne vastly outpaces her. By the time Lottie takes in the sprawling courtyard and the grand beige palace beyond, Vivienne has already reached the first of five rifle-bearing, white-belted guards and appears deep in conversation, despite the guard's valiant efforts to stare past her.

She turns and waves to Lottie. The guard cocks his head.

Lottie jogs to greet them, hurriedly fixing her blonde waves behind her ears. "Hello!"

"This is Lottie Lawrence," Vivienne says with great emphasis on her name.

The guard looks mystified, as well he might. But then his eyes spark under his tall helmet.

"'What did you find, Millie?'" he recites, a little mischievously.

Lottie lets out a giggle. "That's right."

"*Vous venez du concert?*" he asks. "*Un peu tard, mais . . .*"

Lottie recognizes at least part of what he's said. "Yes, *oui, très tard*, we are . . . exhausted." She mimes putting her head on her hands and falling asleep. "*Si fatiguées.*"

Vivienne stares at her as if more appalled than impressed, then steps forward.

"Princess Grace won't be expecting us, but it's very important that we—" she starts. "*Excusez-moi?*"

The guard has already walked away to a wide, white-columned doorway where a man in a smart suit stands watching them warily. After a brief exchange with the guard, the man nods, and two of the stationed guards break from their lines to escort Vivienne and Lottie toward the palace.

"Well, that was easy," Vivienne says, sighing in relief.

Lottie nods. This is good news, of course, but Lottie can't help but flinch. Being marched into a big house by armed gentlemen feels uncomfortably like getting arrested.

The suited man stands rigidly in the doorway. A butler? Is that what you call it in a royal household? Something about his appearance suggests fastidious professionalism, but there's a wild glint in his eye that signals this is a man at the end of his tether.

"*Mesdames, bienvenue au palais,*" he says smoothly, a sheen of sweat shining on his forehead. "Please disregard the mess."

Despite how messy she looks herself, Vivienne glides straight inside like she owns the place, while Lottie calls out an awkward "*Merci*" over her shoulder.

The butler shuts and bolts the door, grousing to himself, as a much more cheerful, if equally harried, footman appears to usher them into a grand hallway, so dazzling Lottie feels sure she's hallucinating. Even Vivienne's mouth falls open in awe. There's not an inch in sight that hasn't been gilded, carved, painted, or otherwise ornamented. The walls are painted in gold leaf, the trim molded into flowers and leaves, frescoes fill the ceiling, and enormous vases stand sentry in every corner.

As for the "mess" the butler referred to, Lottie is left confused. Was that some kind of Monégasque joke? Sure, there are a few areas that bear the signs of restoration work being done, but she's not sure that's worth remarking on.

Then, with his eyebrows raised as if in warning, the footman opens the door to the royal apartments. Lottie laughs in shock.

The dissonance between the sitting room itself, which looks like an enormous rectangular Fabergé egg, and what's filling it is so jarring that she hesitates to even walk inside.

"What on earth has happened here?" Vivienne squawks, her eyes wide with horror.

The footman shrugs. "You are late for the party."

9

That isn't strictly true, Vivienne realizes as she follows Lottie through what looks like a scene from the siege of Troy: Tipped-over cocktail glasses, half-finished champagne flutes. Towers of picked-over charcuterie and half-eaten hors d'oeuvres littering the credenzas and tabletops. This party has definitely lost its steam, but the revelry is still raging on in some quarters.

In one room, jazz musicians riff on their instruments, pausing between solos to smoke "funny cigarettes" and swig from bottles of Pol Roger. In another, she spies a sleeping man in a tuxedo sprawled across a Louis XIV fainting couch with a fedora blocking his eyes from the chandelier's light, while a pretty woman sits on the floor next to him, eating shrimp cocktail out of a bowl. Sensing Vivienne's gaze, the woman gets up, slurs a whisper, "Don't wake up Frank," and then slams the door in their faces.

The last of the raging partygoers stagger from room to room, giggling, arguing, some of them belting out garbled renditions of the tunes from *High Society*, but there's an air of staleness to it all, a good time turned sour.

"Bet you've never been to a party like this one, Miss Rhodes." Lottie's eyebrows rise pertly.

"On the contrary," Vivienne mutters. "My entire childhood was spent on the sidelines of bashes like this one."

She thinks of her parents now, the glamorous Damien and Lia Rhodes, who arrived in Los Angeles and grabbed its scene by the neck, ferocious in their desire to reign supreme as Hollywood A-listers. How dashing they looked at the start of every affair at their grand Santa Monica home, how perfect and glittering, their usual animosity for each other tucked away safely before the company arrived. At some point during every party, they'd drag her out of the shadows, parade her around to wave to their guests, then shoo her off to bed with an airy kiss. Vivienne could never sleep from the noise. She'd sneak down, watch from the stairs sometimes, the slow transformation of her parents and their well-pressed guests into strung-out monsters.

It's that memory that keeps her from startling when a cigarette-smoking, middle-aged man staggers into view, wearing a loosely belted polka-dot dressing gown—and nothing else.

"Ah, more lovely ladies," he says wryly, his British accent dripping with derision. He's familiar-looking—Vivienne thinks she might know who he is—even though they've never met. "Invited guests? Or were you hired in for the occasion?"

They're spared from answering by the arrival of an older, gray-haired fellow wearing even less, just a sheet pulled loosely around his waist.

"Somerset, Willie darling, I told you to stay in your room," the middle-aged drunkard chides. Now she's positive this is Noël Coward. "Now where is your minder?"

As Coward escorts the gray-haired man past them, Lottie grabs his shoulder, smiling sheepishly, nodding toward his cigarette of all things. "You wouldn't happen to have another one of those, would you?"

"Assez!" The door to the apartments flies open. The butler storms inside, face stricken at the sight of the chaos, his immaculately combed hair flipping and flopping. "Enough!"

The musicians stop playing.

"You are in the home of the sovereign Prince of Monaco, not some Vegas motel. *J'en ai marre d'Hollywood.* Out! Out! To bed now. We will clean up your mess." And then, under his breath, "You swine."

As partygoers grumble and stumble deeper into the house, Vivienne seizes the chance to beeline for the butler, who's directing beleaguered staff with mops and wastebaskets to clean up everywhere he points.

His eyes narrow as she and Lottie approach. "There are no beds remaining," he snaps. "And no, you may not sleep in the parlor."

As if on cue, a maid escorts Frank Sinatra and his date out of the sitting room.

"We actually don't need beds," Vivienne presses, exhaustion revving into panic. "We really need to speak to Grace, immediately."

"The princess is sleeping. We will see you out now." The butler sniffs. "The party is over. I suggest you inquire at the Hôtel de Paris." His eyes turn to Lottie, dismissive. "Or perhaps there is a boardinghouse that might take you—"

"I think you're mistaken," Vivienne grits out, trying very hard to ignore the vile insults. "This is Lottie Lawrence. A dear friend of the princess—"

"I wouldn't say *dear* friend," Lottie mumbles, her face going red. "Might not even say friend. We chatted a little once, at a party at Humphrey and Lauren's, but beyond that . . ."

The butler makes a disgusted noise and snaps into the hall, where two of the guards have been waiting.

Vivienne turns to stare at Lottie in utter incredulity.

Lottie shrugs, grinning idiotically, like a child caught with her hand in a cookie jar.

Vivienne can only wordlessly sputter, though when one of the guards takes her arm to forcibly eject her, her brain kicks back into gear.

"Sir, *monsieur*, as I said, we're not here for the party. We're in danger, you see, a very real pickle."

The guards confer in French and then laugh, steering them down the corridor to the great front door.

"We've escaped from a band of criminals on the island of Tavalli and need to alert the police," Vivienne forges on, "and we need your protection in the meantime."

"*Elles ont pris des drogues apparemment.*" Vivienne's guard snorts. "Hollywood."

"What on earth is he saying?" Vivienne snaps to Lottie.

"Something about us being on drugs," Lottie says. "Viv, I don't think you're helping our case."

"You're one to talk," Vivienne shoots back.

They're ushered out into the morning air of the courtyard, the newly risen sun blinding Vivienne's eyes.

"Well . . . ," Lottie ventures after the palace gates slam closed behind them. "I suppose it could have been worse."

Vivienne groans. "I'm starting to think you *are* high." She stomps away, desperate to put space between them. Finally.

"Maybe I am," Lottie calls out. "Maybe I'm hallucinating."

Vivienne rolls her eyes again but doesn't stop.

"In fact, maybe I'm hallucinating these hors d'oeuvres. Let's see, there's oysters Rockefeller, caviar blinis, vol-au-vents . . ."

Vivienne's stomach rumbles in response. She doubles back, plucks a pastry from the assortment in Lottie's hands—what did she do, pilfer from every tray in the palace?—and devours it so fast she nearly chokes on it.

Immediate thought: *Oh, that hit the spot.* Though she restrains herself from sharing the concession. "A bit of a paltry consolation prize."

"Listen, wait, I'm—"

Vivienne waves Lottie off, motioning for her to follow back the way they came, toward the switchback roads winding down into the town center. She must have been firing on one cylinder, delirious with terror, hunger, exertion, to have staked their plan for help on Lottie's "connections." No, she's taking hold of the wheel again and not letting go, not until she's in a hotel room with security. Until Lew is on his way to Monaco. Until Jack Gallo and their cast and crew are out of harm's way and that maniac Ludovico is behind bars.

Lottie calls after her, "Where are you going?"

"Where I see fit."

Vivienne hurries past rows of citrus-hued homes and storefronts, tight cobblestone alleys ribboned through the arrangement like pith. The bay of Monte Carlo glows, rippling gold under the hazy, early morning sun. The whole effect reminds her of an enormous mimosa.

Her stomach begins rumbling once more. Maybe she should have grabbed more appetizers before storming off.

Vivienne pinches her eyes shut, chasing away the food fantasies, then fishes inside her chemise for the film canister, assuring herself it's still there. She can hand this over to the local authorities once she explains the situation.

"Don't you think we should talk about this first," Lottie shouts behind her, "seeing as we're in this together?"

"We are *not* in this together." Vivienne spins around. "I mean, yes, in the corporeal sense we are both, in fact, here, stuck in the middle of this awful situation at the same time and place, but in no way are we aligned."

Lottie's face pinches. "And why not?"

"Because I don't trust you!" Vivienne flaps her hands. "Honestly, how would any sane person trust you?"

"Maybe you should get all the facts first," Lottie snaps back, "before you decide you've got my number."

There's venom in Lottie's tone, a new, searing edge that slices straight through her.

Vivienne blurts a laugh. "Oh, that's rich. You know what? Why not, yes, let's go over the facts. Let's see . . . you stole my fiancé. My role. The crew—"

"The crew?"

"Yes. Oh, I know Charles went on about that poll or whatever nonsense, but it's obvious they all adore you. Don't think I haven't heard their snickers at my expense, their clear delight when Millie's girl bests the Wicked Witch of West Hollywood—"

"Vivienne—"

"You're also a liar. Funny how the damned butler got the truth about Grace whereas I was led to believe you were practically a bridesmaid—"

"Jeez, it was a little fib, harmless at the time." Lottie runs to keep up. "A slight exaggeration, way back on Tavalli. I was, well, I was a little green, if you must know, and—"

"Is that supposed to be an apology, because my lawyer could have written that."

"Fine, I'm sorry! I was jealous, okay? I was only trying to impress you—"

"Impress me? There. Another lie. You're a sore winner too.

Flaunting your victories, shoving them in my face, disguising it all with that false modesty of yours."

Lottie's face is crimson when she catches up, whether from embarrassment or from effort, Vivienne can't be sure.

"It's *actual* modesty," Lottie says evenly.

Vivienne laughs. "You're not as talented an actress as you think you are."

Lottie lunges for Vivienne's arm, but Vivienne shrugs her off and keeps walking.

"And you're not as smart as you think you are!" Lottie shouts.

Vivienne shakes her head. "Everyone talks about what Millie's found, but I wonder, is there a way to lose her?"

"I mean it. You don't know the whole story, but you're too damn arrogant to realize it."

Vivienne drowns her out with an uncharacteristic, almost primal roar.

Because there it is. A small, quaint building on a tree-lined street across the piazza with a large sign in unequivocal red lettering: Police.

This nightmare will finally be over. Vivienne's eyes water, she's so relieved.

She click-clacks in her tarnished kitten heels across the piazza, singular in her pursuit. She looks both ways down the waking avenue, then hurries across the road. Nearly there. Uniformed officers are inside. Already in the midst of protecting the city, it looks like, from the many men she can see through the large windows clustered around a circular table, arms crossed, faces grim, engaging in what appears to be a serious situation. Another man walks in to join them. *Wonderful. Yet another officer sworn to protect the public.* Her brisk walk becomes a run.

"What the— Oof!" she cries as Lottie tackles her from behind.

The pair go careening into the hedges, Vivienne landing with a thud. She spits out a mouth of dirt. "What the hell are you doing?"

"We can't go in there," Lottie hisses, ducking low behind the foliage.

"Don't be ludicrous! Of course we can—"

"No, I mean it. I recognize that policeman, the one who just came in. He's the boat owner, one of the guys exchanging money with Ludovico on the beach."

Vivienne falters.

Without another word, she and Lottie arrange themselves into crouching positions. Together they peek above the hedge line.

"You mean that man there? That towering giant with the dark hair?"

Lottie nods. "We saw him find his boat, remember, when we were walking up the hill?"

Dread snakes up Vivienne's spine. Lottie's right. It's definitely the same man they saw on their way to the palace, although now the fellow's wearing an official uniform.

"Holy cannoli." Lottie lets out a small whimper. "Yep. They've got us."

"What?" Vivienne blanches, wildly peering around. "Where?"

"No, inside, look at what the guy's holding," Lottie says. "Do those gals look familiar to you?"

Vivienne shimmies onto her knees to see better.

Oh. Crap. The boat owner, the Monte Carlo policeman, is handing out a stack of glossy photos to his colleagues. Her eight-by-ten professional headshots—long dark hair curled, hazel eyes staring coolly, confidently into the camera, as if daring them all to find her. Lottie's portraits too, doe eyes wide, glamorous blonde bob poker-straight, full lips pulled into a winsome smile.

Vivienne swallows. "The pictures from the set's promo room."

"After we took off, he must have swiped them to search for us," Lottie whispers. "And not out of the kindness of his heart. He's obviously working for, or with, Ludovico. Whatever the case, he can't be trusted."

Vivienne considers. "If he's running something illegal on the side, that might explain why he could afford a boat as expensive as a Riva."

"And why he wound up here. He's from here; he's on the ever-living police force!" Lottie jabs her finger toward the window. "And if he's crooked, the whole squad could be. We can't risk telling any of them our story. They'd probably call Ludovico and we'll be sent right back to Tavalli to be dealt with. Or worse."

"Worse?" Vivienne whispers hoarsely. Her nerves fire through her exhaustion, buzzing, newly electric. "So what on earth do you suggest we do now?"

Lottie bites her nails. Awful habit, really. "The *Ships* extra, the one who gave you the canister—"

"Emeric, I think," Vivienne supplies, then throws up her hands, incensed by all these question marks.

"You said he also mentioned Interpol."

Interpol. The international crime-fighting organization in Paris. Vivienne barely knows anything about the agency, other than that one of their allies, or associates or agents or whatever, died on Gallo's yacht last night. She nods.

"It stands to reason that he wanted to get that canister to the agency, maybe at all costs, if he gave it to you," Lottie says. "If we deliver it for him, Interpol will help us; they've got to. They'll protect us, Viv, be on our side. We can't say the same about anybody else."

Vivienne stares back through the windows again, stricken.

Lottie's right. If an officer in Monte Carlo is embroiled in Ludovico's dealings, who knows how far his criminal reach extends? Could Ludo have men in every city along the coast? How many crooked cops could be in his pocket . . . and if they trust the wrong authorities, what happens then?

If she and Lottie still aren't safe, even with hundreds of miles of open water between them and the prop master, then the smartest play, no, the *only* play, is for them to go straight to Interpol, give them the film canister, and appeal for help.

"Rotten luck that Captain Criminal came home and found his boat waiting for him," Lottie says. "He knows we're here and there's no getting around it. There's only getting out."

"So we go to Paris," Vivienne says slowly. "But on whose dime, precisely? And look at the two of us."

As Vivienne gestures down at her crumpled, stained charmeuse gown, Lottie reaches out to cup one of her dangling earrings.

Vivienne pulls back a bit, confused. "My sapphires?"

The pair of blue teardrops, sparkling with diamonds and centerpiece gems of her birthstone, had been a gift to herself a few months ago. An uncharacteristic splurge. A self-congratulation of sorts for her Oscar nod, plus a conciliatory purchase after Teddy.

"Remember me pointing out the casino, back on the boat?" Lottie whispers. "It's not far. We could lie low somewhere until it opens, dash in to cash your earrings in for chips, then the chips for cash. Fairly painless. Then we hightail it to the train station, purchase two tickets, and off we go to Interpol."

Vivienne looks back through the station windows at the policemen gathered around the table, conversing, looking grim. They could be talking about her and Lottie right now. They could be minutes from scouring the city for them.

She hates to admit it, but Lottie's plan makes a load of sense.

"There's just one wrinkle," Lottie adds. "You're right. We need to freshen up. They won't even let us through the door of the Casino de Monte-Carlo looking like this!"

"And I take it you have a plan for that too?" Vivienne asks archly.

Lottie winks. "You bet I do."

Interpol

Fumaroli, Pasquale

Wanted by the Judicial Authorities of France for Prosecution

Sex: Male

Date of birth: 11 April 1928

Place of birth: Ragusa, Sicily, Italy

Languages spoken: Italian, French, English

Charges: Murder, assault, racketeering

Height: 5'10" to 5'11"

Build: Stocky

Complexion: Medium

Hair: None

Distinguishing features: Broken nose

Approach with extreme caution. Highly dangerous.

If you have any information, please contact:

Interpol Agent François Aubert

10

We'll pick out an upstart shop," Lottie says, somewhat refreshed after a few blessed hours resting hidden inside a tiny beachside cabana. "High-end, obviously, but not totally de rigueur. Nothing on the Golden Circle. A new boutique."

"You know what's new in Monte Carlo?" Vivienne raises an eyebrow.

"No," Lottie answers patiently. "But there are signs. For example, watch for eagerness. At a new place, the shopkeeper will stand outside, hoping to attract customers, unlike at established shops, which are appointment only."

"Why does it matter where we go?"

Vivienne can't ask a single question without making it sound like absolute agony to voice it. Lottie turns to her with a placid smile. "Because a new shop will be the easiest mark."

Striding ahead, she motions Vivienne to follow her down a narrow road, away from the wide, flashy shopping district, where smaller boutiques and ateliers are open for trade and sparse on customers.

"You seem to know your way around this neighborhood," Vivienne comments.

"There's a bistro near here we went to a few times." Lottie bites her tongue, a millisecond from mentioning the onion soup Max was mad for. No one is supposed to know that Max was with them on their jaunt around the Riviera.

"Sounds romantic," Vivienne says on a breath, shoulders slumping.

"Not really," Lottie says shortly. How can Vivienne not know the score by now? "But it was fun to stroll around in this part of town. I always prefer vacations when you can be entirely spontaneous."

Spotting a shop with freshly potted yew hedges framing the front doorway and, more tellingly, a man in a sharp suit anxiously readjusting the front window display, Lottie grabs Vivienne's elbow and pulls her along.

"Speaking of spontaneous, you do know how to improvise, don't you?" Lottie asks.

Vivienne flinches. "Improvise? As in . . ." Her mouth opens, letting out only silence. "I . . . well, I rehearse. I create a long-range plan and adhere to it and—"

"That's not what we're working with here. No long-range plans. Just quick on our feet." Lottie watches Vivienne with fresh sympathy. This situation's got to be especially hard for a stick-in-the-mud, long-game strategist. "Listen, all I need you to do is trust me. For the next half an hour, tops, I'll take the lead. You just nod along. Right-o?"

After a long beat, Vivienne nods. Good start. Together they glide up to the boutique.

This place is so new you can actually smell the fresh paint. The suited pole of an owner stands just inside the doorway now, back turned, sniping at a harried shopgirl.

As Lottie and Vivienne approach, he turns, the very vision of oiled-mustached obsequiousness. Then, taking in their some-what, shall we say, wilted appearances, his expression closes off.

They'll need to work fast.

"Gosh, Viv," Lottie exclaims, clutching Vivienne's arm like the very best of friends. "This couldn't be the place the concierge meant?"

Vivienne doesn't say a word, as instructed, just presses her hand to Lottie's and sweeps a coolly appraising glance around the boutique that makes the shop owner stand up even straighter.

"Mademoiselles, how may I assist you?" His eyes narrow around his smile. "You are . . . American, I take it?"

Incredible how one little pause can tell you just what this fel-low thinks of Americans.

"Good ear!" Lottie laughs like a glockenspiel—*ding, ding, ding.* "Yep, just taking a break from filming. Walked right off in our costumes! We needed to decompress, and shopping is so re-storative, don't you think?"

"Filming." His eyes light right up. "Ah, I see."

"I'm—" Vivienne starts to say something that sounds worry-ingly like a personal introduction, but Lottie squeezes her hand in warning.

"Pressed for time, both of us are, but so glad we found you," Lottie finishes for her.

Best not to have their full names floating around town. Bad enough that their faces are wallpapering the police bureau.

Lottie slides quickly through the shop's displays, all bustling energy, scanning the gowns on display as she chatters, Vivienne trailing her like a far more restrained shadow. A mute one.

"I'm so glad we managed to find you. You see, we're staying at the Hôtel de Paris, and they said we absolutely *must* come to the new shop on the . . . What did he call it? La petite avenue? Oh gosh, we've gotten it wrong, haven't we? He said you had a relationship with the hotel?"

The shopkeeper looks mystified, as well he might.

Lottie lets her shoulders droop. "We've got the wrong shop."

Vivienne's eyes flash alarm. She starts to turn toward the door.

Lottie grabs her elbow to rein her back in. "What a shame," she says, letting her gaze conspicuously linger on a belted blue day dress, clearly one of the priciest items in here. "That one's rather nice, but, oh well."

And now she steers them both to the door. Slowly.

"*Mais si.*" The man hastens to the doorway, blocking the exit. "This is just the place. If you will allow my assistant to take your measurements, I am sure we can find you several—"

"That one," Vivienne calls, pointing to a smart flared dress in green. She glances at Lottie and adds, quietly, "You are not picking out my dress for me."

Lottie beams. "And I'll have a look at the blue organza."

A few eagerly taken measurements later, accompanied by the fawning compliments of the shop owner, and they are in full possession of two boxed-up dresses with shoes to match.

Still chattering away, Lottie takes Vivienne by the arm and trots with her to the door.

"We'll tell all our friends," she calls. "This is just a gem. *Bonne journée!* Did I pronounce that right?"

Delight is eclipsed by shock on the mustached man's face. "But, ah, there is the matter of payment?"

Lottie stares up at Vivienne's blinking eyes, then clutches her heart, laughing. "Oh, I am a goose!"

The man laughs along in obvious relief. Vivienne laughs too, a low, rumbling sound.

"Room 72." Lottie whirls around again.

The man calls out, "But—"

"Your arrangement? With the Hôtel de Paris? Just charge it to our room, like they said. It's so lovely you've arranged this. No one who's anyone carries cash these days."

"Far too gauche," Vivienne mumbles.

Lottie blinks at her, pleased by that little contribution. Then she turns back to the mark.

"You're really a very current establishment." Lottie winks. "Room 72. Don't forget or I'm going to have to come find you."

At the man's fingers snapping, the poor shopgirl scrambles for a scrap of paper to write down the number, but Lottie and Vivienne are out the door, ducking around an alley corner, before anyone inside that boutique can gather a scrap of their wits to go with it.

"What"—Vivienne breathes heavily beside Lottie—"was that?"

Lottie can't tell if Vivienne's about to serve her a knuckle sandwich or burst out laughing. Possibly both.

"That," she answers, "was the Charge It to My Room. My mother used to dress us up and take me out to fancy hotel tearooms for my birthday. First con I ever learned."

Vivienne stares at Lottie, this time with an odd mix of respect and pity. "Your childhood wasn't quite what I imagined, was it?"

"I sincerely hope nobody can correctly imagine my childhood." Lottie attempts a smirk. "For their sake as much as mine. Now, come on. Let's find another beach cabana and change into our disguises there."

Vivienne wrinkles her nose. "Disguises?"

"Two tourists visiting the casino who are definitely not fugitives wanted by the Monaco police."

They stop walking to stare at each other.

"How has this happened?" Vivienne whimpers. "What are we doing?"

"Steady on," Lottie says, pressing her hand to the back of a woozy-looking Vivienne. "This'll all be over soon."

Vivienne peers worriedly over her shoulder as they step onto a busier promenade. "I feel like we're in a 'walk the plank' sequence in *Bonny*."

Lottie follows her glance and spots the police officers from the bureau ambling in their direction, holding the promotional photos of the two of them. The uniformed officers stop to talk to an old man outside a café, pointing to the photos. The old man shakes his head.

Vivienne yanks on Lottie's arm, nearly pulling her out of her shoes. "Down. Now."

The two swiftly slide on their backsides off the road and down onto the beach, where a couple of weathered fishermen sit in the sand, tying knots into their nets. One of the fishermen graces them with an amused nod before returning to his work. Apparently these sorts of hijinks in young ladies are not exactly uncommon in Monte Carlo.

In a crouch, Vivienne and Lottie make their way down the arc of the beach until they reach one of the candy-colored cabanas and sneak inside.

The canvas falls with a flap, and in unison, they let out a great harrumph of a breath.

"You want me to turn around?" Lottie offers, whispering. "Protect your modesty?"

Vivienne snorts. "You don't come up in Esther Williams pictures and still give a hoot about modesty. Just help me with the zipper."

In the dim light, they help fasten each other into their new dresses, Vivienne adjusting the film canister into her newly rearranged cleavage, making sure it's still safe and sound. They leave their old threads behind, kicked ingloriously into the corner. Lottie does spare a wince of regret at Vivienne's gorgeous evening gown, left behind like trash, but Vivienne doesn't seem to be mourning its loss. Perhaps it's irreparably tainted by the night it lived through.

They'll just have to hope these new glad rags will have better luck than the last set.

Vivienne squints through a crack in the back of the canvas for a moment before turning to Lottie with a decisive nod. "All clear. And the casino must be open for the evening by now. I'm guessing you know the way?"

"Sure do," Lottie says, holding the flap open so Vivienne can emerge out into the evening seaside glow. "You've got me pegged."

"Funny," Vivienne says. "I'm beginning to suspect the exact opposite."

"Hang on a sec," Lottie says, stopping Vivienne in her progress up the beach. Vivienne looks gobsmacked when Lottie reaches out to fix her hair. "There. Perfect."

Vivienne rolls her eyes, but Lottie sees a little smile creep onto her lips before she turns away again.

She wonders how many female friends Vivienne has back in Los Angeles. Lottie's got about a million girls she gossips with; shares gifts with on birthdays; celebrates the big roles with, the awards, the good press. Making friends is a gift she picked up early on, back when her aunt pushed her into that first studio contract. She spent time at the lot school with all sorts of young ladies who could have been competition until Lottie won them over. But Vivienne wasn't one of them. She was attending private schools and sailing on yachts at that age. Maybe they'd be friends now if they'd been in school together. Or maybe she'd have been just as tough a nut to crack at the age of nine.

Friends or not, they are in this together. So Lottie leads the way to the Casino de Monte-Carlo, through streets lined with parked Bentleys, Ferraris, and Maseratis, past the Hôtel de Paris, where well-heeled guests are already filtering out onto the pavement in their evening gowns and stoles, ready for drinks or gambling before dinner. Nobody spares Lottie or Vivienne more than a glance, thank goodness. They're elegant enough to fit in, but not enough to stand out—a nightmare scenario in Hollywood, but absolutely imperative tonight.

A man in a military-looking uniform holds the door for them to enter the casino, and the best word Lottie can think of to describe it is *grand*. Pink-flecked marble columns, warm wood-paneled walls, a ceiling painted with pastoral scenes, chandeliers with electric bulbs spilling gold onto the gathering guests, all illuminated further by the atrium ceiling with stained glass that glows with summer evening light.

There are restaurants beyond, gambling rooms and bars, so much to take in that Lottie has to focus hard to locate the long lacquered desk where the cashier is stationed to exchange cash for chips. She hopes they follow Las Vegas rules here and accept goods in lieu of currency. Probably a more common occurrence later in the evening when gamblers' luck has run out.

The cashier on duty has the look of a well-groomed show dog about him with his thick bristle mustache and puffed uniformed chest, impeccably behaved but ready to bark and snap at a moment's notice. He even sniffs audibly as Lottie and Vivienne approach.

"*Bonne soirée*," he offers, unwelcomingly. "What can I help you with?"

Lottie notes his switch to English, realizing he's tagged them as Americans before they've even said a word, but no matter. She smiles just as sourly back at him, her nose inching higher, sensing that sweetness and naivete are not going to fly in this situation.

"We have jewels to exchange for chips," she says, and as Vivienne produces the earrings and lays them on the desk rather grudgingly, she holds her breath.

"Ah, *très bien*," the cashier answers crisply. Without a beat of hesitation, he pulls a loupe from beneath the desk and lifts the earrings to examine them through the lens. "Van Cleef et Arpels?"

"Good eye," Vivienne answers.

"It is my job," he says stiffly. But one sniff later, he ducks beneath the desk and emerges with a set of neatly stacked chips in varying colors. "Two thousand one hundred and five American dollars."

Vivienne opens her mouth in a squawk. "But I paid—"

"Wonderful, thank you," Lottie coos over her, blocking her view of the desk. "And can we cash out now or . . ."

"Certainly not!" The man's face goes paper-white. "*Mesdames*, this is not a pawnshop."

His eyes dart to the doors of the atrium, through which Lottie can now see uniformed officers entering the casino. Holding photographs. Eight-by-ten and glossy. She doesn't wait to confirm whose faces are on them.

"I was joking." She laughs derisively and tosses her hair. "You French have no sense of humor."

She gathers up the chips quickly, motioning for Vivienne to follow suit, ignoring the cashier's affronted, "I am Monégasque," as they move quickly into the nearest busiest room.

Two women glide past them in extravagantly large hats, lamenting their paltry remaining chips.

123

Lottie turns to them with a gasp. "We love your hats, so very 'of the moment.' How many chips do you want for them?" And just in case: "*Chapeaux . . . si chics. Nous pouvons acheter?*"

Judging by the women's blank stares, they are neither French- nor English-speakers, but a lightning-quick pantomime results in an even quicker unpinning and passing of a fat stack of chips, allowing their new friends to return to the casino floor with supplies replenished. It also allows Vivienne and Lottie to block their faces with enormous brims just as the police stroll past the doorway of the Salle de Renaissance.

"What do we do now?" Vivienne whispers from under her wide, purple bowknot hat. "They're blocking the exit and we're even poorer than we were before."

"We blend in till the cops are gone and we can cash out," Lottie hisses back, scanning the room. "And in the meantime, we win back those chips. There." She finds it—the busiest section of the casino floor, and the farthest from the atrium. "We'll start with roulette."

11

Lottie slides into an empty seat on the near side of the green felt table, motioning for Vivienne to sit down beside her.

After glancing at the trio of uniformed officers still lingering near the casino's grand hall, Vivienne follows, wholly unnerved now. Gripping the brim of her ridiculously ostentatious new hat, she slinks down into the empty chair.

The table is a long, thin, green runway checkered with red and black diamonds, French words, and numbered spaces. At its other end is a stately wooden wheel. There's a buzz to the space too—not just the sounds and whispers of the crowd but a frenetic crackling in the air itself. Vivienne's never been inside a real casino; watching Charlton Heston's debut in *Dark City* is the closest she's ever gotten.

She settles in, listening, detecting various frequencies. The hum of adrenaline. Expectation. Longing too. Ah, the allure of a clear-cut game, a simple crossroads: play and win or play and lose. It was one of the main things that appealed to her about swimming, the reason she stuck with the sport, even after her father's short-lived bubble of pride over his progeny pursuing his passion had burst, long after her coach became Vivienne's sole fan at the meets. There are so few things in this world as elemental as a competition, a race. Such straightforward rules, such honest, palpable stakes.

The Hollywood hustle, for all its charms, is a confounding morass by comparison, victories so tempered by compromises, concessions, and addendums that they sometimes still feel like failures. Case in point, it took five years of nonspeaking roles and sheer tenacity before Vivienne was even credited on a picture, *Grimm's Mermaid,* and that was a catchpenny production.

A slim, wrinkled man in a gold-buttoned uniform interrupts her thoughts, nodding at Vivienne, a dour little frown pulling at his face.

"The croupier," Lottie whispers.

"*Placez vos paris,*" he says. "Place your bets."

"Have you ever played?" Lottie murmurs, carefully selecting two chips as if picking out chocolates from a See's Candies box.

Vivienne takes stock of the other players sitting around the crowded table. To her right, a pair of Japanese businessmen, plus a finely dressed couple in their forties or fifties. Near the wheel, several young men in smart attire. On Lottie's other side is an older, sunburned gentleman in a blinding white suit, along with a pair of prim older ladies. Past them, a colorful group of tourists, likely just here to gawk.

"No," Vivienne finally admits. "Never."

"It's easy," Lottie whispers. "Just follow my lead."

Lottie looks up, scanning the floor, inconspicuously gesturing toward a pair of officers who have wandered deeper into the room. She adjusts her hat to shield her face, then slides one coin onto the square marked with the black diamond.

"It's a game of chance. Pure odds," she explains.

"Well, there must be some skill to it," Vivienne objects.

"Strategy, sure, but leave that to me. We'll keep a low profile, stick to the outer bets, win a little, then cash out and scoot as soon as the coast is clear."

Vivienne affords a weak nod, though she can't help but continue to prickle at Lottie so cavalierly calling the shots. Yes, her scheme with the dressmaker was, admittedly, successful, but her improvising could have just as easily exposed them for the frauds they are.

She can't help but snip, "And what if I'm thinking red?"

"Red?" Lottie shakes her head. "I've already bet."

"And I like the number 36."

Lottie blinks a few times, a deer in a glade, before pasting on her own sham of a smile. "I know what I'm doing, okay?" She spins toward the sunburned, older gentleman on her left and says, in a decidedly admirable impression of a flat Midwestern drawl, "First time overseas *and* at a casino. Wow-ee, this is quite a big trip for two Kansas City farm girls, wouldn't ya say?"

Vivienne eyes the chips on the table and the small stack beside Lottie's fingertips. A part of her aches to play. To feel in control again, armed with just her pure desire, determination, drive against the world. To let her worries fade into a distant dream, like she used to do at the start of every freestyle race; her parents and their soul-crushing refusal to see her, her loneliness, all dissolving away. To be stripped down to the purest of instincts: *go*. It's like an itch she can't scratch, being this close to a competition and not playing. A cloying need to step up. To win.

"Kansas?" the sunburned man beside Lottie says in a posh English lilt. "You girls are a jolly good way from home."

Lottie laughs. "And we forgot to pack our ruby slippers."

Before losing her nerve, Vivienne gently pushes their stack of chips until the pile is on top of square 36.

"*Plus de paris!*" the croupier calls out. "No more bets!"

The old Brit beside Lottie lets out a hearty laugh. "What a charmer you are. I'm Billington. James Billington," he says with a wink. "Didn't catch your name?"

"Dorothy." Lottie somehow manages to wink back while also batting her eyes. "Pleasure to meet'cha."

Vivienne tries to sink into the delicious *clickety-click* sounds of the spinning wheel, which is harder to do now that one of the officers has crossed over her line of vision, passing the center of the casino floor. He seems to be questioning a group of patrons near the bar.

Vivienne squints discreetly.

Oh shit. He's showing them those damn headshots; she can see Lottie's photo clearly from here—her companion's sleek bob, wide smile, glittering blue eyes.

He can't see you. Forget him. Just for a moment. Just for now.

Vivienne pulls her purple hat farther down on her head, hunches her shoulders, and silently commands the wheel to slow, as if it's an extension of her, one of her own appendages. The ball now staggers through the deflectors. *Fifteen* now . . . *Please. Slow down. Stop. Stop! Three . . . Twenty-four . . .*

"Thirty-six!" she cries, leaping to her feet. "Yes! I won!"

Lottie whips her head around, alarmed. She yanks Vivienne back into her seat.

"Thirty-six!" Vivienne hisses, satisfaction racing down her spine like a warm waterfall. "I wo—er, *we* won!"

There are murmurations of approval, nods from around the crowd as the croupier confirms, "*Rouge, trente-six.*"

Vivienne's chips on 36 transform into a matrix of neatly stacked piles.

The croupier tilts his head toward her, a gleam of burgeoning respect in his eye as he rakes the other chips from the table.

"Are you crazy?" Lottie seethes, her smile all gritted teeth. "What part of 'low profile' did you not understand?"

"What incredible odds. What is it, fifty to one—"

"Thirty-five to one, and not the point."

"Quite a pair of lucky farm girls," the man—Billington—coos delightedly over Lottie's shoulder. "I daresay I might have found my muses of fortune. Been bleeding chips for days."

"Beginner's luck," Lottie lobs sweetly.

She refixes her glare on Vivienne, lowering her voice. "You simply refuse to fade into the background, don't you?"

Vivienne's cheeks grow hot. "What are you implying?"

"I'm not implying anything. I'm telling you straight: stop being your bullheaded self. Just take a back seat and be quiet. I said I know what I'm doing—"

"'Bullheaded self'?" Vivienne scoffs. "And I'm most certainly capable of taking the back seat when I trust my costar."

Lottie's eyes narrow. "For the record, that's not your reputation, and as I've said before, you don't always have all the facts."

"I think the facts are clear. I'm a natural at this game and—"

Lottie grips her forearm. "We are thousands of miles from home with corrupt cops crawling this casino with our pictures. The goal is sneaking out of here alive, not reenacting a scene from *Gambling House*. Just trust me!"

"Marcus, Lyle, come, come," Billington turns and bellows. "My lovely new friends just beat the odds."

Vivienne and Lottie look up, mouths gaping, as a veritable

horde of older British gentlemen in linen suits approach with drinks in their hands, crowding all around them to watch.

Vivienne tries frantically to peer through the new crowd, but no. From her table seat now she can no longer see the manic sprawl of the casino floor . . . or spot any of the officers.

"Well, go on then, my angels of luck," Billington crows to Lottie, eyes shining. "Where are you going to place your next bet?"

Before Lottie can answer, Vivienne sneaks another chip from the box. She's feeling *black 26* this time. She was twenty-six when she starred in *X Marks the Spot*, the titular *X* being black, and that was certainly a lucky break, but Lottie grabs her hand again.

"Fine," Lottie snaps under her breath. "Stop. Change of strategy. We can use this crowd. But I mean it—let me take the lead."

"I don't see why—"

"Seriously, can you just"—Lottie huffs—"open yourself up to the possibility that maybe you don't know everything?"

Vivienne's cheeks turn scorching now.

"My sister, I tell ya," Lottie says, leaning back to confab with Billington's cronies. "She don't talk much, but she's got nerve. Always bettin' the farm. But as our grandpa from Old Town Topeka taught me, you gotta play careful, levelheaded."

"*Placez vos paris*," the croupier calls out again. "Place your bets."

Lottie twirls a trio of chips through her fingers a few times before smoothly doling them out over the table. One on the 0, another on the corner of 7. Billington nods approvingly and follows her lead.

"The key to roulette is being smart *and* patient," Lottie tells Vivienne in an undertone. "Playing the long game."

"You mean I need a consistent strategy," Vivienne concedes. Begrudgingly.

"Right. But you also need to be able to pivot, act quickly, re-calibrate every time you're betting." Lottie places another chip on the outer corner of 29. "Add some smart hedges, cover your bigger bets—some double streets, a basket, a trio here or there. You're using the entire table, considering multiple angles. Yes, we want to win—to stay here until we get a window to scram, plus a little more money wouldn't hurt. But we can't win so big as to draw attention."

Lottie pauses her tutorial to toss a gee-whiz "Here goes nut-hin'!" in Billington's direction. Then she refocuses on Vivienne. "Own the table, you see, versus letting the table own you. Think big picture. Endgame. Living and dying on a single bet is for am-ateurs."

There's obviously yet another buried insult in there, but Vivienne's too confused, and, honestly, too fascinated now, to care. She puts her hand to her chest, riveted, her fingers unexpectedly brushing the film canister buried there. A small relief, she sup-poses, that it's still secure.

Then the game is on again, the croupier once more shouting, "*Rien ne va plus!*"

The wheel begins to click with its dizzying spin, the crowd droning and teetering, the ball bouncing, slowing . . . stopping . . . on . . . 30.

Vivienne only understands they've won in some fashion when Billington is whooping and squeezing Lottie's shoulders before grabbing his own pile of multiplied chips.

This time Lottie's wink is for Vivienne. On Lottie's other side, Billington lets out a delighted holler. "I daresay, Dorothy, we're on a roll." He waggles his gray eyebrows. "Tell me, darling, what are you and your sister playing next?"

Lottie somehow narrates her next three bewildering, winning

plays to Vivienne as she did with her first while expertly deflecting questions from Billington's increasingly vocal friends.

"Goodness, darling, you look ever so familiar . . ."

Lottie: "Get that a lot. A cousin. A niece. A neighbor."

"On the contrary, you look like a film star, doesn't she, Henley?"

Lottie: "Aw shucks, don't go givin' me a big head." Followed by that laugh of hers, hitting just the right note between flirtatious and doting.

Meanwhile, the chips keep building. The crowd keeps growing, shielding them from view. The throng of interested onlookers now envelops them like a fortress wall.

Vivienne sinks back in her chair.

Lottie is indeed owning this table. In fact, Vivienne's stray lucky bet has been completely eclipsed. She has, unequivocally, been thrust into the back seat. Reduced to "sidekick." The role of "Mute Sister."

Ordinarily she'd be incensed. And yet there's something exhilarating about watching. Surveying the big picture like a director would. And actually, well . . . trusting Lottie, handing her the reins and watching her perform in a way Vivienne never would have expected—in a way Vivienne never would herself—and finding the performance stunning.

Surprise and delight helix inside her, this new, tangled, complicated feeling so unprecedented that Vivienne chokes out a laugh. Lottie Lawrence, America's "girl next door," pigtailed star of *Millie*, for goodness' sake, is running the roulette table in Monte Carlo.

And the crowd is all-out enamored with her. In fact, Vivienne nearly starts applauding herself, until she notices a man in a distinctive black suit cutting slowly through the crowd ahead, making his way toward the croupier.

"Pit boss." Lottie nods with a fixed grin, noting the suited man too. "And it's time to skedaddle. Wait for my signal."

"What's a pit boss?" Vivienne whispers.

"Hey, fellas," Lottie says, leaning back toward Billington's friends, batting her eyes. "Why don't you try your luck? Take our seats? We've warmed them up for you, wouldn't you say?"

Billington pouts. "Oh, don't go. We're on a tear."

He promptly stops pouting when Lottie edges half their pile of loose chips toward him.

"Dorothy and her sister were never here," Lottie purrs. "Understand?"

Mr. Billington's eyes go wide. Even so, he quickly nods, hungrily gathering the chips. "Yes, why, of course, you have my—"

But Lottie's already grabbed Vivienne's hand and pulled her smoothly through a pocket in the crowd. They expertly thread through the throng, their overflowing box of chips firmly in Lottie's hands. Vivienne finally has a clear view. The police have at long last drifted from the main floor. Perfect time to vamoose!

As they pass by an empty table, Lottie tosses her huge pink hat onto a seat and lifts up the abandoned scarf draped across the seat back beside it. As she's fixing the scarf over her head, she points to a suit jacket on an opposite chair.

Vivienne picks up the jacket. It smells like the studio gym. Stifling a gag, she briskly slips it over her green dress and gratefully ditches her own gargantuan headpiece.

They reach the next-shift teller breathless, waiting in frozen anticipation as the chips are confirmed, counted, taken, and finally exchanged for a crisp stack of bills with a respectful nod as an *adieu*. Lottie slips the money into Vivienne's suit jacket, good a place as any, and then they are past the casino floor exit, down the marble steps, out the doors. All elegance. Composure.

But by the time they emerge into the electric glow of early evening and its searing indigo sky, the lights from Monte Carlo twinkling around the bay, they're both spewing laughter.

"Who *are* you?" Vivienne slips in her heels a bit, her laughter tipping over into exhaustion, a half-manic fit, tears rolling down her cheeks. "That old man's face when you gave him your chips!"

"*Dorothy* gave him her chips."

"Sure, and I'm Auntie Em. And that impassioned monologue about the streets and the baskets and . . ." Vivienne hiccups another laugh as they round a palazzo. "An impressive performance. Just, truly."

"I'd call it a sister act." Lottie loops her arm through Vivienne's, beaming, as they hurriedly weave toward the city center.

"We might just make it to Interpol unscathed."

"Of course we will." Lottie gives Vivienne's arm a little squeeze. "Next stop, train to Paris."

It's the squeeze, for some reason, that tips Vivienne over. She feels exposed, somehow, without the cloak of the casino. Almost reminiscent of how she used to feel after a bedroom scene with George Carvel or Richard Burton or some other costar. Playing at intimacy. Channeling something that, for a few minutes at least, beautifully felt like more than just pretend. A real connection.

She finds herself needing to resist the urge to embrace Lottie, to thank her, to cry in mutual elation at a long-overdue, collaborative win—and reminds herself that this was the same woman standing with Teddy at the Oscars, smiling at her with that shit-eating grin. The catalyst of months of her pain and heartache.

She pulls back a step, placing firm distance between them.

"You mean Marseille," Vivienne says stiffly.

Lottie stops, confused. "What?"

"The train. I consulted the maps near the concierge desk at

the casino. I know how much you love to improvise, but this is hardly the time. Good thing too, because you're mistaken: there's no direct to Paris."

Lottie's face pinches with confusion, maybe hurt. Her eyes drift over Vivienne's shoulder, then widen.

"Marseille, Paris—as long as it's not Monaco." She takes Vivienne's arm. "Cops are out the door, on our tail. We need to move."

On the Q.T.

The Magazine That Tells the WHOLE Story

Vol. 1, Issue 4

JULY 1947

CLOSER THAN FAMILY

Hearts are melting on the set of Apex Pictures' *Seventeen Sweethearts*, and we're not just referring to the titular love interests. Ken Winters, 26, fresh off his star turn in *Lady Be Mine*—not to mention his heroic service in the U.S. Army—has impressed the cast and crew alike by taking little Lottie Lawrence under his wing. The star of Apex's popular Little Song and Dance shorts and, of course, the Millie pictures, Lottie's been tapped to play Ken's college freshman sister—but not everybody has a kid sister who's such a stunner. Maybe that's why newlywed Ken is rumored to be spending oodles of quality time with little Lottie, even into very late hours. Has the lure of forbidden fruit proven too hard to resist? Or is their obvious chemistry both on and off the screen strictly brother-sister? (cont. page 23)

12

They've got a hefty head start on the policemen approaching from the south, so outpacing them these five hundred yards to the Gare de Monte Carlo wouldn't ordinarily be too tough a task. The trick now is to do it while keeping up the ruse of two partygoers heading home on the next train.

So she and Vivienne run arm in arm, like it's just a lark. *How fun to frolic through the streets of Monaco after an afternoon at the roulette table! Whee!* They achieve a sort of rhythm, managing not to step on each other's toes, and most gratifyingly, Lottie is for the first time able to keep up with star athlete Vivienne, if only because she's gripping onto her for dear life.

Vivienne must also feel like she's doing a school three-legged race, because she's the first one to start laughing as they round the corner to the ticket booth and let go. Lottie keeps watch as Vivienne buys tickets, and they're on board the 18:24 train to Marseille safely ensconced in a compartment just in time to see the red-faced, heaving officers reach the platform.

As the train pulls away, Lottie spots the giant joining their ranks, his shoulders straining the seams of his ridiculously ribboned police uniform. Anger swells in her veins, along with triumph.

She can't resist. She opens the window, sticks her head out, and blows him a farewell kiss. She can't be sure in the evening light, but she has a feeling his mammoth face has gone beet red.

As the train picks up momentum, falling into a lulling *click-clack* across the gorgeous countryside, Lottie drapes herself over the comfortable seat and relaxes.

"Golly," she says. "I used to plead with Buster to loan me out for a Hitchcock picture, but I didn't expect one to fall on me in real life."

"I've heard he's a beast," Vivienne says idly, fastening her sprinter's hairdo back into something sophisticated. "Not Buster, Hitch. Obsessive, abusive to his leading ladies. Small wonder Grace quit the industry and married into a house with an entire army protecting it."

"Not to mention a crooked police force at your disposal." Lottie sighs sourly. "I've heard that about Hitchcock too, but I figured I could take it. It's not so different from how the whole town runs, after all."

Vivienne snorts. "Men with their director's chairs, all that power. Never mind that we're the ones who get people to shell out for tickets in the first place. And that more often than not, we're the ones half-directing the pictures ourselves when they're unable to get the job done."

Lottie's eyes sharpen on Vivienne, on the wistfulness in her expression as she gazes out the window.

"You could be a director," Lottie says. "You'd be swell at it."

Vivienne's eyes cut to hers, wary.

"Why not?" Lottie sits up. "Your Cassandra scene. All right, so at the time I was not your biggest fan, but I've got to admit, the changes you made to the blocking, even Max's script, bless him, were brilliant. If you could work your magic with my scenes and finagle your way into the editing room, we might actually have something special on our hands."

Vivienne's eyes drop to her lap, her mouth pulling into a shyly pleased smile. Then she stares past Lottie and sighs. "I think the odds of a major studio handing me the director's seat are slimmer than me winning the Kentucky Derby. On foot."

"Even with Jack Gallo's help?" Lottie shoots her a sly glance. "You two seem simpatico."

"Well, I—we are," Vivienne splutters. "Were. Who knows if he's even still alive."

"Oh. Right. Gosh." Lottie blinks away a wave of dizziness. How quickly everything's changed. "I'm sure he's all right."

"Wish I could say the same." Vivienne's voice is a vault closing.

"Well, I'll be sure for both of us. And once we're back home, when everything's fixed and back to normal, you should make a case for yourself as a director. I'll put in my own appeal, whatever that's worth. Maybe you could even find a small role for me in your first picture?"

Vivienne's eyes narrow. "Now you're teasing."

"Not at all." Lottie shrugs. "I'll happily take orders from you."

Vivienne snorts loudly.

Lottie laughs, caught. "On set, I mean. Out here, I'm afraid we're a team."

Something about what she's said seems to affect Vivienne. Color rises into her cheeks, making her look, uncharacteristically, like a bashful teen making a friend for the first time.

Vivienne peers out again at the dark countryside whizzing past in strokes of emerald and ochre. "So this is France? Pretty much identical to Monaco."

"And yet good riddance to Monte Carlo," Lottie crows. "Here we've got a legitimate gendarmerie, and Interpol and pain au chocolat and crepes and, hmm . . . I think I might be hungry."

Vivienne buries a smile. "They'll serve dinner on the next train to Paris. Not long now."

Not long at all.

Before they know it, the train slows down at the Gare Saint Charles, and they descend the car steps into a large utilitarian station, bustling even at this time of night.

Lottie stretches her arms, her neck, while Vivienne squints at the timetable overhead.

"Ah, good," she says. "Only a sixteen-minute wait for the evening train to Paris. Wait here. I'll be back in a jiffy."

As Vivienne strides to the ticket office, discreetly pulling their stash of money from her borrowed dinner jacket, Lottie savors the summer breeze on the platform, the tantalizing peek at rocky hills in the distance, the hum of voices and swish of bodies moving around her. A moment of tranquility amid all this madness.

She could be anybody here, in this one moment. A French woman commuting to see family. A deposed Russian aristocrat.

Or her real self, whoever that is. Not a person trying hard every minute of the day. Not running, for once, just existing right here. Standing, breathing, feeling something and showing it, damn the consequences.

And yet what this calls most to mind are those days of early childhood, standing forlorn in the middle of bus depots, waiting for some mark to come and offer help. It wasn't the con that she enjoyed about it, Lottie realizes now, surprising herself. Not the win. Not even the break from her mother's manic energy. It was the fact that people came to help her. People saw her struggling and hurried over to wrap her in kindness, however fleeting.

Maybe that's why she feels so safe now, in the in-between. And she's not so very famous that anybody would recognize her.

"Lottie Lawrence?"

That voice—that familiar baritone—makes her throat tighten like fingernails are digging into it. No. Not here.

She forces pretty blankness into her expression before she turns, but when she catches sight of Ken Winters arm in arm with his wife, Betty, she has the sense she hasn't quite nailed it.

"Hot dog! I thought it was you," Ken says, turning to his wife. "What did I say, Betty? I do believe you owe me a franc."

Betty shrugs, laughing. "I thought it was a little far-fetched, but oh my goodness, here you are! So good to see you."

And she means it. Even after all this time, Lottie can tell by the warmth in Betty's gently crinkling eyes that she's never heard the rumors or read that damn *Q.T.* article. Ken probably made sure his wife never laid eyes on it, because look at them. They're still such a pair, Ken and Betty, both elegantly sliding into middle age, slim and bronzed from the sun, like a set of expensive candlesticks.

Betty leans in for a cheek kiss, and what can Lottie do but kiss back? Her eyes flit, unwillingly, to Ken, and she sees him eyeing the two of them with a wolfish glint in his eye. Lottie feels the blood drain from her face.

Betty grabs her arm. "So tell us, what on earth are you doing in France? We've snuck away on vacation while the kids are back in Iowa with my folks for the summer—so needed, for all of us, don't you think, honey?"

Ken *hmms* in agreement, his eyes still fixed on Lottie as if he owns her, poor Betty as ever none the wiser. Registering what Betty's said, Lottie remembers now that the childhood sweethearts have six children. Betty married Ken right out of high school and moved with him to California so he could pursue his Hollywood dreams. Didn't take long for that charm of his to land him a contract at Apex, but after a few small roles, Pearl Harbor put the brakes on his aspirations. He wasn't in service long before a mysterious but honorable discharge took him out of action and gave Apex the opportunity to brand him a war hero and bump him up to major roles, first in battle stories, then domestic romances. In the decade since, Ken's gone from win to win and is now one of the biggest film stars in the business. And all this time, his beautiful wife has been by his side. Raising miniature beautiful people. Burying her own pretty head in the sand.

The wind blows down the platform.

Betty stares at Lottie, eyebrows raised, and Lottie realizes she's waiting for an answer. What's brought her to France?

Good lord, where to start?

"We're shooting a picture," Vivienne supplies.

Lottie whirls around, sinking with relief. Reinforcements.

Vivienne slides past Lottie to offer a hand, the other clutching newly purchased train tickets. "Vivienne Rhodes."

Ken outright kisses Vivienne's hand, the slimeball, but she seems to take it in stride.

"Oh my goodness, Vivienne Rhodes," Betty says, even more delighted. "I'm such a fan of yours, aren't I, Ken? Let me tell you, we were at the premiere for *Bonny*, and I went straight out the next day by myself and saw it again. Didn't I, Ken?"

As they laugh, Lottie shrinks away like a kicked dog. Betty might be approaching her forties, but she's still the genuine girl next door Lottie's always pretending to be. The thought of her being tied to someone like Ken for life is physically revolting.

As Vivienne visibly unwinds in the face of Betty's adulation, launching into behind-the-scenes details about her training on

142

the ropes and in swordplay, Lottie drifts gradually backward and away, praying for the train to arrive and break up this little quartet.

But as the train arrives with a clatter and roar, Vivienne trots back to Lottie. "You all right? Obviously a little awkward for you, but they've invited us to join them for dinner and I don't see how we can refuse. This might be a real boon, you know. We might consider spilling the beans to them about the mess we're in. Ken's a war hero, for goodness' sake. He could protect us while—"

Lottie's mouth goes very dry. "No. Don't tell him anything. You cannot trust him."

Vivienne's eyes narrow on hers, but before she can say anything, the train stops and Lottie hurries past her to hoist herself aboard.

She watches Ken and Betty head to the right to pick out a compartment and turns on her heel to the left, determined to find a space away from them where she can breathe. Vivienne joins her in loaded silence, using the mirrored lacquer of the door to adjust her dress, jacket, and hair. Lottie doesn't bother. She'd quite frankly rather look like mad Cassandra at dinner tonight than Helen of Troy.

The train starts away, but any relief Lottie might have felt at getting that much farther away from Tavalli and Monaco has been smothered completely by the arrival of Ken Winters. Her first feature film costar.

Her first a lot of things.

"Shall we?" Vivienne suggests, and Lottie flinches.

"Already?"

"It's past eight." Vivienne blinks, as if Lottie isn't quite right in the head. "They're serving now. Just think about the food. You were starving twenty minutes ago."

"I was. I am. Let's go."

She can do this. Her whole life has been playing the friendly gliding duck, legs scrambling frantically under the water's surface. Why should tonight be any different?

They're waiting at a prime table in the dinner car. The waiter obviously recognizes Ken, but his eyes go even wider when he sees Vivienne and Lottie walking in to join them. A movie fan, then. So much for keeping a low profile, but Lottie supposes it doesn't much matter on this side of the border. *Vive la France!*

Vivienne carries the society chitchat, apparently her comfort zone, through the entrée course and wine service, and by the time Lottie's steak frites arrives—her carefully mandated studio diet can go straight to hell today—the conversation has swung around to the trend in historical epics.

"Now, I for one have got to hear the dirt on *A Thousand Ships*," Ken says, leaning in with a conspiratorial wink. "That's what you're shooting, isn't it? Surprised the studio let you out of their sights. From what I've heard, Apex isn't just in trouble; it's barely a going concern. Or was until . . . what's his name? The new president?"

"Gallo," Vivienne says. She sips her wine, and Lottie watches her swallow down the catch in her throat. "Jack Gallo."

"Right, right." Ken swirls his own cup without drinking. "You know, Sammy Zimbalist was telling me MGM made a play for Apex, but Gallo's offer blew Vogel's out of the water. An absolute nobody. Now, Sam's a fellow with vision. He offered me *Ben-Hur*, you know."

Lottie can tell from the way he shifts his eyes to the left that he's lying.

He steals a roasted potato off his wife's plate. "Filming in Rome as we speak. I couldn't bear to be away from the rugrats that long, so they gave it to Charlton."

Betty presses her hand to his arm and flashes him an adoring look. The family man. What a star.

Lottie chokes on her steak. Loudly. Half the dining car turns to look as she doubles over, coughing.

"A little water?" Ken offers, alarmed, passing her glass closer.

His pinkie does a tango against her hand and she jumps up from the table like a scared cat, coughing even worse.

"Just . . . need a moment," she gets out and hightails it straight past the giddy-eyed waiter, down the rattling train corridor, and safely into their compartment.

Funnily enough, once the door slams shut, her coughing stops. She sits down and breathes, treacherous tears springing to her eyes.

After all this time, he can still scare the life out of her. It's infuriating—and absolutely the last thing she needs while she's fleeing for her life from actual criminals.

Although he's a criminal too, isn't he?

The door careens open, clapping against the frame before it slides back with a thump.

Vivienne stands before Lottie, hands on her hips. "You want to tell me what's going on with you? Because it looks a hell of a lot more dramatic than scarlet letter guilt, and I really didn't peg you as one to self-flagellate. That's a compliment, by the way. And why can't we trust him, exactly? Surely he'd help us. Unless you think he's in league with Ludovico Despetti, which seems extremely unlikely to me. Though who the hell knows anymore."

Vivienne sits down with a sigh—her version of delicacy, Lottie supposes.

"Let's cut past the rumors, shall we?" Vivienne offers. "First, did you have an affair with that man?"

"Well . . . y-yes," Lottie stammers. "But it's complicated. It's not what people say. It's . . . worse."

Vivienne raises a single eyebrow. She should win an Oscar for that ability alone.

Lottie looks away, gathering her courage. Then:

"I'd just turned sixteen."

Vivienne draws in a hissing breath. Surprised, maybe.

Lottie goes on doggedly. "I'd been living with my aunt and uncle in Pasadena for the past nine years. They're the ones who pushed me into the pictures, and not out of the goodness of their hearts. They put me up for this two-bit variety act first when they saw an ad in the papers and realized I could sing. It wasn't too bad, as those things go. Two old fellows doing a clown act and I was the rascal urchin, causing mayhem. I had a little song at the end, 'At the Picture Show.' Do you know it?"

Vivienne shakes her head.

"Anyway, Buster Smith came to one of the shows. Brought me in, signed me up, little roles at first at Apex. Comic shorts, that kind of thing. My aunt pushed me to lie about my age to get around the labor laws so I could work longer hours. I was an early reader, so they bought the act, and suddenly I was ten instead of seven. Over time, things started to get rolling for me. I'd gotten a pay bump for the Millie pictures. But my uncle seemed to resent it more and more, the fact that I earned more than he did. Like it made him less of a man or something. He started coming home absolutely soused, and my aunt defended him at every turn. She wasn't much better than him. She'd only adopted me when my mother got arrested—"

"Arrested?" Vivienne flinches. "What for? Wait." She closes her eyes. "You don't have to tell me. I know this is all rather personal."

Lottie waves off her concern. "Mama was a confidence woman. Small time. She did what she could to support us both after her family kicked her out for getting in the family way, but anyway, that's beside the point. You asked about Ken Winters."

Lottie's fingers are trembling. She balls her fists to steady them.

"The night in question, dear Uncle Jimmy came back around two in the morning and barged straight into my bedroom demanding money. Started going through my drawers looking for cash. It wasn't the first time, but I knew right then it was the last. I pointed him toward my handbag, let him take whatever was inside, then once he passed out, I packed my bag and ran."

"You must have been terrified," Vivienne says softly.

"You know, I'd love to say I wasn't, that the school of hard knocks had already taught me well, but that's not the truth." Lottie lets out a cold laugh. "I *was* terrified. I had no idea where to go, what to do, but I knew Ken Winters had an apartment up in the Valley he'd stay in after long shooting days. We'd been working together the past five weeks or so. I was his kid sister, playing older than my age, but still sort of the younger comic foil. He knew I was younger than the line they'd been selling the public and he'd been so nice to me on set. Really treated me like he was my big brother. He was, what, ten years older than me? More? Offered me advice on the business. Said I could come to him if I ever needed help with anything. So I did. I showed up on his doorstep. He took me in. And then . . . he took advantage."

"You were sixteen," Vivienne whispers.

"Yep. I didn't know a thing. Thought I did. But when he

offered his bed, I didn't know how to insist I'd take the sofa. When he crawled in with me, over me, I said no, stop, but he didn't listen, and eventually I just gave up. I figured this was the price of freedom. I was becoming an adult, and this was how you did it."

She finally meets Vivienne's eyes and sees faint tears glistening there, a reflection of her own expression.

"I stayed until the shoot was done; then I went to Buster and asked for an apartment on the lot with the rent deducted from my pay. By that point, I was getting good press, they liked me, and they were happy to help. Ken transferred over to MGM and, lord, I was thrilled, but the damage was done to my reputation. Permanently, apparently."

Lottie shoots Vivienne a wry glance, expecting some sort of apology, perhaps, for her harsh words back on Tavalli, even in the form of sheepishness.

Instead, livid red circles form on Vivienne's cheeks, her nostrils flaring. She looks like she's going to explode with rage.

She stands. "I'll kill him."

Lottie jumps up to grab her. "Vivienne, don't."

"You were a child," Vivienne fumes, staring daggers at the compartment door. "And he damn well knew it!"

"He did," Lottie says, taking her wrist. "But listen to me. Betty is a doll. She doesn't know, I'm sure of it, and I don't want to be the one to ruin that for her. Besides, we can't afford to make a public scene right now."

Vivienne blinks as if waking from a dream. She nods, curt. Then she peers at Lottie, plaintive. "I'm sorry that happened to you."

Lottie laughs. Shrugs. "Yeah. Me too."

"I'll go make excuses. Grab our dinners and bring them back here. I'm not letting that bastard rob us of a first-class meal."

Vivienne straightens her shoulders and glides from the compartment, leaving Lottie to flop limply against the train window.

What a turnaround for the ages. Vivienne Rhodes, her staunchest defender!

Truth is, she's never told anybody that story. Not even Teddy, who knows about her childhood, her money-grubbing aunt and uncle, her early days in vaudeville.

But Lottie's glad that Vivienne's turned out to be her confessor. Her terror of Ken gives way to a sense of relief. Safety, even. He's nothing in the face of the wrath of Vivienne Rhodes.

The door flies open. Vivienne runs to Lottie, pulling her upright.

"Where's the steak frites?" Lottie murmurs, confused.

"Never mind that," Vivienne snaps. "We've got to go."

"What? Why? It's hours until Paris and—"

Vivienne grips Lottie's shoulders. "The man from the boat. Gallo's boat. He's here."

"The guy from Interpol?"

"No, he's dead. Keep up, Lottie. I'm talking about the guy who shot him!" Vivienne says. "One of Ludo's goons, the bald fellow, Syd's assistant. He's pacing through the dining car, wearing a hat now, but it's him, I know it is. I don't think he saw me, but . . . he's got a gun in his back pocket."

"I *am* a dumb blonde," Lottie says on a breath. She grits her teeth in frustration at herself. "Why, oh why, did I blow that kiss? They might not have been able to confirm it was us if I hadn't felt the need to gloat. Oh my God, he called his cronies, didn't he? That big lummox must've picked up the phone and told them we were on the train to Marseille . . . and your goon must have tracked us from the Marseille station onto this train."

"I think it's safe to say the goon belongs to both of us now," Vivienne corrects tightly.

"We might be dead already if it weren't for Ken and Betty," Lottie realizes.

She meets Vivienne's wide eyes, then, as the train starts to slow, holds on and peers ahead out the window. She can't tell where they are, only that it's a stop, and that's enough for her.

"Right," she agrees. "Let's get the hell off this train."

MOVIE STARS PARADE

JUNE 1958   25¢

HOLLYWOOD STARS SAY OUI OUI!

Hollywood has been enamored with Europe's *mode de vie* for ages, but these days celebrity culture seems gripped by Euro mania. Indeed, the prestigious Cannes Film Festival this May turned the Cote d'Azur and surrounding areas into a monthlong party, with stars and staffers extending their time overseas, jetting to luxurious locales along the French Riviera, Provence, Costa del Sol (pictures, below, of Yul Brynner sunning himself in Nice; Ken Winters and longtime wife, Betty, stepping out in Paris's 11th Arrondissement).

With more tentpole projects being filmed abroad this summer, such as Apex Pictures' *A Thousand Ships* and MGM's epic, *Ben-Hur,* which is filming in Rome's Cinecittà Studios, this "Los Angeles by way of the Louvre" trend is sure to continue . . .

13

Vivienne sprints through the train corridors after Lottie. The two of them elbow around a young English couple jostling their bags down the aisle, past an elderly man waiting near the vestibule, all the while glancing over their shoulders for Ludovico's thug. When the train finally shudders and sighs into a full stop, they're the first passengers down the steps. The platform is narrow, crowded, the small headhouse glowing eerily against the blackberry sky.

"Where is he?" Lottie whispers. "Did he see us get off?" She pulls the scarf she swiped from the casino tighter around her head.

Vivienne warily scans the platform, then the long steam locomotive behind them, peering inside every one of the illuminated windows running its length like yellow crochet trim. "I don't think so."

Lottie shivers, taking Vivienne's arm. "Come on, we need to go."

They hurry past the station into the surrounding Provence village. St. Rambert, according to the wrought iron sign Vivienne spots on the platform. It's small, a crisscross of winding cobblestone streets, faded pastel storefronts, a row of lampposts twin-kling in the night. In the distance, a sprawling expanse of vineyards borders the town on all sides like a dark emerald moat. The place is undeniably charming, a romantic place to vacation, even, were her circumstances wildly different.

Her thoughts immediately turn to Gallo; she can't help it. Is he alive? Did Ludo's man get to him too? Could he have escaped? Or did Ludo decide to spare the producer in order to continue his criminal endeavors? She hopes to God that's the case.

Vivienne swallows, surprisingly gutted by the prospect of never glimpsing Jack's dashing smile again. Look at her, of all peo-ple, falling for the studio boss. Now, when it might be too late.

"I think we're safe," Lottie says. "Let's try to find a restaurant. We can hole up a little while, figure out what the heck is going on while we wait for the next train."

"And eat," Vivienne adds, still mulling over her dark thoughts. "I can't stomach another interrupted meal."

Though as soon as she says it, she wishes she could take it back. Did she just make light of their run-in with Ken Winters?

"Hopefully the kitchens aren't closed," Lottie whispers back.

Vivienne nods, though she aches to recalibrate. Ken Winters. That bastard. She's furious at herself for being so taken by sur-prise. Shouldn't she understand by now that appearances are only masks, that they can hide a world of heartache and trouble? How could she of all people assume, like everyone else, that she knew the terms of Ken and Lottie's relationship?

She wants to tell Lottie that she didn't deserve it, that she's a good person—anything more than just pledging to murder the son of a bitch—but can't seem to find the right words. Ad-libbed lines, wandering off script, riffing, it's all fairly uncomfortable for her. And off-the-cuff, heart-to-heart monologues? She simply doesn't have the skill set. It's like attempting to speak Italian or French. She doesn't know the language, never had any practice, not a lick, especially when it comes to female friends.

Not that Lottie is a friend, per se. But she certainly no longer feels like an enemy.

Despite her ineptitude at burying hatchets, Vivienne forces herself to try. Lottie deserves that.

She feels her cheeks flaming with anticipated awkwardness as they follow the curve of the road. "Hey, Lottie?"

Lottie stays silent. Her brow is stitched tight, her eyes scanning their new surroundings. Vivienne follows her gaze. St. Rambert's center square has come into full view. There is indeed a bistro up ahead, its lights on, revelrous patrons laughing, chatting, spilling onto the sidewalk. Vivienne can smell the savory aromas from here.

"Lottie, listen, I just want to say I'm—"

The departing train shrieks. Both women flinch and turn around.

"Crap." Lottie grabs Vivienne's elbow, ushering her forward.

"What?"

"The scary-looking bald fellow with the crooked nose? I'm pretty sure he's behind us."

Vivienne's heart starts clattering. She attempts to peek, but Lottie keeps her hold firm.

"Don't look, just take my word for it. He got off the train."

Vivienne eyes the bistro up ahead. "Should we duck inside? Hide?"

"Nope, too risky."

"So, what then, a back alley? Should we run into the vineyards?"

"I think we need to split up." Desperation rings through Lottie's voice. "Confuse and lose."

"What?" Vivienne balks. "No, thank you, no—"

"I don't want to either, but it's our best shot. My mom and I used to run the double con all the time. You beat feet in two different directions and confuse the mark. It works in nine out of ten situations."

"And what about the tenth?"

"Vivienne." Lottie inches closer, discreetly nodding toward Vivienne's décolletage, where the film canister that Emeric gave her is safely stowed.

In response, Vivienne raises her other hand over her chest in protection.

"This can't end unless we reach Interpol," Lottie whispers. "And we can't get there unless we lose this guy. Believe me, if there's one thing in this world I'm good at, it's running."

Vivienne can't help but discreetly glance over her shoulder. Sure enough, she spies a figure in a Panama hat, no more than about forty paces back. She homes in on their pursuer's tanned face, his lopsided nose, his feigned carefree smile, his hands in his pockets as if he's a tourist on holiday, due at a wine tasting or a rustic dinner in Provence. He's even whistling.

But his acting job is subpar, as to be expected. His stance stiff, his shoulders rigid. The obvious way he's surveying, scanning hungrily.

Vivienne spins, now rigid herself. "We might have made eye contact."

"I told you not to look back!"

"It was a reflex!"

"Gah!" Lottie steals a breath. "Fine, just . . . see that oncoming fork in the road? Go left and find a way to loop back to the bistro. I'll go straight. Hopefully he tails me and I can shake him."

Vivienne's nerves are electric now. A mere twelve hours ago, the idea of splitting up from Lottie would have felt like a grand idea.

But now? A death sentence.

"I do think it's prudent to share my experience here," Vivienne sputters, "as we had a scene similar to this in *Bonny*. Once my character split up from her crew, she was captured by rival pirates, and didn't you say your mother wound up getting arrested?"

"Please, it'll work, just—" Lottie sighs, flashing her an exhausted smile. "Trust me, one more time? I'll find you near the bistro, and then we'll figure out a way to scram."

She squeezes Vivienne's elbow before hurrying off.

Vivienne blanches, feeling a bit like a woman scorned, though who's her audience, this henchman?

Right. No time to dally.

She quickens her gait, veering left as instructed, tottering down the curving cobblestoned road in her new scammed heels, which have already started to blister around the toes as if in punishment.

As she passes a windowed storefront, the butcher at the counter cutting a hunk of sirloin pauses, knife raised. He glares at her ominously.

Vivienne hastens away, her brisk walk more of a scurry now. Around her, in the dark, the shadowed facades of the storefronts and crooked homes look like looming ghouls.

She pinches her eyes shut, attempting to quell her rocketing pulse. Her heel folds, sending her stumbling.

"*Mademoiselle?*" an older woman locking up a flower shop calls out, her voice laced with concern. "*Mademoiselle, bonsoir, tout va bien?*"

"I'm fine, everything's fine," Vivienne grumbles, hobbling. "Don't make a fuss!"

She takes the corner in a sprint, glancing back wildly now, but the only person on the road is the florist, still watching her pityingly. Up ahead, the road appears to loop farther left, away from town, the bistro, Lottie. Damn it!

Impulsively, Vivienne darts into a narrow alley wedged between a sleepy-looking residence and a shuttered antiques store.

Her body ripples with fear as she tiptoes down the cluttered passage. In the dark, the boxes and trunks stacked against the antiques store transform. Even more ghouls, shadowed watchmen. *Wonderful.* She nearly squeals when a rat squeaks, scurrying across her path.

She stops.

Gather yourself.

How she wishes right now that she was someone like Lottie, or even her father, for that matter. Someone able to decide with their gut, who doesn't need a map or a script or a very detailed outline to consider their every move. But Vivienne has always been a long-term planner, top-down, a strategist, and even here in this disgusting, vermin-infested alley, she finds herself running a quick list of pros and cons for either retracing her steps or trudging forward.

"Forward," she tells herself, at last decisive. As she begins walking again, she tries to avoid a loud clatter of her heels. Did she choose the right way? Is that . . . is that lamplight up ahead?

Oh yes. Yes! And there's a sign flapping in the distance too. She can make it out if she squints: Bistrot St-Rambert.

Hope rises like a tide.

But before Vivienne can take another step, a hand wraps around her wrist, jerking her toward a pile of clutter. She lets out a shocked yelp and spins.

It's the man who's been following them, new hat and all. She never got a good look at him on set, but this up close and personal, he's even more intimidating. Wild eyes, sun-beaten skin. Every bit of him seems to snarl.

"*Aspetta*," he whispers. "Shh."

She shrieks, drowning him out, instinct finally kicking in. She yanks her hand away, hard, causing him to trip forward and temporarily lose his firm hold. Just enough for her to slip away.

"*Ferma!*" he hisses, chasing after her. "You cannot run forever."

She tears through the alley full tilt, heels click-clacking, heartbeat thrashing through her ears. Careening for the bistro sign, Lottie, anyone.

"Help!" she shrieks. "Help!"

The man's footsteps quicken behind her.

"Quiet," he hisses. "*Silencio!*"

"Help me!"

But they're alone in this alley. She's so close, but still too far. She feels him narrowing the distance between them. Growing closer. What should she do? Her mind flitters to Lottie's ramblings in the Casino de Monte-Carlo, about betting, strategy, hedging. *Maybe it's time to try something else, time to take the offensive?*

She spins, fast as a flip turn, stares at his looming face, and with all her might—slaps!

Damn it. So much for improvising. The goon lets out a primal snarl and tackles her, throwing his body into hers. They go down together, crashing into the debris-littered alley.

Vivienne kicks and screams as the man swiftly moves his hands, first restraining her, then covering her mouth, and then, when she bites him, wrapping them around her throat.

"*Cagna! Puttana!*"

Stars begin to collide behind her eyelids. She lunges for **his** eyes, swatting at his hat, nails out, clawing for blood. But the pressure around her neck keeps tightening, a noose, a swimmy feeling growing in her stomach.

"No, I'll . . ." The words come out in a heave as she gasps for air. "Ne-ne'er . . . surrender."

It's a line from *Bonny*. Even in her last moments, she's sticking to script. One of her own revised lines, but still, the woeful absurdity.

Vivienne blinks furiously, her panic hot, coursing through her, every nerve singing a swan song.

This is my last performance, she thinks numbly as she weakly thrusts for freedom. *My final scene*.

She closes her eyes, reality collapsing to a pinpoint.

"Get! Off! Her!"

The piercing cry is abruptly followed by the sound of shattering glass.

A gasp of surprise.

Then a thud.

The pressure releases from Vivienne's throat as she slumps onto her side.

"Vivienne? Vivienne!"

The ground of the alleyway is cool, rancid smelling. Her throat, neck, insides raw. Is she dreaming now? Dead?

A different pair of hands shakes her. Hard.

"Stop," Vivienne moans, hoarse, the word torture to utter. "P-please . . ."

"Vivienne, come on, wake up. Look at me!"

Another tug, a shake, and somehow Vivienne is on her knees, blinking alert, staring straight into Lottie's worried blue eyes.

There's a smashed, jagged wine bottle nose in Lottie's hand.

Beside her, the body of Ludovico's hatted goon is sprawled out, tangled in a heap. He lets out a faint moan, rolling to his side.

Still conscious. Still dangerous.

"What . . . ?" Vivienne blinks, swooning. "I . . . What did you—"

"I hit him with a bottle!" Lottie hoists the vessel's jagged nose. "Keep up, Viv. Come on. He won't be down for long. We need to go!"

Vivienne shakily clambers to her feet, accepting Lottie's hand. "I don't want to split up ever again."

"Note taken!"

They scurry past the overflowing bistro, the oblivious diners, festive music playing, ringing out across the village square. Lottie looks both ways, then decidedly ushers them toward a vineyard tasting room set a little off an adjacent road. It's called, encouragingly, a cave, but what they find is a plain old farm building.

They round the structure, traipsing through its sprawling side yard overgrown with lavender, and find a trio of delivery vans parked in the gravel drive near the fields. The back doors of one of the trucks are open, and inside, a tiny labyrinth of crates. Hundreds upon hundreds of wine bottles. And just enough room to crawl in between.

Lottie lets out a shaky, satisfied breath. "He won't look for us in here. And if he does, plenty more bottles to clobber him with."

She leads Vivienne up the ramp. They duck inside the truck, round the nearest tower of crates, and slide down in the back.

Without a word, Lottie passes Vivienne half a baguette, swiped from the bistro, she assumes, sneaky devil. Her searing throat screams in protest, her parched mouth choking on the scratchy texture. Still, she takes another bite, murmuring in gratitude.

"We can wait here all night if we have to," Lottie whispers. "He'll give up the hunt eventually; we just need to sit tight. We'll get on the first train we can, and then straight to Interpol."

A loud groan answers before Vivienne can. From *beneath* them. Before she can register exactly what's happening, the soft light filtering through the truck's open doors pinches out.

Vivienne freezes. There are French voices now, if she's not mistaken. Men. Talking. Bickering?

She finds Lottie's eyes as the voices continue around the truck.

Doors from somewhere up ahead creak open. Slam closed. The engine revs loudly. And with them inside, the truck rolls away.

14

We're going somewhere." Lottie perches, incredulous, against the truck flooring with the palms of her hands.

"Yes, I'd noticed." Despite the valiant attempt at sarcasm, Vivienne is clearly just as panicked as Lottie.

"Someone is driving away with us." Lottie takes in the clinking crates around them, the glass bottles inside. "In a wine truck!"

"Well, that's one consolation. Along with the fact that we're escaping. Again."

Vivienne's voice trembles slightly. Lottie reaches for her hand. Vivienne lets her hold it for a full second before pulling away, which Lottie considers progress. But Vivienne's still shaking, teeth chattering. Shock from what she's just faced down.

Lottie's surprised she's not as rattled herself. Maybe it's still to come, once they find a way out of this new predicament. But for now, she wants to gather poor Viv up in a comforting blanket of a hug, and the only thing stopping her is knowing it's the last thing Vivienne herself would want.

"We don't know where we're going," Lottie says, and yes, her voice does seem to be pitched a little higher than usual, funny that. She picks her way through crates to peer through the crack in the back doors. "We're far enough away from him now. Should we jump out?"

"Are you insane? We'd break our necks. And then have to keep running."

Vivienne has a point. Lottie can't make out much in the darkness, through the narrow slit of the metal doors, but what she can see of the road is passing by extremely quickly.

"Besides." Vivienne slouches against the van wall. "As you said, it's a wine van, and it's full. They're probably headed up to Paris, to sell from this local vineyard to the restaurants there. That must be why they're traveling by night, for morning deliveries. We'll ride along, hop out when they stop, and take the canister straight to Interpol. Let's just sit tight and try not to question our good fortune."

Lottie lets out an unladylike snort.

"Fine. Our less ridiculously catastrophic fortune than anything else that's happened in the past two days. Past week," Vivienne corrects, her voice growing fainter. "Six months, if you add it all up."

The sound of Vivienne's yawn is contagious. Lottie takes a page from her book and finds a more stable position among the stacked crates, where she's less likely to hit her head on anything as the van lurches down the road. She kicks off her shoes, getting comfortable.

She can hear occasional voices from the cab in front, separated from them by a thin bit of metal. Two, low and laughing, and another, higher, like a child. French, she thinks, from the cadence.

Vivienne starts to softly snore.

So I'm not the only one. Lottie smirks, filing that bit of information away for later strategic use.

The van careens along its merry way. Someone's voice rises in the cab. Singing. Lottie doesn't know the song.

She closes her eyes.

A slap of sunlight hits Lottie's face.

She blinks, eyes adjusting with difficulty until they focus on a girl of about twelve years old with long pigtail braids staring at her in abject astonishment.

"Pierrot, Antoine? Venez voir?"

The sound of the girl's yelling rouses Vivienne, who snorts to life, instinctively fixing her hair and dress as she straightens imperiously.

"Y a deux femmes ici, j'ai pas, mais qu'elles sont belles!" The girl lets out a wild giggle, then claps a hand over her mouth as she turns her attention to them. *"Qu'est-ce qui se passe, mesdames? Vous êtes perdues, ou . . . ?"*

"Lottie?" Vivienne closes her eyes again with a groan. "Care to translate?"

Lottie blanches. "She's speaking very quickly."

Two rather strapping young men join the twelve-year-old in the van's doorway. The girl's brothers, Lottie guesses. There's something alike in their angular features and olive-tinged complexions. Politeness wars with bewilderment and dawning delight in their expressions as they take in Lottie and Vivienne, lounging amid their cargo.

"Américaines, je pense," the girl says behind her, then turns back to the van smartly. "I learn English in school; it is not problem."

"Are we in Paris?" Vivienne pipes up. Then, at the girl's fuzzy expression, adds a broadly French pronunciation: *"Paree?"*

The French trio glance at one another.

Lottie seizes the opportunity to jump into the conversation a little more diplomatically. "We're very sorry. *Désolées.* We had to hide. We were in danger."

"Danger?" The little girl puts her hands on her hips, either skeptical or confused.

"Danger," Lottie repeats gravely. "Gosh, how do I describe this in French?"

Perched on her knees, she gives up, instead miming running, then ducking into the car, hands over her head, then shutting the doors.

The young men's eyes go very wide. She looks completely bonkers, no doubt. Hopefully charmingly so.

"And then," Lottie soldiers on, "the car . . . you . . . drove away. I don't know the word for that either." Here she mimes steering an invisible wheel, waving goodbye to imaginary bystanders. It's a regular vaudeville act. She's still got it.

By the end of that little performance, Vivienne is staring at Lottie in utter horror, but the French folks at last seem to understand.

"Oh my very gosh," the girl says, giving an American accent a good go. "What a catastrophe!"

Lottie smiles. That must have been on the school vocabulary list recently. Then her gaze shifts. Her grin falls, and her jaw right with it.

"Yes," she agrees. "*Total* catastrophe." Behind the brothers' broad shoulders, she can see the landscape.

Not Parisian buildings. No Eiffel Tower or Arc de Triomphe. No city whatsoever, only verdant hillsides, wispy clouds, piercing blue sky, and beyond that, snowcapped mountains?

Oh my very gosh indeed.

Except the word Lottie blurts out is, "*Merde*."

Vivienne's caught up too. She scrambles between wine crates and slides out of the van, eyes wide with incredulity.

Lottie joins her outside, ignoring the pins and needles stabbing her feet as they touch rocky ground.

"Are those . . . ," Vivienne breathes, "the Alps?"

"Yes!" The little girl beams. "They are beautiful, no?"

"*Oui*," Lottie agrees dimly. "*Très belles.*"

"The absolute wrong direction," Vivienne squawks.

"Also *oui*," Lottie says.

The young men have drifted out of hearing range, chatting to each other over cigarettes. Damn, would she like one. If ever there was a time for a smoke, it was now. Both boys toss covert looks over their shoulders at Lottie and Vivienne, who are apparently even more delightful now that they're in full view, still in their full Monte Carlo casino party dress glory.

"I am Cecile," the girl says, offering a jaunty handshake.

Vivienne steps back, watching Lottie. Letting her take the lead. Heaven's sake, is she afraid of children on top of everything else?

Lottie shakes her hand. "Grand to meet you, Cecile. I'm Lottie."

Vivienne lets out a relieved breath, and Lottie realizes now why she'd hesitated. She wasn't sure whether to give their real names or not. Lottie just hopes she herself made the right call.

"Vivienne," she says, and Lottie notices that Cecile looks a little more awed shaking her hand than Lottie's. A fan?

"Do you recognize us?" Lottie asks.

"Re-cog-nize," Cecile repeats slowly. Not a word she knows, Lottie guesses.

"Have you seen us before?" she tries.

Cecile shrugs, eyebrows scrunched. "In the village? No."

Vivienne looks at Lottie, then adds, "Do you watch movies? Cinema?"

Cecile makes a little gagging noise that startles a laugh out of Lottie. "No. I detest the cinema. So boring. Stuck in a dark room watching pretend. I like real life. Outside. You know?"

"You must have a good life, to prefer it to the movies," Vivienne says. "When I was your age, I felt the exact opposite."

The little girl stares, uncomprehending either the English words or the sentiment behind them. Then she blinks and skips quickly away, calling behind her, "Come! Meet my brothers."

"We're in the Alps," Vivienne says again. "On a mountain pass. With strangers."

"Not strangers for long," Lottie says, taking her hand to drag her along. "Let's go meet *zee bruzzers*."

"This is Antoine, the short one," Cecile announces, her eyes sparking with mischief. Her brothers clearly have no idea what she is saying; they just smile along. "This very ugly one here is called Pierrot."

In truth, neither of them are short, nor ugly in the slightest, all bronzed arms under rolled-up sleeves, muscular shoulders, brown hair tinged gold by the sun. Both men are a good deal too young for Lottie and Vivienne—too young even for Lottie's real age—but that doesn't seem to deter the fellows from trying.

In lieu of a handshake, the French boys swoop in for cheek kisses, one on each side, and then trade partners, like a country dance. Lottie feels a blush rising to her cheeks at all this sudden intimacy, but if anything, the boys look even more gallantly bashful.

Even Vivienne gets visibly flustered. But with a toss of her hair, she recovers. "So where are you all headed? We're trying to get to Paris. It's very important."

"We go to Rome," the girl says.

Lottie's heart stops.

Vivienne spins around, hands in her hair. "Italy. We're headed back to Italy."

"This is . . . We can't . . ." Lottie catches her breath, winces a smile. "You can't go to Paris instead, by any chance?"

Cecile stares at her with pity, as if realizing she is, in fact, an idiot.

"We go to Rome. We deliver the wine from our *terretoire*." At their appalled expressions, the little girl adds reassuringly, "It is a long way, but we have fun."

She turns her back to confer in feverish whispered French with her brothers.

Lottie takes the chance to link elbows with Vivienne and draw her away.

"What are we gonna do?" Lottie hisses, taking in the sweeping, isolated landscape around them. Hill upon hill upon valley and mountain, rock-cragged and endless. The road itself, while well-paved, is quiet at this early hour. By the angle of the sun, it must be just after dawn. "Walk back?"

"Through the mountains? In heels?" Vivienne kicks one foot behind her to demonstrate.

Lottie rolls her eyes. "It wasn't a serious suggestion."

"We could wait for a car heading in the other direction," Vivienne says, squinting eastward. "Hitchhike."

She spits out the word like a bitter pill.

"And cross our fingers that we get good sorts, no one who would take advantage of two young women in party dresses, traveling alone?" Lottie fights the urge to bite her fingernails. "Pretty risky."

Vivienne eyes Lottie with open sympathy. Likely remembering her big confession back on the train. Which feels like a lifetime ago.

"Let's find a place to lie low, then, and recalibrate." Vivienne shields her eyes and scans the horizon, like a wartime scout. "A mountain resort, perhaps. We still have those francs."

She pats the pocket of her borrowed jacket in demonstration.

"I know, but they won't last us long." Lottie sighs. "Not at a resort, anyway. Maybe a hikers hostel?"

Vivienne goes a little green at that suggestion.

"And again, we run into the same risk," Lottie adds. She turns to look at the young French family, now smiling shyly in their direction. "Now *they* seem like good sorts. Pity they're leading us into the lions' den."

"Lions' den. Gladiators." Vivienne seizes hold of Lottie's shoulders. Lottie gasps at the terrifyingly electrified look in the taller woman's eyes. "Rome. Sam. Sam Zimbalist. *Ben-Hur!*"

Lottie stares. "Are you having a fit?"

"They're filming *Ben-Hur* in Rome right now. Zimbalist is on the picture. He's wanted to sign me to MGM, been chasing me for a year."

Lottie cocks her head. "I'm guessing you're not just bragging here."

"Only a little. What I'm saying is . . . forget Interpol, forget Paris. We'll take the path of least resistance and go to Rome instead. All roads lead there, isn't that what they say?" Vivienne snaps a wild laugh. "We'll get to the set, find Sam, and when he hears everything we've been through, he'll help us! It'll be like being safely home in Hollywood but, you know, six thousand miles away. He'll call Interpol, get us flights back, maybe with a security detail. The cast and crew will be safe, maybe even . . ."

Vivienne closes her eyes, cutting off that last thought, perhaps a little too painful in its hopelessness. Then she blinks alert again, resolute.

"He'll put a stop to all of this. It's a good plan, Lottie, it is."

Lottie's inclined to instinctively agree, but for once in her life she quickly rifles through their options first. Of which there are very few. Another car hasn't driven by in all this time, and there isn't any kind of lodging, hostel or otherwise, anywhere in view.

"What do you think?" Vivienne asks. "Are you with me?"

Lottie can't help but reel at the humility in Vivienne's expression, something that would have been unthinkable just a few days ago.

Before Lottie can agree, Cecile steps between them, hands on her hips, a bossier expression on her face than either of them could ever muster.

"I make a plan, yes?" Cecile announces. "You come with us to Rome. Then you take train to Paris. We stay with our aunt tonight. She make good food. There is phone. There is inside toilet. It is not bad for the mountains, you will see. You stay in the, ah . . . studio? Where my uncle work? Because no room in the house, *ça va*? It is fine. We will check on you."

Vivienne blinks, thrown for an absolute loop by Cecile's assertiveness.

"*Ça va bien*," Lottie says, reaching the absolute limit of her flimsy French. She shoots Vivienne a wink.

And with that, they are off once again.

Antoine and Pierrot rearrange the crates to make more space for their guests and offer a few more warm but unnecessary cheek kisses while they're at it, before shutting the van doors with apologetic grimaces. The darkness doesn't feel so ominous now. A little light streams through the gap in the doors, making the tops of the bottles glow.

As the engine starts, a rap sounds on the wall separating them from the cabin and Cecile calls through, "Have some wine! We bring extra!"

Vivienne squints at Lottie. "Did she just say—"

"Give me your shoe," Lottie says, a bottle already in hand.

Deftly, she twists Vivienne's sharply pointed heel into the cork, working it loose with a satisfying *pop*, not even any damage to the shoe. It's too dark to assess how impressed Vivienne is, but she has to say, she's pretty darned impressed with herself. And the wine is some sort of red—tart, fruity, hints of cherry. Absolutely what the doctor ordered.

"Hand it over," Vivienne says, and she doesn't mean her shoe.

They pass the bottle back and forth, swigging like sailors, giggling like schoolgirls.

"We should pace ourselves," Vivienne suggests.

"Long journey," Lottie agrees.

And do they follow their own advice?

Absolutely not.

Hollywood Reporter

APEX PRODUCER WAGNER OFFICIALLY DECLARED "MISSING"

BY JAY GRIER

JUNE 15, 1958

William Wagner's family has appealed to the Los Angeles city police department, which has officially declared the producer "missing" this morning, according to sources close to the family. Authorities in the Hollywood area and surrounds are working with international counterparts to piece together what happened to the man who stormed off the Tavalli set of Apex Pictures' production of *A Thousand Ships* over ten days ago.

"The force won't rest until we find him," said Chief of Police Harlan Rogan. "We ask any individuals who might have pertinent information to please come forward . . ."

15

"You know what would elevate this tasting?" Lottie purrs as she passes another bottle of red to Vivienne.

Vivienne blinks. Is this their second bottle? Third? She's lost track inside this rumbling van, lulled into a dreamy sense of nowhere, no time, given the engine's melodic hum and the stuffy, textured darkness.

"A really, really good cheese plate," Lottie continues, slurring and wistful. "What I would give for a hunk of cheddar"—Lottie raises her hand like a claw—"This big. A real shame Pierrot and Antoine aren't dairy farmers."

"And that their Mourvèdre is so bad." Vivienne puckers from the wine's thick tannins.

"Shh, you snob!" Lottie swipes the bottle from Vivienne, leaning against a tower of wine crates with a sloppy grin. "Can you imagine if they overheard the famous Vivienne Rhodes slandering the fruits of their labor? You're very influential in your opinions." She winks. "In my experience."

Through her swirling stupor, it takes Vivienne a full ten

seconds to put together what Lottie is talking about. "Oh, you mean . . . Oh."

"The poll." She poses glamorously. "What a poor choice I was."

"Lottie, come on. In no way did I suggest to that drunkard Charles that we should poll the cast about you playing Helen."

"But you were ragging on me," Lottie pushes playfully. "Did you tell Gallo I was wrong for the role too?"

"No!" Vivienne clears her throat. "I mean, I suppose I might have implied it when I first arrived."

"Knew it!" Lottie thrusts the bottle into the air, triumphant.

"But you proved yourself during shooting," Vivienne stresses. "Besides, I was focused on my new vision for Cassandra, thrilled about it. Honest, that's what I was talking to Jack about—"

"On your dinner date." She cocks her head. Way over.

"I told you, it was a business meeting!"

Lottie giggles, passing the bottle back to Vivienne. "Whatever you say, dollface."

Vivienne can't help but laugh too as she takes another swig. Though thinking of the yacht, of Gallo, of that fateful night turns the wine sour in her stomach.

Gallo's dark eyes fixed on hers. The candlelight animating the creases around his smile. The shots. Shouts. Emeric covered in blood . . .

"I hope to God Jack's okay," Vivienne mumbles. "All of them, I mean. All the cast and crew." Her eyes flit upward. "I'm sure you're, um . . . worried about Teddy too," she adds, the concession akin to coughing up a knife. "I know how close you two got during *Bovary*."

Lottie's eyes shine in the dark. "We . . . did."

"And I know"—Vivienne forces out the rest—"how he feels about you."

Lottie stares at her curiously. "He's a real pal, that Teddy, sure." She leans forward, blue eyes wide, hands resting on her knees. "But I get the sense . . . I mean, do you . . ." Her laugh is thin, light, wavering like a butterfly. "Do you actually think there's something going on between me and Teddy?"

A strange knot tangles inside Vivienne's belly. She doesn't answer.

"Viv, Scout's honor," she presses, "it's an Apex setup. A total publicity stunt. Granted, it's lasted longer than I thought it would, and I'm glad it has, because he's such a good guy—but that's just because we're popular. Folks loved us in *Bovary*. We boost each other's fame. That's the reason we were cast together on *Ships*. There's nothing romantic between us. Nada. Zilch!" She squints, her face broadcasting confusion. "You know the studio plays these games. Why would you ever think it's something more?"

Vivienne blinks. Her head suddenly feels so much heavier now, weighted down by all the memories. She and Teddy strolling down Sunset. Their talks under the stars. The way he'd sometimes look at her on the set of *Beach Holiday*, the piercing sun igniting his glass-green eyes. Then the months of waiting for the phone to ring, the nights of staring, bleary-eyed, at her ceiling. And finally that fateful evening of the Oscars, when she saw him with Lottie. So glowing. So happy. So adamant to get Vivienne alone and set the record straight, to explain to her that she'd been forgotten, eclipsed.

"Because Teddy told me himself."

"Teddy?"

"At the Oscar pre-party." Vivienne wills her tears away. "We hadn't talked in so long. He'd completely disappeared on me, and still, I held out this naive hope that when we saw each other, all the time and distance would disintegrate and we'd, I don't know, have our happy ending. But . . . he told me he'd found the love of his life."

"Oh, Viv." Lottie pauses, her face softening. "I promise, it's not me."

Vivienne closes her eyes. The world transforms on her again, rearranges itself—though this time, the tangy wine has nothing to do with it. So many of her thoughts, decisions, reactions have been informed by a lie? All the ill will she wished upon this woman seated across from her in this dingy truck. Goodness, the hurricane of emotions she brought onto set . . .

And Lottie and Teddy are a stunt?

She blurts a laugh. So much wasted hatred. Exhaustive, soul-consuming loathing.

"But that doesn't make sense," she mumbles, mind scrambling to thread it all together. "Why, then, would he tell me that he'd found true love with someone else? Just to hurt me? Or to spare me? To let me down easy, easier than 'I don't feel the same way'?"

She nearly forgets she's wondering aloud when Lottie interjects quietly, "Maybe you should talk to Teddy about it."

Vivienne glances at Lottie, flush with fresh embarrassment, along with a new, hesitant sort of concern for her. "So I don't understand. If you aren't in love with Teddy, then what are you doing?"

"What's that supposed to mean?"

"We aren't anywhere near done filming," Vivienne says. "We're at least a year out from *Ships'* release, and that's if everything goes smoothly from here on out, which, given the project's history, is a really big assumption. Then there's all the surrounding promotion, releases, events . . ."

"So?" Lottie takes another swig.

"So, by my calculation, that equates to years of your life consumed by a pretend relationship. And we're not getting any younger."

Vivienne stops when she notices Lottie squirming. But she has to know.

"I just suppose I'm asking if that's enough for you. Don't you want . . ." She thinks, painfully, of Jack's words back on Tavalli. "Don't you want something real?"

Lottie takes another languid pull of the wine.

"I've never expected true romance. I'm not built for it. I wasn't raised that way." Lottie hesitates. "Now that I think about it, all my relationships have been 'you scratch my back, I scratch yours,' you know? Even in my family. Especially my family. And after things happened with Ken . . ." She clears her throat. "I don't think I believe in real love. Never experienced it, anyway."

"I'm not sure I have either," Vivienne admits. "But I know that I want it."

And maybe it's the wine, or the fuzzy dark of the van, but for a wild moment, she's twelve again, back in the Santa Monica Cinema. Watching Rosalind Russell and Cary Grant, wanting to live inside their banter, ready to pack her bags for a honeymoon in Niagara Falls.

"I want the real deal," she adds quietly.

"Makes sense." Lottie nods, thoughtful. "We're products of our environment, right? Or so the scientists say."

It takes Vivienne a moment to parse the implication.

"Are you suggesting that my parents had some great love affair?" She barks a laugh. "They're a pair of shams."

Lottie gasps in genuine horror, hands flying to her mouth. "No."

"Oh yes, they've hated each other since before I was born.

My mother would throw dishes at my father's head when she'd get ape mad. We went through three sets of chinaware before I was ten. My dad would storm out, leave for days. Lather, rinse, repeat."

"But all those celebrity papers," Lottie presses. "The glossy pictures I'd see in the mags when I was growing up. Of you even, in *Life*, their darling champion, the perfect little family—"

"You read about me when you were a kid?" Something about this mortifies her.

Lottie shrugs, but she's grinning. "Maybe once or twice."

Vivienne looks away.

"'The glamorous family Rhodes.' Ha. They wanted the world to see what they wanted them to see. They're showmen. My father, a professional one, after all." She swallows hard. "Though they both blamed me for being stuck with each other."

Lottie's face pulls. "Oh, Vivienne."

"It's fine. I accepted, eventually, that I was just a pawn. I mean, I tried for a while to make my father truly adore me with the swimming. Then moving on to acting, when Buster showed an early interest in me. But I realized if I was only gunning for Dad's approval, I would never win. As soon as I signed with Apex, I let that all go. I had to."

The well-worn memory comes to her again, her very first picture, *This Time for Keeps*. The frenetic pulse of that set, the glamorous stars like Esther Williams and Johnnie Johnston, all those prop pieces, the fancy stages, the bathing beauties in their glittering swim caps and suits. That palpable feeling of something starting, like a whispered welcome to a different kind of life, a life where one could make dreams come true. Where happy endings were a regular occurrence.

Vivienne glances down. She's taken the film canister out

again, she realizes, rolling it between her fingers like a twitch. She stuffs the cartridge away.

"Everything I know about real love, I learned from the movies," she adds quietly.

"So how can you call that real?" Lottie asks.

"It's a . . . different kind of real," Vivienne concedes. She finds herself drifting back, again, to her last conversation with Gallo. "A more magic kind of real, I guess. Aspirational. True because it makes us believe. Makes us all, for a little while, feel so deserving."

She startles to find Lottie's hand winding through hers and squeezing, like a sister's might.

"I hope you get it, Viv," Lottie says quietly. "You do deserve it."

Vivienne's eyes unexpectedly prickle at that. She closes them, letting her head loll back against the crates.

She's not sure how long she's out, but a sharp hitch to the left jostles her awake. Another jarring bump, another turn.

Vivienne rubs her eyes. Still woozy. "Is it my imagination or are we slowing down?"

Lottie blinks alert, shifting onto her knees. "We're slowing down. Hallelujah!"

The van gives another yawn before stopping altogether. In moments come the muffled tones of Antoine and Pierrot around the side, trailed by that snippy songbird, Cecile.

The bed opens to reveal the brothers' muscular silhouettes. Dazzling light bursts around them, spearing the van like shards, searing Vivienne's eyes. She and Lottie spill into crisp, lavender-scented air like fawns on new legs.

"We are here," Cecile announces so theatrically she'd give Charles Brinkwater a run for his Shakespearean money.

Vivienne blinks, spinning slowly around.

They're parked on a gravel drive in front of a sprawling farmhouse. Sloping slate roof, squat stone walls, charming wooden balconies. Just behind the home are fields, an orchard—and to the left of the house, a little stone path that winds around to some sort of artist's studio. There are a few easels, tripods maybe, stacked outside. In the distance, punctuating the picturesque scene like an exclamation mark, are the shadowy blue peaks of the Alps.

"Breathtaking," Lottie whispers.

Cecile nods, waving them to follow her up the drive. "The beauty is why Ramon and Hermione are here. For *mon oncle*, every day bring surprise. Every day make a new picture."

"And where do you keep your telephone?" Vivienne asks, itching to call Lew, to right this mess immediately now that they've finally arrived.

Lottie lets out an easy laugh. "Maybe we say hello first? Anyway, my first priority is that inside toilet."

They reach the home's stoop, where a woman in her thirties with handsome, Joan Collins–like beauty waves them across the threshold.

"*Bonjour*," she says warmly, stepping aside. "*Entrez, entrez.*"

Cecile offers quick but animated introductions to their hosts in French.

"That is Hermione, *ma tante*," she says of her aunt to Vivienne and Lottie. "Good cook, but not so clever, my mother says."

She gestures to the oafish, kind-looking man standing beside Hermione. "And *Oncle* Ramon. He is photographer. Very good. Very . . . what is the best word in English? Messy?"

They walk through a rustic, delicious-smelling kitchen, its stovetop cluttered with simmering pots, and into a lovely open parlor with teeming bookshelves and a record player.

Cecile nods toward the wooden telephone, complete with a

handset, resting on the corner table. "I told them you are big famous people and you will pay for the call."

Vivienne practically lunges for the receiver. "How do we connect internationally?"

Cecile relays her request to Ramon, who chuckles, sweeping forward to assist.

"Lew first, right?" Vivienne's heart is hammering with anticipation.

Lottie nods.

"His Rolodex knows no bounds," Vivienne explains. "He can call Interpol for us. Call Sam. Hell, maybe he can arrange for more suitable transportation—"

She stops when she hears a bleating ring on the line. Here it is. The beginning of the blessed end.

Lottie slides beside her. "What's the buzz, cuz?"

"It's ringing." Vivienne swallows, disappointment blooming, a weed in the base of her core. "Still . . . ringing."

"Maybe Lew's out," Lottie says. "It's, what, eight or nine o'clock in the morning in Los Angeles?"

Vivienne bites her lip. Lew Binkle is a schmoozer, a firm believer in the deal-over-breakfast meeting. "He's probably at the Polo Lounge or something. Damn it, I should have thought of that."

Lottie glides Vivienne's hand, which is death-gripping the receiver, back down to the cradle. "Maybe we can call Interpol ourselves."

"Sure." Vivienne huffs out a laugh. "How?"

Lottie smiles at Cecile. "You wouldn't happen to have the number for Interpol, would you?"

Cecile blinks. "That is neither English nor French."

Lottie sighs. "I mean the number for the International Criminal Police Org—"

"Can you call your agent?" Vivienne interrupts.

Lottie throws up her hands. "Viv, I'm a contract player—"

"Right, right, you don't have an agent. How do you get any-thing done?" Vivienne flops on the sofa, dread cresting over her like a wave. "What about a reporter? Or hell, Zimbalist himself? Could we ask the operator to connect us with Cinecittà Studios?"

Lottie grabs the phone again. "We can at least try the opera-tor." She stops her dial, frowning, listening, frowning again. "And now it's dead."

"Dead?" Vivienne cries.

Ramon releases a long ostensible explanation for the faulty line in French, while Vivienne's angst threatens to pull her under completely. If they aren't able to reach Lew, or anyone else, for that matter, what the hell do they do? Are they really going to just journey on to Rome on a wing and a prayer?

"Phone is like the weather," Cecile assures them. "Ramon says maybe tomorrow it is better."

Hermione pops her head in from the kitchen, adding a few sentences in French.

"Dinner is nearly ready," Cecile translates. "And everything is better with a full stomach, yes?"

Unable to argue with that, Vivienne relents.

A short while later, they're arranged for dinner on the patio, a quaint stone terrace framed by a canvas of startling color, the lavender fields spread out before them like purple tarmacs lead-ing toward the mountains. The meal, too, is exquisite—tartiflette, sautéed greens, a massive bake of ratatouille. And the wine keeps flowing.

By all measures, it should be a welcome interlude, especially since she and Lottie finally had a chance to first quickly freshen up before putting their party dresses back on.

Vivienne pulls the film canister from her décolletage again, fidgeting. Relaxation has never come naturally to her, and with everything at play right now, her nerves are frayed, her stomach stitched like a crocheted blanket, complicated patterns, despite finally feeling satiated. She finds herself obsessively cataloging all the many ways their situation could worsen in this relentless game of cat and mouse.

What if they can't reach Lew or anyone else on that godforsaken phone tomorrow? What if there's no way to connect with Interpol? What if journeying to Cinecittà Studios is a mistake? What if they can't get onto the set of *Ben-Hur*? Or Sam isn't even on location?

Vivienne pictures this possibility now, she and Lottie left to wander the streets of Rome, the target of corrupt *Italian* cops this time. How long would they last before they'd get scooped up and delivered right back to Tavalli, to Ludovico, or whoever he really is? How long before he'd "take care of them"?

She barely says anything through dinner, she's so consumed by her own spiraling fears.

So consumed, in fact, that she startles when Lottie grabs her hands, stopping her twiddling.

"Come on, gloomy-face." Lottie nods back to the house. "Let's dance."

Vivienne blinks. "Dance?"

Lottie's right. The party has relocated inside, and Vivienne can hear the sound of a jumpy tune emanating through the window.

"Get you out of your head for a little while." Lottie winks, extending her hand. "If you can stand it."

Vivienne sighs, placing the canister down, smoothing her dress. "Fine. I fold."

Inside, the lights of the parlor have been turned down, the

music crooning loudly from the record player. Pierrot is already shuffling along, laughing, with Cecile, while Antoine is sprawled across the couch, watching. He stands quickly, though, gallantly, as Vivienne approaches.

He glances at Cecile, who nods in encouragement, mouthing words that Vivienne can't quite make out.

Antoine slides closer to Vivienne. "May I . . . 'ave . . . this dance?"

Her cheeks flush in spite of it all. She tries to muster an appropriate level of delight. "Why, yes. Yes, I'd be honored."

Antoine takes her hand and spins her fluidly, then pulls her in, like a swift and impromptu version of a tango.

"Look at you cutting a rug, Viv," Lottie calls across the room.

Cecile must have bowed out, because Lottie and young, strapping Pierrot are now feigning a waltz.

They all take a break after a few songs for another glass of wine, a new bottle that Antoine opens. The wine goes down easy, one of their better varieties. Vivienne tries to remember the label. Pierrot, meanwhile, changes the records. The next song crackles to life with fervor, and Cecile manages to coax Hermione to stop with the dishes and join them as her dance partner.

It soon turns into an honest-to-goodness dance party. Lottie teaches the boys the foxtrot, after which Vivienne demonstrates the Charleston, to whoops and laughter. At some point she and Lottie switch partners. They dance until the record player again turns to static.

"I need a break," Vivienne says, laughing, flopping herself down on the couch.

Lottie flops beside her. "More wine?"

Vivienne grabs her chest dramatically. "Goodness, no, are you mad? I—" She sits up, ramrod straight.

"You okay?" Lottie says.

Vivienne's heart starts humming, her fingers scrabbling. "The film canister." She flies to her feet.

"What do you mean?" Lottie touches her arm. "What's wrong?"

"The film, the canister!" Vivienne sputters.

She begins frantically foraging around the bookshelves, the table with the telephone, the coffee table that's been set aside. "I don't understand. Where is it? I always tuck it in my bra, never put it down. It must have fallen out dancing . . ."

Her search comes up short. She stops, arching her back, near ready to burst into tears . . . when her eyes lock on the open window, the still half-set table on the patio outside. She was fiddling with the canister at the table, wasn't she? "I must have put it down at dinner!"

She runs through the mudroom, back to the patio, Lottie and a curious Cecile trailing her.

"It has to be here. It has to!" Vivienne rifles through the crumpled napkins. Shifts the dirty plates. But it isn't on the table, and it isn't on the ground underneath, and her heart is a bona fide rocket now.

"Where is it?!" she cries. "Oh my gosh, how have I lost it?"

"Just calm down," Lottie assures her. "We'll find it."

"I will get Ramon," Cecile says.

Vivienne grips a chair back, the steady stream of alcohol over the past however many hours catching up to her, knocking her down like a wave.

"How could I be so careless?" She blinks back a swell of nausea, an onslaught of dizzying stars. "How could I . . . ?"

"I so sorry!" Ramon is jogging up the stone path from his studio, arms raised like a stickup.

Cecile jogs beside him, listening to his flurry of French.

"He took the film," Cecile explains as they hurry toward Vivienne. "He thought it was his, as he is always leaving around . . . what do you call them? Rolls? I told you. He is messy."

Ramon launches into additional indiscernible elaboration while Vivienne's body slowly unknots itself.

"Oh thank goodness," Vivienne moans. "Could we please have it back, then?"

"*Alors . . .*" Cecile winces. "It is not film anymore."

"What?" Vivienne and Lottie say in unison.

Ramon begins to speak animatedly.

"He has already started . . . what is the word? *Developing*," Cecile says, eyes alighting with pride at having remembered the parlance. "If . . . you want to see?"

They burst into Ramon's studio, Ramon leading the charge, still chattering in apologetic-sounding French all the while.

The place is more spacious than it appears from the outside, nearly as first-rate as Apex's own headshot studio on the lot. Light stands, key lights, and backdrops of various colors are draped across the walls.

Ramon ushers them toward a door on the far side. *"Chambre noire. Soyez prudent."*

"The darkroom," Cecile explains. "Be careful."

They enter a black hole of a room, all shadows swallowed whole. No sensations other than sounds. Ramon fumbling, cursing in French, before there's a click.

A soft red light punctures the darkness, casting Ramon's features in a diabolical haze. He stands beside a long counter, upon which rest nearly a dozen identical trays.

"See." He gestures downward. *"Ici.* Here, here."

Vivienne steps forward, transfixed.

The film Emeric gave her is now a collection of waking images on glossy paper, each photograph resting in its own bath tray.

Ramon takes a set of large tweezers, lifting a few of the images from their pungent vats and carefully settling them into the final tray on his counter.

Vivienne peers over the trays. The images are becoming ever crisper before her very eyes, the shapes taking on harder lines, more distinct edges.

A story materializes, a narrative conjured like magic—explanations to questions she didn't even know to ask.

The first picture, on the left, is a hazy rendition of Ludovico's prop hangar.

The next: a photo taken inside the warehouse of a long rectangular table. Vivienne squints, peering closer, and gasps. On the table's far side are a plethora of pure white bricks, as if an Alaskan igloo had been deconstructed, piece by piece, on top of the table. She's never seen these types of bricks before, but she senses immediately they're made of something illegal.

"Cocaine?" Lottie whispers. "Or maybe opiates."

Leave it to Lottie to hazard a guess.

The next picture is of the crewman, Syd's assistant—the one who attacked her in Provence, the relentless bald thug who's been pursuing them—along with a few other men off-loading a small schooner parked at the marina.

The next picture is the most horrific. A bloated, unidentifiable body, strung out and tangled in a web of maquis brush.

Vivienne swallows a gag.

Lottie whips around to Vivienne. "This is evidence."

Vivienne nods tightly. "What Emeric must have uncovered before he was killed."

"So they're using the set for . . . for trafficking?" Lottie says tentatively, as if tasting the word and finding it noxious. "The drugs come in and then Ludovico, what, hides them? In the props. I noticed they were hollow, flimsy, but I didn't think how it might be an easy way to ship the contraband back to the States." She bites her nails. "I saw it on the beach, didn't I? Saw the exchange but didn't know what I was looking at. And saw him too . . ."

Lottie nods to the photo of the corpse, then turns away, distraught.

"*Ça a l'air très mauvais,*" Ramon chimes in grimly.

Cecile's wide eyes look haunted under the red overhead light. "Do you know these criminals?"

Lottie squeezes Vivienne's arm in warning. "Oh, Cecile, no," she says airily. "We're talking about a movie, our movie, of course."

Vivienne picks up Lottie's subtle cue, recognizing the very real need to pivot quickly, recalibrate, improvise for the sake of their audience. They cannot, will not, worry these poor people, their kind and gracious hosts, with the full extent of the trouble she and Lottie are in. No need to inadvertently place them in danger.

"Ah yes, the film we're working on happens to be a murder mystery. Er, a mythical murder mystery, with all the trappings of a big-budget epic."

Cecile and Lottie both stare at her.

"Been a bit of an evolving production, mind you," Vivienne forges on. "Imagine it much like an Agatha Christie novel set in ancient—"

Her throat suddenly closes. The last picture, now developed, silences her utterly.

In the final photo, Jack Gallo—debonair movie mogul, film aficionado, charming dinner date—stands with Ludovico on a beachy shore, passing a large handful of cash to a man she's never seen before. Behind them, several other men load production props—marble columns, a miniature throne, a vase—onto a smaller freighter.

"Holy cannoli," Lottie whispers. "Jack's involved too?"

But Lottie's voice feels far away, like she's standing onshore, and Vivienne is drifting out to sea, all the way back to Tavalli, to Gallo's glamorous yacht.

To his clearly well-practiced act that she fell for hook, line, and sinker.

THE TIMES

No. 52, 101   WEDNESDAY   June 1, 1958

INTERPOL CRACKS DOWN ON DRUG TRAFFICKERS; MAJOR BUST IN CORSICA

By Todd Gumfeld

The fight against the drug-trafficking pandemic continues, with the International Criminal Police Organization (Interpol) scoring a victory today when two agents arrested well-known narcotics dealer Galfonso Nortega, 33, as well as intercepted an incoming shipment of over twenty pounds of opiates on the northern shore of Corsica in the early hours of Friday.

Interpol has been tracking Nortega's activities for nearly a decade, having marked him as a key player in international trafficking circles and an actor with ties to infamous Italian crime families. Interpol senior agent François Aubert hopes that the arrest and questioning of Nortega will ultimately lead the agency to identify and close in on higher-ranking players within the mafia . . .

16

Monday, June 16, 1958

Lottie wakes up to a dull, insistent headache—her own damn fault, she recalls now—and, more inexplicably, the sound of . . . is it yodeling? They are in the Alps, she remembers, and gosh, the air smells fresh, but do people really yodel?

What's more, it sounds an awful lot like Vivienne.

Lottie sits up, stretches, rubs her eyes, straightens her clothes, and emerges into a clear, crisp Alpine day. Late into it, by the height of the sun. Birds chirping, rabbits gamboling, breeze blowing, and . . . yep, Vivienne Rhodes caterwauling inside the farmhouse. Not yodeling, exactly. Just shouting.

As Lottie makes her way to the main house, outside of which Cecile sits idly whittling a stick with a pocketknife, she spots Vivienne framed in the parlor window, beautifully picturesque except for the telephone receiver she's holding up, blocking her face.

"Can you hear me now? Don't hang up, Lew!" Vivienne shouts. "Bad telephone line. In the mountains!"

She sings every word individually, her eyes squinting with desperation.

Lottie looks to Cecile.

The girl shrugs. "We told her it will not work well."

"No, I'm not on the picture right now! Gallo. Is. Bad. Bad guy. I need you to call Sam Zimbalist. Tell him we're coming. Me and Lottie Lawr— Lew? Can you hear me? Ugh!" Vivienne does a stamping dance in the window, her teeth clenched tight. "Going. To. Cinecittà. Rome. Tell Zimbal . . . Oh, for heaven's sake."

Vivienne stares at the receiver, then hangs up.

Lottie rounds the house, Cecile on her heels, and heads inside. As soon as Vivienne spots them, she droops. "That's the line gone. Again."

Hermione says something in French, cheerfully setting the table for breakfast behind them.

Cecile translates. "The wind tears down the poles very often in the mountains."

Vivienne flumps into an empty chair at the table. "Well, better than last night, anyway. At least I got through. Hopefully he heard some of that so they'll know to expect us at the gates."

The studio gates, she means, but Lottie can't help imagining a triumphal arch, the shining gates of Rome itself. Any other time she'd have been thrilled by the prospect of visiting the Eternal City, seeing the sights, the famed Cinecittà Studios. The past few days, though, have made her long to stay put right here, in a farmhouse with a sweeping view, with crusty fresh bread and honey and fruit for breakfast and no one the wiser as to who she's supposed to be. No game, no goal, just life.

But this is not her life. It's Hermione and Ramon's. And she and Vivienne have everybody back on Tavalli to think about.

After breakfast, Lottie insists on washing dishes, Vivienne following suit a beat later. As they stand side by side, hands deep in a soapy tub, Vivienne glances wryly over and Lottie bursts out laughing at the incongruity of it all.

"I'm sorry about Jack," Lottie says, nudging Vivienne with her elbow as she scrubs. "To find out this way . . ."

"I only wish we'd found out sooner." Vivienne's jaw clenches. "Like before he bought the damned studio."

"Maybe we should have known." Lottie grabs a dishrag and starts drying cutlery, probably more vigorously than necessary. "A mysterious, deep-pocketed Hollywood outsider? We were all so relieved our contracts wouldn't be canceled we never stopped to think what the source of all those millions was. Jack's got to be big-time to afford a deal like that. And if he's involved in narcotics, bringing drugs to North America? That's very dirty business."

"And here we are in the middle of it." Vivienne slumps, elbow-deep in suds. "Well, at least our hands are clean."

"But only our hands." Lottie gives her dress a wary sniff and bursts out laughing.

As if in answer to her unspoken wish, Hermione emerges from upstairs brandishing two dresses, their sizes or near enough. Hermione has a trim figure herself, the result of farm labor, obviously, rather than a gymnastics regimen and a hovering nutritionist.

"For you," she insists, over their protests. "Yes. More . . ."

She looks to Cecile for the word.

"Comfortable," Cecile offers with a dismissive wave of her hand. "And less *ridicule*."

The dresses are indeed less ridiculous than the ones they scam-bought in Monte Carlo—simple, practical, patterned like tablecloths and tied with thin fabric around the waists. But when Lottie follows Vivienne in putting hers on, leaving that belted blue dress blessedly behind on the floor of the upstairs bedroom for Hermione to do with as she will, she finds it soft and comfortable and wonderfully clean. It smells like sunshine and mountain air and makes her even more loath to leave.

Downstairs, Vivienne stands in front of a mirror with comb and hairpins and is deftly arranging her wavy chestnut tresses. Beside her, on the table, rests the flat leather pouch Ramon gave them, their developed photographs stacked neatly inside.

"By the way, when you said that Gallo might be big-time," Vivienne says, almost idly, as Lottie comes into view, "how big-time?"

"Back home, I'd say mafia," Lottie says, sitting opposite her at the farm table. "I suppose we could say the same here, although I think in Europe they call themselves Cosa Nostra. Maybe Gallo's a leader, a boss. A don, I think they call them. Either way, it's got to be a powerful organization, with ties to North African opiate suppliers, European smugglers. Their role in it must be getting the goods to California and selling them there. No shortage of buyers, I'd imagine."

"How do you know all this?" Vivienne looks more concerned for Lottie than wary. How times have changed.

"I read the newspapers. That's all," Lottie answers reassuringly. And then, at Vivienne's raised eyebrow, adds, "Don't look so surprised. I do know how to read."

Lottie reaches for the comb, but Vivienne jumps up and grabs it from her.

"I'll do your hair," she says, brooking no argument. "Easier for me to hide your roots from this angle."

"Oh no!" Lottie claps her hands to her scalp in fresh horror. "I forgot all about that. Ginger was supposed to touch them up this past weekend. Are they terrible?"

"Terrible? No. Dark brown? Oh yes." Vivienne smiles. "I can

hide it. Although I must say, I'm dying to see what you'd look like with your natural hair color."

"One day maybe," Lottie murmurs, letting her hair be fussed with. It's a nice comforting feeling. Like what people with sisters must feel like. "When I've retired."

An empty promise. The idea of retirement has always filled Lottie with outright panic.

And yet I could be retired already and not even know it, she thinks. *The both of us. On the lam from our film shoot. It doesn't matter how much explaining we do, this is a heck of a mess, and if Hollywood despises one thing, it's messy actresses.*

"Why do you do all this?" Cecile asks, sitting atop the table, plucking a strawberry from the center fruit bowl. "You will sit in the back of the truck and no one will see you but the wine."

Lottie turns to her with a wink. "You'll understand when you're older."

Cecile makes a sound of disgust recognizable in any language and slides from the table to stalk away.

Lottie watches her go with an indulgent smile. Oh, to be twelve again, not a care in the world about your so-called beauty. But then, when she was twelve, she was already contracted at Apex, going to classes at the studio school for not only academics but also cosmetics, dance, fitness, fashion. She'd started dyeing her hair then too; it was in her contract. She may have entered Apex Pictures as the brunette Loretta Dudek, but within a year she had been rebranded as Lottie Lawrence, all-American blondie. Lord, how that bleach used to sting. She'd cry through every treatment those first few months.

She would never put her own child through that. Though odds aren't high she'll have a child . . . or, given current circumstances, that she'll even live long enough for it to be an option.

"What if the crew's in on it, back on Tavalli?" Lottie thinks aloud. "If they're all mafia, from Gallo down? Then Teddy, Max . . . they're in even more trouble than we anticipated. How far does this go?"

"All the more reason to get to Rome," Vivienne says decisively, stepping away from her finishing touches on Lottie's hair. "To *Ben-Hur*. There is no love lost between MGM and Apex. If I were Sam Zimbalist, I'd jump at the chance to offer us safety and take down Apex in one fell swoop. So we stick with the plan. Get to safety, get the photos to Interpol, get that rat fink Jack Gallo into handcuffs, and get our friends the hell off that island."

Lottie leans back, arms crossed. "See? You do make a swell director."

Accustomed to traveling by night, to make it into the city for early morning deliveries, the boys wake up from their long daytime snoozes just before dinner is served—another hearty, rustic French offering that Lottie and Vivienne tear into with such gusto that even Cecile lets out a low whistle.

"It is a good thing *ma tante* gave you new dresses. Looser in the middle, *non*?"

Dinner done and tidied up, it's time to depart, with many thanks both to Hermione for her hospitality and Ramon for his part in uncovering the truth. She could tell from his warily sympathetic expression that he didn't buy their line about the photos being part of a mystery they're shooting, but he's done his part in keeping the secret from Cecile and her brothers.

"*Bon chance*," Ramon says worriedly at the door, taking their hands in his as if praying. "*Faites attention*."

He and Hermione make a show of waving cheerily from the

house as Lottie and Vivienne crawl back into their berths at the back of the wine truck. Then the doors slam unceremoniously shut and the truck rumbles away down the rocky road.

"How long do you suppose this leg of the trip is?" Lottie asks.

Vivienne closes her eyes, cradling the pouch of photos like a blankie. "If you don't mind, this is all hitting me. Hard. I think I need some shut-eye or I'll hardly be able to chase down Zimbalist."

"Good thinking," Lottie says, using her own small bag as a pillow. "Night night."

And she is out like a light before she can even add up the miles between them and Rome.

The truck drives steadily, only one brief roadside stop for the family to relieve themselves under the cover of a copse of trees, which Lottie and Vivienne both decline, opting to keep sleeping instead. By the time the rolling Italian knolls give precedence to the seven famed hills of Rome, there's just enough predawn light for Lottie to spot their outlines. Finally, the doors are opened again, allowing the two of them to peel their aching limbs upward and out into the Eternal City.

They find themselves parked outside a restaurant, still dark inside, with only small signs of life: noises from the kitchen, the door opening to greet the delivery.

There's a quick restroom stop for everyone before the boys set to work unloading crates of wine from the back into the kitchen stores. Cecile seizes the moment to confer with the restaurant owner, speaking in rapid Italian.

What a whiz kid, Lottie thinks, she herself only able to make out a few words. Dové *means "where," doesn't it? And Cinecittà? Well, that speaks for itself.*

Apparently it speaks something to the restaurant owner too,

who grins at Vivienne and Lottie in open amusement. "*Si, si, tutti vogliono essere nel* 'Big Hollywood Film.'"

Vivienne draws in a breath and leans close to Lottie's ear to whisper, "He recognizes us."

Lottie thinks not.

There's something definitively dismissive in his expression, especially as he reiterates, with a belly laugh, "*Tutti!*"

He does give Cecile detailed directions to Cinecittà, at least, and shouts, "*Buona fortuna, stelline!*" as they clamber back into the truck.

After another half hour of driving through jolt-and-jerk traffic, there's a jaunty knock on the back of the truck, and past Cecile, Lottie sees the shining gates they've been waiting for. The studio looks like something out of Burbank, apart from the letters sprawled across the top of the gates: Cinecittà.

Lottie's pretty damn sure she has never seen a line of extras this long outside a Hollywood studio in her life. It snakes thickly around the sprawling compound, with police cars lined up to keep them from clumping into an out-and-out riot. It's a sort of party, people sharing food, beer, and wine despite the morning hour, some folks running up to greet friends ahead of them in the queue before being shouted back into their places half a mile back.

Lottie's so stunned, she barely registers that this is goodbye.

More cheek kisses from the misty-eyed farm boys. Cecile translates that they hope she and Viv will come see them again in St. Rambert so they can take them out dancing, and then a hefty handshake from the far less sentimental twelve-year-old.

"Your mystery film looks okay," Cecile says appraisingly. "I will go see it in the cinema."

High praise, Lottie thinks, laughing to herself as the little girl walks away.

When the wine van pulls away through chaotic studio traffic, Vivienne's gaze lingers longer than Lottie's. She must have felt the same reluctance to leave their welcome detour into pastoral domestic life over the past twenty-four hours.

But now, once again, it's showtime.

They waste no time marching straight up to the guard booth set into the tall terra-cotta gates, though Lottie does take circumspect note of the angry shouts flying in their direction from the endless line of aspiring extras. She can't tell what they're saying, but she guesses it would be too rude to be found in any Collins Italian phrase book.

Vivienne doesn't bother with Italian. "Vivienne Rhodes and Lottie Lawrence to see Sam Zimbalist. He'll be expecting us."

There's a pause that might be thoughtful from the sweating guard. Then his thick brows furrow, and Lottie realizes it was more of a confused silence.

"*Entrambi dovete mettervi in fila,*" he says with a grunt, and then if it weren't clear enough from his tone, he repeats, more emphatically, pointing to the line, "*In fila. Nessuna eccezione!*"

Vivienne, undeterred, repeats, just as emphatically, "Sam Zimbalist. Vivienne Rhodes." She turns to Lottie. "How do you say we have an appointment?"

Lottie blinks wide. "I don't speak every language, Vivienne."

The guard's face has gone red. "*Nessuno ha bisogno dei tuoi nomi, ora vai. Vai!*"

He sticks his hands out the window to shoo them, to jeering calls from the queue. This is probably the most entertainment they've had for hours. Two guards emerge from another gatehouse, brandishing sticks, and the fuzz have turned their way, sensing trouble.

"This is ridiculous," Vivienne says, opening her mouth for yet another escalating round, but Lottie takes her arm, motioning behind them.

"He thinks we're extras," she says.

Vivienne squawks, "How could he possibly?"

Lottie motions down to their dresses, up to their coiffures, despite all best efforts now hopelessly frazzled by the humid Roman air. "Do I look like a movie star to you?"

The guards, droning in Italian, herd them away from the booth, pointing to the miles-long line.

"Maybe we just go in with them, then?" Vivienne looks a little dizzy. She's clutching the pouch of photographs like it's a life raft.

Lottie offers a steadying hand on her wrist but nearly slips when Vivienne sprints toward the front of the line.

Predictably, the crowd instantly protests. Loudly. Cacophonously. Far too chaotically for Lottie to urge Vivienne to back up and take stock, but no need.

With impeccable timing, the studio door opens, like the pearly gates, and just as reverently as a crowd awaiting salvation, the queue's din becomes muffled. A giant of a woman in red heels and matching lipstick scans the group, including the frozen Lottie and Vivienne at the front, with eyes narrowed critically.

Suddenly she points and barks, "*Lui, lui, lui, lei, lei, lui, voi quattro, si, e . . .*" Her eyes slide past Lottie and land on Vivienne. "*Lei. Grazie.*"

She turns around and walks off, and those miraculously selected hurry inside.

"Go!" Lottie says, pushing Vivienne forward.

But Vivienne's got an iron grip on Lottie's wrist. "Not without you," she says with a wink.

Before anyone's the wiser, the two of them march into Cinecittà, letting out a relieved breath in duet. *That's got to be the end to the chaos*, Lottie thinks, hankering for the organized bustle of a typical Hollywood studio lot.

"I'll find a production assistant," Vivienne says, her voice pitched high with tension. "Someone American. They'll get us to Zimbalist. This will all be over soon."

But the minute the gate clangs shut behind them, it's clear it will not be that simple.

If the outside of Cinecittà was a powder keg, the inside is a detonating bomb.

Hundreds, no, thousands of extras mill about like refugees, orders shouted between different factions in Italian, while beyond the fray, production vehicles drive frantically between backdrops, soundstages, offices, and even a fully operational, American-style restaurant. There's an enormous structure in the distance, far more vast than any set Lottie's ever laid eyes on. As she gawks, as stunned as any of the others in the crowd, a hand lands roughly on her shoulder, ripping her from Vivienne's grip.

It's the extras coordinator. The giantess. She scowls down at Lottie in open irritation, then barks behind her, "*Schiava!*" She points to Vivienne. "*Patrizia.*"

Two male assistants appear, chattering unintelligibly, and with astonishing skill wedge themselves between Lottie and Vivienne, herding them in opposite directions.

"Lottie!" Vivienne shouts behind her. "Wait, we can't—"

"You can do this," Lottie shouts back. "Take the lead; I'll find you!"

But the general melee drowns out Lottie's voice. She can just see Vivienne mouth, "*What?*" as her face bobs between the others being herded toward a massive tent. Lottie nearly trips over a man in a toga lounging on the ground and fanning himself with a magazine. By the time Lottie has righted her balance and turned back to Vivienne, she's been entirely swallowed by the inexorable horde.

"Schiavi," reads the sign on the tent they bring Lottie to.

And underneath, in English: "Slaves."

17

Tuesday, June 17, 1958

Assistant? I need an assistant!" Vivienne cries, fighting, albeit uselessly, against the crowd's swell. She grips the photo portfolio tightly. This is harder than swimming against a current. "An English-speaking assistant, *por favore*!"

The horde pulls her forward, its hold as intense as a Pacific undertow. She gives up the battle, realizing she has little choice but to ride the tide of chattering extras toward the set's dressing areas. If the rules of Hollywood change and she ever does manage to find herself in charge of a production, it will never, ever be this chaotic—like the running of the bulls without the bulls. The crowd finally crests at the tent's entry flaps, and Vivienne floods in with the rest of them.

Once inside, as she attempts to get her bearings, she's accosted by a thick, noxious heat. Body odor. Perfume. Stale clothes. She resists a gag as she wades through the morass of jostling elbows and limbs.

One of the male production assistants from earlier, the one

who separated her from Lottie, reappears—a lanky young man with a pencil tucked behind his ear. His face is now marred by an overwhelmed frown.

"Sir, please," she starts, "my friend and I, we're in danger. We need to speak directly to Mr. Zimbalist, and immediately."

The crew member blinks at her blandly.

"It's a matter of life and death," she overenunciates. Not that it will help matters if he doesn't speak English. "Sam Zimbalist. We have photos to give him. Pictures he's hopefully expecting. Pictures that incriminate someone very important—"

"Yes. We make picture."

The assistant thrusts a long red stola, matching tunic, and gold-leaf headpiece at her, then motions toward the far side of the tent, where scores of women are forming messy lines in front of a row of portable changing rooms separated by threadbare curtains.

Vivienne grabs his arm before he can dart away. "I hate to pull rank, but I am Vivienne Rhodes. American film star? Up for an Oscar a few months back?"

Behind her, a gruff American voice growls, "Yeah, yeah, sweetheart, we're all Oscar winners here."

Vivienne makes the mistake of turning around, which allows the damn production assistant to skirt away.

"Wait," she cries out.

Too late, he's gone.

"Thanks a lot," she snaps at the interrupting American, a beefy man who's flung his own costume around his thick neck like a scarf.

"'I hate to pull rank,'" the man mimics in a breathy, haughty tone. "Gotta earn your way, doll." He smirks, eyes roaming over her. "And Vivienne Rhodes, my ass."

She snorts, indignant. "I beg your pardon."

He leaves her too, roughly navigating his way with an extra dose of shoulders and elbows toward the cluster of men opposite who are gathered in queues for what she can only assume are the male dressing rooms. And all the while, new hordes of extras are filing into this stuffy, claustrophobic tent, angling past her with their costumes. The serpentine lines, growing ever longer . . .

"Oh, for heaven's sake," she mutters.

She huffs toward the lines, staking her place, her impatience growing, then wilting, then resurrecting inside her with fresh blooms of panic and indignation. These lines are a creative form of purgatory—at some point she swears she moves backward— but eventually it's her turn inside one of the cramped, standing dressing stalls. If she has to put an end to this madness *in costume*, so be it.

She thrusts off her borrowed day dress. Her noblewoman costume is loose in the hips, a bit worse for wear and smelling like mothballs, but sufficient. She can't help but take some time adjusting her gold-leaf crown just so, the beefy extra's words, *"Vivienne Rhodes, my ass,"* still rattling. Of course Zimbalist will recognize her, and hopefully will be expecting them, if Lew was able to decipher her cries for help over the phone line. Zimbalist is a stand-up producer, a pillar of good taste and judgment, with plenty of incentives to assist. He'll help them; he must. She just needs to somehow find him in this morass.

She manages to tack onto the tail end of the latest group of extras filtering out from the tent and onto set. Fresh air and searing sunlight accost her at once.

She blinks. Peers around. And has the sudden, unshakable sensation of falling into a dream. Before her, parading down a road of sparkling white sand, are thousands of costumed extras. The road is flanked on the left by a column-adorned shrine with a dozen glimmering porticoes, the gigantic set piece appearing to be carved out from a looming, red-toned mountain face. What on earth did that cost?

To her right is what appears to be the underbelly of a colossal, tiered, custom-built amphitheater. For a stunned minute, she can do nothing but gape.

Scores of assistants are situated all along the road, as are several police officers in uniform, directing traffic, signaling the crowd forward, then steering them sharply to the right, into the theater.

Vivienne is funneled, right along with the rest of the extras, into the heart of the largest, most impressive set she's ever seen. The stunning, sprawling Circus Maximus come to life. *This* is why she's always been enamored by the movies, their spell work; how they can transform history, aspirations, our collective imagination into tangible, enveloping reality. *This!*

Inside the theater, Cinecittà has somehow built a quarter-mile-long, full-fledged arena, the entire track covered in pristine white sand. Dwarfing, gold-painted statues of Roman gods at least four, maybe five stories high adorn the track's center island, and surrounding the track on all sides are horizontal sections of tiered amphitheater seats. Story upon story of stone benches ascend into the clouds.

Still astounded, Vivienne rides the relentless tide farther into the stadium, her haste to find Zimbalist eclipsed for just a moment by total admiration for the scope of William Wyler's directorial vision. Various teams of stallions are being groomed near the statues—quartets of white, brown, and black horses hitched to ornate chariots. In every direction, production crew members bustle about, shuttling weapons, helmets, and other props to and from the sidelines. In the distance—is that a tour bus? What the heck is this film's budget ceiling, the moon?

Down the track, there are half a dozen parked automobiles. Some sleek Italian cars, Ferraris maybe, or perhaps Bugattis—she has never been a car person, yachts and schooners more her literal and figurative speed—and beside them, a few trucks arrayed with filming platforms and camera equipment.

Vivienne kicks into a higher gear, revved by the sight of the camera cars. Wyler and Sam Zimbalist must be nearby.

Before she gets very far, the six-foot female assistant who greeted them at the gates sweeps in front of her, brusquely ushering Vivienne back into the throng, impatiently gesturing toward the stands.

"*Signorina*, please!" Vivienne says. "I need to speak immediately to Sam Zimbalist. It's life or death, and he's expecting me."

Again, she is ignored.

Despite the crisp, businesslike way they're all being handled, the vibe of this innumerable extras crowd is decidedly . . . *boisterous*. It can't be later than ten in the morning by now, and it feels like an all-out rager. The two young bucks beside her on the stairs are sharing a flask, for goodness' sake. Ahead, an older lady polishes off a late breakfast. Vivienne blinks. Is that a hot dog? There was that American-style restaurant—wasn't there?—on the way in, tasked with serving this village of extras, she supposes. The lady swallows the last bite and dusts her fingers off on her toga dress.

The crowd bottlenecks, and groups around Vivienne cluster off and start gossiping, comparing costumes. This is ludicrous, not to mention a waste of precious time. How is she going to get to Zimbalist from here?

"*Spostati sui sedili!*" the female assistant shouts, adding in clipped English: "Move! Into the seats! No empty!"

Vivienne peers around for an opportunity to break away, to

make herself seen, and peers up. There are at least ten currently unoccupied rows at the top of the stands.

She angles through the extras dutifully filling into their rows, soon reaching the section's apex. She hurries across an empty row and turns down the first aisle.

As she doubles back down the stairs, she spots Charlton Heston below in the arena, bronzed and brilliant in his ornamented cape and toga. She passed on the opportunity to meet him at one of the Oscar after-parties in March, went home in a funk instead, and now she's kicking herself. Vivienne frantically scans the rest of the track. Aha, yes, there's William Wyler, directing a team of men standing near the cars. Zimbalist can't be far away.

Wyler turns toward the stands, megaphone in hand. "Quiet! Quiet on set! *Silenzio per le riprese!*"

A thick, surprising quiet blankets the stadium. He's got the touch. Below, crew members assist Heston into his chariot. His counterpart, Stephen Boyd, another actor she doesn't know personally, settles into his own, taking the reins of his black stallions.

Vivienne forges ahead, determined, angling past stragglers still filtering into their seats. And then she sees him: Sam Zimbalist, settling into a tall canvas chair near the camera cars. Thank goodness. Their knight in shining armor, glistening with sweat in his white linen shirt!

"Sam!" she cries. "It's me, it's—"

"Chariot race!" Wyler booms from the filming platform of one of the trucks below, his voice amplified by a megaphone, then repeated in an Italian echo by some unseen translator. "Scene 45, day 21, take one! Extras, we need to hear you. Cheering, booing, cries!"

He stalks off the track, out of sight.

"Excuse me, wait!" Vivienne shouts.

"Annnd . . . action!"

"No, wait, Sam—" Vivienne cries, but her words are swallowed by the extras' thunderous calls, the scene igniting, the actors in motion. "Please, someone—"

A sharp tug on her arm stops her cold. "Not. One. More. Move."

She freezes. The voice is Italian, accented, menacingly familiar. The words, hot breath in her ear.

"No," she whispers. "Impossible."

"Anzi." His laugh is edged, a serrated blade. "You led us right here. *La tua richiesta di aiuto.*"

Vivienne shuts her eyes, mind spinning, head dizzy. "I'll scream. I swear, I'll—"

She stops as something hard—a pistol's edge—pokes into her back.

The henchman's lips graze her neck, his bald head brushing her cheek. "Now you come with me."

Variety

Vol. 210, No. 24   NEW YORK, TUESDAY, JUNE 17, 1958   25 CENTS

MGM'S "BEN-HUR" REBUILDS ROME

BUONGIORNO, or should we say GOOD MORNING from Cinecittà Studios in Rome! The set pieces that MGM has commissioned for *Ben-Hur* defy belief—and description. The Circus Maximus, which was built for the famous chariot race sequence, covers a whopping eighteen acres, with gold-painted, four-stories-high statues created by MGM's Edward Carfagno. The chariot sequence alone is estimated to cost over a million bucks.

As *Variety* reporter Alex Archerd reports, "Standing in the middle of the Circus is like standing in the middle of L.A.'s Coliseum (sans Dodgers, of course)." Although the hordes of screaming Italian extras might give Dodgers fans a run for their money . . .

18

Lottie feels fully in character by the time she's shoved into the crowd of other "slaves" awaiting their turn on camera.

She's been prodded rudely from one station to the next, her hair wrenched into a stark bun under a conical felt hat, her farmhouse dress unceremoniously removed by a burly costume matron and replaced by a long, coarse tunic that turns Rome's thermostat dial up to at least 120 degrees.

And she has the distinct impression that she's been cast as a man.

When the horde of slaves reaches the absolutely colossal walls framing the set—Lottie gets dizzy looking up to find the top of them—she can hear the roar of the crowds, shouts from a loudspeaker, the angry whinnies and snorts of dozens of horses, but can see nothing beyond.

"*Silenzio per le riprese!*" a diminutive production assistant shouts.

Lottie can understand his intent, if not the language. *Quiet on the set.*

Fat chance.

The PA's Italian accent was dreadful. He's got to be a California import. Her heart starts to thud with fresh hope. If she can reach him, maybe she can explain the situation. Perhaps he'll even recognize her if she takes off this awful hat.

She picks her way through the crowd—yep, all of them are men apart from her—trying to pry the cone hat from her head, only to remember it's been pinned on. Sweat gathers on her forehead, along with absolutely everywhere else.

"Excuse me," she says to a big bearded man, who responds by cursing at her in Italian. Three others form a wall in front of her and she has to dodge and dive to get closer to the PA, who's now retreating around the corner of the set walls, nearly impossible to see because he's so much shorter than everyone else.

She manages to wrench herself free, loose from the throng, and sprints the rest of the way to the last place she saw the PA's pomaded head.

And then she has to blink away her delirium.

This is unbelievable. It's another world. Not the chintzy sets filling the Apex lot in Burbank. Frankly, this even puts the Tavalli set pieces to shame. It isn't really a set at all; it's ancient Rome come to life. A full Circus Maximus! Horses, chariots, and charioteers standing ready, hills painted realistically, towering above the scene. Stands in every direction, packed with extras—thousands of them!

And somewhere among those thousands, one little Vivienne Rhodes.

Lottie's wonderstruck smile drops right off. How on earth is Vivienne going to make her way through that to find Zimbalist?

And now that she's looking around, her one American contact appears to be gone too, replaced by his physical opposite, the Italian giantess, who is shoving the extras quickly into position all around Lottie, penning her in entirely.

In the distance, on a megaphone, she hears, "Action!" and the chariots set off, the horses already lathered into a shine from the heat. The dust they produce clouds her eyes, so she makes her way closer to the arena's edge to gain a better view of the stands across the way. The crowd of slaves follows, like she's Moses parting the Red Sea.

A rig drives past with a camera fixed on it. When her eyes adjust to the blur of the sand it's kicked up, she sees a movement in the stands opposite—someone making their way down through the crowd of spectators. Maybe a set hand?

No, now that she squints she can see the woman is wearing a deep-red costume and has dark hair pinned up under a gold headpiece, with a certain haughty insistence in her downward progression that screams Vivienne.

But she's not the only spectator on the move.

Lottie feels a chill ripple over her sweat-drenched arms. There are three others. Two behind Vivienne, one approaching from the side.

Tall. Bald, and though she can't tell from all the way over here, Lottie would still wager cash money that the man's got a broken nose. The extras part for him as soon as they glance up at his ugly mug—the power of intimidation in obvious effect. And Vivienne not yet the wiser.

"She needs me," Lottie says with a gasp, backing away through the cheering, swaying, sweating extras, keeping her eyes on Vivienne's crimson shape all the while.

"Excuse me?" From nowhere, the short American PA appears in front of Lottie. "Where do you think you're going?"

Startled, she steps back, just far enough to be swallowed by the crowd again.

"You're on the clock. Get back in the scene; it's not break

time . . ." The PA curses to himself, then bellows, "*Non ancora! Vattene!*"

"Sir?" Lottie shouts over the roar around her. "I'm not Italian! I'm—"

But a chariot is passing again, and the extras' din has been turned up to fully deafening. Lottie has to jump to see past the shoulders of the others, and in that quick blink at the stands opposite, she sees the bald man reach Vivienne. As a final confirmation of ill intent, he leans down, his mouth close to her ear.

"I'll kill him," Lottie snarls.

A bearded slave turns to her, shocked. "You are woman?"

"Sorry to disappoint." She sprints past him, past the hapless little PA, past even the lurching giantess, to nowhere in particular except out, away, through the labyrinthine inner halls of the set, toward Vivienne.

She's got to get to her. This is a bust, a setup, maybe. How did these criminals know to find them here?

Right now it doesn't matter. The only thing that matters is getting out.

It's like a real stadium, Lottie thinks despairingly as she scrambles closer to Vivienne's side of the stands, through anterooms and tunnels. She sprints through an archway into what turns out to be the horses' stables, right beside a covered parking lot for the producers' luxury vehicles. There's a cherry-red Ferrari she might be tempted to get a closer look at if she weren't running for her life, but when she races past it to find the next route through, she's met with a solid wall.

Dead end. Only way out is back.

Back to the crowd, to failure, to danger, to Vivienne getting nabbed and Lottie powerless to do anything to stop it.

She feels like a little kid again, hiding behind a dumpster, watching her mother get pulled into a police car, sitting balled up, holding her breath tight, waiting for them to find her too.

Lottie's breath comes in short bursts now. She presses her hand to the wall, closes her eyes tight, and stomps her sandaled foot.

No. Stop it.

There's always an exit. Always an angle.

She turns, and she sees it.

There.

The way the chariots go. Straight through the set. Into the Circus Maximus.

Her eye catches on that cherry-red sports car. Whichever big shot owns it must be impossibly complacent. The keys are dangling right there on the dashboard mirror.

An idea sparks, a wild one.

And Lottie's adrenaline revs it to life.

19

Vivienne swallows, her entire body falling still. She hugs the portfolio tightly, hissing, "Let me go."

The bald thug only grips her tighter, pressing the pistol deeper into her back.

"Mr. Gallo very upset you left . . ." He perches his chin over her shoulder, his rancid breath on her skin. She can feel his stubble on her neckline and can't resist a violent shudder. "He only want to talk."

"Not really up for conversation," she grits out.

Below, the horse-drawn chariots thunder through the arena, a deafening crescendo of pounding hooves. The camera cars race a few feet ahead of the action, swerving around the track's bend, capturing all the angles. Movement on the stadium stairs to her left catches her eye. It's another man from set—she recognizes him, one of Ludo's prop assistants—heading their way, two stairs at a time. For all she knows, the gang's all here.

"We go," her captor seethes. "Now."

He edges her up the stairs.

The cheers from the sea of extras rattle through her bones.

There are literally thousands of witnesses, and yet no one registers what is happening. Vivienne's all alone, the hapless star of her own doomed production. No Lottie Lawrence to cook up a last-minute plan, an off-the-cuff, ingenious pivot to save her now.

She squints against the harsh Roman sunlight, frantic. Maybe Lottie was right, maybe Vivienne can—must—do this on her own. She blinks, rapidly recalling Lottie's little tutorial at the roulette table. Every strategy needs improvisation. Quick thinking. The ability to recalibrate.

Maybe Vivienne can save this wretched day after all. For both their sakes.

The crowd jumps to its feet as the chariots rumble past once more. *Use the crowd—just like we did in Monte Carlo.* Against the new commotion, Vivienne ducks and spins, throwing her full weight into her captor's stomach. The goon staggers back, arms splayed out like a startled baby, heels teetering on the edge of the stair.

There's a flash of dawning horror in his dark beady eyes as Vivienne winds up and lands a swift kick to his groin.

He folds over, bellowing, "*Cagna!*"

"Watch out!" she cries as she darts into the nearest row of patrons. "Watch out, that man's got a gun!"

There are a few gasps and affronted cries, but for the most part Vivienne's declaration is absorbed by the crowd like bad stage direction.

"*Una pistola?*" An extra guffaws. "*Nell'antica Roma?*"

Another extra groans, "Wyler *ha perso la testa.*"

She edges down the row with a frantic litany of "excuse me's," "pardon me's," "watch out's," peering over her shoulder to see if she can spot that bald head bobbing through the crowd or his crony amid the madness.

All the while, below, the chariot race rages on, Heston's Ben-Hur and Boyd's Messala breaking around the far bend. Heston's majestic white horses have inched out in front. Boyd snaps his reins, goading his black stallions to retake the lead.

"Stop that woman!" Gallo's gunman shouts. "She is fugitive! Stop!"

The rest of his words are swallowed by the throng; the extras' cheers are textured now, the canned hoots and calls laced with groans, questions, curses in Italian as the gunman and Vivienne awkwardly cat-and-mouse their way through them.

She's nearly reached the next aisle over—a clear path straight down to the arena itself. *Faster, faster, go!*

Vivienne careens into the aisle, grasping her costume's skirt with her free hand else she trip down the steps. The aisle's staircase winds down toward a stunning, two-story columned section of Roman architecture. She can see a pathway from there that leads to the arena's lowest level.

Inside the sandy arena, the chariots charge into their third lap; she can only tell because of the silly ornate dolphins on top of a statue, marking the laps. The camera-laden trucks race past once again—and, oh goodness, she can see Wyler across the arena now, through the island's statues. He's passing by on one of the camera cars. And as the vehicle clears out of view, she sees Zimbalist again, in the tall canvas chair. Mere yards away.

"Sam!" she blurts, her voice devoured by the cacophony. She hurries down another flight. "Mr. Zimbalist, please!"

The megaphone booms, "Cut! What the— I said, cut!"

The camera car stops with a screech.

Zimbalist jumps up from his chair while Wyler climbs down from the car, both of them charging into the arena. In moments, they're waving their arms, faces waxed with shocked fury. A nervous clutch of assistants trails behind them, fully breaking the fictive dream.

The chariots all halt along the track.

"What the hell is that Ferrari doing?" Wyler cries, stomping across the sand. "It's ruining the damn sequence!"

"Vicky? Rob?" Zimbalist shouts. "Find out who authorized this!"

"Wait!" Vivienne cries. "Mr. Zimbalist!" To no avail.

No, no, no, he and Wyler have already left the stadium, disappeared into one of the Circus's arched exits and off set.

She hears footsteps and whips around. Sure enough, the bald gunman is right on her heels, running at full tilt toward her on the stairs. The other thug is trailing her too, she realizes, along with two additional men crawling out of the set like cockroaches. And quickly scuttling closer.

She grips the portfolio and takes off in the direction of the exit where Zimbalist and Wyler disappeared. But she can hear them behind her. She's not going to make it in time. She's not going to—

A red sports car screeches to a halt in front of her section, sand splaying in swirls, the extras in the lower level coughing, complaining.

"Vivienne!"

Lottie?

"Vivienne, get in!"

Vivienne wipes the dust from her eyes.

Yep, Lottie Lawrence is leaning across the Ferrari's console, shouting at her through the car's open passenger window. "Now!"

She does as she's told, cutting through the remaining stands, hopscotching across the stone benches' empty slivers until she reaches the amphitheater's walled divider.

Vivienne throws her legs over the edge, ignoring her thrashing heart, the nearly two-story drop to the ground. She swings around, lets go—

And lands on the arena floor on two feet, like a cat.

Portfolio still in hand, she scrambles into the car, slams the door, and squeezes Lottie's shoulder in gratitude.

"Where's Zimbalist?" Lottie says.

"I lost him." Vivienne buries a sob, pointing ahead. "He and the director went through that exit right there—"

"Back to the production area?" Lottie's forehead furrows. "Maybe we can cut them off."

She reverses abruptly, doubling back the way she came, toward the columned shrine. Then she takes a hard left, heading toward the production tents.

"Nice ride," Vivienne huffs out.

Lottie grips the wheel, nodding. "Agreed, it's pretty smooth."

Vivienne can't resist turning around. Gallo's men are still in the arena, literally left in the dust. The foursome run into another archway below the stands and out of sight.

"How the hell did they find us?" Lottie takes a hard left, swerving past a prop area.

Vivienne shakes her head, eyes welling now. "He said . . . he said we led them here."

"What? How? I don't understand."

Neither does she. An errant tear escapes, splattering onto the dusty leather portfolio cradled in her lap. "Maybe we get out, search the tents, look again," Vivienne says. "Zimbalist is here, Lottie. I saw him. He's got to be somewhere around here—"

"Half a dozen of Gallo's buddies are already on our tail." She thrusts her chin at the rearview mirror.

Vivienne follows her line of sight. Sure enough, at least three motorcycles are on the road now, behind them. Gaining on them.

Lottie makes a sharp right, back onto the massive set's main entrance road.

"Wait, stop!" Vivienne shouts, a gust of hope rising like a geyser.

"Stop, stop where?"

"On the left there. Quick, pull over!"

Lottie throws on the brakes, parking with a lurch between a cluster of offices and the set's cast and crew restaurant.

Vivienne kicks open her door, besieged by manic determination.

"You there!" she shouts at the lanky Italian assistant from the tent. "Stop!"

The man must be on break, grabbing an early lunch. He stares at her with that same infuriatingly blank stare, mouth agape, a hot dog in one hand and a Coca-Cola bottle in his other.

She grips the portfolio, beelining for him. Does she just hand all the pictures over? Isn't that a risky move? What if this man's a bad bet? And yet what options do they have left?

The roulette table materializes in her mind, Lottie's advice once more. *Play the long game, hedge, work multiple angles.*

Decided, Vivienne pulls out half the photos from the portfolio—with any luck they'll tell a somewhat condemning narrative—and waves them above her head like a surrendering flag. "I told you, these pictures I've got here, they're shocking—"

"Dirty pictures?" The assistant's eyebrows quirk.

"Not for you! Or you'll be fired. For Mr. Zimbalist, his eyes only, right away." Vivienne thrusts the pictures into his hands. "He's expecting them, promise me. Say they're from Vivienne Rhodes, Viv *Rhodes*. Understand?"

"Viv, come on, we're not alone!"

Lottie's correct yet again. Coming around the bend from the direction of the tents are those motorcycles, now roaring at top speed.

Relenting, Vivienne scrambles back to the red Ferrari and slides in.

And then they are off, barreling forward, past the assistant, the restaurant, the remaining offices and grounds.

Straight through the Cinecittà gates and into Rome.

20

"What are we doing, what are we doing, what are we doing?" Lottie squeals, narrowly avoiding the crowd of hopeful extras spilling onto the roadside.

"You tell me," Vivienne shouts, craning her neck to keep a lookout. "You're the one driving!"

"Good point." Lottie shifts one gear up. When she hits the gas, burning rubber, both women's backs slam against the polished leather seats.

Behind her, over the Ferrari engine's growl, Lottie can hear the high insect hum of motorcycles drawing nearer and nearer. Maybe even multiplying.

As they floor it past the police officers keeping the crowd in check, Vivienne waves her hands, shouting, "Help us!"

For her part, Lottie just hopes they don't get pulled over, handed over, run over. Can they trust anyone anymore?

She rounds the corner with a squeal onto a wider avenue, busy with traffic.

"Is Zimbalist in on this too?" Lottie asks, weaving between cars.

"He'd better not be," Vivienne barks back. "I just handed him half the evid— Duck!"

"Duck? I'm driving!"

A new sound joins the melee—the sharp whine of a bullet flying past Lottie's ear. She does duck, late—thank goodness he missed—then glances back to see one of the men on motorbikes pointing a gun in their direction. She returns her attention to the road—and talk about timing. Traffic is stopped and she's about to slam into it.

She yanks hard on the steering wheel, careening up onto the sidewalk, shouting, "Sorry! Sorry!" to all the pedestrians jumping out of the way.

To be fair, they're not the only car weaving wildly in and out of traffic. Road lines seem to be mere suggestions in Rome, which is at least one stroke of luck for them.

"They've gotten logjammed!" Vivienne shouts to Lottie. "I see two of them trying to get around a bus that's blocking traffic and—"

"Are there more?" Lottie says, peeling a right onto a cobbled street.

Vivienne's eyes go wide as yet another bike rounds the corner. "Sure are!"

The front right bumper of the Ferrari clips a metal trash can someone's left out, full of loose rubbish. The can ricochets against a stone wall. Lottie keeps her eyes on the street but hears a satisfying *clang* and *screech* behind them, punctuated by Vivienne's whoop of triumph.

"We'll lose them now," Lottie crows, as if either of them knows where they are heading or to what. The embassy, maybe? Beg for protection from the good old US of A?

Lottie has no idea where an embassy would be. She just knows that this road can't be the way. It ends up ahead with a sharp left. She takes the turn at a slightly saner speed, only to find this new road heading straight back to the avenue.

And waiting at the corner . . . four men, four motorcycles.

Vivienne curses like a sailor—language she picked up along with her boating skills?—but Lottie doesn't flinch. A beast of a Ferrari versus a flock of lightweight Ducatis? Not exactly an equal jousting match.

But then the men on bikes remove guns from their pockets. That evens the odds considerably.

"I have an idea," Lottie says in a low tone. "But it's a little bit crazy."

Vivienne shoots her a look of fresh alarm.

"When I say get down, get down," Lottie adds.

A bullet hits the roof of the Ferrari with a ping.

"Get down!" Lottie grips the steering wheel with clammy hands and crouches low next to Vivienne, her foot firmly on the gas pedal. She slides the other foot onto the clutch, lets go for a mere moment, and shifts up to fifth, fighting the urge to close her eyes, even though she can't see anything from down here but Vivienne's screaming face.

And then—impact. But not a huge one. She can hear the men screaming around them. They'd all gotten out of the way except for one, a direct hit that's sent the motorcycle and rider flying over the carriage of the sports car and . . . yep, crashing hard behind them.

A deafening honk announces their arrival back on the avenue. Lottie shoves herself upright and yanks on the wheel just in time to slide past an oncoming oil tanker.

"What the hell are we doing?" Vivienne asks this time.

The possible answer comes in the form of another engine

roar—this one from above. A small airplane, flying low to the ground. Taking off? An airfield must be nearby.

"We're getting the heck out of Italy," Lottie announces and veers through winding traffic until she can see the distinct line of an airstrip to the west. A tiny airport, surrounded by parkland, but still. A way out!

"You have got to be kidding me," Vivienne groans, and Lottie thinks for a second she's arguing with her, until she hears that mosquito buzz again and dares a glance behind them.

Yep, three surviving motorbikes, still on their trail. Though a little ways back, they're nimble, darting in between cars with alarming speed.

"Hang on," Lottie announces, then turns into oncoming traffic to reach the strip of grass verge leading up to a reassuringly tarmacked entrance.

Vivienne looks like she might be sick if she tries to answer. She nods queasily.

They reach the lone airstrip and stop with a jerk. Lottie peers around frantically for a terminal, office, anything, but there's nothing except a small spindly tower. Maybe there's someone in there who can help.

"Look out, look out, look out!" Vivienne shouts.

Lottie tugs the car back into gear. "Is it them?"

"Yes, but no, but . . . *look*!" Vivienne points upward.

Lottie follows her finger to see the nose of a landing airplane bearing down on them. Damn it, no, they're blocking the runway!

She swears she can feel the landing wheels shiver against the roof of the Ferrari as they race off the asphalt and onto the grass of the surrounding park.

And here come their old buddies, relentless as flies. Lottie can't keep track of them anymore. The motorbikes seem to come from every direction, and the grass is rutted and bumpy, so it's all she can do to keep her hands from flying off the wheel as they judder in their seats. This car was not made for off-road adventures.

She cranes her head to look for a road, or something approaching one, before the axle gets ripped off the car. Vivienne is holding her head in her arms, preparing for flying bullets, probably wisely, so Lottie doesn't have the benefit of a lookout this time.

The car smashes into something intractably hard, the hood crumpling like a tin can. Lottie's mouth collides with the steering wheel so that she tastes blood, but she can make sense of little else. Everything spins. Smoothly. They're no longer moving.

Vivienne releases herself from her seat belt—that brace position seemed to have helped her come out of this crash unscathed. Lottie scrambles out of the car and away. She's not a fast car aficionado, per se. For all she knows, this thing might very well explode. She runs her hands along the thing they've run into. Not a building, just a long, arched wall. An archaeological site. A ruin.

"I think we've found ancient Rome," she calls to Vivienne, but the sound of wheels on grass turns her around.

It's not just the motorbikes greeting them now. It's a long gray limousine.

The driver stays put. The back door opens on its own.

"Looks like you're having a little car trouble." Jack Gallo stands, then leans against the limo, his legs crossed at the ankles, the very picture of careless charm. He flashes a dazzling smile, as if this were all a fun game. And he's the winner. "Please allow me to give you ladies a lift."

A cold pistol barrel presses against Lottie's waist. She glances frantically to Vivienne, who stands cornered by a sneering Ludovico, but she has her eyes closed, her face a mask of disgust.

So Lottie looks at Gallo once more. Coolly. Calmly. Dizzily, yes, but still.

She licks the blood off her lips and smiles charmingly, preparing for the performance of a lifetime. "Well, hello, Mr. Gallo! Fancy seeing you here."

"SHIPS" STARS TAKE UNEXPECTED HOLIDAY

By Everett Kain

Apex Pictures' *Titanic* of an endeavor, *A Thousand Ships*, has garnered countless headlines for production hurdles and surrounding drama. But a secret source on-set confides that yet another controversy hasn't even been disclosed: two of *Ships'* stars have fled the picture.

"Our two leading ladies have taken off, gone missing," an actor involved with the production, who chooses to remain nameless, told *Confidential* in an exclusive interview. "I know the movie is about Helen running away with Paris, but *our* Helen, Lottie Lawrence, has split town with Vivienne Rhodes. We're all pretty worried."

A second source, who also talked to *Confidential* off the record, confirmed sighting the co-stars at the Monte Carlo train station. So are these starlets taking an unplanned holiday? Hitting the casinos, perhaps? Is it a tactical play, a contract renegotiation strategy?

And last we checked, weren't these ladies sworn enemies?

21

Vivienne glares at the flat expanse of blue sea through the yacht's small circular window. She's been trapped here, in one of the ship's lower guest rooms, for so long that the coastline of Fiumicino has completely vanished. Along with the portfolio containing the incriminating photos, confiscated by Gallo's men when they were dragged on board. Nothing to look upon now but the thin thread of horizon stitched underneath a swath of broad clouds.

Is Lottie in another room on this same hall? Is she all right, physically, at least? Is she scheming how they might get themselves out of this wretched nightmare? Gallo, she supposes, was smart to keep them separated. Right now Vivienne feels like half a person—stagnated, defeated. Weak.

She shakes her head, still unable to fully process the chain of events that led them here. A swarm of motorcycles hunting them down. A car chase through the switchback streets of Rome to a damn airport, and in a Ferrari, no less, with no stunt doubles. They're lucky they weren't killed—although it's possible their luck has only delayed the inevitable.

Vivienne spins away from the window. Begins pacing the tight horseshoe of space around the room's satin-sheeted bed, its cherrywood furniture, the little golden sea-inspired trinkets accenting the bedroom. Gallo has impeccable taste; she can't deny that. She remembers now, how the grand ship had totally wowed her that first night she'd stepped foot onto its decks, how impressed she was by the decadence of the salon, the extravagant setting of the dinner table. As if it were all a sign of good character.

Shame washes over her once more. Gallo and his self-deprecating charm, his infectious passion for storytelling, for cinema. His showstopping smile. A devil in sheep's clothing.

What a damn fool she's been. Again.

She perches on the edge of the bed, shivering. She's still wearing her thin noblewoman costume, which is now ripped at the hemline, reeking of that musty tent back on the Cinecittà lot. If Gallo was going to kill them, he'd have done it by now, surely, yes? Strangled them in the limo? Hidden their bodies in Rome? Thrown them overboard? He's some type of mafia don, after all—or however Lottie put it—their studio chief. Obviously high up enough to orchestrate a criminal enterprise on this large a scale, his stature further evidenced by the obsequious way his scores of minions cowed to his demands when their limo arrived at the Fiumicino docks. A guy like Jack Gallo can likely snap his fingers and—*poof*—people disappear. A man like him doesn't go to the trouble of keeping two women alive, dragging them all the way across the Tyrrhenian Sea, unless he needs them.

Or unless he's completely sadistic.

Her room door clicks open. Vivienne stiffens at the sound, expecting Gallo himself, or that ubiquitous bald goon she can't seem to shake, but instead, it's a sheepish-looking deckhand. The same young man, actually, who helped her onto the yacht all those nights ago, her literal escort into this fiasco. The deckhand steps forward quickly, feigning authority, but won't meet her eyes. Still a bit starstruck, Vivienne realizes, which almost makes her smile. He hands her a long garment bag, then places a leather satchel on the bed, nodding.

"You change now, *Signora* Rhodes."

He locks the door behind him.

Vivienne opens the garment bag first. Inside is a long, twilight-blue charmeuse dress in just her size—a gown nearly identical to the one she wore during that private dinner with Gallo. Same low neckline, same flutter sleeves. She opens the satchel to find a pair of crystal-studded heels, toiletries, even a bag of makeup.

How unnerving. Does Gallo think they're going to pick up where they left off?

She showers quickly, even though the warm water feels luxurious on her skin, practically a spa treatment after so many days on the road. She hates to play dress-up for Gallo, but between the gown and that foul-smelling Roman costume, there's really no contest. Once ready, she enters the hall, where the deckhand lingers, waiting. Together they traipse along the outer decks below the flybridge—Vivienne notes a helm, control board, and a marine radio buzzing with chatter—and then into the salon, where Gallo and Lottie, too, thank God, are seated at a table near the floor-to-ceiling windows. Behind them is the tapestry of blue sea and tired, twilight sky, rolling out in all directions.

Gallo stands as she enters the room.

"Vivienne," he says. "You look stunning."

He does too, as much as it pains Vivienne to admit it. Jack's dark hair is slicked back, his chiseled features arranged into a careful smile. His taut, athletic body, accentuated by his shawl-collar tuxedo. Lottie, for her part, looks like a new woman: her blonde bob, sleek and styled; her mauve, capped-sleeve evening dress flattering. The table between them is splendidly set, the same as it was during her previous dinner. Fine china, tall crystal glasses filled with champagne, even fresh-cut flowers to complete the effect.

Vivienne's eyes lock on Lottie's. She tries to telepath her thoughts, to rouse a current of wordless connection between them, to summon that same force Vivienne has felt pulling her toward Lottie, toward actual trust, building, invisible wave by wave, during their time together on the road. *Should we run? Ask to break our contracts? Grovel for our lives? What's the play here, Lottie?*

The silence stretches far too long.

Vivienne clears her throat. Best to keep things neutral, she supposes. Let Gallo play first. "Thank you for the dress, Mr. Gallo. Most certainly an upgrade from the, ah, threadbare costume I arrived in."

"Everything about MGM is threadbare. Second-rate." Gallo winks. He waves her forward. "I was just telling your costar that even though we're in a predicament here, we might still come to a civilized arrangement. Please, sit."

Gallo pulls out Vivienne's chair. He hands her a flute of champagne, then takes a large sip of his own, signaling for Vivienne and Lottie to follow suit.

"Ladies. I must say, I am disappointed," he finally says. "Running away from a picture during production is a very serious breach of contract. And to run in such a dramatic, messy way. You took out Georgio's Ducati, I heard, and totaled that beaut of a car." He *tsk, tsk, tsk*s. "Actresses through and through. Had a hard time finding you, I'll admit." Gallo arches a brow. "Thank goodness for Lew."

Vivienne's head whips up. "Lew?"

"Lew Bickle. Your agent?" Gallo sinks back in his chair, triumph gleaming in his eyes. "He called me—yesterday, was it?—saying he'd gotten a panicked, nonsensical call from Vivienne Rhodes about some trouble on set." Gallo pauses dramatically. "Mentioned you were upset, in the midst of dashing across Europe to talk to Sam Zimbalist, of all people. He was worried, naturally, though he couldn't make much out, given your bad connection."

Gallo's infuriatingly handsome face curls into a full Cheshire cat grin. "Never really understood the point of agents as middlemen, but I must say, Lew proved quite useful. He's changing my mind."

Lottie throws Vivienne a doleful look. Vivienne's stomach sinks to the floor. So it's her fault that they were found. That they're here. Her dogged insistence to reach Lew halfway across the world, to let him handle everything for her. She never played out the repercussions, never considered the various angles, never saw the whole table, as Lottie tried to explain. And now they've lost.

Gallo swirls his champagne, his perfect profile on full display. "If you'd only, I don't know, slowed down, used your heads. I sent several of my men to talk to you, but you—"

"*Talk* to us?" Vivienne growls, the words rumbling out of her. "Your creepy bald goon nearly strangled me in Provence!"

"You have to admit, Jack," Lottie interjects lightly, "he doesn't make the greatest impression. You see that guy coming toward you, you run the other direction."

There's a tense beat before a smile quirks Gallo's lips. "I suppose you raise a fair point. I should have considered appearances. But you see, I sent Pasquale because I trust him to complete the job he's been hired for. Which, alas, is more than I can now say for the two of you."

The table falls silent as a waiter appears beside them with their salad course. As soon as he disappears, Gallo retrieves something from under the folds of the tablecloth—Ramon's leather portfolio, *their* portfolio—and carefully lays it between their plates. He opens the flap and pulls out the glossy photographs, what's left of them anyway, gleaming under the table's candlelight.

He fans them out, a faint smile on his lips, like an artist admiring his work. "I believe it's time to address the elephant in the room."

Vivienne sways, black algae clouding the corners of her vision. *He knows we know. Of course he does. But what does he want? Why are we alive?* How she wishes she could pause time; yell, "Cut!"; confer with Lottie on the sidelines.

"Those aren't ours," Lottie whispers. "I mean, we didn't take them."

Gallo nods, his eyes still locked on Vivienne. "I can always sense a traitor's presence, you know. A mole. I've been doing what I do for a long time, and I've become an expert, if you will, on people. The rhythms and flow of an operation. I knew there was a lack of synchronicity on set. I just didn't know why." He cocks his head. "In some ways, I'm grateful. The actual damage that bogus extra caused is quite minimal. Reparable." Gallo smiles. "Assuming we can all come to terms."

"Terms?" Lottie echoes hollowly. "What terms?"

Jack briskly flips to a photo of his men on the beach, boats docked onshore, hands exchanging money and those thick, white bricks. "You've obviously seen, from the extra's little picture show, how essential it is that we continue filming. Shipments are scheduled to come into Tavalli slow and steady all through production, which is why we need to finish this picture on schedule, as planned." He flips to another photo, pointer finger stabbing the image. "When we wrap, all these props need to be full before they're delivered back to LA."

Lottie blinks rapidly. "So this film, Jack . . . is it just a front? Is that all *Ships* ever was, an excuse?"

Her blue eyes well with hurt. Vivienne can't be sure how much of it is put-on. Lottie Lawrence really is a very good actress.

"Of course not." Gallo presses his hand onto Lottie's, reassuring, but it's Vivienne he again turns to, his eyes ignited. "I meant everything I said, Viv, about this picture. About movies. The magic of cinema. *Ships* is going to be the biggest blockbuster Hollywood's ever seen. It just so happens to also be my entry point into a new market for a very old and very lucrative product." He downs the remains of his champagne, leaning forward, his face rendered ghoulish in the candlelight. "I can have my cake and eat it too. We all can. All you have to do is keep quiet on set—just you, me, and Ludo's team. Play along and no one has to get hurt, ladies. Hell, everyone benefits. Together we are saving the studio. Maybe even the industry."

Vivienne's thoughts are all-out churning now, her mind a raging storm. Gallo isn't denying any of it. In fact, he's bragging! Flaunting his plan. Fully expects them to support his opiates—or whatever the hell those bricks are—enterprise! Damn it, does this make her and Lottie accessories? How on earth is Gallo going to ensure the Apex board, never mind the police, don't find out either?

"Awful lot of people on set, Jack." Lottie voices what Vivienne's thinking. "The cast, the crew. How do you plan to make sure this stays quiet?"

A shadow passes over Jack's features as he lifts the bottle of Dom from the ice.

"Simple. Insurance. You need it when you've got dirty hands."

He pauses to top them all off. "Though you know that firsthand, don't you, Lottie?"

Lottie flinches but doesn't say a word.

"I'm always prepared for . . . what do they call it in the film world? Unforeseen plot twists?" Gallo takes a lazy sip. "I have compromising information on the cast and crew at my disposal, in case someone tries to make a mess of things. Fortunately, the studio has made it easier, keeping tabs on their talent like they do. Personnel files on everyone involved in the picture. *Extensive* records. On Clay Cooper. Jimmy McClain, the gaffer. Pretty little Ginger. Teddy."

Vivienne glances quickly at Lottie. Her face has gone white.

Gallo leans on his elbows, claiming the table, eyes locked on Lottie.

"Now, I know what you're wondering, Miss Lawrence, and the answer is yes, I have *everything* on you. Your arrest file, your emancipation court records, the coroner's report of your mother's death in prison." Bemused pity, or a facsimile of it, flits across his face. "My condolences on your loss, by the way."

Vivienne longs to reach out and shield Lottie, protect her from this monster, but the damage is done. Lottie is frozen with that same eerie stillness that overcame her in Winters's presence.

Thankfully Gallo doesn't notice. The bastard. Only Lottie's eyes give her away.

"That's reassuring, Jack," Lottie replies with a cool smile. "If we're going to be coconspirators, after all, we need to know there are contingency plans in place."

"See, that's what I mean," Jack says, electrified. He raps his knuckles on the table in excitement. "This is exactly the kind of conversation we could have had days ago if you two hadn't lapsed into hysteria."

"And the Apex board?" Vivienne presses, breathing slowly to keep her fury from tipping over. "How do you intend to keep them from—"

"The board knows." Gallo laughs, as if dismissing a child. "Well, they know to look away, anyway, to avoid enough details to offer plausible deniability, but at the end of the day, they're graciously allowing me to do what I need to do to save them from themselves, to save their precious studio. The studio, I might add, we *all* need."

The walls are closing in, the room pinching to the size of a glass jewelry box.

He must be bluffing. This can't be true. Apex's board has knowingly, willfully cosigned a criminal enterprise? Can they really be that desperate? Cavalier? Foolish?

"They trust me to secure us all a happy ending. So my question is . . . can my two biggest stars afford me the same courtesy?" Gallo gazes out the window at the sea, as if musing to himself. "Or is this going to be another Billy Wagner situation?"

Vivienne sucks in a gasp. The body in the grotto that Lottie found.

It was Wagner. Of course it was.

Lottie's eyes meet Vivienne's fleetingly, a flash of pain confirming her suspicions.

"Good thing I'm a believer in second chances," Gallo says, returning his attention to the table, bright and cheerful. "After all, everyone deserves love and redemption. Isn't that how you put it, Vivienne?"

Vivienne focuses on pushing lettuce around her plate, pulse thundering now, while Lottie remains frozen beside her. Gallo isn't just a criminal. He's not even just a murderer. He's a megalomaniac. A man who expects the world to bend around him, to corroborate the story he wants to tell. A man cut from the same cloth as her father, Vivienne sees clearly now.

She's had a lifetime of appeasing men like him, and she knows what Gallo wants to hear: *Thank you for this second chance. Yes, of course we'll play along.* Her thoughts keep racing. And yet that places her and Lottie—and the entire cast and crew—at the mercy of Gallo's word. His whims. What did Wagner do that pushed Gallo over the edge, that caused Gallo to resort to additional measures, to his contingency plans?

Even if they survive, even if they do exactly as he asks on this picture, what's to say Gallo won't use whatever dark secrets he's dug up to blackmail, manipulate, control all of them for the rest of their lives?

"I'm always prepared." Gallo said it himself. Vivienne cannot place her life, her career, her friend beside her, into this madman's hands.

"What do you say, girls?" Gallo's smooth voice slices through her spiral. "Are we in agreement? Do you understand?"

Lottie gives Vivienne the barest of glances, but Vivienne can sense that unspoken current passing between them now. She's considered all the angles too, and come to the same conclusion. In fact, Vivienne can spot, after their time on the road together, the precise moment when Lottie transforms herself into fiction, into what Gallo's expecting, and anxious, to see.

Lottie tips her chin, bats her eyes, an encore of her classic Millie act—an act that, once upon a time, would have sent Vivienne into a conniption.

"We understand completely," she says smoothly. "If *Ships* sinks, we all sink. Money talks. As you said, I'm not exactly squeaky-clean myself. And we're very grateful that you're looking out for our futures."

Gallo raises his glass. "That's the spirit, Lottie. A team player through and through. A little playing outside the rules never hurt anyone, did it?"

His smile wavers, though, as he turns toward Vivienne.

"You can count on me—on *us*—to deliver," Lottie adds. "Right, Viv?"

For once, though, Vivienne doesn't need a prompt. She knows there's only one play. For now.

"Indeed," she says evenly. "Apex is so fortunate to have a man with vision, a maverick, at its helm."

Gallo's shoulders loosen, his doubt sloughing off, giving way to something else entirely. A hunger that terrifies her. He rests his hand on top of hers for what feels like an eternity before at last languidly pulling away.

"Georgio," he calls out to the young waiter waiting in the wings. "Why don't you bring up another bottle?" Gallo flashes his positively arresting signature smile. A wolf's grin, Vivienne sees now. Vicious. All teeth. "We have so much to celebrate."

STAR POWER

Wednesday, June 18, 1958   Issue 182

SHOOTING STARS ONCE MORE!

Readers of *Star Power* were in a tizzy yesterday, after *Confidential* hastily reported that costars Vivienne Rhodes and Lottie Lawrence had stormed off the set of *A Thousand Ships*, intimating that the stars had walked because of salary disputes and concerns over sharing the spotlight.

Apex Pictures' president Jack Gallo took time out of his busy schedule to explain the situation to *Star Power*, a publication that checks its sources, and has confirmed that it was all a misunderstanding, that his leading ladies are happy as clams and already back on set in Tavalli!

"I'm so pleased that Miss Rhodes and Miss Lawrence have hit it off and developed a friendship, despite our intense production schedule," Mr. Gallo told *Star Power*. "They had a short break in between their scenes, which is rare on this picture. I told them to take some time off, recharge in the Cote d'Azur for a few nights. My stars deserve nothing less."

We, for one, cannot wait to see Vivienne Rhodes and Lottie Lawrence together on the big screen, and we are thrilled to hear there's no bad blood between them, even though they both spent time as Teddy Walters's main squeeze. Sounds like we can thank Mr. Gallo for their truce. Clearly he's got everything under control . . .

22

Wednesday, June 18, 1958

Ah, Tavalli. Solid ground, yes, but also blue seas, idyllic cliff faces, the village fishermen out on the water, waving jovially from their boats. A perfect Italian vista.

There are worse jails, Lottie reminds herself as she finds her land legs on the rickety dock. Even so, she senses more and more how her mother must have felt, walking into the Indiana Women's Prison. And, as Lottie has been reminded only too acutely, her mother wound up never coming out.

That damn donkey cart is waiting for them just past the harbor. The little assistant producer, Johnny, is still the designated cart driver, but his bow tie is off-center and he's looking even more frazzled than the last time Lottie saw him.

"Don't you have any bags?" he asks. "From your trip?"

The question feels loaded, especially with Gallo's men approaching, well within earshot. Instead of answering directly, Lottie looks past him. "Long journey. Gosh. I think I'll stretch my legs."

She gives the donkey a rub on the head on her way past, relating to the tethered beast like never before. The belted shirtwaist dress she's wearing is likely a darn sight more comfortable than the donkey's bridle and bit, but as this getup was a "gift" from Jack Gallo, it represents the same thing—assumed compliance and absolute control.

Hoping to wait for Vivienne, Lottie slows her step up the gravel path, but when she glances behind her, she sees Gallo himself shepherding Vivienne's every move. Vivienne laughs at something he's said, playing her part beautifully, but Lottie knows Vivienne's real laugh by now, and it ain't this one. Lottie can sense the panic barely held in check underneath that alto pitch. She feels it too, hot in her chest, as Ludovico appears by her side.

"Right this way, *Signorina* Lawrence." The malicious glint in her new escort's eye belies his apparent gallantry.

Ludo might not be as physically imposing as Pasquale, but in his wiry, leering way, he's no less sinister.

"We have missed you here, *principessa*," he croons, smoothing his thin mustache. "We have dreamed of you at night, hoping you would return."

"Gosh," she tosses back. "All that fuss for little old me?"

"Not so little," he says, staring flagrantly at her bosom. "Not *all* of you."

She hastens her pace up the hill to the Albergo Tavalli, feeling Ludo's eyes shift to her backside as she passes.

She breathes, gathering herself, remembering the game. *Play along, be nice, get the shoot done, make it home without any bullet wounds, figure out the rest from there.*

"The rest" being a lifetime of blackmail and coercive control from a worldwide criminal organization, but who's keeping track?

It's an odd relief to open the door to the Albergo Tavalli, faint

243

memories of feeling safe here lingering in the air of the lobby as she strides inside. She'd anticipated some irritated looks when they gallivanted back in, some jabs about holding up production, so she's not surprised to see some raised eyebrows and snide greetings among the assembled cocktail clutch this evening upon her arrival. Even professional nice guy Clay Cooper shoots her a sour "Well, look who the cat dragged in" look after she offers him a wave.

"Don't you look sun-kissed," Brinkwater slurs from across the room. "I'm sure Ginger will fix it. Methinks Helen of Troy does not have freckles."

Lottie scans past the old snob, hoping for a glimpse of someone she actually cares about, until finally, elated, she calls, "Teddy!"

Teddy gasps, shoving himself away from his stool.

"You look like you've seen a ghost." Lottie attempts a laugh as she hugs him.

"Are you one?" he says. "I'm not sure of anything these days."

Gosh, he's gaunt, Lottie thinks. *He looks like he's barely slept.*

She glances over her shoulder, remaining careful. A reedy young man from the prop department is standing in the hotel lobby corner beside the reception desk, no doubt placed there to listen in.

"Hope you weren't too inconvenienced," she says lightly, leaning on the bar while working a pebble out of her shoe. "Mr. Gallo said it's all been going gangbusters without us here. You wrap all the battle scenes?"

"Maybe," Teddy answers as Max descends the steps, his own eyes wide behind his glasses at the sight of Lottie, the prodigal friend. "Unless there are more to come I don't know about."

"So," Max intones as he joins in the huddle. "You gonna tell us where you've really been? Because we've had a betting pool going, and it's time to pick the winning guess."

"Jack's gone around telling everyone you and Vivienne lobbied him for a vacation," Teddy says, his voice tight. "A girls' trip. But I had a peek into your room when the maid was cleaning and—"

"You're too funny, Teddy." Lottie laughs, squeezing his arm extremely hard, then blinking meaningfully past him to the man in the lobby.

He takes the hint, cuts himself off just as a deeper hush strikes the room.

Lottie turns to see Gallo ushering Vivienne inside the hotel, his hand pressed to her lower back in a way that sets Lottie's teeth on edge.

Lottie smiles so that Gallo can see it, all friendliness, act fully in place. As he lingers well within listening distance, she turns energetically to Teddy and Max, adding, "Just needed a little R and R. You know how close Viv and I have always been, but we hadn't had a chance to catch up since the Oscars, and it's been all work and no play since we got here."

"Don't mind me, I'm just jealous." Teddy's such a good actor Lottie almost believes she's got him hoodwinked. His shoulders relax, that megawatt smile flashing with relief. But as he goes on, he covertly reaches to her arm and pinches back. "So where did you two crazy birds fly off to?"

"Well, first we went to see Grace, of course, then to the sweetest little French village, way off the map. We stumbled into it really, *so* charming. And then the Alps."

"The Alps," Max repeats, his glasses slipping with his incredulous expression. But before he can probe further, a deep voice rings out through the lobby.

"Everyone, gather around," Gallo commands. "Let's welcome back our two leading ladies! Don't they look refreshed?"

Vivienne has a Mona Lisa smile fixed to her red lips, an insouciant sophistication to the lift of her chin as Gallo interrupts his speech to whisper something into her ear, but Lottie can see her hand trembling at her side and has to fight the urge to run to her, to physically place herself between Vivienne and danger.

No need. Gallo steps away, claiming the spotlight for himself as he goes on.

"Now, I know we had to shuffle a few things around, but I'm sure you can agree that this production will be all the better for giving our stars what they need. And here they are, back in the fold, rested, energized, and ready to make *A Thousand Ships* the biggest success Apex has ever seen. So let's hear it for Vivienne Rhodes and Lottie Lawrence!"

As the crowd breaks into dutiful but decidedly lackluster applause, Gallo squeezes Vivienne's arm, then bustles away through the lobby, his underlings in tow, including the young man at the reception desk.

As soon as the hotel door shuts behind them, Vivienne slumps with a low exhalation. Lottie bounds to her in two long strides, slinging an arm around her waist for support.

"What do you need?" Lottie asks, leading her to an empty stool at the bar. "Whiskey, wine?"

"Water, I think." Vivienne groans. "And a washcloth." She rubs peevishly at the spot where Gallo was touching her.

Teddy mimes to the Italian-speaking bartender to pour Vivienne a glass. "You got it, Viv."

She looks a little surprised as he hands it to her. Almost touched.

Lottie nudges him, murmuring, "What was that you were saying, Teddy, about searching my room? We should be safe to chat over here. Just keep your tone light, pretend you're telling us a joke."

"What about . . . ?" Vivienne nods at the bartender's back, eyebrows high.

"Doesn't speak a lick of English," Lottie says.

"Not even a sniff of it," Max agrees. "It's made for some interesting cocktail mix-ups this week, let me tell you."

"And we're certain that he can't understand?" Vivienne presses.

"Watch this," Lottie says, then straightens, knocking on the bar. "My good man, I will offer you two thousand dollars for one sip of your finest whiskey."

The bartender turns. Stares back, absolutely uncomprehending.

She points to the closest bottle of whiskey, mimes drinking, then holds up four fingers. That he understands. Four glasses are dutifully poured.

"Teddy." Lottie nods, vindicated. "You were saying?"

Teddy clears his throat, grinning like he's about to say the funniest thing in the world. "So, first of all, I snuck into your room and, golly gosh, you hadn't packed a bag, had you? Everything was still there. So I thought—"

"And I agreed," Max cuts in.

"I'd better get the word out somehow, do some digging. So I called up Everett Kain. Snuck a little mention into the gossip columns."

Lottie slaps her hip, cracking up. "Oh, Teddy, you didn't."

"He sure did," Max murmurs into his whiskey.

"Don't know what came of that, but I think it probably hit the morning edition, because you'll never guess what happened here. Tell 'em, Max." Teddy smiles wider, his eyes manic.

"The phone lines went out," Max says dryly. "All over the island. Isn't that a crazy coincidence? And they still don't work now."

"Hey." Down the bar, Ginger cranes her head over. "Are you folks talking about the phones? Do you know what's going on?"

She slides to join them with her glass of red in hand. Lottie notes the uncharacteristic circles under the younger woman's eyes.

"I haven't spoken to my daughter in days," Ginger says, gripping her glass tight enough to snap the stem. "She's been expecting a nightly call. It's in my contract, my conditions for booking this job, and now I can't reach her, even to say, 'Don't worry, honey, Mama's okay.' But am I even okay? Call me paranoid, but it's starting to feel like something funny's going on here."

Vivienne and Lottie share a glance. In silent agreement, Vivienne takes Ginger's arm and pulls her into their group.

"Don't worry," she assures Ginger. "None of us think you're being paranoid."

"In fact, why don't we take this conversation to that empty table over there?" Lottie offers, tossing her hair in the direction of the corner of the room.

"Not upstairs, to one of our rooms?" Vivienne suggests.

Max makes a low grunt of dissent. "Having a friendly chat in plain sight is what one might term 'normal behavior,' whereas going upstairs en masse into a bedroom will raise all kinds of eyebrows."

"I suppose," Vivienne admits.

They casually make their way to the table, Max armed with a fresh bottle of Montepulciano to share. Normal behavior indeed.

As soon as they're all in their seats, Teddy leans forward, dropping the party boy act for a breath. "So you wanna tell us what the hell happened to you two? You honestly had us worried sick."

He looks to Vivienne when he says it, and Lottie's glad for

that. She knows only too well how concerned he's been for Viv, and not just in the past week. Whatever Vivienne might think of Teddy, he really does care about her.

But how to answer his question? Lottie gives the room one more scan. And then she cheerily fills them in on everything they know about the production's real purpose, the harsh truth delivered quickly, directly, like ripping off an eyebrow wax treatment.

It might have been the wrong decision to bring Ginger into the fold, Lottie realizes, seeing the unvarnished horror in her eyes. There's a reason a girl that good-looking is working the makeup tent and not in front of the camera herself.

"How do you know this?" Ginger at least has the good sense to whisper.

"I saw one of the exchanges going down, in a cove near the hangar," Lottie murmurs back. "The drugs coming in. It was a cop, actually, from Monaco bringing them over. There were broken props down there, a sort of dump, and all the set pieces for this shoot are hollow, ready to be loaded up and shipped back to sunny Southern California once we're wrapped. Ludovico's running the trade, but Gallo's the man in charge, and we think a good chunk of the crew's in on it. The prop department, anyway."

Max laughs ruefully. "Of course the only set I'm invited back onto winds up being a criminal enterprise. You know, for all his flattery, I did wonder why Gallo insisted on me as the script doctor. Convinced myself it was because he really did love my punch-up work on *Two to Tango*. That I was the most able writer, despite my political associations. Turns out it's because those associations make me the least able to squeal."

Teddy presses a reassuring hand to Max's back.

Max shoots him a crooked smile. "This is not gonna get me off the blacklist."

"I'd worry more about getting off the hit list," Vivienne cuts in. "They've murdered at least two people since production began, one of whom was an Interpol agent. The other?"

She turns to Lottie.

Lottie presses her lips together, apologetic. Then out with it: "Billy Wagner."

"Oh my God." Teddy slumps against the table, pain filling his eyes. Wagner had been the producer on several of his early war movies. "I thought he'd just quit the picture and was lying low in Palm Springs or something."

"Sadly not," Vivienne says. "Looks like he stumbled onto something during preproduction."

"And then I stumbled onto him," Lottie says.

Teddy's eyes go buggy. "Wait, *you* found Wagner's body? And then—"

"We ran for our lives," Vivienne says impatiently. She looks to Lottie. "Long story short?"

Lottie nods. "They caught us."

"I don't mean this to sound insulting," Ginger says, grabbing the bottle of wine and gripping it tight. "But of all people to wind up in this mess, how are *you two* still alive?"

Lottie shrugs. "Gallo wants to finish the picture. I know it sounds ridiculous, but—"

"He's delusional," Vivienne cuts in, a bit too loud. Lottie flashes her a warning look and she adjusts, relaxing back against her chair. "He wants to make a success of the studio through dishonest means. So he needs us to play our part until filming wraps."

"And to ensure that, he's got dirt on us." Lottie looks at Max. Then Teddy. "*All* of us."

Teddy swallows hard. Then laughs. "So. Right. Then we do what he wants: we play dumb. Get everybody home safely."

"For two more months?" Ginger looks wildly around the room. "You really think we can keep this up that long?"

"Our flame-haired friend here is right." Max refills Ginger's glass, his stare pointedly encouraging her to drink. She does. "Think how much 'stumbling upon' has occurred in a matter of, what, weeks? What are the odds that no one else will see something they shouldn't see, say something they shouldn't . . . ?"

They all follow his oh-so-casual glance across the room at the ever-monologuing Charles Brinkwater.

"And meet with another 'accident.'" Max tops off Lottie's wine. "Along with anybody else unlucky enough to overhear."

Lottie takes a sip. "Not to mention all the dirt he has on us. This doesn't necessarily end when shooting wraps. Not if Gallo gets his way."

"The longer we stay here, the more danger we're in," Vivienne says with a toss of her hair to hide her nerves from anyone who might be watching. "There's really only one option."

She leans on the table, resting her chin on her fist, and they all inch forward in tandem to listen, as if she's about to share some delicious Hollywood gossip.

But no need for the pretense, as it's Lottie who confirms what Vivienne's thinking with a raise of her glass: "Ladies and gentlemen, we've gotta get the hell out of Tavalli."

23

Saturday, June 21, 1958

"Scene five again!" Sydney shouts, so exasperated that smoke is practically spewing from his ears. "From the top. And, Charles, can we *please* add that extra line from Priam?"

Vivienne watches as Charles nods his assent and lurches onto the throne, while Syd ushers Teddy and Lottie swiftly across the elevated stage and Max trails the trio, dashing frantic notes to himself across the printed script pages in his hand.

They picked up right where Vivienne and Lottie left off—the series of Cassandra's "vision" scenes—with today's filming focused on the prediction of Helen and Paris's love affair toppling Troy. Syd had to spend the better part of the past week or so shooting battle sequences, despite the full arsenal of extras not having arrived on set yet. Her and Lottie's "outing," as the team has taken to calling it, obviously took the shooting script and flung it to the high heavens. Apparently, though, Syd managed to pull off the impossible, keeping Gallo's blockbuster roughly on schedule, although he most certainly looks worse for wear from the effort.

Vivienne glances around the frenetic palace set, the elevated stage, alive and bustling with actors, lighting people, assistants, crew. The stunning marble columns loom large over the throne, the gilded floor sparkling, tiled with an elaborate mosaic of gods and goddesses seated under the clouds at Mount Olympus. The set's sheer detail, the scope of this film, is extraordinary. She knows this objectively, and yet she can't deny that the headlining emotion she feels standing on this stage is acute disappointment. Partially because she bore witness to the breathtaking spectacle and the true directorial vision of Wyler's Circus Maximus in Rome.

But mainly because this whole thing is a lie. A beautiful, expensive, dangerous lie.

Vivienne glances nervously at the trio of production crew members conferring at the base of the stage—one of whom she knows quite well, seeing as she spent the last eight days running from him. The bald hit man with the unnervingly crooked nose. Pasquale. His gun and holster are well-hidden now under his linen jacket, no one else the wiser. Now that she is in the know about Gallo's dealings, though, all the little cues, the signs, that something untoward is afoot are so glaringly obvious to her that she cannot believe anyone can miss them. *How many prop people are carrying guns? How much of this extensive crew is muscle, Gallo's underlings posing as assistants or extras? How could I not have noticed it immediately?*

"Vivienne?" Syd interrupts her internal condemnation. "You ready to go again, doll?"

She realizes she's been just standing here, pressing her lips together tightly, running her hands down her chiton, as if that's going to iron out all the wrinkles of this cursed production.

"Yes, right." She swallows. "Ready."

Syd waves his arm in a "Take it from the top, and quickly" motion. The lighting team shines that otherworldly green "prophecy spotlight" on Lottie and Teddy, who stand, waiting, atop the mosaic.

Syd huffs down the stairs, counting down aloud. "Annnd . . . action!"

Vivienne sets to dramatic pacing. "I, Cassandra, am a mere vessel of the future's secrets . . ." She burrows into her lines, attempting to take solace inside her character. "I have seen the great despair Paris will bring down upon our people as he listens to the call of the temptress across the sea . . ."

As she delivers her monologue—her own revised version of it—she spots Max next to Syd below, nodding along.

Instead of cutting her off, Max Montrose, shock of the ages, seems to be accepting her changes to this scene. All of her changes. Every damn edit. Maybe he finally saw the wisdom of her suggestions, although Vivienne must admit imagining Cassandra with true power, autonomy, right now feels a bit ironic and infuriating. Perhaps it's just that Max has learned to trust her a bit—or at least, given Lottie's endorsement, to trust her by extension.

Though it's just as likely that Gallo spoke to Max and forced him into it.

Vivienne swallows, nerves tightening like a bustier, her eyes scanning the crowd. At least Gallo's not on set this afternoon, a small consolation. Whenever he's around, she can feel his stare, heavy with desire. With expectation. *What happens if he decides to stop being patient? To just take what he wants from me?*

Somehow she manages to finish her lines.

On delayed cue, Charles Brinkwater, looking far too ruffled in his royal Trojan cloak and feathered headpiece, pitches forward, reeking of whiskey and sweat. "My dear Cassandra, your concern is, ah, unfounded. My own gaggle of oracles assure me that—"

"Cut!" Syd says, jumping up from his chair. "Just cut."

Their director looks beyond fried as he takes the stairs again, his thinning gray hair splayed near his ears like an unkempt troll. "All right, let's tone this green spotlight down. Everyone's looking like they're about to wretch."

"Please don't say that," Charles mumbles.

As the lighting team wheels the monstrous spotlight back, Vivienne studies Charles, who indeed looks like he's about to be sick. From his steady diet of booze for breakfast, yes, but she wonders, does Charles sense that things are gravely amiss on this island? Does anyone else understand the true stakes of this production?

"And, Charles, *Charles*." Syd stomps toward him. "Come on, we need the right lines. And more conviction. Let us feel indisputably that *you* dismissed Cassandra, that *your* hubris caused Troy's down—"

"May I take five?" Charles covers his mouth, hurrying off the stage, past Pasquale and another one of Gallo's thugs-posing-as-crewmen.

The goons ascend the stairs, conferring softly in Italian, pointing at the towering columns as they pass by Vivienne.

"*Quelle colonne . . .*" She catches traces of their comments as she steps aside. "*Bisogno nell'hangar stasera.*"

"Mr. Gallo want to make changes," Pasquale barks to Syd when he reaches him. "Some changes to set."

"Set changes? Mid-scene?" Syd rubs his temples. "You know what? It's lunchtime anyway." He turns, shouting to the crowd, "Everybody, back here at one! Not a minute later."

With relieved murmurs, the cast and crew disperse.

"Thank God. I'm famished," Lottie whispers, sliding beside Vivienne. "Do you think the village restaurant is catering again today?"

Vivienne raises an eyebrow as they descend the stairs. "What's the alternative, popping over to Schwab's and . . ." She trails off.

Lottie lets out an uneasy laugh and stops walking.

Jack Gallo is hovering behind the cameras. Here after all. Watching.

Watching her.

Vivienne's stomach curdles as Gallo stands up, hands raised in a slow, menacing clap.

"Well done, you," he says with that Cheshire cat's grin, his eyes locked on Vivienne as he saunters forward. "Your changes to Cassandra's prediction were spot-on. The whole scene feels so much more authentic now, doesn't it?"

Vivienne swallows. "Thank you, Mr. Gallo."

"Oh, please, Viv." He laughs. "It's Jack."

He takes off his straw fedora, revealing his thick swath of black hair. The piercing sun, now igniting his eyes, spangles the dark brown with flecks of gold.

"That's what we've been talking about all along, isn't it? The magic of pictures." He edges closer, blocking out the path, the hotel, the world. "How a scene can envelop you. Transport you . . . even *save you.*" He gently but possessively rests his hand on her shoulder.

Vivienne shivers despite the heat.

"You all right, Viv?" He squeezes.

She forces a smile. "Fine, yes. Fine."

Gallo hasn't been able to keep his hands off her since they stepped off his yacht, their illuminating dinner conversation serving as some kind of unofficial green light for him. As if she and Lottie had any choice but to agree to his "deal."

He's getting more forward, and aggressive, with each passing day. The fact that he's charming, attractive, and so seemingly transfixed with her only adds insult to injury. Some of the cast and crew think they're an item. She can tell by the way the cameramen whisper, how they shoot her glares when they think she isn't looking. It's mortifying, not to mention insulting, given what's truly going on.

Lottie, no stranger to rumors herself, bless her heart, has made it her mission to quell the gossip.

"Are you joining us for lunch, Jack?" Lottie chimes in, edging around Vivienne in such a way that Gallo has no choice but to break contact.

Vivienne takes advantage of the interruption and puts some more space between them.

"Not today. Too much work to do." Gallo gives a meaningful nod toward Ludovico's prop hangar. He turns to Vivienne. "But maybe a drink at the hotel bar soon."

Vivienne gives another shudder as he saunters off.

"You okay?" Lottie offers her arm.

"You know me. I'll survive."

Lottie gives her a reassuring nudge as they join the tail end of cast and crew members trailing up the walk, the snake of people filtering into the lobby of Albergo Tavalli. The past three days have been the same. Calls at 7:00 a.m., and now filming straight through the weekend. Lunch taken al fresco in the gardens off the hotel lobby, then back to work until sunset.

The unexpected run-in with Gallo has dashed her appetite, but if Vivienne's learned anything from her and Lottie's time on the road, it's that when food presents itself, she needs to eat it. She loads her plate with a filet of whitefish, a bit of pasta, and sautéed vegetables.

She follows Lottie over to the far table where Teddy, Max, and Ginger are sitting, voices low, careful.

". . . nothing in the production trailers," Ginger is murmuring when they approach.

Max sighs. "No luck on the lobby phone either."

Teddy looks up and smiles, scooting over to make room for Vivienne.

"Are you still trying to figure out a way to reach the authorities?" Lottie whispers, plopping down on the opposite bench between Ginger and Max and promptly digging into her antipasti.

Max nods, glancing behind him, but the coast is clear. "After Ted fell asleep, I came down and scouted the lobby. Guards are patrolling the grounds all night. There's no way to even sneak down to town to find a phone."

Vivienne freezes for an instant. Though not because of Max's mention of the guards.

That casual aside: *"After Ted fell asleep."* It confirms something that's been snaking through her mind since she learned that Lottie and Teddy were a setup, when her memories flip like a Rolodex at night. Through the recent whirlwind events with Lottie on the road, yes, but older recollections too. The past winter with Teddy. On set for *Beach Holiday*. All the little offhanded remarks she's noted these past few days when Teddy and Max are together. The way they look at each other. Lottie's suggestion that Vivienne should ask Teddy about the real love of his life.

Answers—true answers, finally—click into place.

Teddy *and* Max.

Vivienne looks away for a moment, overwhelmed by her foolishness, but more than that, by a serene relief. There is a certain rightness about it all. A satisfactory conclusion.

What's between Teddy and Max is the real deal.

"I doubt the fine businesses of town would even help us." Lottie cuts into Vivienne's thoughts. She gestures to the catering spread behind them. "If one thing's true about Gallo, it's that he has people loyal to him everywhere, Monte Carlo to Hollywood."

Ginger stabs a carrot, mumbling, "Bully for him."

Vivienne suddenly remembers. "There is a working line on Tavalli, you know." She turns toward Lottie. "Or just off Tavalli, I should say. Gallo's yacht? Not a phone, but—"

"The yacht!" Lottie turns to Teddy and Max. "Viv's right, the yacht has a radio—"

"And it works. Or at least it did," Viv says. "I heard it buzzing on our lovely dinner cruise over."

"Okay, but . . ." Max lets out a dismissive snort. "There's no way Gallo would ever let us within a hundred fathoms of that yacht."

"Not you maybe." Lottie shucks a thumb at Vivienne. "But definitely her."

Vivienne blushes when all eyes turn in her direction, then immediately grows nauseous over the idea of stepping foot on that yacht again.

"Even if I could finagle an invitation to his boat, how would I get to the radio without Gallo or his minions noticing? And who would I radio?"

They all fall silent, thinking, waiting as a crew member slides by their table with his heaping plate.

"Wait," Max murmurs once the guy is gone. "There *are* boats around to radio!"

"What do you mean?" Teddy asks.

"The shooting script. Hang on." Max pulls his tattered, marked-up copy off of the bench, fiendishly flipping through it. "We moved the battle scenes up in the schedule because you two had flown the coop. But also because Syd was sweating that delaying the establishing panorama shots for much longer might result in freighters cluttering ancient Troy's horizon."

Ginger and Lottie lean toward Max as he keeps flipping through the pages, stopping when he gets to a calendar grid.

"What we've got here is the maritime schedule for this part of the Mediterranean." He looks up wildly. "The cruisers USS *Des Moines* and USS *Boston* are both due to pass through these waters in the next twenty-four hours. If we can get onto the yacht tonight, we stand a chance of reaching them, sounding the SOS."

"You really think that could work?" Teddy says.

"I think it's worth a shot." Max bites his lip. "Though there's still the problem of using the radio without Gallo or his guards being any the wiser."

Vivienne frowns, thinking, remembering Pasquale. "One of Gallo's men mentioned something about set changes to Syd. I think he was talking about the hangar. *Stasera*. That means 'tonight,' doesn't it?"

Lottie raises her eyebrows, impressed. "So you're saying . . ."

"They might be busy working in the hangar, on a new shipment."

"But what about Mr. Gallo?" Ginger frowns. "You think he'll be there with the grunt workers? Man like him doesn't do his own heavy lifting."

Lottie chews her lip, wheels visibly churning. In sync with Vivienne's own. "Wait! Maybe—"

"I could draw him away," Vivienne finishes.

"Take him up on that drink at the bar tonight?" Lottie squeals. "Just like a—"

"Long-awaited date." Despite everything, Vivienne can't help but smile at their synergy. It's been like this between them, even on camera, since Provence. Able to glean what the other is thinking. Playing off each other like a seasoned two-hander act.

Ginger looks doubtful. "The hotel won't work. He'd be able to see his yacht from any of the windows."

"Dang it, you're right." Lottie pauses, mulling. "It'd have to be farther, yeah. We need to get Gallo away from set, buy us more time. The village?"

"The village?" Max echoes. "What is this, *Brigadoon*? Gallo's never going to jaunt off set for a date down among the commoners."

Lottie clicks her tongue. "I think it's obvious that when it comes to Viv, there are *always* exceptions."

Vivienne lets out a groan.

"Sorry." Lottie winces, adding quickly, "You know I'd do it if I could. I'm just—well, I'm clearly not Jack's type."

Ginger grunts. "That makes two of us. And phew to that."

"You can tell him you need a change of scenery," Lottie says. "That you have personal things to discuss, away from all the prying eyes."

"Right. *Personal things.*" Vivienne shudders at the implications of those loaded words.

"It won't be long, just enough time for one or two of us to sneak on board the yacht and radio for help." Lottie takes her hand. "And by the time you've ordered dessert, that help should already be on the way. The US Army!"

"Navy," Max corrects.

"Navy!" Lottie chirps in the same tone. "All you need to do is stall."

"It's fine, Viv." Teddy shakes his head. "You don't have to do this. We understand. It's a lot to ask. If you're not okay with—"

"No, that's not what I—" Vivienne swallows, straightening her spine. "I suppose I'm just trying to envision the type of character who might waltz up to a hangar full of hidden opiates and invite my warden out for a night on the town. How's this?"

She tosses her dark hair over one shoulder, attempting to channel Rita Hayworth in *Gilda*. The brazen gun moll through and through.

Ginger claps while Max barks a laugh. "Well, I'll be. Vivienne Rhodes!"

Max's eyes sparkle with something new. Surprise? Respect?

"You're the face that helped us sneak aboard a ship." Lottie nudges her shoulder. "Far more impressive than launching a thousand. Helen's got nothing on you, Viv."

Teddy, though, merely furrows his brow. Vivienne remembers this look. A question. His check-in to make sure she's truly all right with this Hail Mary plan. The small gesture warms her, reminds her of so many nights last winter at Chasen's and Romanoff's when they'd enter a room full of eyes and all he'd have to do was look at her and she'd know someone was on her side. His palpable concern—his *friendship*, she sees now. A friendship that, maybe, she can have once more, assuming they all survive this.

And they *will* survive. They'll escape, the lot of them, out from Gallo's hold. Vivienne didn't finally break free of her father's influence just to end up living under the thumb of a man even worse.

She nods, newly resolute.

"All right," Teddy relents with a slow exhale, looking around the table at her, Lottie, Max, and Ginger. "If I had to bet my life on any one of us delivering a scene, it's you, Viv."

Lottie smirks. "I'll pretend I didn't hear that."

"Wish me luck." Vivienne attempts a smile.

Max tips his Chinotto soda grimly. "I think you mean *break a leg*."

24

Max raps on the hotel room door with his secret code. *Boom, badda, bop bop.*

Lottie answers promptly, scooting back to let him slide inside the dark room.

"How very *Rear Window*," Max whispers, nodding to Teddy, who's crouched beside the window, staring out to sea with a pair of binoculars. "Where did you get those?"

"Johnny Preem," Teddy says idly, still squinting through the lenses.

"He's a bird-watcher," Lottie explains.

Max coughs a laugh. "Of course he is."

They join Teddy at the window, bending down to follow his line of sight. Even without magnification, Lottie can make out the scene. The beach, empty. The sky, deep dusk-blue. The sea, ever rolling. And the yacht, not docked beside the wharf like usual but anchored out in deeper water, a precaution on Gallo's part, perhaps, in case anybody gets cold feet and decides to try to make a break for it.

Which, to be fair, is kind of what they're doing.

"There," Teddy murmurs, leaning forward at the sight of something Lottie can't make out with the naked eye. "Heading out."

Now she sees it, the shadowed shape of the boat's dinghy pulling swiftly away. She might not have been able to pick it out at all if it weren't for the white line written across the dark surf. The remaining interior lights on the yacht blink out, leaving only that sole anchor light aglow.

"You were right," Max whispers. "They're all going to the hangar job. All hands on deck. Actually, *no* hands on deck. We hope."

Lottie and Max share a loaded glance. "We hope" is the only assurance they're going to get at this point.

Teddy sets the binoculars down on the windowsill. "That's our cue, boys and girls."

Lottie hesitates for one panicked second before following them to the door. "Do you think this dress is going to be easy enough to swim in? I do have a bathing suit."

"I think that might be a smidge conspicuous, darling," Max teases gently.

But Teddy takes her clammy hand. "You really can leave this to us, you know. Keep watch with Ginger on the beach instead."

"And leave all the fun to the boys?" She scoffs.

"I know how you feel about the water," Teddy frets.

"I've had much more exposure to it over the past week. Honestly, I'll be fine, just a little slower than you two. Anyway, swimming out to a yacht is a hell of a lot easier than what Vivienne has to go through tonight."

They fall silent thinking about it.

The last image Lottie had of Vivienne this afternoon was one for the ages—her friend standing in full resplendent evening-gown glory, hair and makeup impeccable thanks to dear Ginger's ministrations, then disappearing into Gallo's waiting grip as Lottie casually sipped prosecco at the bar. There was no hint of apprehension in Vivienne's upright posture. She'd taken Gallo's hand smoothly, eagerly even. The consummate actress.

"She'll be all right," Max says, wrapping both arms around the two of them. "Vivienne's tough as Teflon."

Lottie knows better. But she smiles at his attempt at reassurance. Besides, they've got their own roles to worry about now.

Chatting away about absolutely nothing, the three of them stroll languidly down the hotel steps, past the bar, and through the lobby, where Ginger sits reading a dime novel on the settee. Lottie's eyes flick to her as they pass, and Ginger gives no more than a hard blink of understanding before returning to her reading. Her acting skills are proving better than Lottie expected, but her hands are clenching that book tight enough to crumple the cover.

Per the plan, Ginger will wait for a few minutes before putting her book down and going out for a walk, following them as if by coincidence, in case of any spies among the hotel staff. She'll then keep watch from the shoreline with a flashlight in hand, ready to signal if danger approaches.

The view they take in as they stride out of the hotel and into the night confirms that most of this evening's activity is centered up at the hangar, which is lit by lanterns like balefires in the darkness. It's a moonless night, dark as ink now. Farther down the island, past the set, Lottie can see the warm glimmer of the village. A few paces away, down the hill, is the vague outline of the beach that stretches beside the docks, rendered clear only by the lapping of waves on rocks and the anchor light of the yacht.

Teddy wastes no time stripping off his shirt and trousers. Max follows suit much more awkwardly, and when he wades into the water after his boyfriend, he lets out a breath like a steam engine. "Holy Arctic narwhal, that is bracing."

Lottie clenches her fists. No sense faltering now. She reaches the waterline, kicks off her flats, and runs straight in.

She draws in a hissing breath to keep from squawking. Even with Max's warning, it's colder than she expected. Each inch that she sinks deeper into the water is a fresh agony.

Next to them, waist-deep, Teddy laughs under his breath. "Babies."

He silently slides his whole body under the water, coming up with a slick head like a playful seal.

"Come on in, the water's fine."

"Show-off," Max whispers back.

Lottie bites her lip and lets herself fall backward, fully submerged. "Not fine." Her teeth are already chattering when she pops up, dripping. "D-definitely not fine."

"Agreed," Max huffs over his shoulder, but as he adjusts into a breaststroke, he skillfully glides away, another natural swimmer, apparently.

And Lottie's left in his wake.

This might have been a bad idea, Lottie admits, but she didn't want to let the team down, and she figured adrenaline might propel her to the yacht.

She was half right. With a sort of doggy-paddle motion, she manages to keep most of her head above the waterline, but despite his occasional glances back, Teddy gets all the way to the stern of the boat before she's even made it halfway there, and Max is a close second. Lottie's eyes have adjusted enough to the dark now to see Teddy raise two fingers in a gesture he must have picked up in a war movie. Lottie guesses that means "meet us inside."

Sure enough, Teddy hoists himself onto the back platform

and clambers up the ladder into the yacht, Max right on his dripping heels. Lottie stifles the urge to call out to them, *Wait for me!* Or perhaps, *Never mind, I'm going back!*

She turns around to peer at the beach. It's too dark to tell whether Ginger's made it there yet. Not too dark to see that it's a closer swim to the boat than to the shore.

The shore of Tavalli. Their prison.

Versus a boat. The chance of escape. Even . . . immediate escape.

They could go, the three of them, as soon as she's aboard. Start the engine, take off full speed, and save their own skins. Get away from this godforsaken island, ensure their lovely life together as a trio will continue, and, from safety, send the authorities back here for the others.

Including Vivienne.

Lottie's body goes even colder with that realization. She ignores the sensation and focuses back on the task at hand:

Dog-paddle faster.

25

Tavalli's restaurant, La Giostra, is almost impossibly charming, with its ornate arched entrance, potted ferns, and shelved alcoves teeming with wine bottles. Not faux-rustic like so many posh spots in Los Angeles, but actually so. One bistro wall is all open windows overlooking the turquoise Ligurian Sea and the horseshoe of cottages hugging its shoreline, the island's southern-point town no more than a labyrinth of crude roads, a piazza, and this lively bar and restaurant.

In theory, Vivienne has longed her whole life for a romantic night just like this one. A date with a gorgeous, attentive man who worships her; a perfect bottle of rosé; a salty breeze winding off a glamorous far-flung sea.

In reality, the past hour has been pure torture.

"I suppose I'm a product of my upbringing, same as you, Viv," Gallo purrs as he tops off both their glasses. "In some ways, as strange as it sounds, I was raised for Hollywood."

Vivienne grabs her drink reflexively, taking another sip. Liquid courage. She's been drinking more than usual, though not so much as to lose control. She's impressed herself tonight, she'll admit, playing her part of doting dinner date, a totally improvised role, mind you, and to a seemingly captivated audience. Gallo appears engaged enough that he hasn't once checked his watch or mentioned the need to get back to set, the hangar, or worst of all, the yacht. The fact that this restaurant offers a five-course menu is helping matters. Vivienne just prays it's been long enough for Lottie and the others to successfully board and radio for help. That their Hail Mary plan comes to fruition.

Max had agonized over the notes on that shooting script all day, as well as cross-checked it against the hotel's own vessel schedule. The USS *Boston*, he confirmed, was passing through, would be less than a mile away, at precisely eight o'clock tonight. Lottie, Teddy, and Max must have reached the yacht by now. Help could already be en route. Right this moment, navy ships could be heading their way to storm onto set, to free her fellow cast and crew and end this nightmare.

Although it's not over yet.

"Yes," Vivienne says breathily, leaning forward. "We do have that in common, don't we?"

They pause a moment while their waiter slides beside them, serving Gallo his canederli, Vivienne her tilapia. He bows with a "*Godere.*"

"We do indeed." Gallo flashes Vivienne a sheepish-looking, and clearly practiced, grin. "Never would have thought it, but producing pictures and running a business like my family's?" He points his fork at her in emphasis. "They really aren't so different."

"How interesting," she intones, forcing herself to pick at her tilapia. Rule one in improvisation, it turns out, is to let the narcissist do most of the talking. "Do explain."

Gallo's grin turns wider, as if he thought she'd never ask. "To start with, my family's line of work lets me connect with people,

Viv. Learn about them in interesting ways. *Collect* them, if you will, for a rainy day, and use them to my distinct advantage, should the opportunity to do so ever arise. I've had my eye on the flick business for a while; I told you that." He stops to take a monstrous bite. Vivienne resists the urge to grimace when he starts talking again with his mouth full. "So I started learning the players. Where they went, the circles they ran in. Their flaws. Or if you'll forgive me a Trojan War metaphor, their Achilles' heel."

Vivienne laughs dutifully, taking another bite, her thoughts returning to her last meal with Gallo, to what he'd told her and Lottie during their passage from Rome. How he always makes sure to have a contingency plan in case of "unforeseen plot twists." It sounds like an overall strategy: he chooses his targets based upon their weaknesses. His ability to exploit them. Apex Pictures' money troubles were common knowledge, for example. Clearly Gallo took advantage of that situation, presented the board with an offer they couldn't refuse, a chance to save the studio from ruin in exchange for free rein over his methods. Maybe he even had leverage, dirt, on the higher-ups too. Perhaps Buster Smith had been caught gambling—the only plausible vice Vivienne can imagine Apex's head of production falling prey to. Or one of the board members got involved in extortion himself. Or drugs. Or once called upon Gallo's people to clean up loose ends on a messy deal. Or, Vivienne thinks now of that slime Ken Winters, something even more salacious.

"Is that how you chose this cast and crew?" she asks, breathy with feigned admiration. "There were so many changes to the production after you took over. Do you have something on everyone on *Ships*?"

"Bingo, my dear." He beams. "You see the brilliance of it, don't you?"

What would be brilliant is slapping that grin off your face.

She nods, matching his smile. "How did you phrase it on the boat, Jack? Insurance?"

"Precisely." Gallo winks before taking a swig. "Didn't take too long to uncover Lottie's criminal past. Imagine how the public would react if they found out about that."

He hardly lowers his voice, she notices, as she surreptitiously glances about the dining room. Could the owners, even the patrons of this restaurant, be part of his collection too?

"And there's Ginger's status as a single mother," he adds. "Knocked up at fifteen. Poor old Sydney's been in and out of sanitariums for the past decade, suffering annual nervous breakdowns. Brinkwater's drinking problem is so thinly veiled in interviews, it's laughable. All he needs is a steady supply of aged Scotch—"

"And Max," she supplies. "His political affiliations?"

"He was already vulnerable, yes. But there's more to that story. He and that very good pal of his, Teddy, are both of a particular . . . how shall we say . . . persuasion." As Gallo's eyes twinkle under the restaurant's dim lights, Vivienne's stomach twists tight as a constrictor knot. She imagines Teddy and Max now, finally happy, luminous really, when they're together.

Out of all of Gallo's secrets, this one might hold the most capacity to destroy.

"Not much detective work needed there," Gallo murmurs. "I knew the instant I heard Teddy had barely protested when Apex broke you two off before *Bovary.* Any man who can walk away from Vivienne Rhodes . . ."

Gallo *tsk*s. He takes another sip, never breaking eye contact.

Dread tightens in her throat. And yet she has to know. "What about me?"

"What do you mean?"

"What's your advantage when it comes to me? What's my, er, my weakness?"

Vivienne braces herself. Perhaps it's her father. Maybe he got involved with this gangster at some point and couldn't pay his debts, so he pledged Vivienne as his guarantor. *Is this par for the mafioso course, to come after the kids?* Or maybe one of the actresses on her early aquatic pictures started rumors, claimed Vivienne was a literal Medusa to work with. She wouldn't have put it past Esther, that's for sure. Her mind keeps free-falling through the past, every run-in she's ever had with a director, a costar. Makeup artist, costume designer, agent, assistant, operator.

"You're the exception." Now Gallo lowers his voice, leaning close to whisper. "From the very first time I saw you up there on a cinema screen, I knew you were extraordinary. Your talent, elegance, force. I simply wanted you here, Viv. I wanted *you*."

Vivienne almost forgets to breathe, let alone to smile for this monster. The devastating irony. To be wanted so badly, to be seen as extraordinary, an exception to the rule. His line feels lifted from a movie, something a dashing actor would whisper into his leading lady's ear in all those cinematic love stories she'd worshiped as a child. It's what she's always wanted to hear. What she wanted from Gallo, once upon a time.

But her time on the road with Lottie has taught Vivienne something, or at least it has honed an ability that was swimming inside her, nascent and malleable, all along. A capacity to see the whole picture, all the players, the various angles of any given situation. The courage to remove herself *from* herself long enough to notice the flow of the bigger scene, the wider perspective, just like any "swell" director might.

And right now, Vivienne can clock the raw truth tucked behind Gallo's steady gaze, his slight hesitation. The touch of vulnerability seeping through all that bravado.

He really does want her.

All she has to do is keep him talking, to ensure the others have enough time.

Vivienne leans forward, lowering her lashes. "If I didn't know better, I'd think you were calling me perfect."

Gallo's posture matches hers. "I'd argue more perfect than Helen of Troy."

"Aha." She smirks. "Is that why you cast me as the priestess?"

He laughs, gently reaching for her hand. "You and I, side by side, we could take Hollywood by storm. I see it, Viv. I want that too. Although . . ." His lips quirk, his eyes flitting to the door. "Maybe we should continue this discussion somewhere even more private."

Oh no, oh no. Stall. Stall!

"That sounds lovely, but how about dessert first? It's a gorgeous night, after all."

"I can think of something sweeter."

"Ever hear the best things come to those who wait?"

Before Gallo can parry that riposte, she stands, placing her napkin on the table.

"Need to powder my nose. Let's stay, can't we, Jack? It'll be fun. Order me the tiramisu? I'll be back in a jiffy."

Not the best improvisation by any means, but right now it feels like a more crowning achievement than nabbing that damn Supporting Actress nomination. By the time Vivienne dashes into the bathroom, she's shaking, hyperventilating with fear.

She folds over the counter, swallowing a sob. "How can I keep this up? Oh, Lottie, Teddy, if you could hear me now—"

A toilet flushes.

An older woman in a collared sundress slips out from the stall.

Vivienne wipes her eyes. "Sorry. Ah, tough date."

The woman edges past her for the sink.

"I mean, my date himself is wonderful," Vivienne says, remembering herself, trailing the woman. "I'm the problem, really, always. Far too much wine, blabbering on—"

The door slams closed on her.

Vivienne glares at her reflection. Her face is covered in tonight's war paint. Her rosy cheeks, swirls of blue eye shadow, those perfect brows Ginger sculpted before heading out to play her own part in their escape tonight.

Goodness, how she wishes they were all together right now. Her friends. The thought nearly takes her breath away. She's never had friends before. Colleagues, of course. Advocates, even— Lew's as steady and true as they come. But friends? This is a first.

They are all counting on you, she tells herself, then stalks out of the restroom, ready to make a small plate of tiramisu last as long as humanly possible.

Sauntering back through the restaurant, she startles to a stop.

Ginger, of all people, is standing near the door, on the arm of Gallo's bald minion, Pasquale. Is Ginger on a date herself? Is this part of their plan she wasn't privy to?

Vivienne continues to walk, more slowly, across the dining room. Her table is empty. She scans the restaurant, looking for Gallo, only to find him sidling beside Pasquale and Ginger, who appears to be pinioned by the goon's elbow.

As Vivienne steps forward, she and Ginger lock eyes.

"Are you okay?" Vivienne mouths, heart practically ratcheting out of her chest.

Ginger's face falls, eyes fluttering rapidly, as if staving off tears. She looks positively terrified.

Oh my God, no, she's not okay. Was she caught? Are the others in trouble?

Wait. Vivienne blinks, reassessing with a director's eye. *That's not terror.*

It's guilt.

"Vivienne." Gallo's voice is flat, like a gavel.

The world slips into slow motion. Gallo crosses the room in two bounds, grabs her arm, and wrenches her toward the door.

"Heavens, is something wrong?" Vivienne's tone surprises her. It's still even, somehow, cool and collected, even as her pulse is all-out rocketing now, even as the boisterous restaurant falls silent, the locals watching, an eager audience.

"Cut the act. You know damn well."

"Jack, please, where are we going? Why are we leaving?"

"Fun is over. It's time to return to business."

He shoulders her silently out into the warm night air, all light extinguished now, the expansive Ligurian Sea a black hole.

Vivienne wants to reply, to argue her case, but the words stay lodged in her tightening throat. They stagger up the hill in silence.

When Jack speaks again, dragging her behind him, it's almost to himself, his words chilling in their certainty: "Time to cash in my insurance."

26

Lottie lolls like a beached whale for a moment on the swim platform of the yacht, letting gravity siphon the great weight of salt water out of her dress. Teddy thought this one would be lightweight enough. Good grief, was he ever wrong.

A few labored breaths and she heaves herself upright again, up the ladder and into a salon that would surely be gleaming if the lights were on, leather banquettes and bucket chairs leading up to a lacquered bar, against which Teddy is leaning as if he owns the vessel.

He mimes pouring himself a martini. "Thought we were going to have to fish you out."

Max paces the carpet, swiping at puddles with his bare feet.

"When we get back," she snaps, still panting, "I am asking Vivienne for swimming lessons."

"Are we worried about leaving evidence we were here? Anybody? No?" Max waves at the drips pooling off of Lottie's dress. "Just me?"

"Let's just be quick, be quiet, and be gone," Teddy says, instantly serious. "Radio should be up in the helm, right, Lottie?"

"Thatta way," she agrees, motioning to the shallow stairs.

Teddy starts up. "The only trick will be finding the channel for the navy cruiser."

"Listen for the one with American accents," Max offers dryly, following Teddy up into Gallo's dining area.

"Brilliant, Maxy." Teddy shoots him a killer grin over his shoulder. "As I keep saying, that's why they pay you the big bucks."

There's a small stairway off the dining room leading to an interior cockpit. No communication equipment there, alas. And from there, one more small flight to the helm. And beside the great silver steering wheel, as promised . . .

The radio.

It's playing quietly, maritime messages in Italian passing between local ships and harbors.

"Care to do the honors?" Max offers, stepping back in deference to Lottie.

She's flattered to be given this task, even though she's never worked a ship radio in her life. How hard can it be?

She turns the dial and the volume skyrockets, the radio's crackling absolutely deafening.

Max jumps forward, wildly waving, and Teddy nearly shoves her out of the way, but she hisses, "I've got it, I've got it," turns it down with a slow exhalation, then adjusts the other dial to change the frequency.

She puts her ear to the speaker, listening hard, like a safecracker in a movie. "You look out for a signal from Ginger, Ted. Any lights on the beach?"

"All clear," Teddy says. "So far so good."

Even so, Teddy pads about in peevish silence, and after about ten turns of the dial, darts down to whisper in Lottie's ear, "Any American accents?"

"Yes," she whispers back, swatting him away. "Yours."

She turns the dial again, and this time Max crouches down eagerly, joining her, ear to ear. "You hear that?"

She nods to him, listening harder.

It's static-spattered, but the voices behind the interference are speaking American-accented English. Military jargon too, though Lottie can't begin to understand what any of it means.

No need to. She grabs the receiver, presses the button, and hisses into it. "USS *Boston*, USS *Boston*, come in. This is an emergency; multiple American citizens in . . . um . . ."

Lottie looks to Teddy, who shrugs wildly. He never could improvise.

Then to Max, who offers, "Mortal danger."

"Really?" Lottie winces at him before pressing the receiver button again, "Mortal danger. Require army . . . No, sorry, navy assistance?"

There is no answer at all, just crackles on the line, and then: "This is a maritime military channel, ma'am."

"Well, I realize that! That's why we're contacting you, why I asked for navy assistance. We're on a maritime, um, boat, ship radio. Island is called Tavalli and you're passing by within fifty nautical miles—"

"State your name and coordinates."

Lottie glances at Max in exultant relief. "I don't know our coordinates, but my name is Lottie Lawrence and—"

There's a sound like the receiver's been dropped, and then the other voice snaps, "Lottie Lawrence? 'What did you find, Millie?' Did Jones put you up to this? Let him be informed that misuse of official military channels is subject to court martial procedures."

Even the navy makes Millie jokes? Lottie seethes through gritted teeth. *I've been in plenty of other pictures!*

Teddy gently takes the receiver from her: "I can confirm that she really is Lottie Lawrence and I'm—"

"Out of time," Max mutters low. "Ladies and gentlemen, I'm afraid we've got company."

Teddy lowers the receiver and Lottie's too dumbstruck to pick it back up.

"Company" is an understatement. Three boats are racing to the yacht from each direction of Tavalli, their motors an animal snarl in the night.

"We could go," Max sputters, his hand gripping the wheel. They turn to him. "I hate to say it, bless all the lost souls on Tavalli, but we could turn on this engine and get the hell out of here."

Lottie bites her lip. She'd had that idea herself, hadn't she? And yet . . .

Teddy himself looks stricken. "But Vivienne."

"We'll still call in the troops, of course we will, just from somewhere, I don't know, safe?" Max snaps. "Gotta decide now. They're closing in fast."

Teddy looks to Lottie. She swallows, hard, staring behind her at the dark ocean horizon. The wide expanse of freedom.

This is what she's best at. Running. Surviving to see another day. Just her two legs and her wits and—

"No," she says, pulling Max's hand off the wheel. "I'm sorry, but I won't leave her. Not any of them. They'd be in even greater danger the second Gallo found out we took off with his boat. By the time help arrived, it could be too late."

Looking relieved at not needing to make the decision himself, Teddy is starting to attempt another radio transmission when they feel a thud judder the side of the yacht.

Time is absolutely up. A dinghy has arrived, tying to the platform at the stern of the boat. Three men hurl themselves aboard with frightening speed. Ludovico takes the lead, waving the others into position.

Three of them, three of us, Lottie thinks, already balling her hands into fisticuffs. But when she sees the glint of guns in their hands, she turns around and pries the receiver from Teddy's rigid grip, shouts into the radio, "We're about to get shot, damn it, and when you read the news tomorrow and find out beloved movie stars Lottie Lawrence and Teddy Walters were found dead on Tavalli, you'll be kicking yourself you didn't answer the radio call—"

"Teddy Walters," the radio operator repeats dully, cutting her off. "Sure, lady. I repeat, it is a criminal offense to interfere with the broadcast of military telegraphy . . ."

A throat clears just behind her ear. *"Buonanotte, principessa."*

Lottie slowly pivots.

Beside her, Teddy and Max have already raised their arms in surrender.

Ludovico motions with his gun to Lottie's hand. "Shall I shoot it out?"

She drops the receiver.

As they're marched away at gunpoint, Lottie can still hear the empty drone of the navy operator citing specific code violations she could be court-martialed for, then a thumping *click* as the radio, their last hope, is turned off entirely.

Ludovico guides Lottie into his own dinghy, while Max and Teddy are yanked apart into separate vessels. Over the growl of idling engines and the ocean surf, Lottie can hear the sound of a scuffle, a blow landing, a muffled shout.

"Please don't hurt them," Lottie whimpers to Ludo. "It . . . This was all my idea. I'm the only one who should be punished."

Ludo chuckles, gripping Lottie's elbow as they motor away toward the shore. "You want to be spanked, princess? It is too bad

I don't get to pick your punishment. You will have to wait for Mr. Gallo to decide."

After they hit land, Lottie teeters onto the sand.

"Where are you taking us?" she asks Ludo, picturing that grotto again, the trash heap, the corpse of poor Billy Wagner waiting there for company.

"You will go where all naughty children go." Ludo laughs. "Straight to your room."

He means it, she realizes as they reach the Albergo and she's guided upstairs through the now empty lobby to her very own bedroom. Full relief doesn't strike until he shuts the hotel room door and leaves, rather than following her inside.

But being alone and shivering her stunned way out of her drenched clothes and into a dry nightgown is faint comfort when she can hear the rustle of someone's back resting against her door, physically blocking her way out.

A light glints in the darkness outside her window. She crouches near the sill and picks up the binoculars that Teddy left, training the lenses on the illuminated yacht, now docked at the marina. Several of its rooms are lit up—could they be holding Vivienne in there?—but right now Lottie can see only one figure inside. Male, tall, broad-shouldered.

She focuses the lenses. Yep, it's Gallo. He's in the salon, and judging by his pacing and reddening face, he's shouting—into a phone receiver.

This whole time there was a phone on the boat?

Lottie has to close her eyes for a few breaths until her fury at herself passes. When she opens them again, Gallo is no longer in view. The salon is empty.

The other lit cabins are obscured by curtains. No chance of knowing who else is on board, and it takes some searching and refocusing for Lottie to find Gallo again, now a dark silhouette on the bow of the wavering yacht. A small red glow emanates from his hand. A cigarette.

And there were cigarettes on the boat too, she registers dully. *So many missed opportunities.*

Lottie's worry hardens into outright despair as she takes stock of the ruins of tonight's plans.

They got caught, no rescue imminent. All of them captive in this hotel. Vivienne must be locked up somewhere too, maybe in her own room down the hall. Unharmed, Lottie prays. Gallo wouldn't have hurt her, would he? He's too besotted with her for that, surely. But it's that kind of obsession that can most easily turn violent.

Lottie bites at her thumbnail, dizzy with worry.

Oh, Vivienne, where are you? Why did we ever send you into that lion's den?

At the window, she watches Jack Gallo's dark silhouette for as long as she can stand it, desperately searching for clues as to what he's done, what he's planning to do.

And he seems to watch right back, staring out at the island of Tavalli as if it's a great white whale he's planning to harpoon.

"*You will have to wait for Mr. Gallo to decide*," Ludovico said.

Lottie has the awful suspicion that he already has.

27

Sunday, June 22, 1958

Vivienne can hear Jack Gallo pacing, his heavy footfalls across the bedroom's ceiling like an ominous thunder soundtrack on loop. *Warning. Danger. Oncoming storm.* She can hear his voice too, seeping through the walls. Not clearly enough to make out his words, but that tone—frustrated, insistent—is enough to chill her spine, singe her nerves.

His thugs dragged her and Ginger on board the yacht as soon as it docked at the marina. Immediately, she and Ginger were shoved into this lower deck bedroom, shades drawn, one lone night lamp casting the room in an unsettling glow. Their entire ride back from the restaurant had been monstrously tense. Gallo stayed silent most of the way, wearing that trademark manufactured calm of his like bad cologne, his vague, earlier promise—*insurance*—sending Vivienne's mind spiraling with horrible possibilities for how he plans to punish them. Lottie, Teddy, Max are nowhere to be found, and they were supposed to be here, radioing the shining USS *Boston* for help, that savior cruiser somewhere out along the horizon that by now is surely gone.

She's been trying to get details out of Ginger for what feels like hours. She clearly betrayed them, yes? That's the only way Gallo could have found out about their plan. Ginger had to have told him herself. But the cosmetic artist is a certified mess right now, crying in the corner, her once flawless makeup smeared in blacks and reds across her face.

"Ginger," Vivienne tries again. "Pull yourself together and level with me."

Ginger sniffs but says nothing.

Now her patience is wearing thin. "Ginger, I understand you feel bad, but there are more important things to worry about right now. Where are the others?"

"I don't know."

"What did you tell him?"

Ginger just shakes her head.

"Why?" Vivienne snaps. "We could have escaped, you know! You could've been on your way to your daughter right now! Do you understand the type of man you've just sold us out to, what he's capable of?"

"Yes, I've gathered enough, thank you." Ginger's haunted eyes pin on her. "In fact, I haven't slept since you and Miss Lawrence got back on set and unloaded all this on me."

She wipes her hand across her nose.

"You and your harebrained schemes, your half-baked plans to escape the damn mob. You seem to think real life is like the movies and you're still the heroes, happy ending guaranteed. Men like Mr. Gallo don't just let a bunch of bigmouthed, fame-hungry starlets learn his secrets and then *waltz away into the night*! You're so damned naive, all of you. Pampered. Sheltered." She rubs her eyes fitfully, painting a streak of mascara across her face, mumbling, "I'd rather make a deal with the devil than never see Jackie again. So I did."

Vivienne smarts from the sting. Pampered? *Sheltered?* "But that's just it, don't you—"

Her retort is cut off, the bedroom door flying open, orders coming fast from Gallo's crooked-nosed henchman, shouts laced in Italian: "Up. Mr. Gallo *è finite. Ora!*"

He grabs her by the elbow, but Vivienne shakes off his death grip, huffing. "Anyone ever tell you you've got quite the gentleman's touch, Pasquale?"

"Out," he seethes, waving her and Ginger out the door. "*Now.* Back to hotel."

Vivienne brushes past him, tailing Ginger into the lower deck hall, where several of Gallo's other thugs jostle down the corridor and up the stairs. They follow the crowd off the boat, into the island's small marina. She can see Gallo up ahead, a trail of cigarette smoke in his wake, as he walks up the docks. In the distance, on the hill, the Albergo Tavalli shines ominously, like a set piece from a Jack Arnold picture.

Her pulse beats in her ears. Call it intuition, her newly awakened instincts put to use, but Vivienne can actually feel that the bigger picture has shifted, the stakes changed. That while she and Ginger were locked in that stifling room, Gallo rewrote the rules of whatever dark game he's playing.

"Jack," she calls after him, dread mounting. "Wait, please, Jack, let's talk!"

"Too little, too late, Miss Rhodes." He doesn't even turn around. He sounds almost amused.

The hotel's vaulted lobby is nearly empty given the late hour, only Gallo and a few of his men hastily conferring in the corner.

As she's ushered inside, Ludovico and two other crewmen brush past her, out the door.

"Pasquale, *sveglia gli altri*," Gallo tells his bald-headed goon as he swoops in between them. He gestures toward a few other thugs clustered near the reception desk. *"Digli che abbiamo una scena da girare."*

The group of heavies moves forward like a unit, up the hotel's marble staircase.

"Jack, please," Vivienne grits out. "Tell me, what's going on?"

He ignores her entirely, as if she's a mere piece of furniture, and slides away.

A cacophony of sounds filters down from the higher floors. Footsteps creaking across the hotel's old ceiling. A swell of tired greetings. Whispers of speculation soon cascading toward them like a tide.

Dozens of cast and crew members slowly wind down the stairs, Lottie, Teddy, and Max leading the confused parade. Lottie, looking harried in a floor-length nightgown; Max, with his glasses askew, one eye mottled purple and rapidly swelling. But all of them alive, thank God.

Lottie must feel Vivienne's gaze, because she turns, her entire body wilting when they lock eyes. "We tried, Viv," she calls out weakly. "We really did."

Most of the other cast members have clearly been roused straight out of bed. Johnny Preem looks like a lost little boy in pajamas, rubbing his eyes as he descends the stairs. Syd is sporting striped loungewear, his gray hair standing on end, tired eyes dubiously roaming the heavily guarded lobby, as if he's not quite sure how he took a wrong turn into this bizarre lucid dream.

"What time is it?" Syd mutters.

"Three a.m.," Gallo says evenly. "But I was struck with inspiration and simply couldn't wait. I'm fired up!"

He takes a few jaunty steps forward to address the befuddled-looking crowd, the cast and crew gathered like a large choir on the stairs.

Gallo adds, louder, "I want to film the city of Troy at the moment the horse arrives!" He glances at Syd, then turns back to the others. "Indoors this time. The lighting was all wrong when Syd filmed last week, and it shows on the dailies."

"You want to reshoot the Trojan horse scene . . ." Syd's face contorts in anguish, as if he's just woken up on a tightrope. "Now?"

Gallo's eyes broadcast venom. "Yes, Syd. *Now*."

He claps his hands, rousing the crowd. "Come on, everybody, where's your team spirit? No need to fall behind another day. Time is money." Gallo snaps his fingers at his thugs stationed around the room to get moving.

"But, Mr. Gallo!" Clay Cooper calls out, his southern drawl echoing across the marble foyer. "We don't have our costumes on!"

Gallo turns, flashing Clay his disarming smile. "Don't worry, my young buckaroo, everything is waiting in the hangar. Now go. Go!" He turns to shoot Vivienne a cruel wink. "It'll be fun."

As he sets off, striding ahead, his men close in, urging the crowd forward.

Ships' major players, the goddesses, throngs of extras, lighting and set people flow like a steady stream across the lobby's gleaming white floor. Lottie, Teddy, and Max are subsumed, caught up in the current.

Vivienne too. She careens along with the rest of them into the steeped summer air, slick with humidity, cicadas croaking an ominous overture. Gallo, their Pied Piper, leads this strange, unsettling procession off the hotel grounds and onto the island's central dirt path.

As they traverse along the cliffside, Vivienne's gaze snares on the long row of sets tucked below in the valley and the new, looming shadow hovering in the water beyond.

She blinks. *It's another island*, she thinks blearily.

No . . . another *boat*. One so large that it dwarfs Gallo's yacht.

Wild hope surges in her chest. Is it the navy? Did they get through to them after all?

But the outline is wrong, she realizes now. Long. Flat.

Some kind of transportation vessel, from the looks of it. She squints. There's a cluster of what look like storage containers aboard. A freighter?

That isn't good.

Even this far away, she can spot several figures on the decks loading hefty objects of various shapes and sizes on board. Down on the beach, there's a cart headed toward the marina, its bed filled with an assortment of pottery and fake period antiques.

Vivienne feels a devastating coldness spread through her limbs.

They're taking the props off set. Shipping them away.

Why now?

"My agent warned me this picture would be a challenge, but I never anticipated dead-of-night calls," Charles Brinkwater slurs, a failed attempt at a hushed whisper to her and Clay Cooper as they trace the cliff's curve toward Ludo's hangar. "At this hour, I am firmly in a retired, regenerative state of mind—"

Clay waggles his eyebrows. "You mean a *libations* state of mind."

"It's only framing shots, Charles. Very little effort involved!" Gallo calls from up ahead.

Charles startles, chastened. "How on earth did he hear me?"

"He is omnipotent." Pasquale laughs behind them. "Like a god."

As Vivienne's stomach keeps plummeting, Clay dopily glances around. "Oh! So he's one of the gods and we're the mortals. Maybe this is a like a role-playin' game, Charles. I've read about this type of acting. *Method*, I think it's called—"

"*Sei un imbecille*," Pasquale growls.

Vivienne tries to break away, to move faster through the crowd, desperate now to catch up to Lottie, Teddy, and Max, who are bobbing along up ahead. None of this makes sense. They need to reconvene, right now, and figure out what the hell is going on.

As they loop toward the hangar, she spies Ludovico standing sentinel at its entry, pulling peevishly at his mustache. It's grown in quite a bit, Vivienne notices. He hasn't had time to trim it for days.

Gallo pulls Ludo aside as the others file in. It takes Vivienne a moment to notice that Ginger is behind them, hovering in their shadows.

"*Portateli dentro*," Gallo says.

Ludo nods. "*Siamo quasi carichi.*"

"*Chiudete le porte . . .*"

Despite her best attempts, Vivienne can't understand a word of what they're saying. Pasquale puts an end to her eavesdropping anyhow, elbowing her toward the doors.

Gallo spots her just before she enters the hangar. He reaches out to coldly cup her chin, turning her face this way and that. "Viv, darling, you're looking a little sickly."

Oh, how she longs to spit at him.

Before she can, he drops his hand and reaches behind Ludo, grabbing Ginger's arm and pressing her forward, into the fray.

"Hair and makeup for Miss Rhodes, immediately."

Ginger recoils, avoiding Vivienne's glare. "I think I'd be more comfortable out here, Mr. Gallo—"

"Nonsense! You're a key member of the crew. A professional. You belong in there."

Ginger folds her arms over her chest, head down, as she hurries through the doors after Vivienne. Vivienne turns around, just once, to find Gallo smirking. He even gives her a little wave. So he's not coming in.

The massive hangar looks sparse, gutted. Cheap folding tables and chairs are scattered around the room, and almost no props at all remain, other than a few errant columns lying on their sides.

There is one exception, of course: the gleaming, two-story, wooden Trojan horse, proudly positioned in the center of the room, like the centerpiece of a museum exhibition.

"This doesn't look like a city," Vivienne whispers to herself, uneasy, as she wades deeper into the warehouse, more people closing in behind her.

"What did you say, Miss Rhodes?" Johnny Preem, who still appears half asleep, asks her above the buzz of the throng.

"The scene Gallo said we were filming," she says, claustrophobia squeezing her. Too many bodies, too many smells, too much heat. "The city of Troy. When the horse was delivered by the Greeks. Except there is no city backdrop here. How on earth can he expect us to—"

He doesn't expect us to film at all. He expects something entirely different.

There's a sudden chorus of gasps ahead, a dizzying, disorienting shock wave that buffets Vivienne further. She angles herself to spot the new source of commotion. No luck. She shoulders forward to see. "What? What's going on?"

Vivienne rounds the back side of the towering Trojan horse and sees it. The prop, the setup, the plan, all of it.

The horse's trap-door stomach is distended, the horse's innards fully in view.

She sways, a dull buzz cresting, roaring through her ears. Inside the horse are hundreds, if not thousands, of sticks of dynamite.

Clay Cooper joins her side. "Well, I'll be," the actor clucks. "That's the stuff they used on *All Cowboys Are Heroes*. Blew that farmhouse sky-high."

"Oh my God," Vivienne whispers, realization finally dawning. The disparate pieces of this horrific night sliding into place. The props being loaded. The freighter. Everyone shoved inside one space. Dynamite. *Insurance*.

Vivienne's mind starts free-falling as the overcrowded hangar turns suffocating. *Insurance*. The pieces keep clicking. As in *actual* insurance. Gallo and the Apex board can wipe the slate clean, cut bait on the film. Write it off as a mishap. A real-life tragedy. A sinking *Ships* payday . . .

And then they start anew, out from under this money pit.

Oh my God.

"Move!" Vivienne blurts, desperation igniting, consuming her in flames. She has to find Lottie, the others, now, right now. Where are they?

She turns and shoves Clay toward the doors. "Come on!"

"Viv?" Charles swoops between them, hands out to calm her. "I see you're getting into character. Commendable, but I'm worried you're taking this artistic choice a bit far."

"What? Don't you— That's *dynamite*! Turn around, go!" Vivienne shoves past him, wading through the crowd, which is proving disturbingly dense in more ways than one.

"Move!" she barks at the trio of goddesses, yawning prettily as they fuss with their silk pajamas. Then she spots her director. "Syd? Syd! We need to leave. We're in trouble!"

"Trouble," Syd repeats as he surveys the hangar, lost in thought. As if he's actually playing out the scene. "No, I can do this. Breathe now, Sydney. Does he want something postmodern here? An empty hangar. A dose of wartime reality? Hmm."

How does no one else see what's really going on?

"Lottie!" she cries out. "Teddy! Max!"

She finally spots them on the other side of the Trojan horse.

Lottie plucks Vivienne from the crowd and hugs her tight. She smells like Chanel and seawater. Like home.

"Oh, Lottie, this is bad," Vivienne sobs.

"I know." Lottie pulls back. "They took the drugs, the props—"

Vivienne nods. "They've already loaded them onto a freighter, meaning—"

"We're all going *kaboom*." Max slides beside them, the new shiner to his left eye on full display, violet and swollen under the hangar's dim lights. He looks like he's about to vomit.

Teddy takes his hand. "How do we get out of here?"

"All of us," Vivienne sputters. "We need to get *all* these people out."

She sidesteps the guys, spotting Brinkwater stumbling through the crowd toward Syd.

She grabs him by his shoulders. "Charles, I need you to listen. Those explosives inside the horse are *real*. If we don't leave right now, we're all going to die—"

"Doesn't have quite the same impact as a hidden army." Charles frowns. "I really do hope Gallo knows what he's doing."

Clay Cooper, truly the dimmest of all the bulbs, starts laughing. "You know that Mr. Gallo," he drawls, leaning against the horse. "Every chance he gets to add fireworks to the production . . ."

Utterly exasperated, Vivienne turns to a group of chattering extras. "This isn't a joke. You need to turn around, *leave*, right now!"

One of them whimpers, "I don't wanna get fired. Just got my SAG card."

Vivienne throws up her hands. "What the hell is wrong with these people?"

"They're clueless, Viv." Lottie sidles beside her, biting her fingernails with vicious intensity. "Think about all those extras on *Ben-Hur*. The only thing they cared about was getting on camera."

"That's it," Vivienne says on a breath.

She grabs Lottie by both shoulders and plants a loud smooch on her cheek. Then she turns to the crowd.

"Listen up, everybody!" she shouts. "It's time to start filming."

28

Syd, trembling in his loungewear, clings to the wooden armrests of his director's chair like they're flotation devices. "But we're not ready to film. I'm not ready. There's no set, no—"

Lottie rushes to his side, consoling. "Shh, not now, Syd. Why don't you take a little breather? You've already worked so hard, under impossible circumstances. I'll see if I can get Johnny to fetch you some water."

She eases Syd, still muttering to himself, out of his seat and past the horse. Lottie's still not sure exactly what Vivienne's plan is, but she knows they don't have time for Syd to get in the way of it.

Behind the still-milling crowd, into which Lottie deposits their erstwhile director, she can see the wide hangar doors starting to shut. Frantic, she looks around and spots two of Ludo's goons picking their way out of the throng to safety.

They don't have long. Minutes, tops.

Spotting an opening in the crowd, Lottie runs to Teddy and Max.

"Filming?" Max sputters. "There aren't even any cameras."

"Extras in position, by the doorway!" Vivienne calls out. Nobody budges.

Lottie growls in wild frustration. Then she sprints to Syd's chair, snatches up his bullhorn, and deposits it into Vivienne's outstretched hand like they're in a relay race.

If I manage to make it back home, my trainer's not gonna recognize me, she thinks, heart pounding.

Vivienne lifts the bullhorn. "Extras, I need you in position! Back, back, by the doorway!"

There is some movement now, a little wary shuffling, but not enough. Amid the din, she hears one male extra snorting, "Since when is she the director?"

Lottie snatches the bullhorn out of Vivienne's hand and screams into it: "Since now! For God's sake, listen to her!"

The shock that ripples through the echoing hangar is enough to stop even Ludo's goons in their tracks. A lucky break, since there's only one wide door left open and its gap is narrowing fast.

She tosses the bullhorn back to Vivienne, who catches it handily and wastes no time—a necessity, given that now they have the goons' full attention and they are making their way over.

"All right, everybody, we're shooting a new scene. The horse has arrived, the Greek army is spilling out of it, and what I need the crowd to do is flee. You got that? When I call action, you run for the hangar door and you do not stop. And . . . action!"

And with that, Vivienne has spoken the one magic word that can possibly affect this group of starstruck hopefuls. Never mind the lack of lights and cameras, there is still immediate action, the eagerest of extras starting the charge first, from the back.

It would have been a bottleneck, even more dangerous, a stampede, if not for the extras filling the area by the doorway. With a roar of enthusiasm, they shove at the hangar doors, knocking the goons onto their backsides in their shock at the wave of bodies coming at them.

"That's the extras taken care of!" Lottie yells, running alongside Vivienne to freedom. "What about the others?"

"We have to trust in the power of the crowd!" Vivienne yells back, but she takes care, Lottie notes, to grab Max's shirt as they pass him, ensuring he keeps pace with them.

The crowd is indeed powerful, as intractable as the currents of extras who ran through Cinecittà, a true force of nature. The cameramen, goddesses, even Ginger, are all being pulled out of the hangar in its wake.

Teddy runs a few feet ahead, finding gaps for them to run through. When one of the goons steps into his path—the young deckhand from the boat, Lottie recognizes—Teddy doesn't hesitate. His hand flies out and clocks the guy straight on the jaw, sending him toppling backward.

"Nice work!" Lottie cries, sprinting alongside him.

"Ow, ow, ow," he mutters. "I've never hit anybody for real before."

With one final burst, they are out, they are *free*, running in the open air, over gravelly soil, away from that deathtrap and toward the front of the horde, ready to lead them anywhere but here.

"Vivienne, you were brilliant," Lottie crows, grabbing her arm. Vivienne laughs as if incredulous herself. "I cannot believe that worked. I told you that you were a natural at—"

A sound rings out. Deafening. Sharp. Much too close.

And then a surprised shout.

Teddy holds his hand to his shoulder. Takes it away to stare at the red pooling there. Spewing out of him, quickly.

"No!" Lottie shouts, grasping at Teddy. "No!"

Max breaks his fall, tumbling to the ground with him.

Lottie screams into the crowd, "A cloth! Get me a cloth! Fabric, a tie, something!"

It's Ginger who rushes forward through the stunned mob, yanking the scarf from her hair. "Here, take it. I'm sorry. I'm so sorry . . ."

Lottie swiftly ties the scarf around Teddy's shoulder, his wound, her eyes spilling over at his cry of pain as she fastens it tight while Max whispers reassurances into Teddy's ear.

She's so preoccupied with staunching the bullet wound that it takes her a moment to look up at the crowd, all of them sinking slowly to her level, to their knees.

And in front of them, backing up one step at a time, Jack Gallo.

With a gun to Vivienne's head.

29

E veryone, stop!" Gallo shouts. "Just stop!"

The noise of the crowd halts on a dime, an eerie silence descending over the cliffside.

All Vivienne can hear now is her heart galloping between her ears and Gallo's heavy breathing.

He lets go of her wrist, winding his arm around her throat, positioning himself behind her. His other hand firmly retrains his pistol to her temple.

"You Hollywood people." He pops a disbelieving laugh. "You really are impossible, aren't you? A bunch of spoiled brats."

Vivienne's entire body thrums, electric with fear, eyes watering from the wind whipping off the sea. Before her, Teddy is splayed across the ground, his handsome face warped with pain, teeth gritted, curled around his blood-soaked shoulder. Lottie and Max huddle beside him, eyes wide with terror. Syd, Charles, Clay, Johnny, the extras, the lighting crew, the goddesses, this entire godforsaken team a sickly panorama of horror and defeat.

"All I tried to do was save your pathetic studio, your careers, and you made it such a chore."

Jack yanks her farther down the path, where his gunmen are waiting, backing away from the crowd now too. Guns still drawn, a slow, reactive dance away from the hangar.

She notices a small box on the ground, a few paces away from the receding goons. Jack stoops to lift it, pulling her down with him. Box firmly in hand, he edges them farther backward.

"Here I am, trying to save a Hollywood institution from ruin, and what do I get as thanks? Ingratitude. Mutiny."

"Save us?" Max scoffs, now hovering protectively over Teddy. "You were going to light us up like fireworks, you psychopath."

Jack takes a break from digging his gun into Vivienne's head to point it at Max. "I gave you all the chances I could, you commie hack. Gave all of you damaged goods a chance!"

Gallo yanks Vivienne backward again, his gun now sliding down to rest against her neck.

She shifts, resisting his new grip, and finally focuses on what he's holding. A small brown box. Batteries exposed, along with a conspicuous switch. She's never been this close to one before, but she knows in her bones what this is.

A detonator.

"In my line of work, you do what you're told or you die," Gallo says. "But you people!"

He snaps another cold laugh as Vivienne feels her knees go weak, dizzy with panic, the crowd blurring. All those faces. Those stricken, defeated, beautiful faces.

"'Put me on the marquee.' 'Cassandra's not a big enough role,'" Gallo mimics caustically, voice dripping with sarcasm. "'My room's a box, I need more lines, more money, creative control . . .'"

The wind sends Vivienne's tears whipping in cold streams. She teeters in her heels, eyes flitting to the cliff drop—astoundingly high, she sees, now that she's so close. The angry waves of the Ligurian churn below, indigo whitecaps folding under the predawn sky, as if sending up a prayer . . . or an invitation.

A wild idea besieges her.

She remembers Lottie, a lifetime ago, describing the water beside the grotto. *"The depth drops right off. They couldn't catch me . . ."*

"You're all making me seriously question my latest business venture." Gallo *tsk-tsk*s as he tightens his clutch on the detonator, inching them farther away from the crowd.

All her fellow cast and crew, still in range of the blast.

Vivienne finds Lottie's eyes amid the throng, suddenly consumed by a fierce, bone-shaking certainty that everything she's ever done—her entire career of competitions, victories, failures, auditions, roles—may have led her, in some strange twist of fate, to this very moment. *Right here.*

Across the cliffside, Lottie's eyes widen with understanding. She shakes her head firmly at Vivienne.

"No," she mouths, lips trembling.

But if Vivienne can see the entirety of this game, surely Lottie can too, the absolute necessity of her next move. How all their prior gambles have been anticipated, thwarted, outmatched.

How there's only one more bet-it-all play.

"Fortunately, I'm not a quitter. I'll survive this tragedy, and Apex will rise from the ashes." Gallo's voice echoes across the sky. "Trust me, the world won't miss any of you. What a pathetic, sorry lot, some of the weakest and whiniest people I've ever—"

"Everyone has flaws, Jack," Vivienne whispers into his ear.

She uses his surprise, the brief moment of Gallo hesitating, to inch them both backward, right against the cliff's edge. To ready herself in position.

Gallo reasserts his grip. "What did you just say?"

"Everyone has flaws. A weakness," she repeats, stealing a fortifying breath. "Yours, it turns out, is me."

And she jumps.

No overthinking, no overanalyzing, just pure instinct.

Go.

As she lifts off, she tightens her grip around Gallo, feeling his body tip, his balance giving way, his startled cry reverberating through her own bones.

Vivienne's back arches into a seamless, perfect, gravity-defying U as the ground gives way—and Gallo goes down with her.

The chilly sea air whips at Vivienne's face, stealing her breath, burning her eyes. A mounting sound of pure terror jolts through her, a disorienting moment before she realizes that they are not *her* screams.

She releases Gallo as they fall, scrambling to right herself, to survive the staggering drop. She swiftly welds her body into a pencil, wheels around midair, riding momentum, muscle memory, struggling to find balance. To plant her feet below her once again. Before impact. Before—

Vivienne smacks into the water, hard, whiplash wrenching every vertebra.

The frigid water consumes her hungrily, the force of the undercurrent batting her around like a weather vane in a thunderstorm. She makes the mistake of opening her eyes and sees nothing but a dark, streaky blur. The unexpected sting sends her reeling, choking, clawing for relief, for air.

Calm. Stay calm. It's Lottie's voice she hears. *Trust your instincts.*

She ignores the burning swirl behind her eyelids, her lungs pinching with the need for air, and leans into the shallow undertow, surrendering for a moment. Allowing the current to pull her sideways, have its way with her, before finally letting her go.

She sneaks a look once more, following the rippling threads of light, breaking the surface with a glorious, grateful . . .

Gasp.

Lightheaded. Dizzy. Battered. *But free.*

Treading against the oncoming waves, she whirls around. Beach. Cliff. Hangar. There's movement up there, on the cliff's edge, the mob advancing again, a trail of people fighting its way down toward the beach. She hears shouts, cries . . . Of joy? Relief?

A pink eraser of a sun emerges on the horizon, effacing predawn's murky blue so it becomes a canvas of waking gray. Her stomach churns along with the tide as she spots something near the grotto in the distance. A cluster of sea stacks. And a tuxedo-clad body, face down amid the jagged basalt rocks, moving listlessly in the waves like a bundle of laundry.

Jack.

Relief surges through her, a new lightness.

Dead. *Dead and gone.*

But that's not what the crowd is looking at. Not her either, not entirely.

She splashes, turning around. There's something else out there. An oncoming ship. Not the yacht, not the freighter. Advancing toward them fast.

She dives under again, avoiding the ship's wake, swimming championship fast, fighting her way to shore.

Dragging herself out of the shallow water, heels long gone, Vivienne sinks her toes into the coarse sand. She staggers onto shore, evening dress clinging like a mummy wrap, and falls onto the wet stretch of coastline, dimly aware that she has never in her life looked more like a sea witch.

She looks out at the water and sees the blue-hulled ship heading straight for the docks. The small letters written across the bow arrange into a miracle. One beautiful acronym, one powerful enough to propel her and Lottie across the Ligurian Sea and back again.

INTERPOL.

The behemoth of a ship turns to dock, dwarfing the pier, then a multitude of ladders are thrown over the decks simultaneously.

"Vivienne!" Lottie's warm voice rockets across the beach.

Vivienne turns right as her friend envelops her in a full-body hug, nearly toppling her onto the sand. Chanel. Salt. The clean laundry smell of Lottie's downy nightgown. *Home.*

"Don't you ever pull a move like that on me again, you hear me?" Lottie grips Vivienne's shoulders now, studying her like a miracle. She's smiling, tears in her eyes.

Vivienne whimpers out a laugh. "I worried you wouldn't approve."

Lottie cocks her head. "I wouldn't approve?"

"Back in Monte Carlo, r-remember?" Vivienne says, teeth starting to chatter. "You told me living and dying on a single bet was for amateurs. The j-jump felt like the only play left to me, but still, if my gambling mentor doesn't concur, I'll accept notes for next time—"

Lottie pulls her in tight again, laughing herself.

"You did good, Viv," she whispers. "Perfect play, award-winning performance. Hitchcock couldn't have directed it better himself."

Lottie takes her weight, lending Vivienne support as they settle onto the sand and watch the activity on the docks.

"Holy cannoli, can you even believe it?" Lottie says. "After all that. *They came.*"

Vivienne nods, resting her head against Lottie's shoulder, still shivering.

A swarm of blue-uniformed Interpol agents have begun to flood the docks, dividing and scuttling onto the beach. From the opposite direction, the horde of cast and crew members descend down to the shoreline. Johnny and a pair of extras now hold Pasquale hostage. Clay Cooper is corralling another goon like an untamed horse. Teddy, bloody, wincing hard but mobile, thank goodness, hobbles along with Max's support. Ginger, arms crossed, head down, trails behind the crowd.

All of them safe and alive.

"*L'Organisation internationale de police criminelle*," a voice booms through a megaphone. "*Cesser et s'abstenir!*"

Vivienne peers back around.

One of the officers, pewter-haired, tall and slim, stops at the mouth of the pier. He calls behind him, "Jack Gallo *est le premier objectif. Allez le trouver, vite.*"

Several of the agents nod in response to that apparent command, pivoting, hurrying up the path in the direction of the cliff.

"*Je cherche* Vivienne Rhodes," the steely-looking officer calls out to the assembled crowd of cast and crew. "I am looking for Vivienne Rhodes!"

"Here!" Lottie cries, gesturing manically. "She's right here!"

Vivienne's breath hitches as he approaches. She might honestly cry. A bona fide, honest-to-God happy ending. Is it possible?

"Vivienne Rhodes." The Interpol agent's storm-colored eyes crinkle as he stoops down, considering her, wet and shivering like a drowned rat. "Let me get you a blanket."

She chatters out, "I'm f-f-fine."

He smiles, and his angular face transforms, warm and spirited now. "Fine. And brave. But cold." His French accent, thick and melodic.

As he shouts another quick but indecipherable order in French, Vivienne notes his striking profile, softened by the smile lines around his eyes.

What is the matter with me? Vivienne thinks. *I'm clearly in shock.*

"Your friend, Sam Zimbalist," the officer continues as he helps Vivienne up. "He told us to come right away."

His colleague joins them, offering a thick woolen blanket. The officer drapes it around Vivienne's shoulders.

"The pictures you gave him . . . They were . . ." He trails off with a slow grin. "They were dirty indeed. Just not in the way he perhaps expected."

Vivienne sputters out a laugh. "I'm so glad he got them, that he called you. We never actually meant to develop the film Emeric gave us. Oh, that was his name, right?"

"Agent Corbin, yes," he says, his tone grave. Perhaps he picked up on her use of past tense and has gathered his colleague's fate.

"But our host in Provence made a mistake," she goes on, "or, not Provence—where were we by then?"

Lottie puts her arm around Vivienne again. "The Alps," she supplies.

Vivienne blurts out the rest in one breath. "I think Mr. Corbin wanted me to bring the film to you directly, but Gallo's men were following us and— Oh, it's been such an ordeal."

The officer's eyebrows rise farther. "I can imagine."

They're cut off as a pair of Interpol agents lead a scowling Ludovico down the beach in handcuffs.

"I th-think Jack is dead." Vivienne shivers, gesturing out to the sea stacks. "I saw his body in the water."

The officer nods somberly. He steps back, surveying the cliff, the hangar looming above them.

"Wait here," he says. "Wait here and we will talk."

He takes off.

Vivienne keeps shuddering while she and Lottie watch as the officer and his team restrain the remainder of Gallo's team. The last vestiges of Gallo's master plan, dragged down to the docks.

She shakes her head. The man, the mogul, the demon, is *dead*.

The rest of the cast and crew have broken into smaller groups, some recounting details about the night they've just endured, others sinking to the sand in relief. The trio of goddesses are crying and speaking to a few other officers, explaining their versions of the past few hours with dramatic gestures. Across the sand, a pair of medics help Teddy toward the Interpol boat. Max stays unabashedly by his side, shepherding him forward by the waist, comforting him.

Despite everything, Vivienne smiles. Teddy's going to be all right, she knows. She can see it in the determined set of that square-cut jaw. And good for him, not just for living but for finding someone he can't live without. And maybe she's going to be just fine herself.

She surveys the cast, the crew, then glances at Lottie and musters a shaky smile.

Maybe friendship is its own rare treasure.

It's not long before the officer joins them again.

"Emeric Corbin and I, our team, we have been tracking Gallo's family for years," he tells her and Lottie as they stroll down the beach together. "Waiting for a moment just like this one. They are one of the largest and most powerful families in organized crime, trafficking between continents for over a decade. Without ramifications. When we heard Jack Gallo was involved with Apex

Pictures, we of course began watching closely." The officer clears his throat. "We assumed Jack had plans to branch out to America. Emeric was posted here, undercover, in the hopes of gathering intelligence. So, if you please, ah, let me get the facts? When the producer, Monsieur Zimbalist, called our office, he said he found you in Rome."

"That's right." Vivienne nods tightly. "Well, no, he didn't find us, but we were there looking for him."

"And yet you said that you were trying to reach our team in Paris?" The officer's eyes twinkle in the breaking dawn.

"We were indeed," Lottie says. "That was most certainly the plan."

"I see," the officer says in a tone that clearly indicates he does not. He dislodges a notepad from his pocket. "But you decided to go to Rome instead?"

"To Monaco, actually," Lottie says. "But only because we thought Princess Grace might help. We picked the *wrong* night to pay a social call—"

"Total mayhem at the palace," Vivienne says. Then quickly amends, "That should probably be off the record."

Lottie laughs. "Monaco led to Provence—"

"And *then* into the Alps," Vivienne supplies.

"And dancing and way too much wine . . ."

"I guess it's actually quite a long story." Vivienne has a sudden urge to laugh, cry, flop onto the beach and make angels in the sand. The relief is almost overwhelming, joyful, bubbling up and over now, like shaken champagne.

And speaking of libations, could she ever use "way too much wine" right now. She suppresses the manic desire to ask this officer to join her and Lottie at the bar. To sit down and recount their fateful adventure, step-by-step.

Lottie, as always, beats her to the punch. "You know what, Officer . . ."

"François," he supplies, frowning at his small notepad, pockmarked now with scribbles. "François Aubert."

Lottie slinks her arm through his in such a practiced, casual way that Vivienne finally does squawk a laugh. "How about, François, we take it from the top?"

The New York Times

VOL. CVII-No. 36,668   NEW YORK, WEDNESDAY, JUNE 25, 1958   FIVE CENTS

BIGGEST DRUG STING IN EUROPEAN HISTORY; LEADERS OF ITALIAN CRIME FAMILY IN POLICE CUSTODY; RIPPLES FELT ALL THE WAY IN HOLLYWOOD; TWO AMERICAN ACTRESSES REPORTEDLY KEY TO INVESTIGATION

Variety

Vol. 211 No. 3   NEW YORK, WEDNESDAY, JANUARY 14, 1959   25 CENTS

APEX TO MGM, FOR A SONG

In a move surprising few Hollywood insiders, Apex Pictures' beleaguered remaining board members agreed Tuesday to the studio's acquisition by rival MGM Studios. Included in the deal are Apex's Burbank campus and its slate of contracted actors. Although Buster Smith announced his retirement last week, he has agreed to stay on temporarily to help shepherd the studio's upcoming productions under MGM's wing.

When asked for comment, Apex board members declined, citing the confidentiality of ongoing investigations into its financial dealings with Italian gangster Jack Gallo . . .

Hollywood Reporter

RHODES IN THE "HOT" SEAT FOR MGM

BY JAY GRIER

February 15, 1959

Metro-Goldwin-Mayer's vice president of production, Sol Siegel, has tapped actress Vivienne Rhodes for upcoming horse opera *The Hottest Day in June*, but not in the role you might expect. As recent headlines attest, Rhodes is no stranger to stressful situations, which may be why Siegel has opted to send jaws dropping with his choice of director for this Western . . .

30

Tuesday, March 24, 1959

You think you know what I'm capable of? You're a damn fool."

Lottie's hand is steady as stone as she points her revolver, her stare just as unyielding despite the blinding desert light. The man kneeling in front of her squirms, hands raised in silent appeal.

"I'm no victim," she snarls. "Never have been. You want to know who to be afraid of? You're looking at her."

She fires. The man collapses, a look of stunned horror on his face. And Lottie laughs.

"Cut!" Vivienne jumps down from her chair. "And print. And let's break for lunch."

Lottie offers a hand to Andy to help him back up. He's playing his role so well she almost feels guilty for shooting him dead take after take. Almost.

It's a heck of a good time to finally play a villain.

Ginger jumps in to wipe some of the dusty grime off Lottie's face with a damp cloth. A little relief for Lottie in this searing heat. A peace offering, one of many.

Ginger had been blacklisted by MGM after confessing to colluding with Gallo back on the Tavalli set, but after MGM took over Apex and the dust had settled a little bit, Vivienne explained what had led Ginger to do it and insisted that she have carte blanche to hire whoever she liked on her first directing gig for the studio. And she let Ginger bring her daughter to set while she was at it. Vivienne and Lottie didn't *like* Ginger, exactly. It was hard to trust her completely after everything that had happened. But if one thing was clear, it was that in this business, women had to help women or nothing would ever change.

Speaking of which?

"We've got trouble over there." Ginger nods behind Lottie to Debbie Miller's trailer. "He will not let up."

Sure enough, Cal Sherman is leaning against the trailer, blocking any possible graceful exit from a clearly uncomfortable Debbie, who is all of, what, nineteen? And who hasn't yet learned how to escape a much older, much more famous and powerful costar without causing irreparable damage to her career.

After all, if there's one thing Hollywood hates, it's a messy actress.

Lucky for her, Lottie doesn't give a hoot about her own career. She looked death in the face not a year ago. Compared to being abducted and nearly blown up on a remote island halfway across the world, she figures she can take Cal Sherman.

She strides quickly across the loose ground of the Mojave Desert set, quicker in her cowboy boots and trousers than her usual dainty costumes, but Vivienne still gets there first.

"Cal, a word?" Hands on her hips, ponytailed hair flying wild behind her and with not a trace of makeup on her face, Vivienne still somehow manages to look more glamorous than ever.

Cal smirks lewdly at Debbie before peeling himself away to

follow Vivienne, who shoots Lottie a pained blink as she passes.

Debbie gives a shudder once Cal's gone but looks even more alarmed by the sight of Lottie approaching. It's pretty hilarious how easily Lottie can intimidate people in this getup, but that's far from her intention with Debbie, their leading lady, stepping from TV stardom into her first big movie role. Debbie's got serious jitters, and the Cal Shermans of this world aren't helping one bit.

"If he ever bothers you again, come to me or Viv," Lottie says. "We'll set him straight."

A relieved grin bursts over Debbie's face. "Thank you, Miss Lawrence."

"Jeez, no, call me Lottie." All easy charm, Lottie links arms with Debbie, careful not to muss her pretty gingham period dress with her own grizzled outlaw costume as she leads her toward the craft services table. "I love *Hawaii Hotel*, by the way. Teddy and I never miss an episode."

Debbie's blue eyes go even wider at the mention of *the* Teddy Walters. "That's such an honor, Miss—Lottie. And I've been such a fan of yours since I was a little girl. The Millie movies were what made me want to become an actress."

Lottie beams back and sets to work filling her plate with salad and cold cuts. Behind her, someone snorts.

"How do you like that?" Vivienne asks when Lottie turns. "Since she was a *little girl*."

"Oh, shut it." Lottie laughs. "She's still a little girl as far as I'm concerned, and I'm still younger than you. So what'd you say to Cal?"

Lottie nods to the far end of the set, where Cal eats a sandwich alone, staring worriedly into the chaparral, sunlight glinting off his sheriff badge.

"I said I had cast him specifically because he didn't have a reputation as one of those guys, and that if my opinion on that changed at any point, I wouldn't hesitate to fire him, cast Teddy in the part, and blacklist him from MGM the way we did Ken Winters. I think he got the message." Vivienne glances over the table at the cute, scruffy sound guy untangling his wires. "Anytime you need me to have a stern word with that one, you let me know." She raises an eyebrow, waits.

Lottie laughs. "Phil? Oh man, I wish he'd harass me more. The lengths I have to go to get him to flirt back, Viv. He's so darn honorable."

"You have got it bad, my friend." Vivienne shakes her head, smiling.

Lottie's eyes meet Phil's across the set. He lights up, his green eyes crinkling, and gives a shy wave. "Ugh, I really have. I'd be out with him straight after we wrap today if I didn't already have plans."

"That's right," Vivienne says faux sternly. "Polo Lounge at eight. Don't forget."

"When have I ever forgotten a double date?" Lottie scoffs, but Vivienne's already clapping over her head for the general assembly.

"Ten minutes and then back on the train!"

Yes, the train. An enormous nineteenth-century train set, a clapboard town, a cast of forty. Not too shabby for a first directorial gig. But anyone who'd ever met Vivienne Rhodes knew instantly she'd never fold under the weight of a challenge.

Vivienne glides into the Beverly Hills Hotel with her arm draped over Max's. The two of them are sure to be mentioned as a hot new item in *Star Power* by Thursday morning at the latest, which should help distract from Teddy and Lottie's impending "breakup."

Lottie is ready to move into more official territory with sound guy Phil. It's downright adorable.

The place is packed tonight. Vivienne spots Joey Bishop and Frank—much more lucid than the last time they saw him—holding up the bar, giving a cheek kiss to Marilyn as she passes. Even with all these A-listers in residence on a Tuesday evening, Lottie and Teddy managed to snag the best corner banquette in the room. They're waiting for the two of them with an open bottle of red, four glasses already poured.

Vivienne glances at the label, unsurprised to see it's the Mourvèdre from their friends' little vineyard in St. Rambert, which they insisted all their favorite hangouts import in order to keep their business booming. Vivienne has to admit, this varietal is growing on her.

"Oh good, you can back me up," Lottie says as Vivienne slides in beside her. "Teddy and I were discussing his next leading lady."

Teddy goes a little red. Max snorts around the rim of his glass.

"Who's the next to be auditioned?" Vivienne asks wryly. "Please don't say Liz Taylor. I know she's game, but—"

"She'll want a ring," Lottie agrees.

"Within a month."

"It's not Liz." Teddy groans good-naturedly, but he closes his eyes and winces when he announces, "Eleanor Curtis."

There's silence at the table for a moment. Lottie and Vivienne squint at each other.

"Over twenty-five," Lottie says with a thoughtful frown.

"And Ellie's a whole lot smarter than you'd guess," Vivienne puts in. "Sat next to her at the Bowl once and she knew every classical music piece and the year it was composed."

"A savant, how delightful," Max drones, clearly piqued.

Teddy opens his eyes, reassured. "And, well, here's the thing. She has something in common with me and Maxy. How do I put this? She needs me as much as I need her."

"You don't need her," Vivienne feels compelled to say. "You don't need anyone. But I take your point."

"Encouraging!" Lottie beams. "But of course we're going to have to audition her as well."

"Lunch in the canteen at the very least," Vivienne agrees.

"Because you do realize there is absolutely no getting rid of us at this point." Lottie rests her head on Teddy's shoulder. And Max, wonder of wonders, throws his arm right around Vivienne's shoulders. She surprises herself as well as she settles comfortably in against him.

"Just picture it," Max says. "The five of us. Six with Lottie's boom boy."

"He's a sound mixer." Lottie laughs, swatting him.

"Anyone in the mix for you, Vivienne dear?" Max goes on.

"Only you, darling." Vivienne winks, shocking herself again with the easy-breezy fib. She really has gotten better at improvising.

There *is* someone, in fact, although it's very new and hard to define. What started as purely professional communication between her and silver fox Agent Aubert about the Tavalli matter somehow kept going, evolving into an outlet for her to process the trauma and then, eventually, their own little rendition of *Love Letters*. Long, soulful ballads about their hopes, dreams, work. Their weekend plans, favorite flicks, the stories that fascinated them from the news. In fact, François was one of the first people Vivienne told about her decision to throw her hat in the ring for director at MGM. Vivienne's trying not to romanticize the whole thing, to rush ahead to happily ever after. For now, it's her little secret.

Which is to say, only Lottie knows about it.

Vivienne raises her glass, adding, "But I'll let you know as soon as anything changes."

"The six of us," Max goes on musing, none the wiser. "Christmases together in Connecticut, all of us waking up in matching woolen socks. Vacations abroad."

Teddy, Lottie, and Vivienne groan in tandem.

Max shrugs. "Too soon?"

"Maybe not," Lottie says. "We can face anything at this point."

Vivienne lifts her glass at that and they all clink.

"Where to, then?" Teddy asks.

Lottie and Vivienne exchange a loaded glance.

"You know what?" Vivienne laughs. "We never did make it to Paris."

A NOTE FROM THE AUTHORS

We've both had a lifelong obsession with the glamorous world of cinema, and there's something so alluring about Hollywood's "Golden Age" in particular. The studio system, iconic stars, the big-budget epics, the lavish shoots in far-flung locales.

For our second collaboration, we knew that we wanted to delve into this heady time, the late hour of the Golden Age specifically, when Hollywood's studio system was in rapid transition. A time when cinematic powerhouses were finding themselves in hot water after a slew of money-pit productions; film stars were clamoring for more money and control; and the threats of communism and the Hollywood "black list" were turning longtime friends and colleagues against one another. An incredibly interesting time . . . rife with incredible story conflict.

We've read several titles that explore this time period through the lens of romance, but we knew we wanted to tell a different type of story. We wanted to examine and press on the way the Hollywood machine commodifies females and pits them against one another. *Rival starlets*, we thought. *Sworn enemies*. Thrill-seeking authors that we are, as we played out scenarios where they'd be forced to team up together, we thought—*let's put them on the run*!

One of the joys of writing historical fiction is getting to meld true places, people, and events with the products of our own imaginations, and we had loads of fun with that here. Apex Pictures, the studio at the center of our story, is fictional, although it's loosely modeled on 20th Century Fox (Fox most certainly did not have a criminal mastermind at its helm, although it was severely struggling in the late '50s and early '60s!). Lottie and Vivienne's film, *A Thousand Ships*, is also an invention of ours, although the headaches and drama surrounding that picture were borrowed from several epics of that age: *Cleopatra*, *Spartacus*, and, yes, even *Ben-Hur*. As far as we know, there has never been a crime boss who's swooped in to save a studio from ruin. But given the prevalence and power of the mafia at that time, it was all too easy to insert those types of sinister players into the action.

As for the starlets' adventures on the run: Lottie and Vivienne traverse through a historically accurate Monte Carlo, arrive at Princess Grace's palace on the night of a very real Frank Sinatra concert, and stumble onto a meticulously rendered *Ben-Hur* production set (with credit to *Variety* articles of the time for help with those details). There have even been persistent rumors of a red sports car visible in the final cut of Zimbalist's picture, so we had a blast imagining our starlets in the driver and passenger seats. The small airport in Rome where they eventually crash their Ferrari is today a city park, although it was operating in the late 1950s, and the cast's attempted escape from Tavalli in the third act also accords with U.S. Navy maritime schedules from that time of year and in that area of the Mediterranean.

And of course every Old Hollywood book worth its salt needs cameos! From Sinatra and Grace Kelly to Sam Zimbalist, Marilyn Monroe, Charlton Heston, and Stephen Boyd, you'll find many celebrities of yore gracing these pages. Our main characters too—Lottie, Vivienne, Teddy, and Max—were informed by memoirs and biographies of iconic actresses, actors, and moguls of the time (including Ava Gardner, Esther Williams, Grace Kelly, Walter Wanger, and Kirk Douglas, just to name a few).

We hope the end result is, as the Hollywood people say, a mash-up: "fiction meets fact"—some real history, serious hijinks, and a whole lot of fun.

ACKNOWLEDGMENTS

Creating a novel is its own type of production, with many experts and champions working tirelessly behind the scenes, helping to transform the clear vision in an author's mind into a finished, cover-and-pages book. Our brilliant editor, Kimberly Carlton, like any great director, understood what we were trying to achieve from day one with this adventure, made the characters of Vivienne and Lottie come alive, and challenged us to elevate every scene with more depth, nuance, and history. We are so grateful, Kim, for your insight, guidance, and advocacy for this story. Working with you is truly a dream.

Every production needs a savvy, devoted line producer—and Julie Breihan, our razor-sharp line editor, brought her stellar insight and commitment to making *The Starlets* the best version of itself. Sincerest thanks to the rest of the Harper Muse cast and crew: Amanda Bostic, Caitlin Halstead, Margaret Kercher, Colleen Lacey, Nekasha Pratt, Kerri Potts, Savannah Summers, and so many others. We're also so thankful to the art and design teams, with special thanks to James W. Hall for his commitment to creating the perfect cover for this novel.

Our superb agent, Katelyn Detweiler, was our staunch and fearless advocate for this story (and every story)! We feel so incredibly lucky to be on this journey with you. Thank you also to Sam Farkas, Denise Page, and the rest of the hardworking team at Jill Grinberg Literary Management. We're thrilled to call you our agency family.

We'd also like to express heartfelt thanks to our writing crew, our community that makes the "biz" not only tolerable but fun: our fellow Harper Muse authors, Freshman Fifteens, Fearless Fifteeners, the writers and faculty at Vermont College of Fine Arts, the Alliterati. Thank you for your ongoing friendship, support, and camaraderie over these many years.

From Jenn: On the personal side, I'd like to thank my Minchinhampton early reader crew, especially Joanna Brett, who I will one day forgive for moving to Spain. So much love to my mother, father, and stepmom, all of whom raised me on classic films and supported my own ridiculous acting stardom dreams for many, many years despite suspecting I was really a writer at heart. (Okay, guys, you were obviously right.) To my boys, Oliver and Henry, the ultimate scene stealers, thank you for letting Lee borrow me for our daily calls. And my biggest gratitude, as ever, goes to my husband, Rob, whose love and support are straight out of a Hollywood romance.

From Lee: It feels a bit odd to call a story about 1950s movie stars a "personal story," but this one is an Appicello book through and through. Since the time I was little, my Dad had us writing, directing, and acting in family-produced movies, and his love of cinema and producing was infectious. Thanks, too, to my sisters Jill and Bridget, my Tidmarsh and Henne cousins, Monica, Natalie, and Michelle for all the many films, dance recitals, soap operas, and TV shows we put on over the years, and to my Mom for being the world's most dedicated "mom-ager" in all those pursuits and passions. Thanks as well to my other incredible and supportive family, the Kelly crew. And endless love and gratitude to my husband, Jeff, my leading man, partner in crime, and buddy cop all in one. Finally, to Penn and Summer—here's looking at you, kids. You're the reason for everything. Love you.

If this is the book equivalent of an Oscars speech, we want to shout before the music cuts off: THANK YOU TO OUR READERS! Having this book in your hands is more than worth all the outtakes and script left on the cutting room floor. We are beyond grateful you picked up this book, and we really hope you enjoyed it.

DISCUSSION QUESTIONS

1. Although *The Starlets* offers readers an exciting romp through 1950s Europe, it also highlights the serious challenges facing women in entertainment during that era, from maintaining picture-perfect public images to silently enduring abusive and criminal behavior from men like Ken Winters. How realistic did you find this view of the "Golden Age" of Hollywood? What do you believe has improved for women in the past sixty years, and in what ways is sexism still pervasive?

2. The plot of *The Starlets* is peppered with allusions to classic films, from historical epics to Hitchcock thrillers and comedies like *Some Like It Hot*. What cinematic references did you notice while reading? What movie tropes do you feel work particularly well in fiction?

3. Although Lottie Lawrence and Vivienne Rhodes begin this book as equals and rivals, the paths they each took to achieve Hollywood success—and the upbringings that led them into film careers—are wildly different. How were their personalities forged by their childhood struggles and even their early filmographies? What does the art of acting offer each of them emotionally?

4. Jack Gallo professes to Vivienne a lifelong love for the cinema that ultimately led to his bid for Apex Pictures. Do you think he truly believes he's doing the right thing to save the sinking studio? In what ways does a character like Gallo fit

well into the Hollywood system of the 1950s despite being an industry outsider?

5. In what ways does the patriarchal society of 1950s America—and in particular, Hollywood—help to make enemies of women like Vivienne and Lottie at the beginning of the novel? What is it about their flight from Tavalli that helps them to break free from seeing each other as rivals and to let go of the entrenched assumptions they've held on to about each other?

6. Alongside fictional inventions like Apex Pictures and the island of Tavalli, *The Starlets* features real-life settings and events, such as Frank Sinatra's concert in Monte Carlo and the filming of *Ben-Hur* at Cinecittà. Do you think specifically accurate details help to ground a historical novel's more fantastical elements? What is the right balance of history and fiction, in your opinion?

7. "If Hollywood despises one thing, it's messy actresses," Lottie observes. Why do you think the Hollywood system of the 1950s sought to control actors' images so tightly—and women's images in particular? What aspects of Vivienne's and Lottie's public images at the start of the story are holding them back from living their lives to the fullest? What is the hidden truth about each of them that they're fearful will be exposed—and in what ways are those the very qualities that create a strong friendship between the two?

8. Would you consider the conclusion of *The Starlets* to be a true happy ending, given that many of the characters still have to make considerable compromises to keep their careers afloat? What do you imagine the future holds for Vivienne and Lottie?

ABOUT THE AUTHORS

Heidefinition Photography

LEE KELLY is the author of *City of Savages*, *A Criminal Magic*, *With Regret*, and *The Antiquity Affair* and *The Starlets* (co-written with Jennifer Thorne). Her short fiction and essays have appeared in various publications, and she holds an MFA from the Vermont College of Fine Arts. An entertainment lawyer by trade, Lee has practiced law in Los Angeles and New York. She currently lives with her husband and two children in New Jersey, where you'll find them engaged in one adventure or another.

JENNIFER THORNE lives in a cottage in Gloucestershire, England, with her husband, two sons, and various animals. She is the author of horror novels *Lute* and *Diavola*, picture book *Construction Zoo*, and, as Jenn Marie Thorne, YA novels *The Wrong Side of Right*, *The Inside of Out*, and *Night Music*. Jennifer is also the author of two historical novels, *The Antiquity Affair* and *The Starlets*, co-authored with Lee Kelly.